POSTAL

CREATED BY MATT HAWKINS

VOLUME 4

D1449852

6/18

PUBLISHED BY TOP COW PRODUCTIONS, INC.
LOS ANGELES

POSTAL

CREATED BY MATT HAWKINS

BRYAN HILL
WRITER

ISAAC GOODHART
ARTIST

K. MICHAEL RUSSELL
COLORIST

TROY PETERI
LETTERER

ASHLEY VICTORIA ROBINSON & RYAN CADY
EDITORS

FOR THIS EDITION COVER ART BY
LINDA SEJIC

ORIGINAL EDITIONS EDITED BY
ASHLEY VICTORIA ROBINSON & RYAN CADY

BOOK DESIGN & LAYOUT BY
TRICIA RAMOS

For Top Cow Productions, Inc.

Marc Silvestri - *CEO* • Matt Hawkins - *President and COO*

Ashley Victoria Robinson - *Editor* • Elena Salcedo - *Director of Operations*

Henry Barajas - *Operations Coordinator* • Vincent Valentine - *Production Artist*

Dylan Gray - *Marketing Director*

To find the comic shop
nearest you, call:
1-888-COMICBOOK

Want more info? Check out:
www.topcow.com
for news & exclusive Top Cow merchandise!

IMAGE COMICS, INC.
Robert Kirkman – Chief Operating Officer
Erik Larsen – Chief Financial Officer
Todd McFarlane – President
Marc Silvestri – Chief Executive Officer
Jim Valentino – Vice-President
Eric Stephenson – Publisher
Corey Murphy – Director of Sales
Jeff Boison – Director of Publishing Planning & Book Trade Sales
Jeremy Sullivan – Director of Digital Sales
Kat Salazar – Director of PR & Marketing
Branwyn Bigglestone – Controller
Drew Gill – Art Director
Jonathan Chan – Production Manager
Meredith Wallace – Print Manager
Briah Skelly – Publicist
Sasha Head – Sales & Marketing Production Designer
Randy Okamura – Digital Production Designer
David Brothers – Branding Manager
Olivia Ngai – Content Manager
Addison Duke – Production Artist
Vincent Kukua – Production Artist
Tricia Ramos – Production Artist
Jeff Stang – Direct Market Sales Representative
Emilio Bautista – Digital Sales Associate
Leanna Caunter – Accounting Assistant
Chloe Ramos-Peterson – Library Market Sales Representative
IMAGECOMICS.COM

POSTAL, VOLUME 4.

First printing. December 2016. Published by Image Comics, Inc. Office of publication: 2001 Center Street, Sixth Floor, Berkeley, CA 94704. Copyright © 2016 Top Cow Productions, Inc. All rights reserved. Contains material originally published in single magazine form as POSTAL #13-16. "Postal," its logos, and the likenesses of all characters herein are trademarks of Top Cow Productions, Inc. unless otherwise noted. "Image" and the Image Comics logos are registered trademarks of Image Comics, Inc. No part of this publication may be reproduced or transmitted, in any form or by any means (except for short excerpts for journalistic or review purposes), without the express written permission of Top Cow Productions, Inc. All names, characters, events, and locales in this publication are entirely fictional. Any resemblance to actual persons (living or dead), events, or places, without satiric intent, is coincidental. Printed in the USA. For information regarding the CPSIA on this printed material call: 203-595-3636 and provide reference #RICH–716157. ISBN: 978-1-5343-0025-5

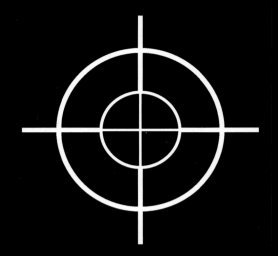

POSTAL

THE STORY SO FAR...

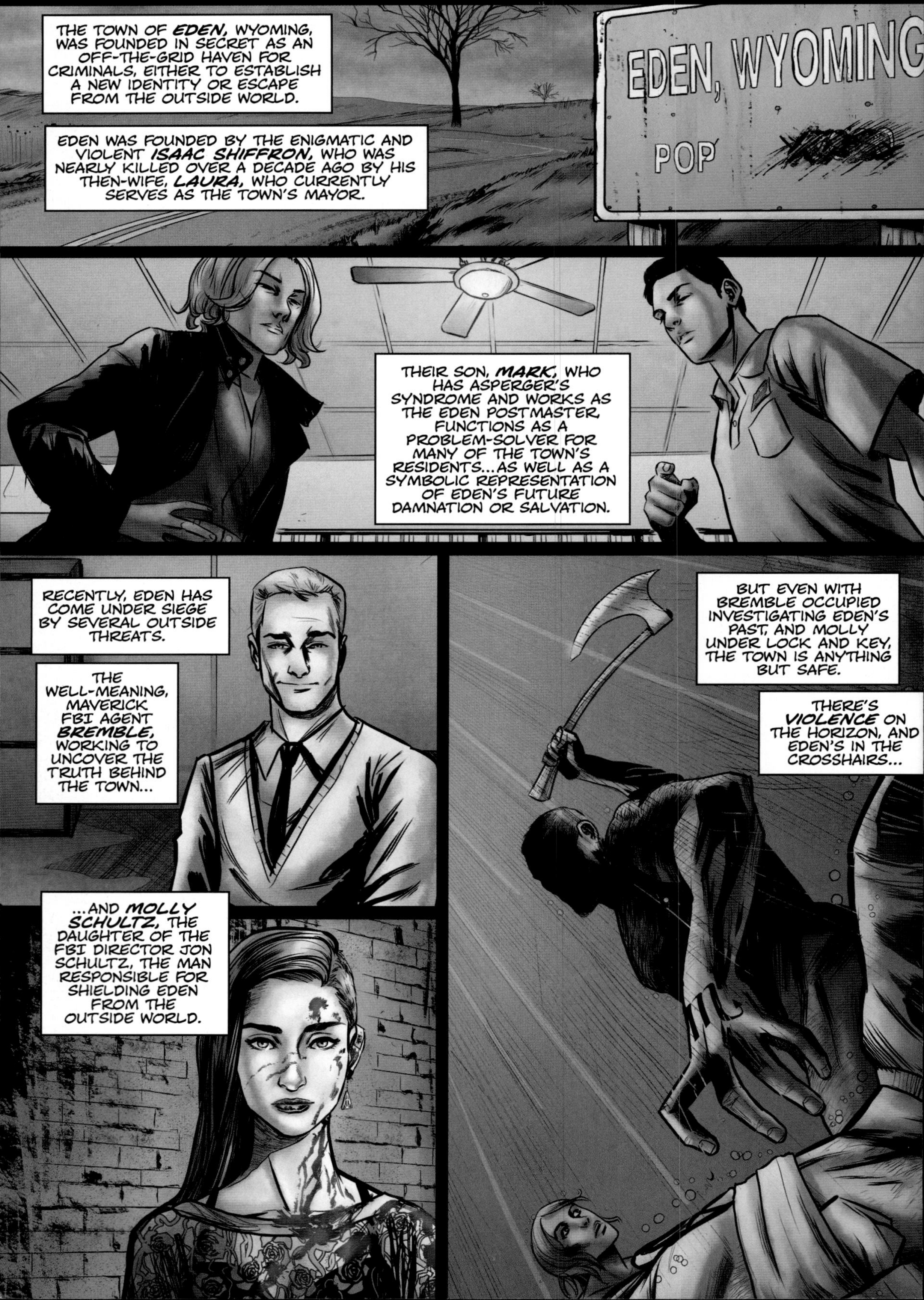
THE TOWN OF EDEN, WYOMING, WAS FOUNDED IN SECRET AS AN OFF-THE-GRID HAVEN FOR CRIMINALS, EITHER TO ESTABLISH A NEW IDENTITY OR ESCAPE FROM THE OUTSIDE WORLD.
EDEN, WYOMING
POP
EDEN WAS FOUNDED BY THE ENIGMATIC AND VIOLENT ISAAC SHIFFRON, WHO WAS NEARLY KILLED OVER A DECADE AGO BY HIS THEN-WIFE, LAURA, WHO CURRENTLY SERVES AS THE TOWN'S MAYOR.
THEIR SON, MARK, WHO HAS ASPERGER'S SYNDROME AND WORKS AS THE EDEN POSTMASTER, FUNCTIONS AS A PROBLEM-SOLVER FOR MANY OF THE TOWN'S RESIDENTS...AS WELL AS A SYMBOLIC REPRESENTATION OF EDEN'S FUTURE DAMNATION OR SALVATION.
RECENTLY, EDEN HAS COME UNDER SIEGE BY SEVERAL OUTSIDE THREATS.
THE WELL-MEANING, MAVERICK FBI AGENT BREMBLE, WORKING TO UNCOVER THE TRUTH BEHIND THE TOWN...
...AND MOLLY SCHULTZ, THE DAUGHTER OF THE FBI DIRECTOR JON SCHULTZ, THE MAN RESPONSIBLE FOR SHIELDING EDEN FROM THE OUTSIDE WORLD.
BUT EVEN WITH BREMBLE OCCUPIED INVESTIGATING EDEN'S PAST, AND MOLLY UNDER LOCK AND KEY, THE TOWN IS ANYTHING BUT SAFE.
THERE'S VIOLENCE ON THE HORIZON, AND EDEN'S IN THE CROSSHAIRS...

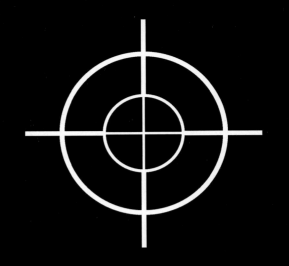

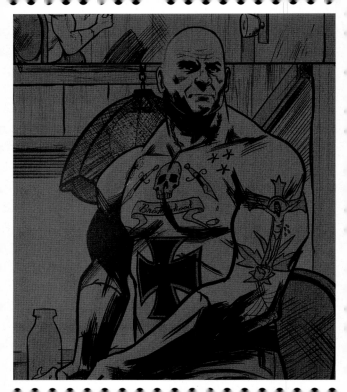

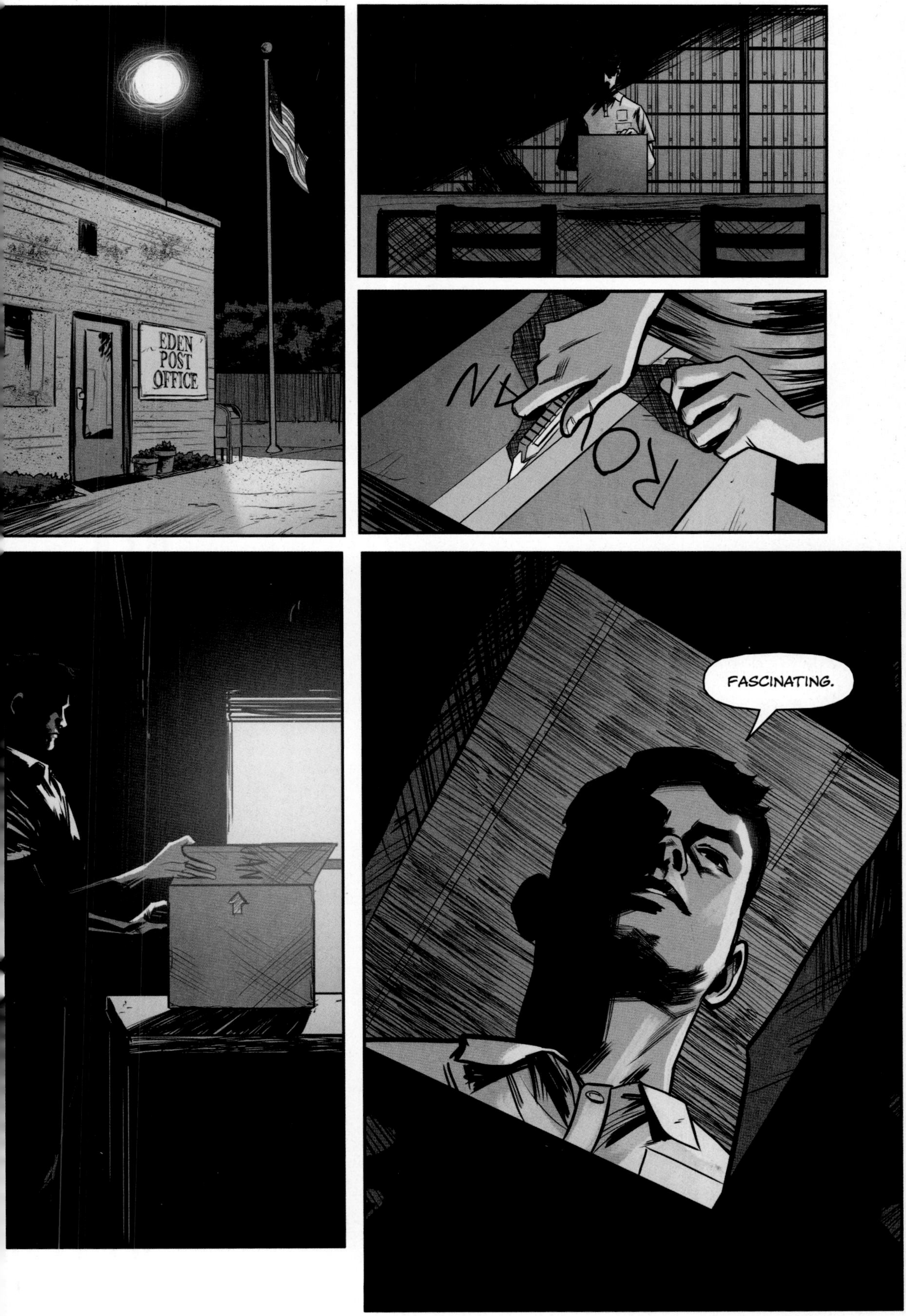
EDEN
POST
OFFICE
FASCINATING.

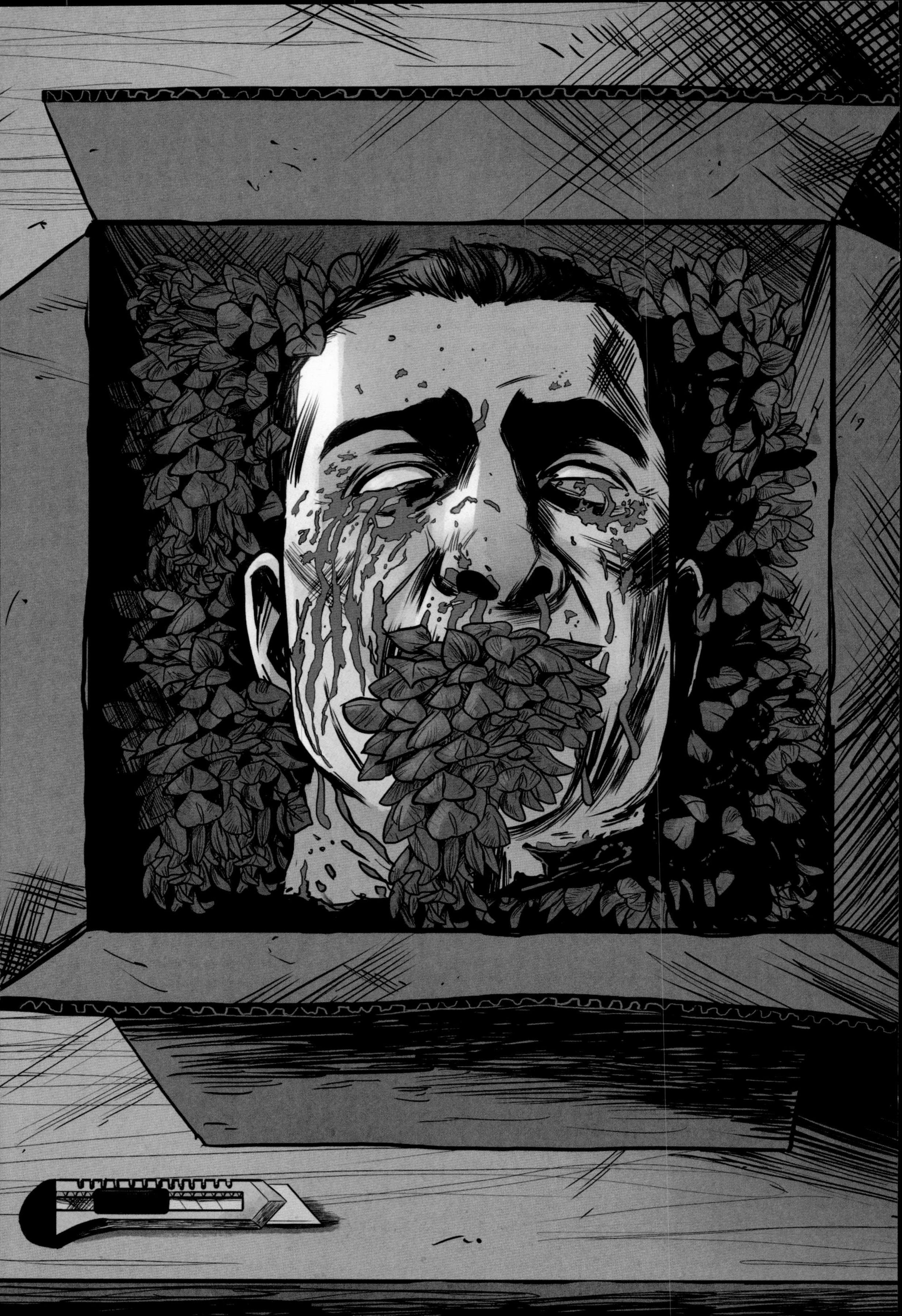

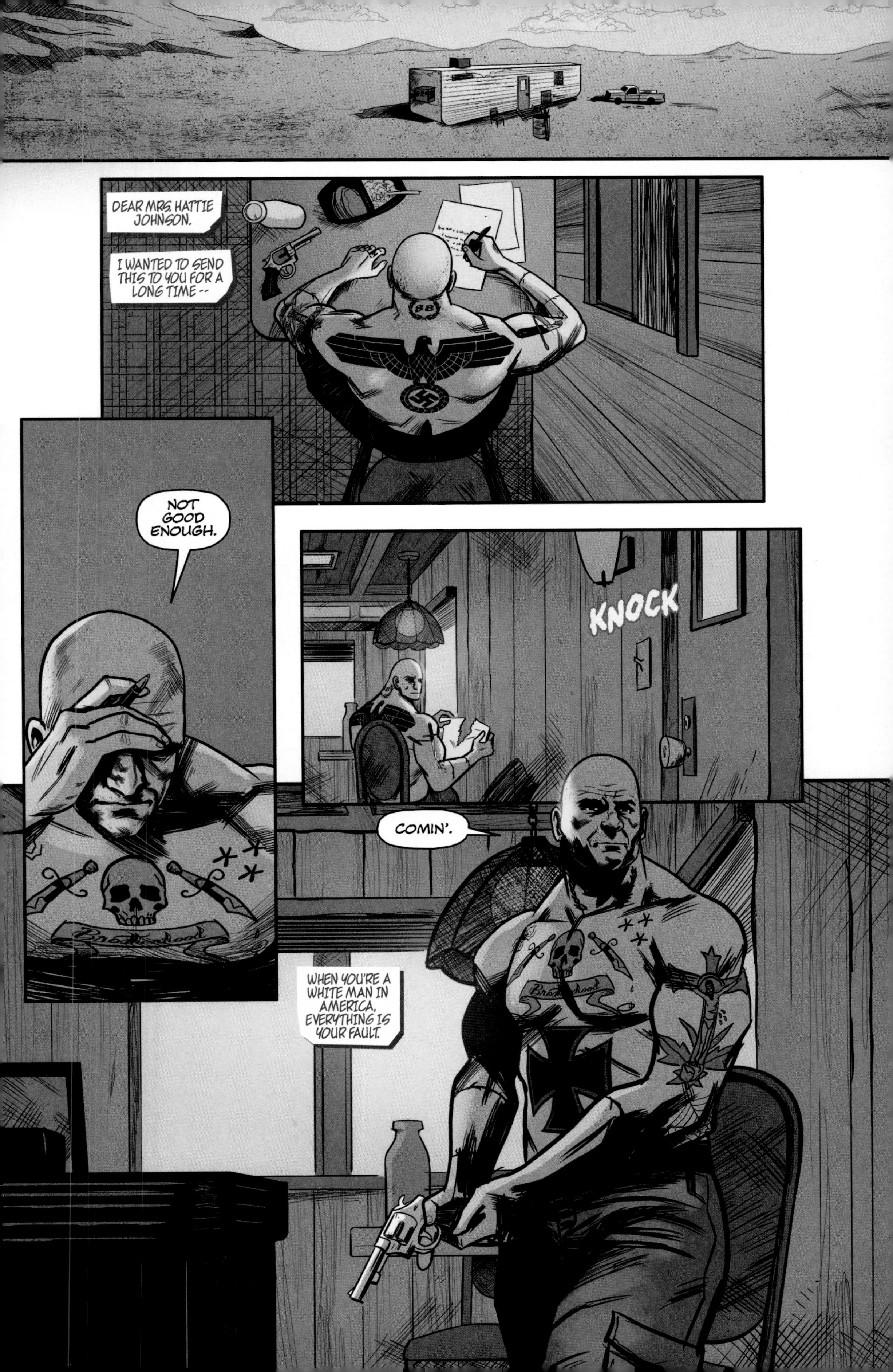
DEAR MRS. HATTIE JOHNSON.
I WANTED TO SEND THIS TO YOU FOR A LONG TIME --
NOT GOOD ENOUGH.
KNOCK
COMIN'.
WHEN YOU'RE A WHITE MAN IN AMERICA, EVERYTHING IS YOUR FAULT.

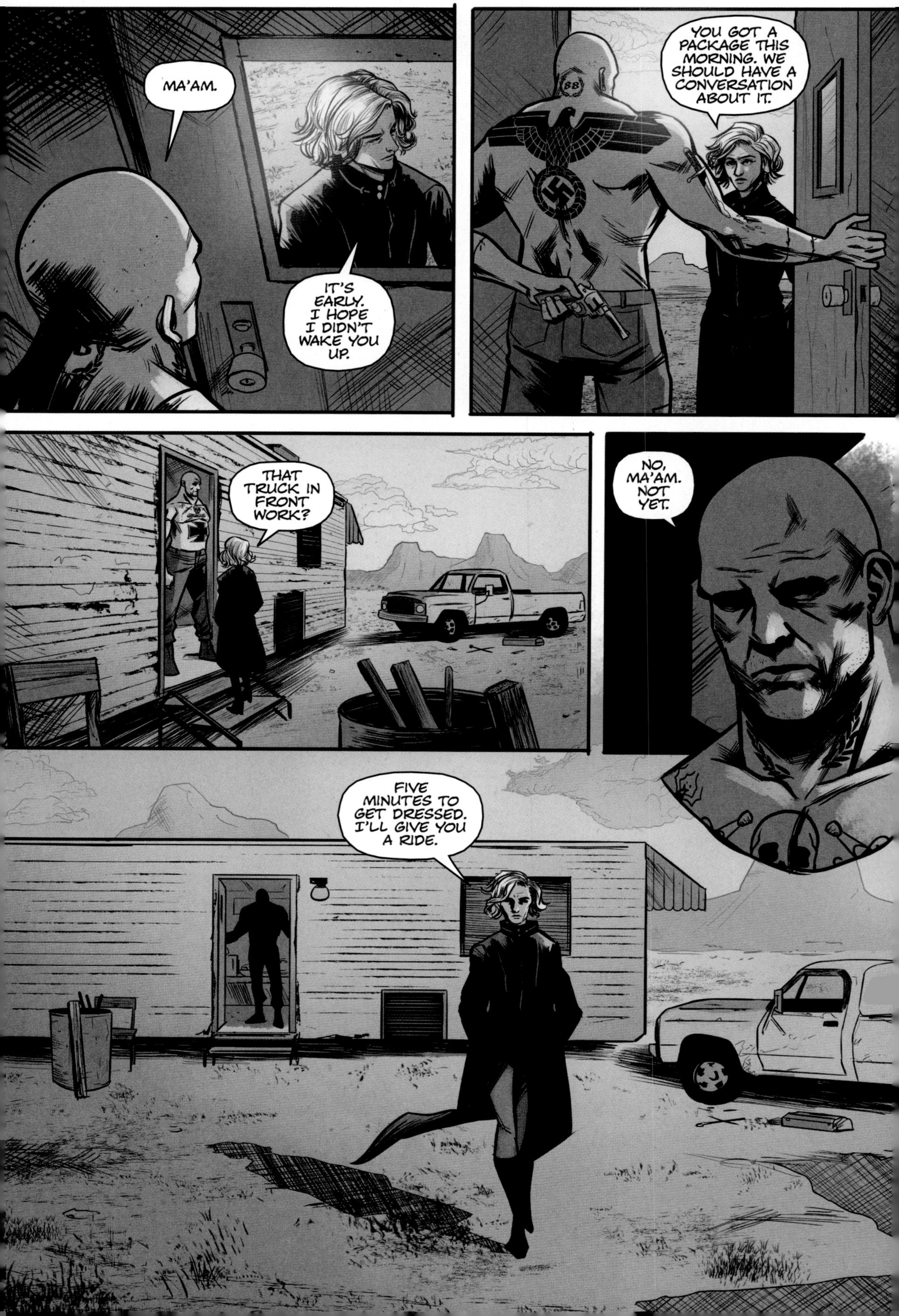
MA'AM.
IT'S EARLY. I HOPE I DIDN'T WAKE YOU UP.
YOU GOT A PACKAGE THIS MORNING. WE SHOULD HAVE A CONVERSATION ABOUT IT.
THAT TRUCK IN FRONT WORK?
NO, MA'AM. NOT YET.
FIVE MINUTES TO GET DRESSED. I'LL GIVE YOU A RIDE.

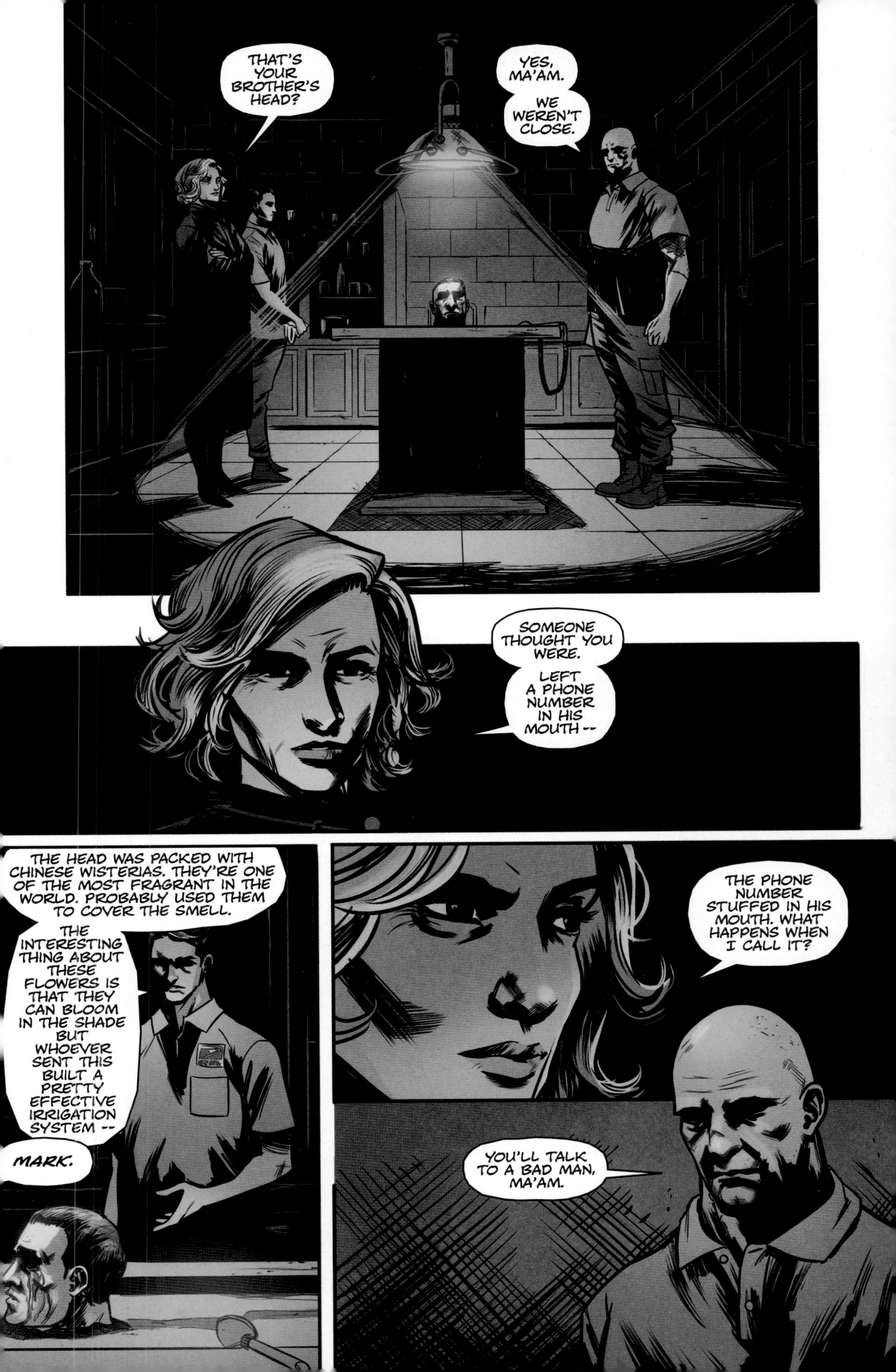
THAT'S YOUR BROTHER'S HEAD?
YES, MA'AM.
WE WEREN'T CLOSE.
SOMEONE THOUGHT YOU WERE.
LEFT A PHONE NUMBER IN HIS MOUTH --
THE HEAD WAS PACKED WITH CHINESE WISTERIAS. THEY'RE ONE OF THE MOST FRAGRANT IN THE WORLD. PROBABLY USED THEM TO COVER THE SMELL.
THE INTERESTING THING ABOUT THESE FLOWERS IS THAT THEY CAN BLOOM IN THE SHADE BUT WHOEVER SENT THIS BUILT A PRETTY EFFECTIVE IRRIGATION SYSTEM --
MARK.
THE PHONE NUMBER STUFFED IN HIS MOUTH. WHAT HAPPENS WHEN I CALL IT?
YOU'LL TALK TO A BAD MAN, MA'AM.

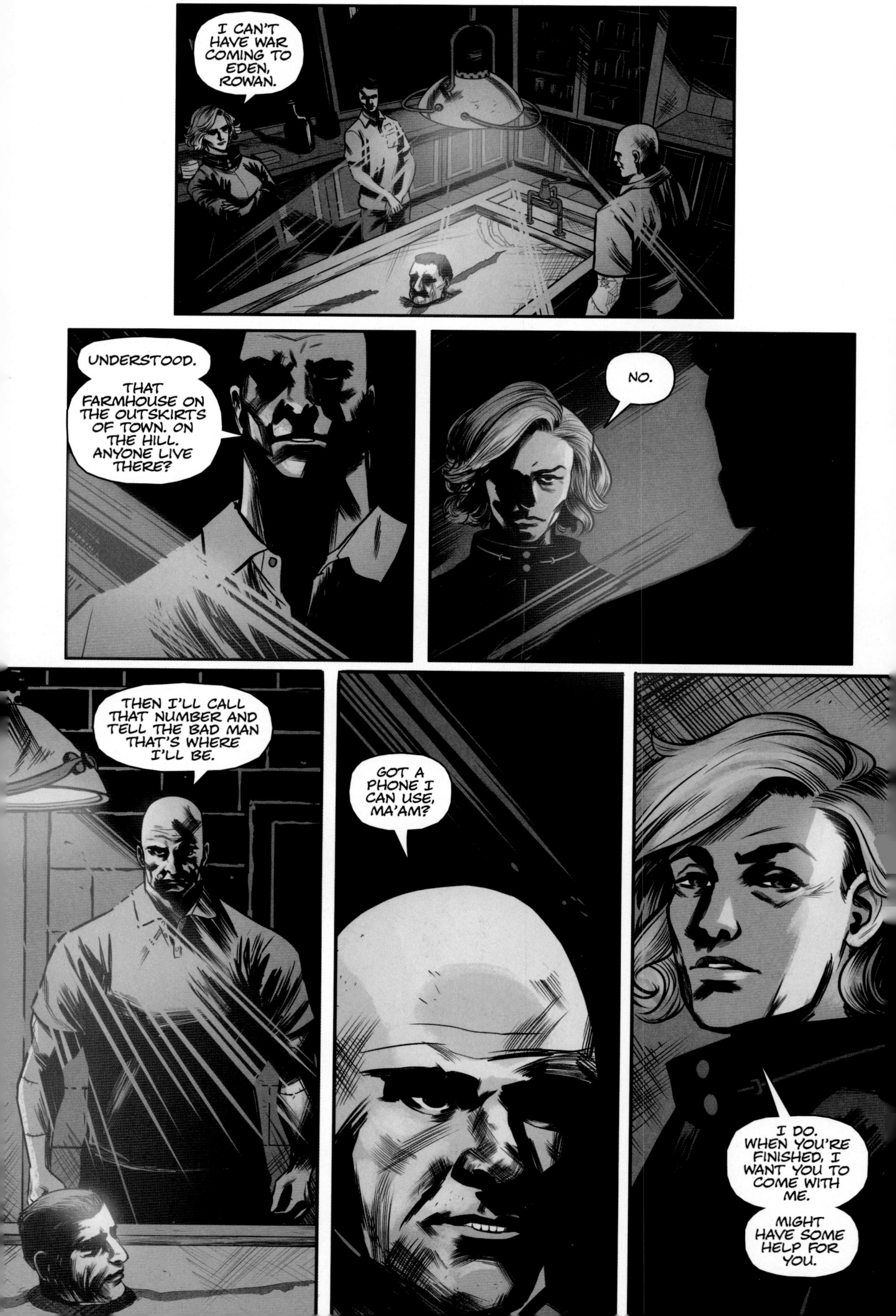
I CAN'T HAVE WAR COMING TO EDEN, ROWAN.
UNDERSTOOD.
THAT FARMHOUSE ON THE OUTSKIRTS OF TOWN. ON THE HILL. ANYONE LIVE THERE?
NO.
THEN I'LL CALL THAT NUMBER AND TELL THE BAD MAN THAT'S WHERE I'LL BE.
GOT A PHONE I CAN USE, MA'AM?
I DO. WHEN YOU'RE FINISHED, I WANT YOU TO COME WITH ME.
MIGHT HAVE SOME HELP FOR YOU.

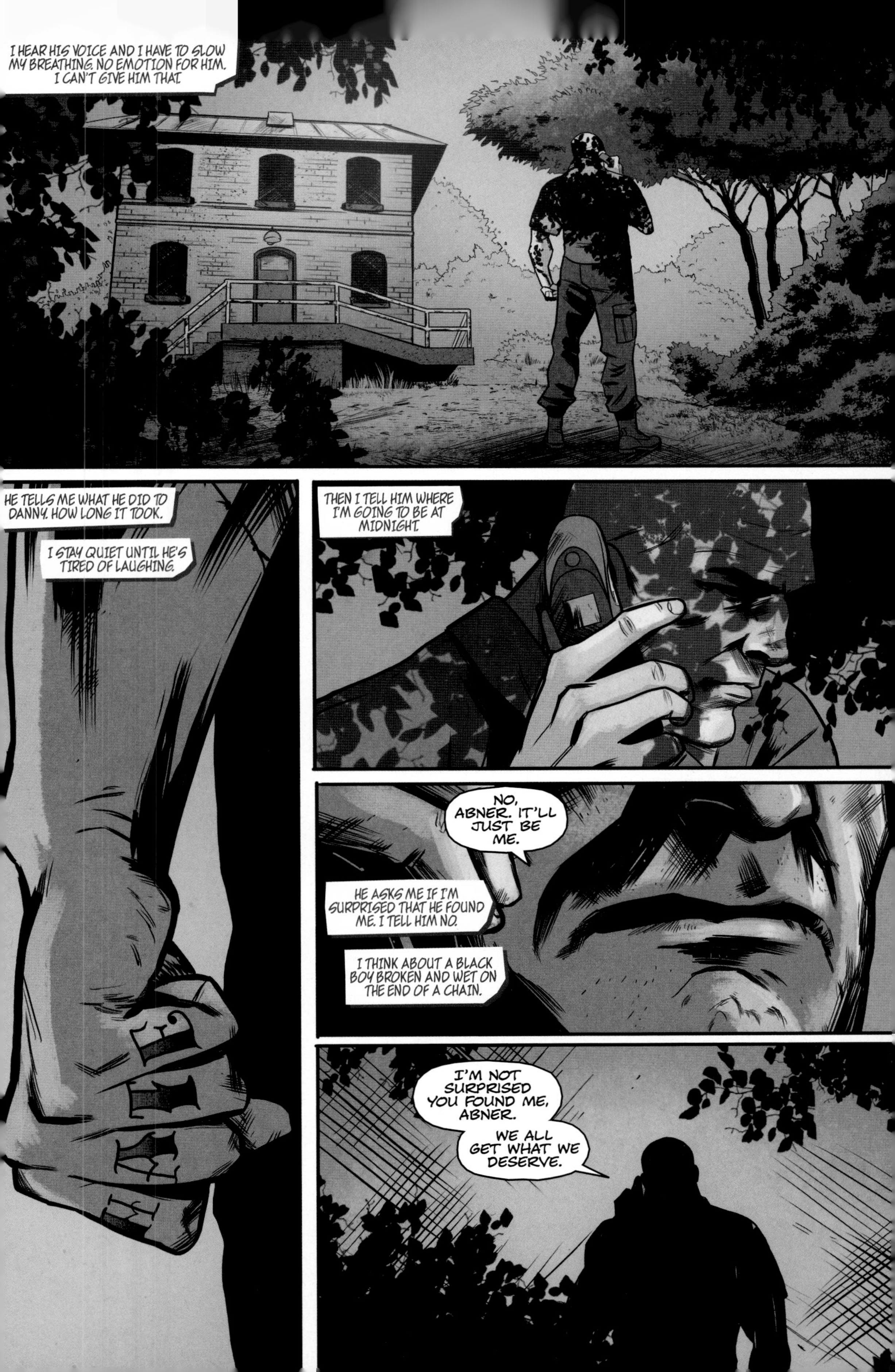
I HEAR HIS VOICE AND I HAVE TO SLOW MY BREATHING. NO EMOTION FOR HIM. I CAN'T GIVE HIM THAT.
HE TELLS ME WHAT HE DID TO DANNY. HOW LONG IT TOOK.
I STAY QUIET UNTIL HE'S TIRED OF LAUGHING.
THEN I TELL HIM WHERE I'M GOING TO BE AT MIDNIGHT.
NO, ABNER. IT'LL JUST BE ME.
HE ASKS ME IF I'M SURPRISED THAT HE FOUND ME. I TELL HIM NO.
I THINK ABOUT A BLACK BOY BROKEN AND WET ON THE END OF A CHAIN.
I'M NOT SURPRISED YOU FOUND ME, ABNER.
WE ALL GET WHAT WE DESERVE.

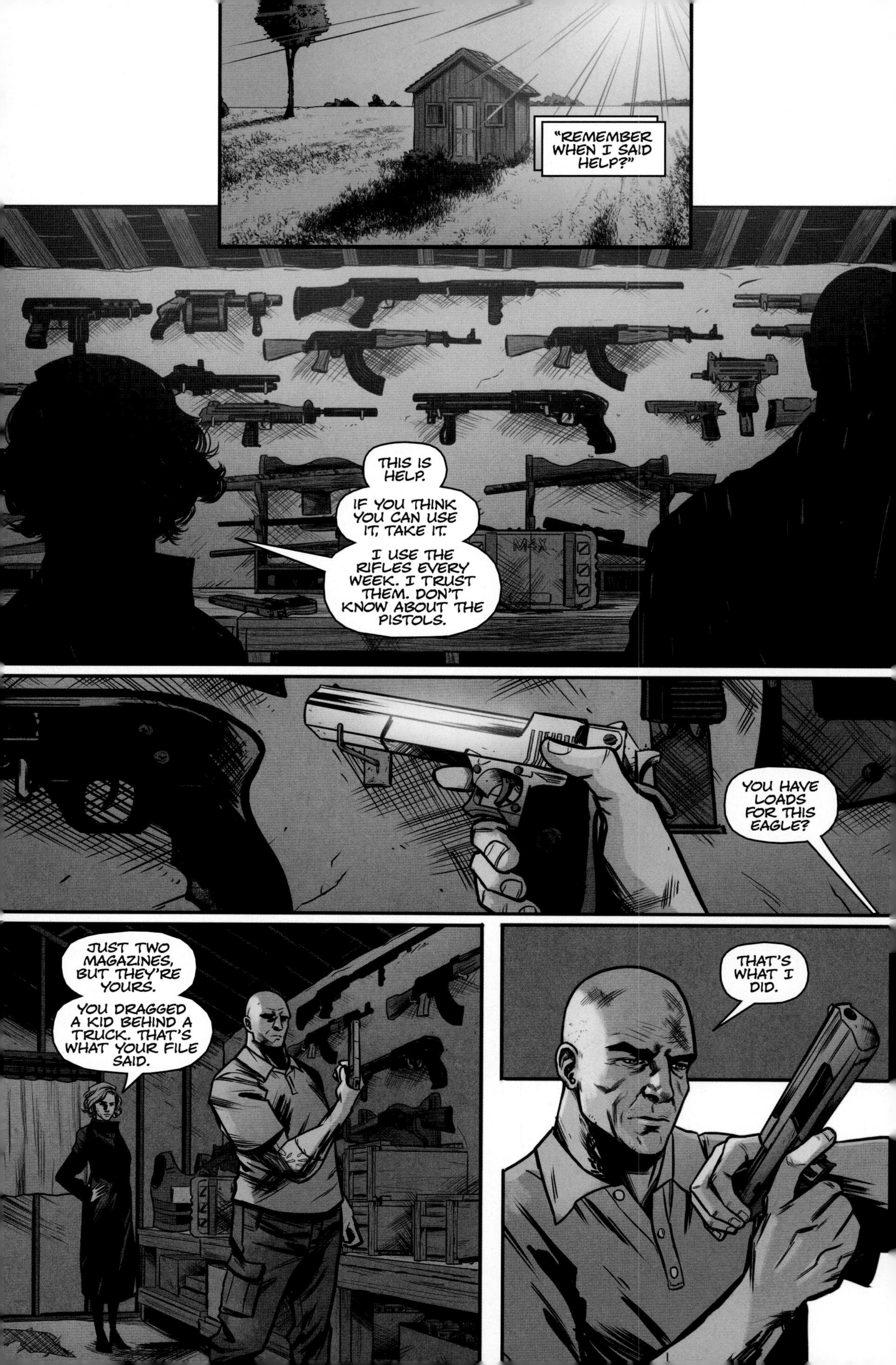
"REMEMBER WHEN I SAID HELP?"
THIS IS HELP.
IF YOU THINK YOU CAN USE IT, TAKE IT.
I USE THE RIFLES EVERY WEEK. I TRUST THEM. DON'T KNOW ABOUT THE PISTOLS.
YOU HAVE LOADS FOR THIS EAGLE?
JUST TWO MAGAZINES, BUT THEY'RE YOURS.
YOU DRAGGED A KID BEHIND A TRUCK. THAT'S WHAT YOUR FILE SAID.
THAT'S WHAT I DID.

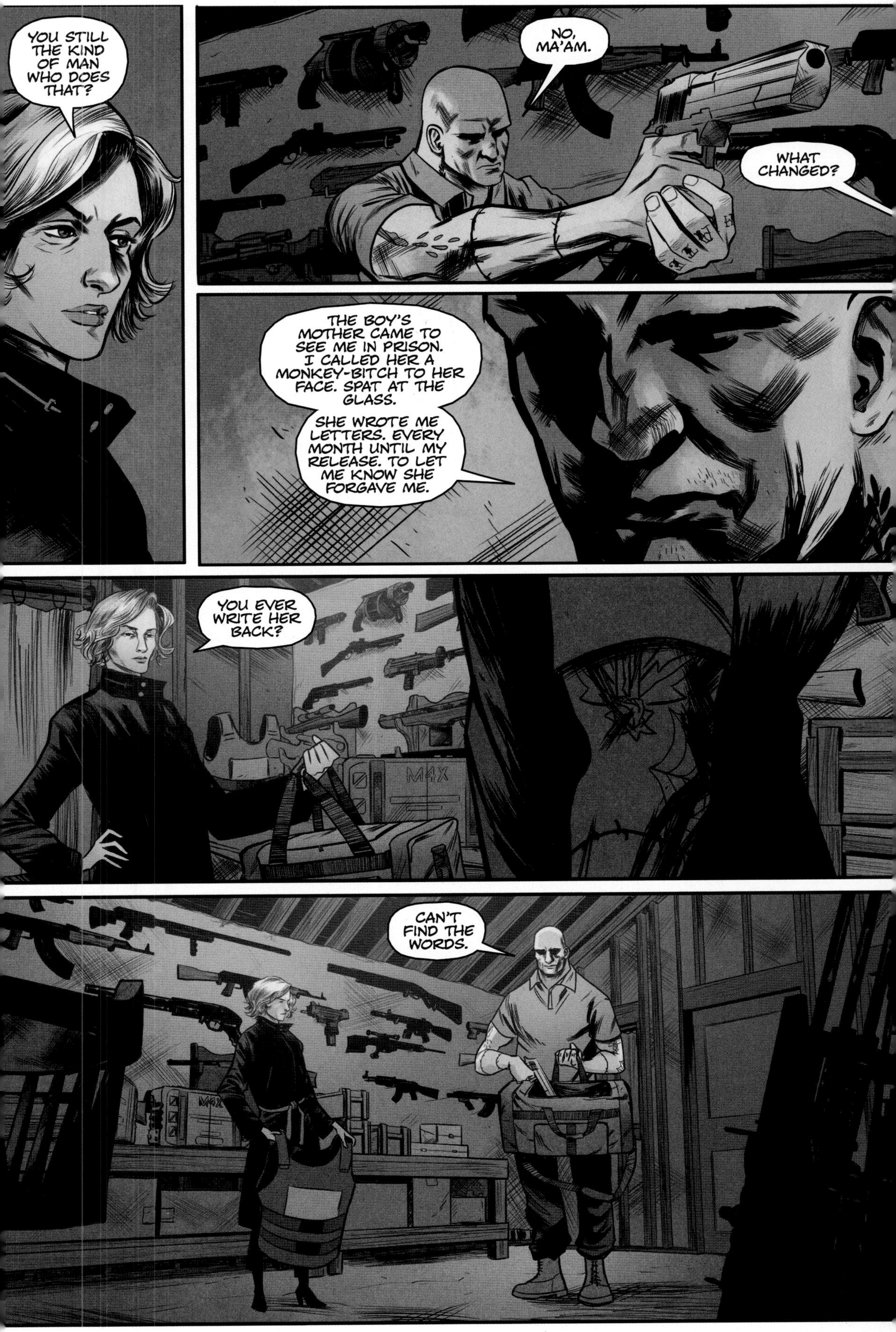
YOU STILL THE KIND OF MAN WHO DOES THAT?
NO, MA'AM.
WHAT CHANGED?
THE BOY'S MOTHER CAME TO SEE ME IN PRISON. I CALLED HER A MONKEY-BITCH TO HER FACE. SPAT AT THE GLASS.
SHE WROTE ME LETTERS. EVERY MONTH UNTIL MY RELEASE. TO LET ME KNOW SHE FORGAVE ME.
YOU EVER WRITE HER BACK?
M4X
CAN'T FIND THE WORDS.

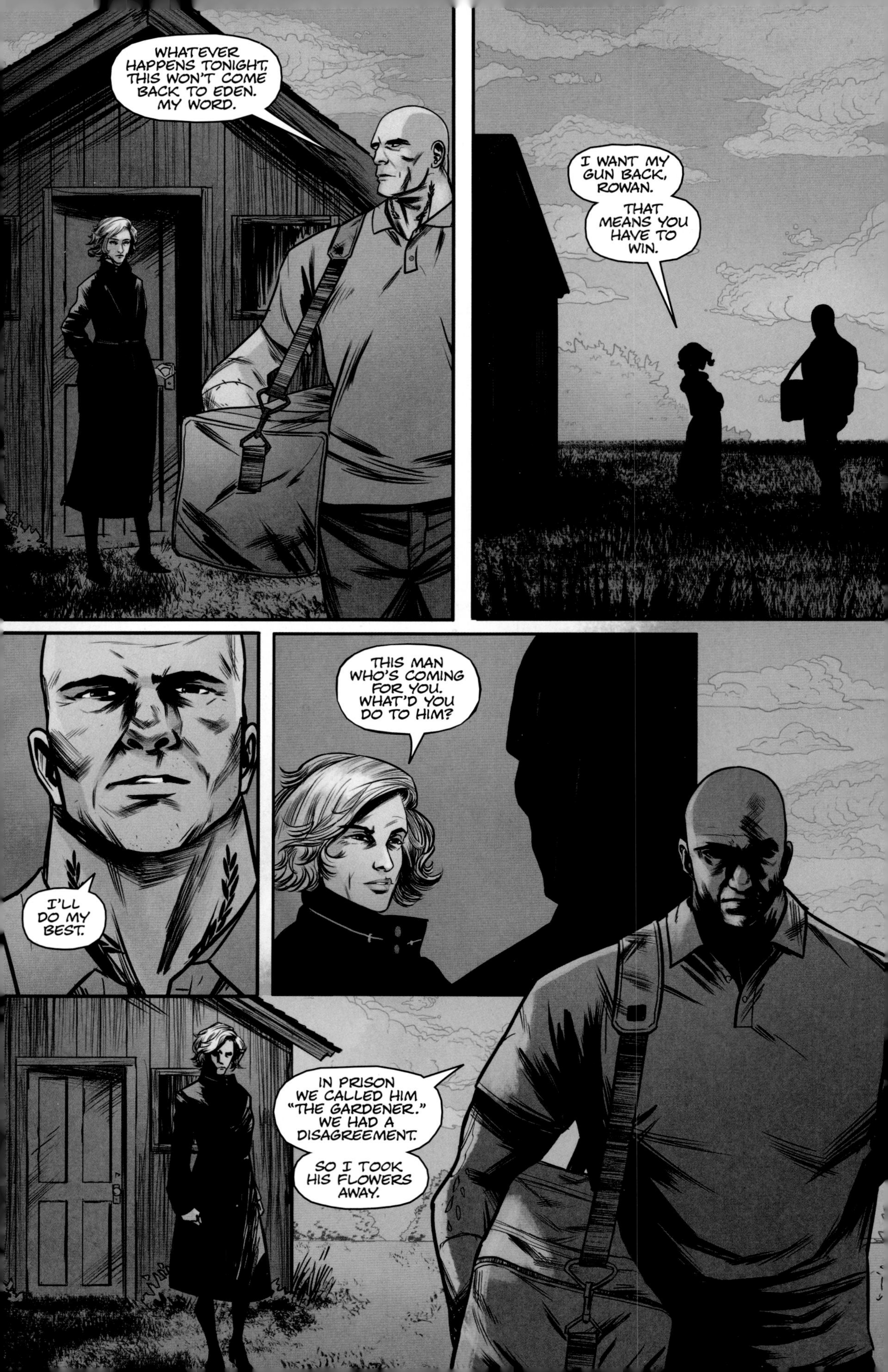

WHATEVER HAPPENS TONIGHT, THIS WON'T COME BACK TO EDEN. MY WORD.
I WANT MY GUN BACK, ROWAN.
THAT MEANS YOU HAVE TO WIN.
I'LL DO MY BEST.
THIS MAN WHO'S COMING FOR YOU. WHAT'D YOU DO TO HIM?
IN PRISON WE CALLED HIM "THE GARDENER." WE HAD A DISAGREEMENT.
SO I TOOK HIS FLOWERS AWAY.

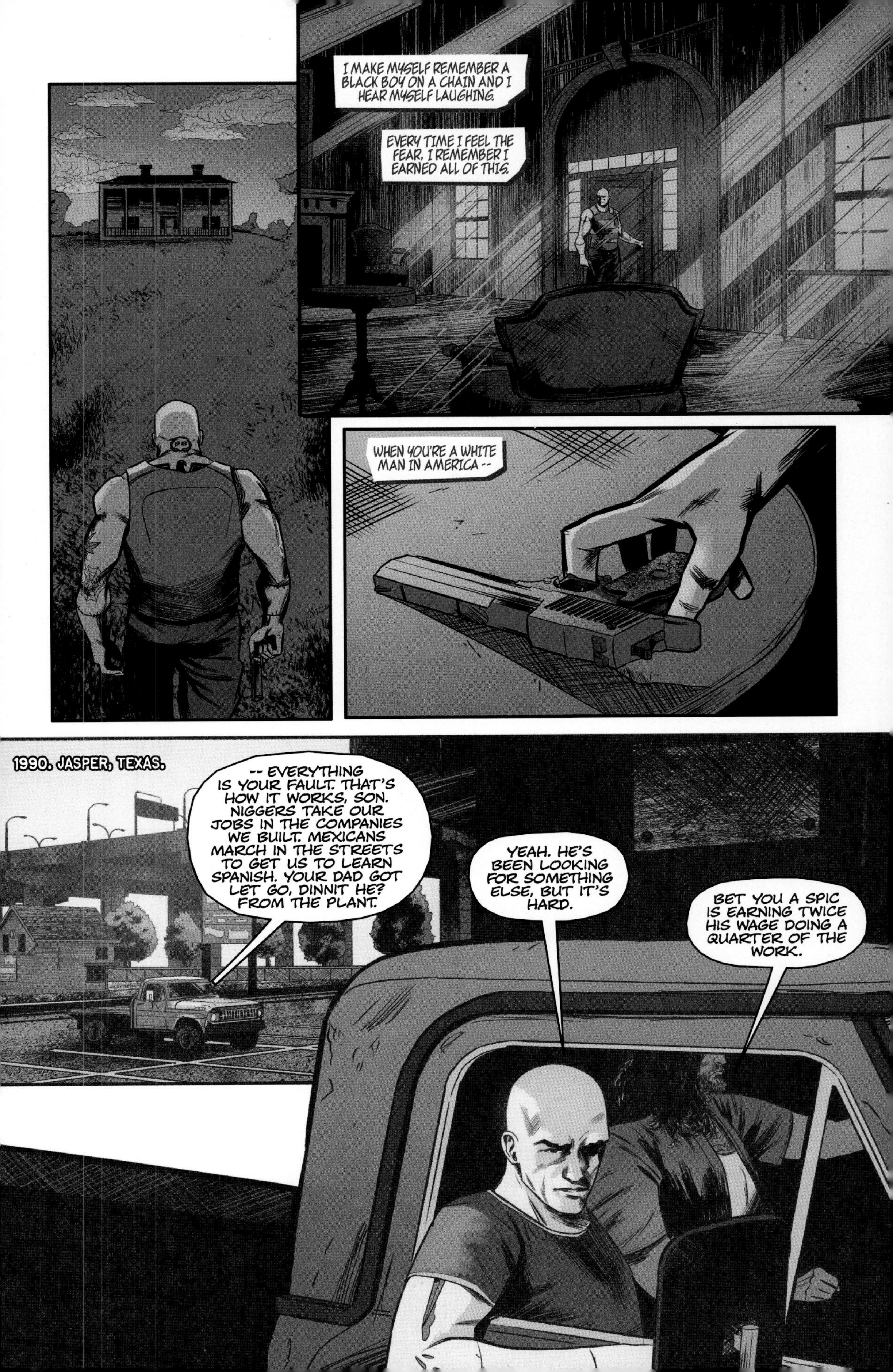

I MAKE MYSELF REMEMBER A BLACK BOY ON A CHAIN AND I HEAR MYSELF LAUGHING.
EVERY TIME I FEEL THE FEAR, I REMEMBER I EARNED ALL OF THIS.
WHEN YOU'RE A WHITE MAN IN AMERICA --
1990. JASPER, TEXAS.
-- EVERYTHING IS YOUR FAULT. THAT'S HOW IT WORKS, SON. NIGGERS TAKE OUR JOBS IN THE COMPANIES WE BUILT. MEXICANS MARCH IN THE STREETS TO GET US TO LEARN SPANISH. YOUR DAD GOT LET GO, DINNIT HE? FROM THE PLANT.
YEAH. HE'S BEEN LOOKING FOR SOMETHING ELSE, BUT IT'S HARD.
BET YOU A SPIC IS EARNING TWICE HIS WAGE DOING A QUARTER OF THE WORK.

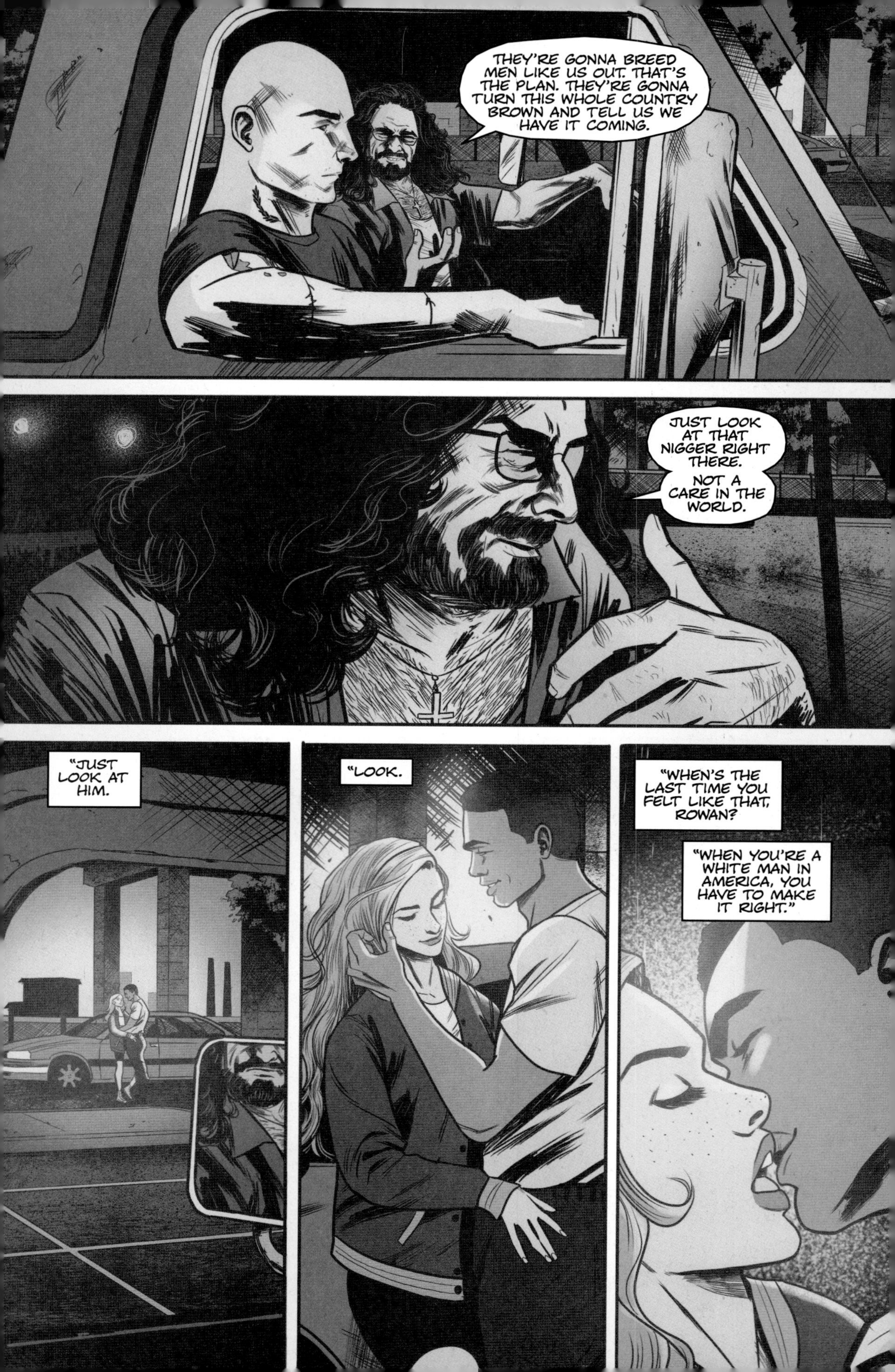
THEY'RE GONNA BREED MEN LIKE US OUT. THAT'S THE PLAN. THEY'RE GONNA TURN THIS WHOLE COUNTRY BROWN AND TELL US WE HAVE IT COMING.
JUST LOOK AT THAT NIGGER RIGHT THERE.
NOT A CARE IN THE WORLD.
"JUST LOOK AT HIM.
"LOOK.
"WHEN'S THE LAST TIME YOU FELT LIKE THAT, ROWAN?
"WHEN YOU'RE A WHITE MAN IN AMERICA, YOU HAVE TO MAKE IT RIGHT."

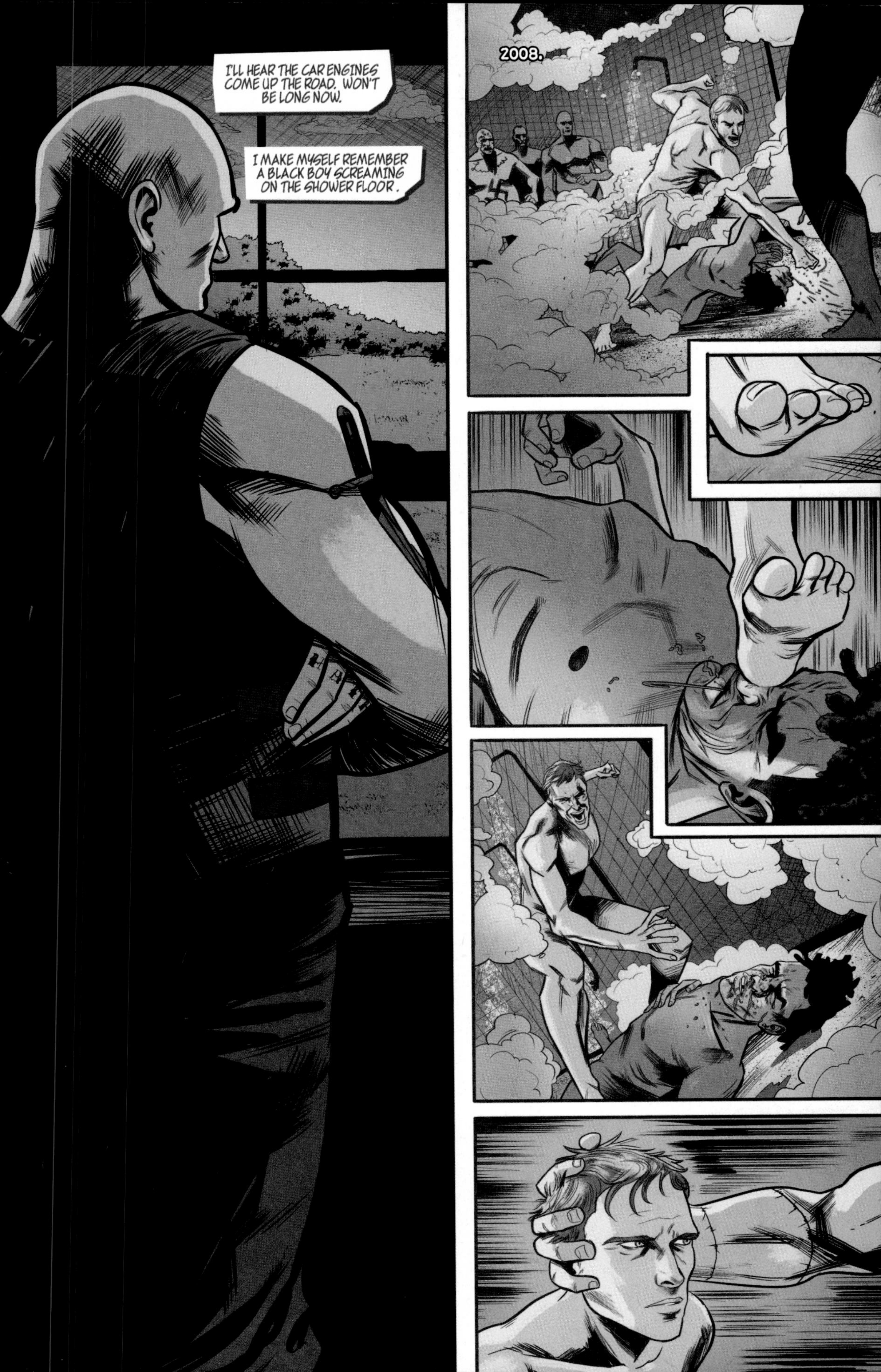
I'LL HEAR THE CAR ENGINES COME UP THE ROAD. WON'T BE LONG NOW.
I MAKE MYSELF REMEMBER A BLACK BOY SCREAMING ON THE SHOWER FLOOR.
2008.

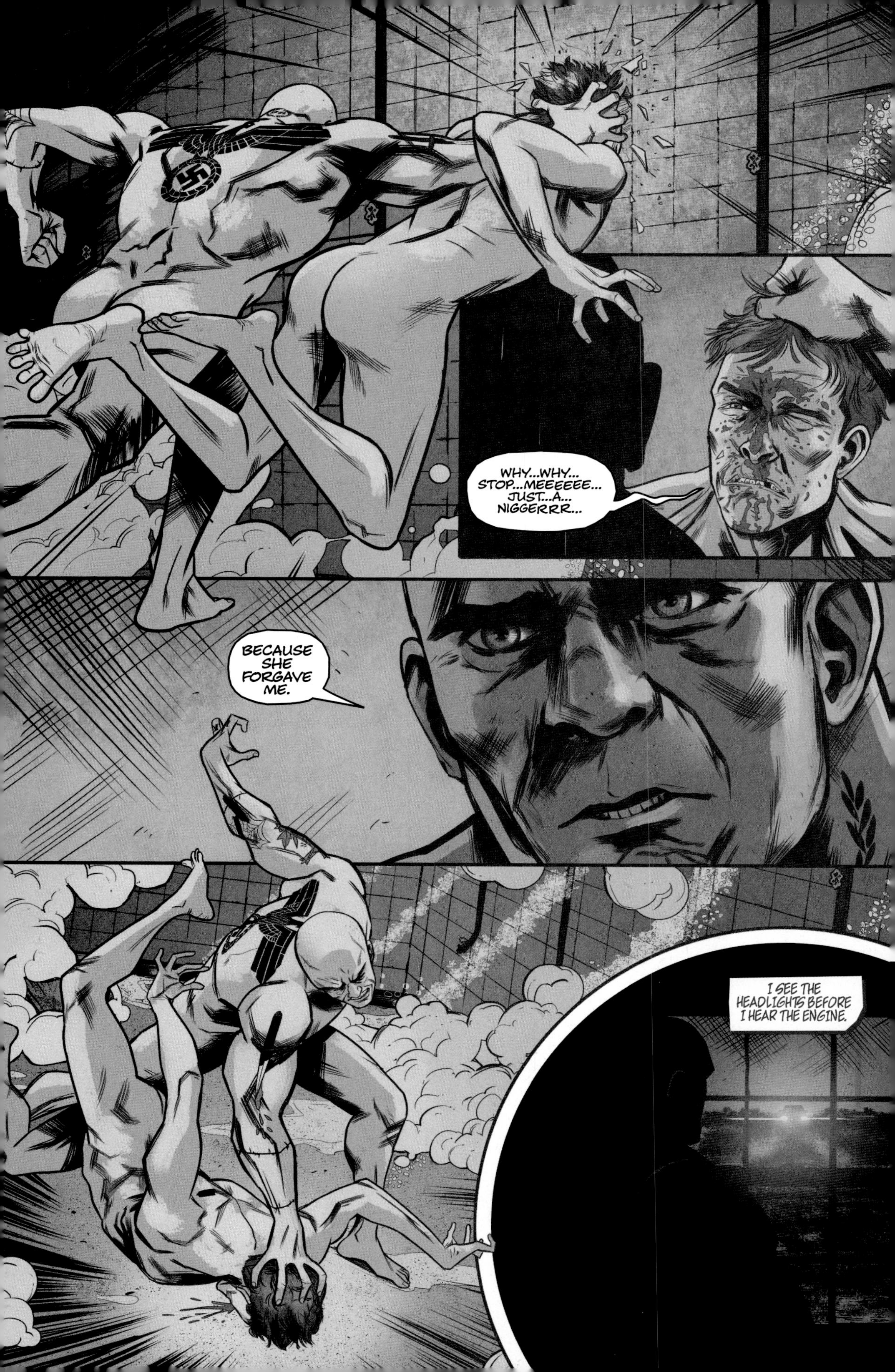
WHY...WHY... STOP...MEEEEEE... JUST...A... NIGGERRR...
BECAUSE SHE FORGAVE ME.
I SEE THE HEADLIGHTS BEFORE I HEAR THE ENGINE.

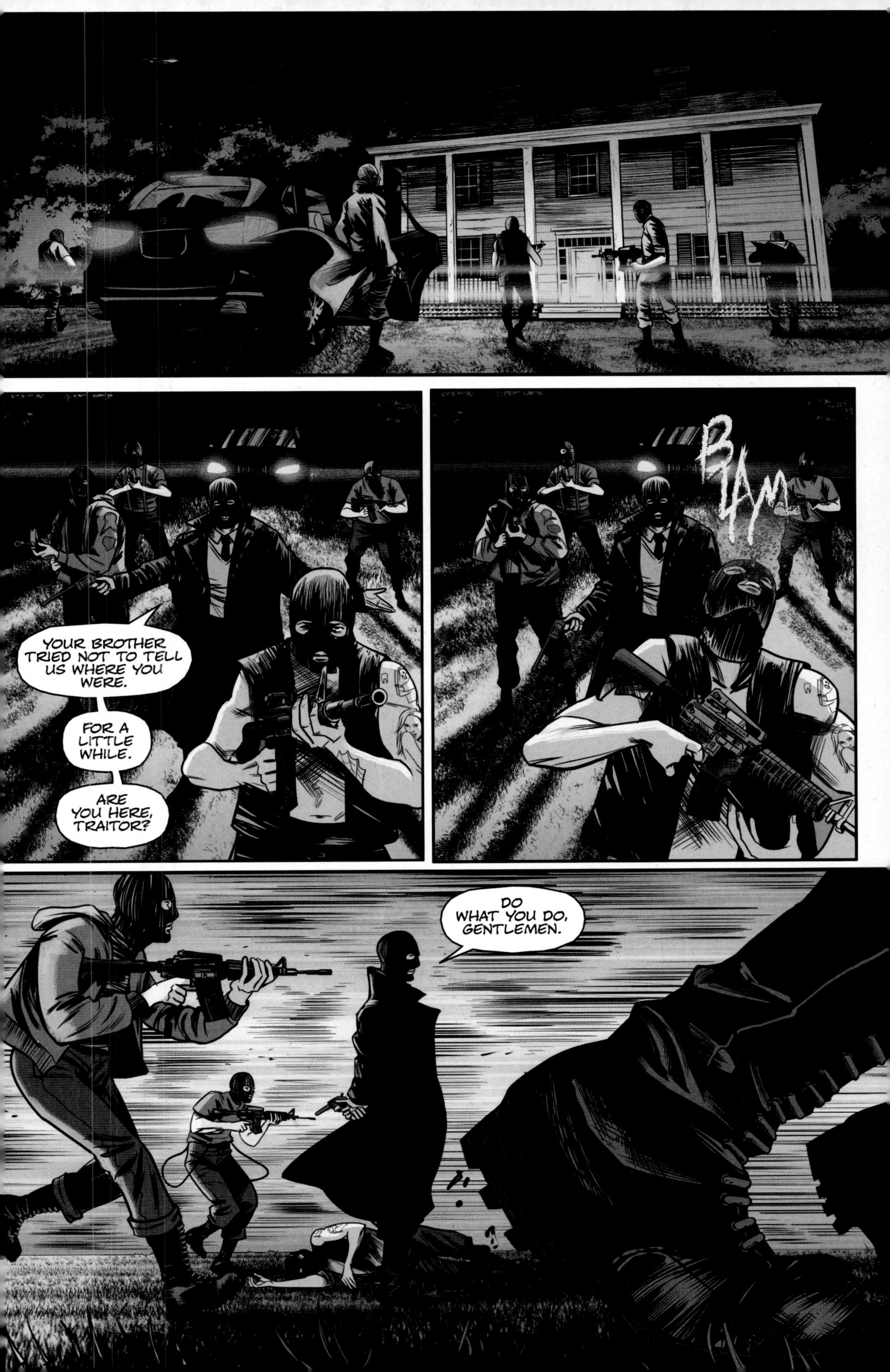
YOUR BROTHER TRIED NOT TO TELL US WHERE YOU WERE.
FOR A LITTLE WHILE.
ARE YOU HERE, TRAITOR?
BLAM
DO WHAT YOU DO, GENTLEMEN.

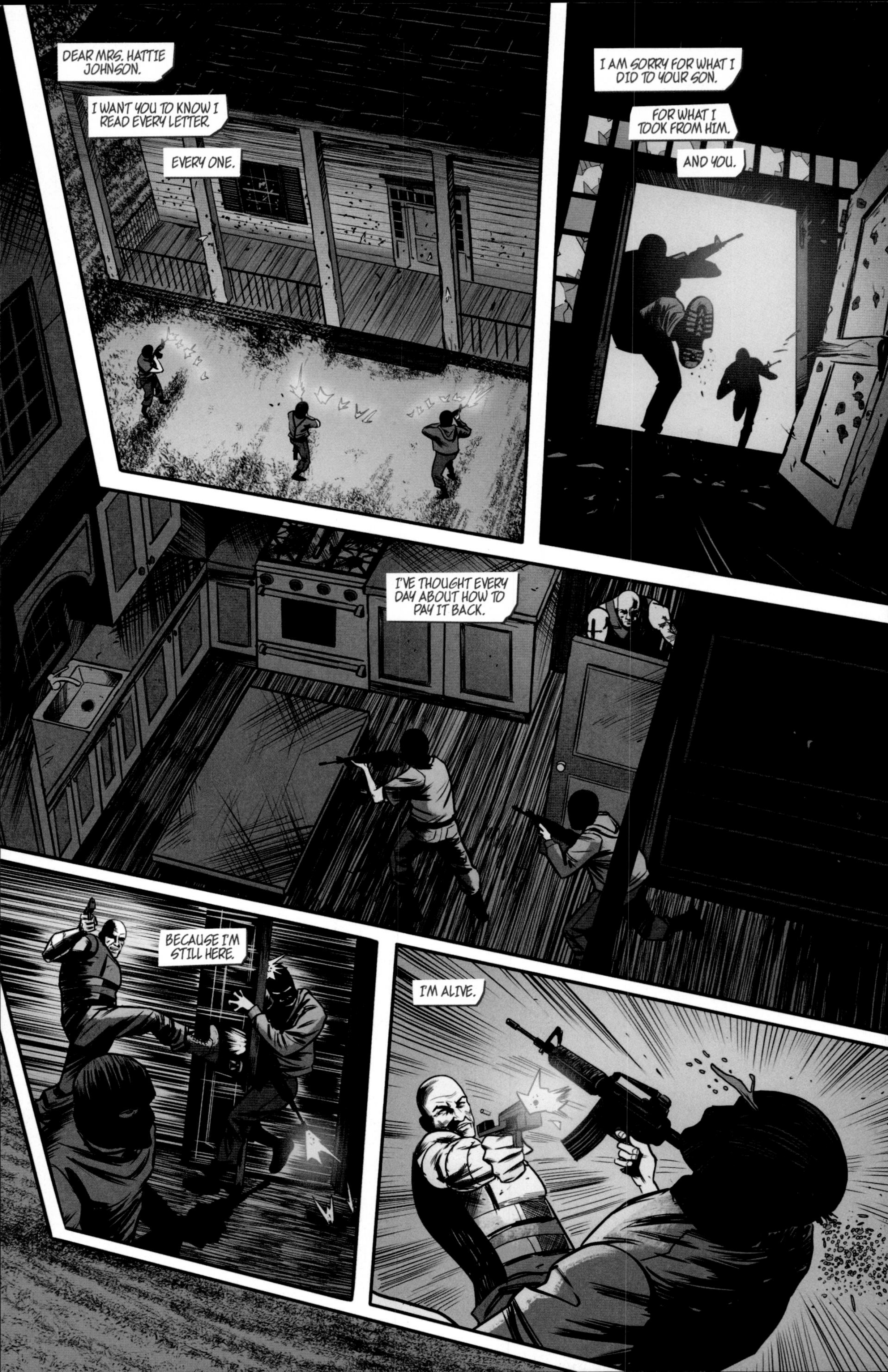
DEAR MRS. HATTIE JOHNSON.
I WANT YOU TO KNOW I READ EVERY LETTER.
EVERY ONE.
I AM SORRY FOR WHAT I DID TO YOUR SON.
FOR WHAT I TOOK FROM HIM.
AND YOU.
I'VE THOUGHT EVERY DAY ABOUT HOW TO PAY IT BACK.
BECAUSE I'M STILL HERE.
I'M ALIVE.

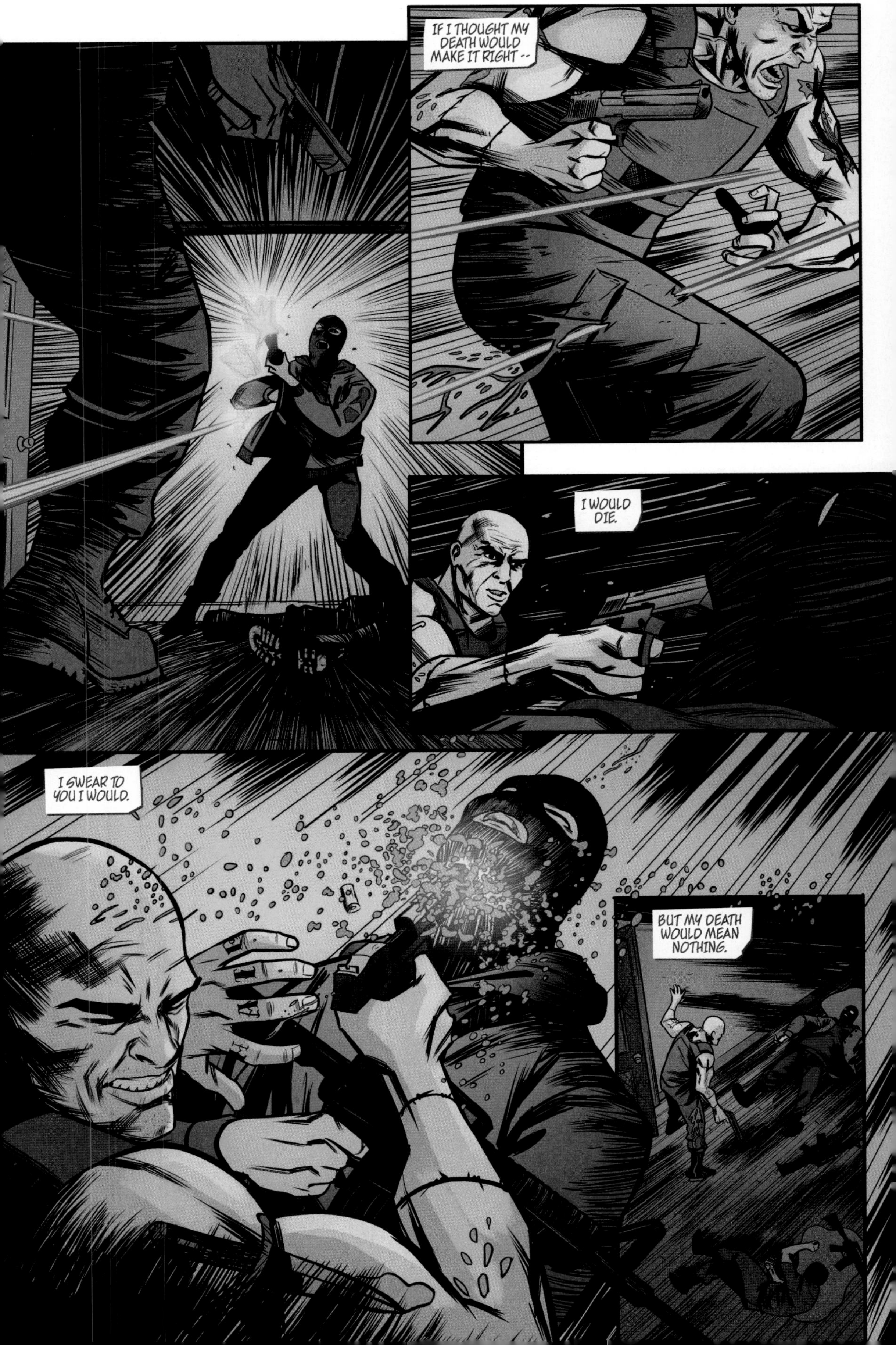
IF I THOUGHT MY DEATH WOULD MAKE IT RIGHT --
I WOULD DIE.
I SWEAR TO YOU I WOULD.
BUT MY DEATH WOULD MEAN NOTHING.

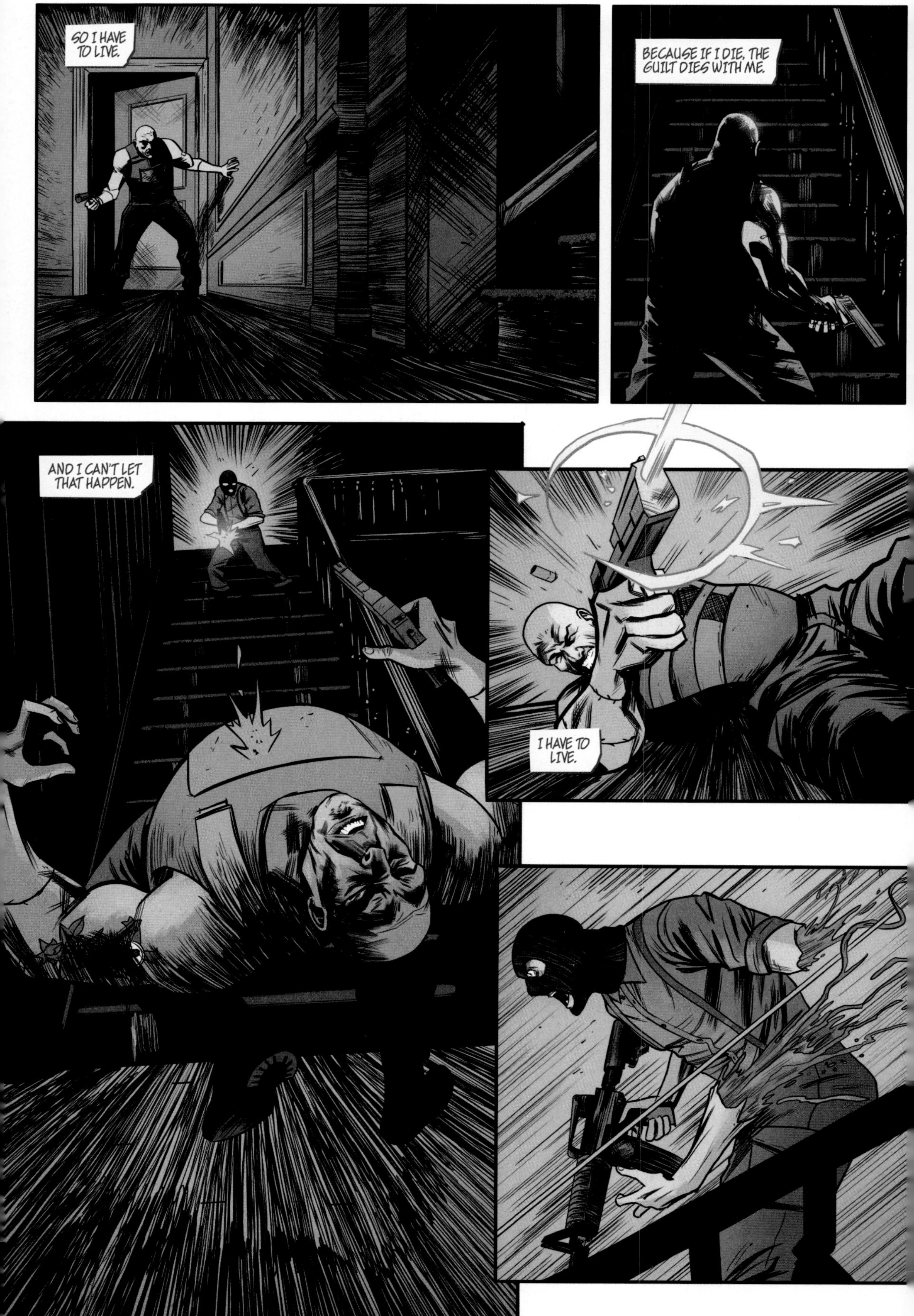
SO I HAVE TO LIVE.
BECAUSE IF I DIE, THE GUILT DIES WITH ME.
AND I CAN'T LET THAT HAPPEN.
I HAVE TO LIVE.

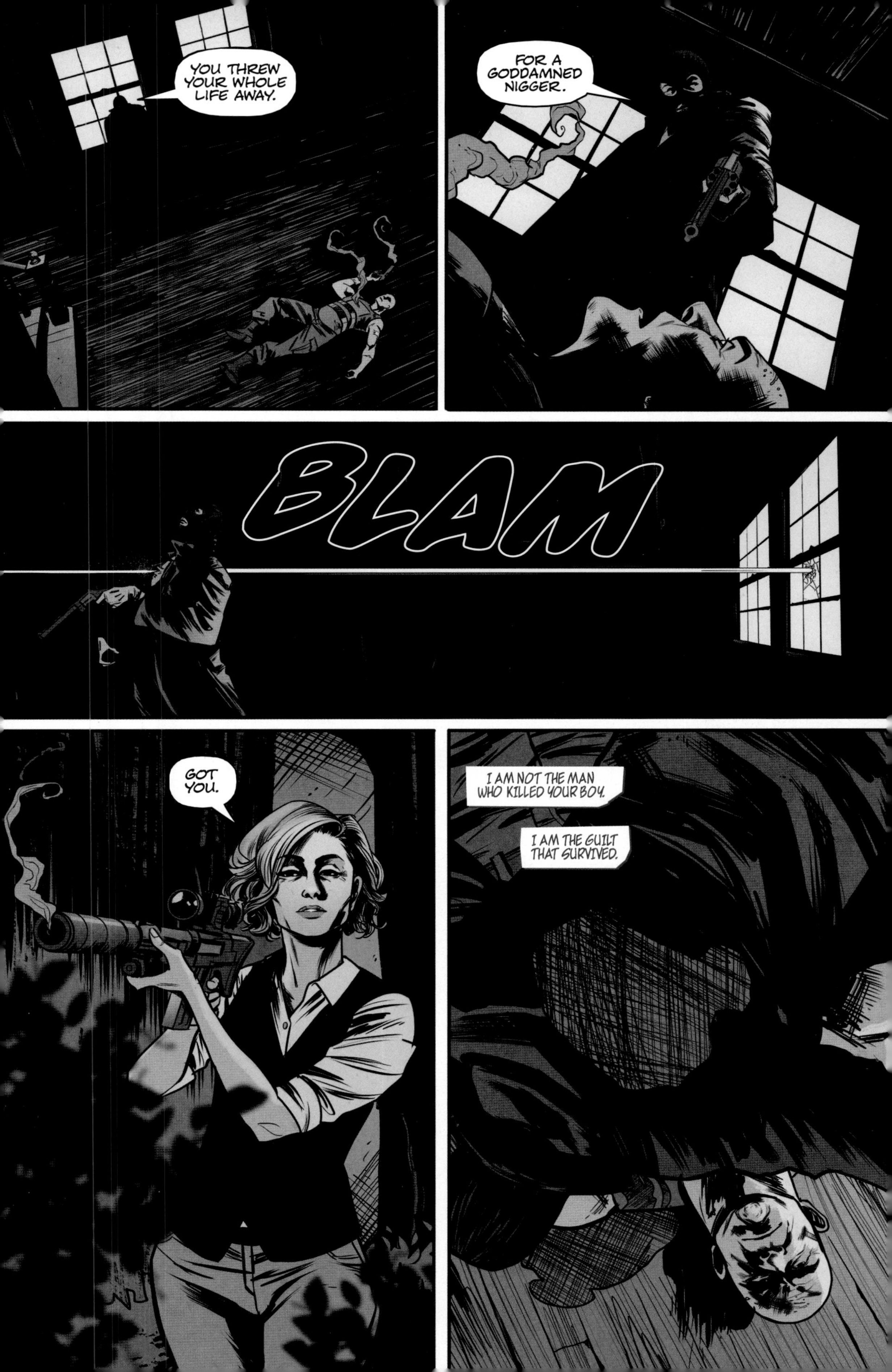
YOU THREW YOUR WHOLE LIFE AWAY.
FOR A GODDAMNED NIGGER.
BLAM
GOT YOU.
I AM NOT THE MAN WHO KILLED YOUR BOY.
I AM THE GUILT THAT SURVIVED.

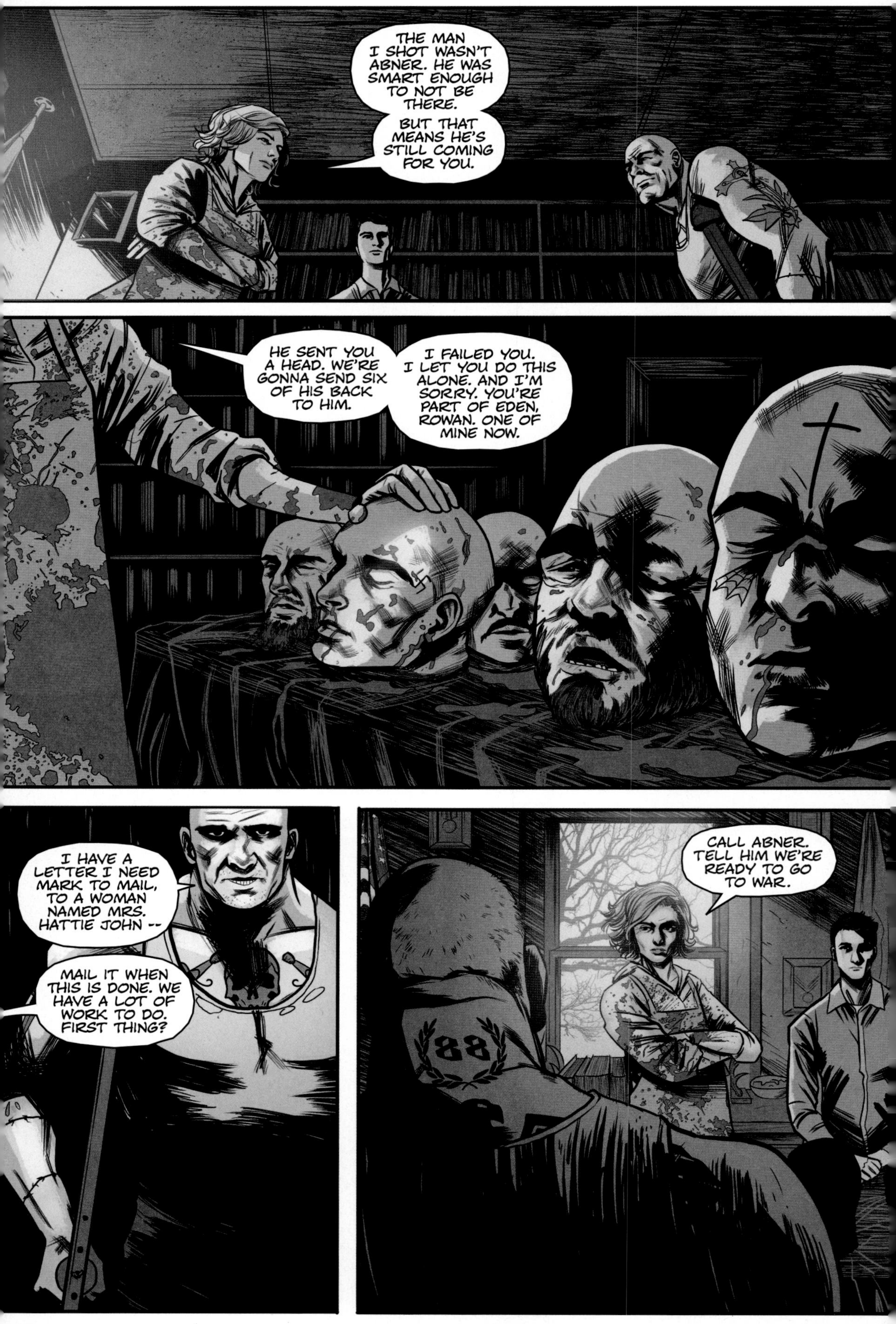
THE MAN I SHOT WASN'T ABNER. HE WAS SMART ENOUGH TO NOT BE THERE.
BUT THAT MEANS HE'S STILL COMING FOR YOU.
HE SENT YOU A HEAD. WE'RE GONNA SEND SIX OF HIS BACK TO HIM.
I FAILED YOU. I LET YOU DO THIS ALONE. AND I'M SORRY. YOU'RE PART OF EDEN, ROWAN. ONE OF MINE NOW.
I HAVE A LETTER I NEED MARK TO MAIL, TO A WOMAN NAMED MRS. HATTIE JOHN --
MAIL IT WHEN THIS IS DONE. WE HAVE A LOT OF WORK TO DO. FIRST THING?
CALL ABNER. TELL HIM WE'RE READY TO GO TO WAR.
88

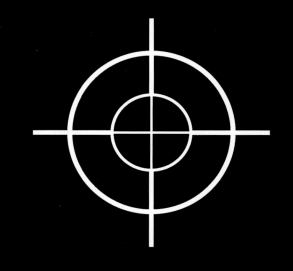

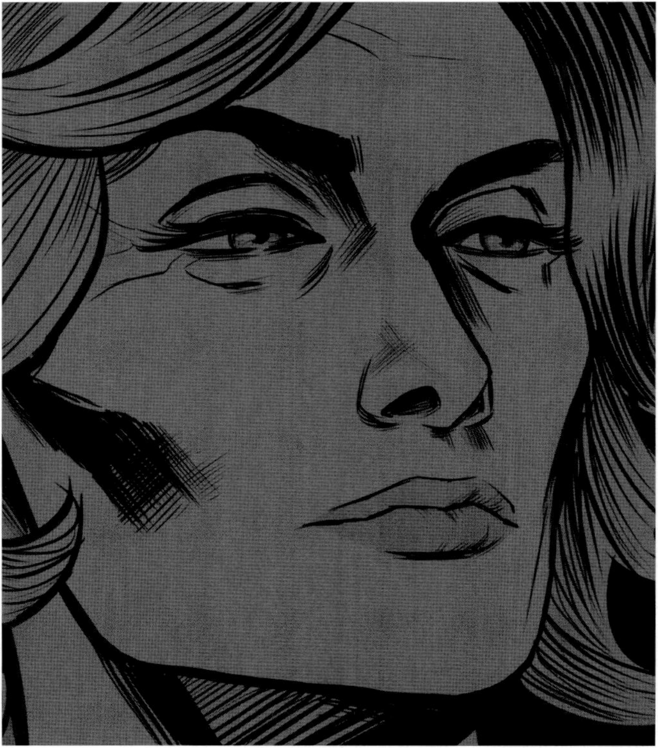

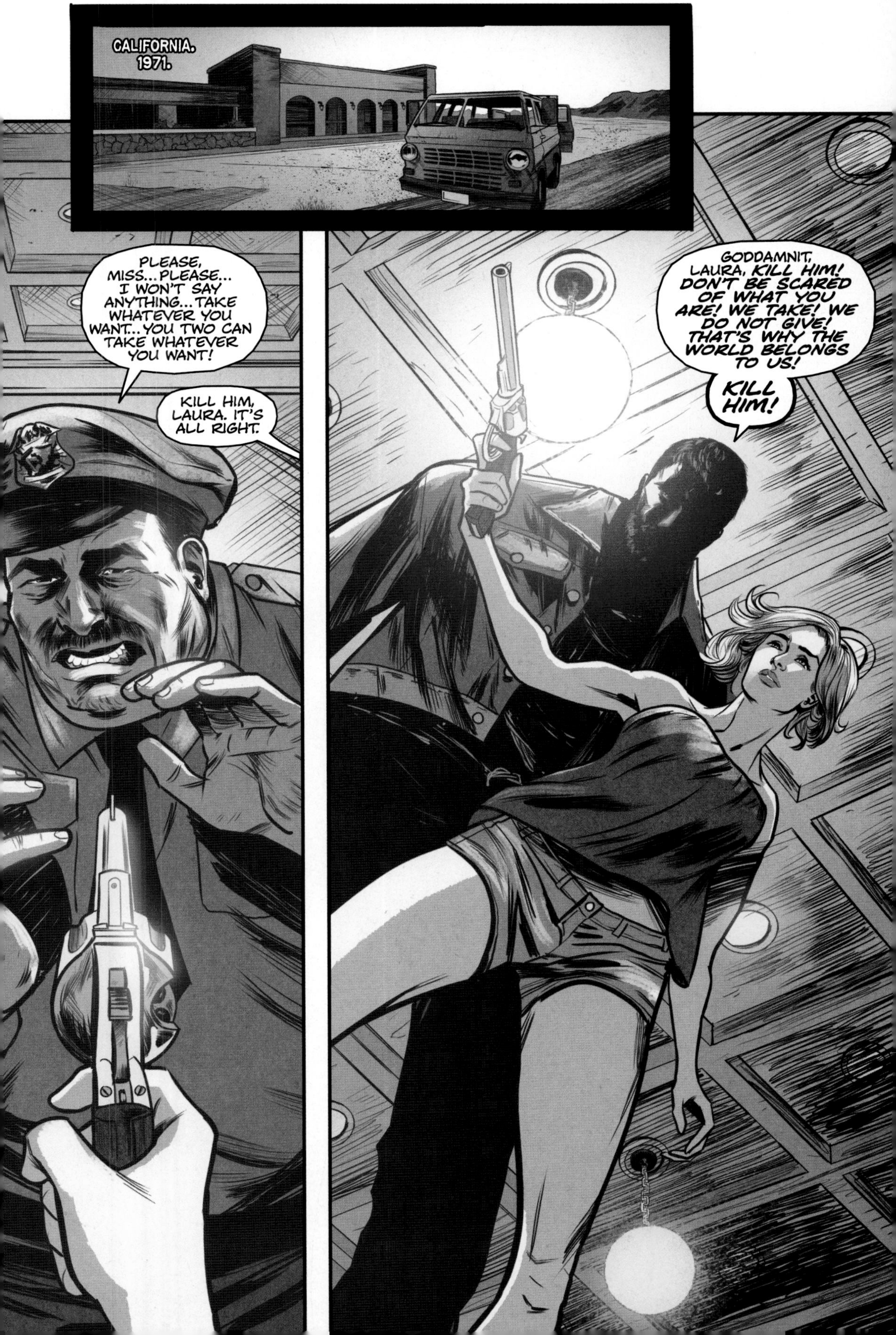
CALIFORNIA. 1971.
PLEASE, MISS... PLEASE... I WON'T SAY ANYTHING... TAKE WHATEVER YOU WANT... YOU TWO CAN TAKE WHATEVER YOU WANT!
KILL HIM, LAURA. IT'S ALL RIGHT.
GODDAMNIT, LAURA, KILL HIM! DON'T BE SCARED OF WHAT YOU ARE! WE TAKE! WE DO NOT GIVE! THAT'S WHY THE WORLD BELONGS TO US!
KILL HIM!

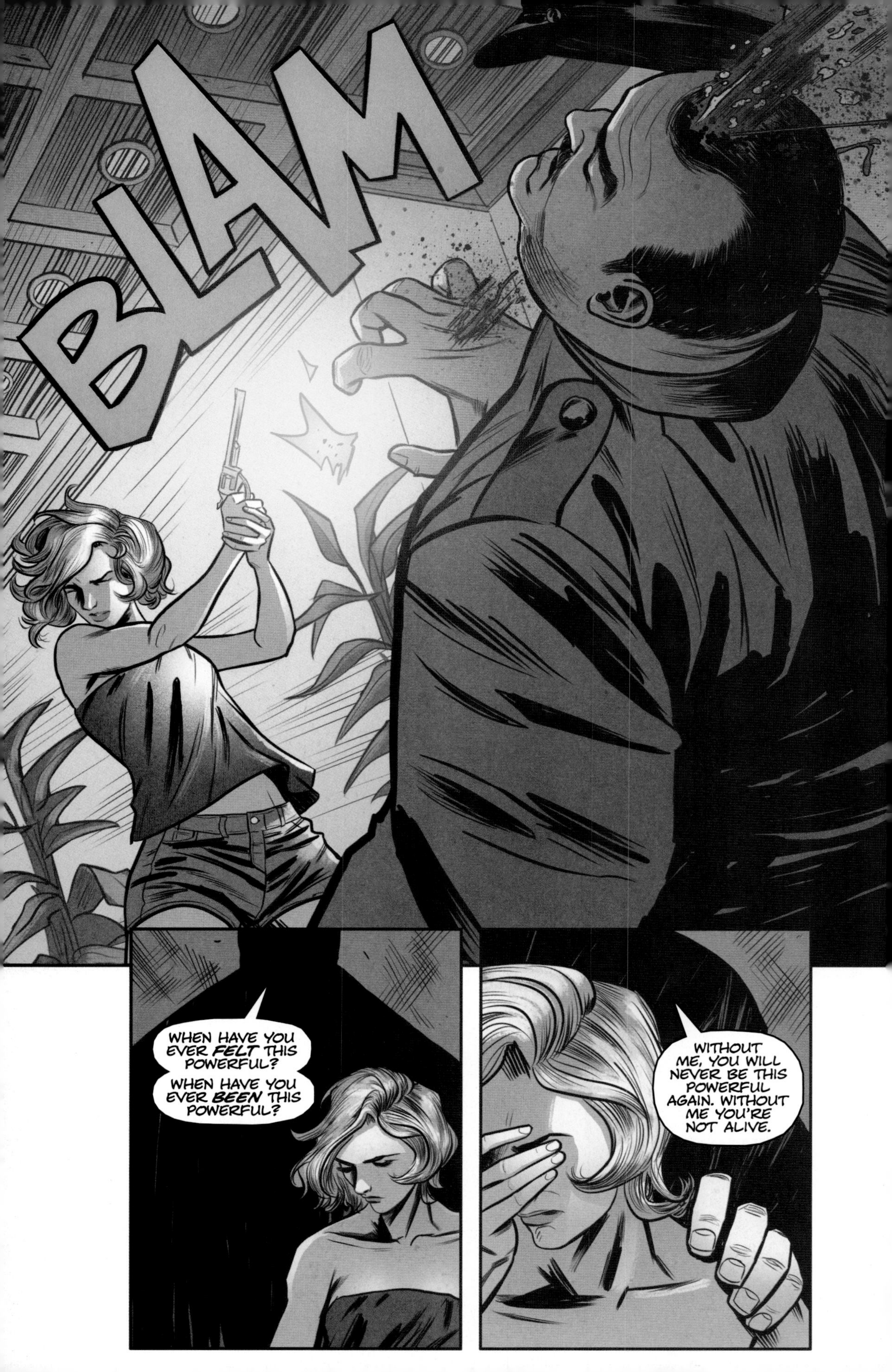
BLAM
WHEN HAVE YOU EVER FELT THIS POWERFUL?
WHEN HAVE YOU EVER BEEN THIS POWERFUL?
WITHOUT ME, YOU WILL NEVER BE THIS POWERFUL AGAIN. WITHOUT ME YOU'RE NOT ALIVE.

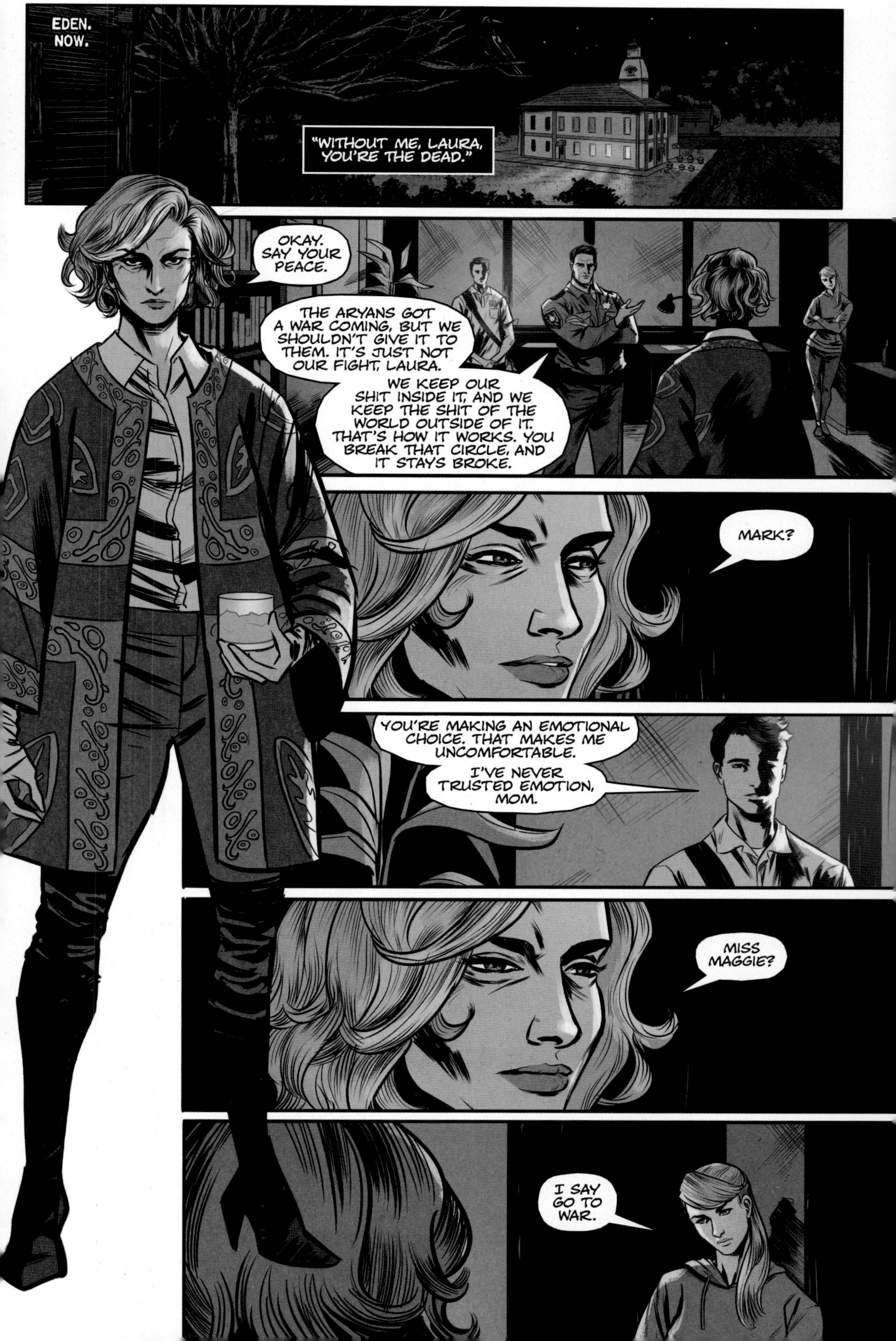
EDEN.
NOW.
"WITHOUT ME, LAURA, YOU'RE THE DEAD."
OKAY. SAY YOUR PEACE.
THE ARYANS GOT A WAR COMING, BUT WE SHOULDN'T GIVE IT TO THEM. IT'S JUST NOT OUR FIGHT, LAURA.
WE KEEP OUR SHIT INSIDE IT, AND WE KEEP THE SHIT OF THE WORLD OUTSIDE OF IT. THAT'S HOW IT WORKS. YOU BREAK THAT CIRCLE, AND IT STAYS BROKE.
MARK?
YOU'RE MAKING AN EMOTIONAL CHOICE. THAT MAKES ME UNCOMFORTABLE.
I'VE NEVER TRUSTED EMOTION, MOM.
MISS MAGGIE?
I SAY GO TO WAR.

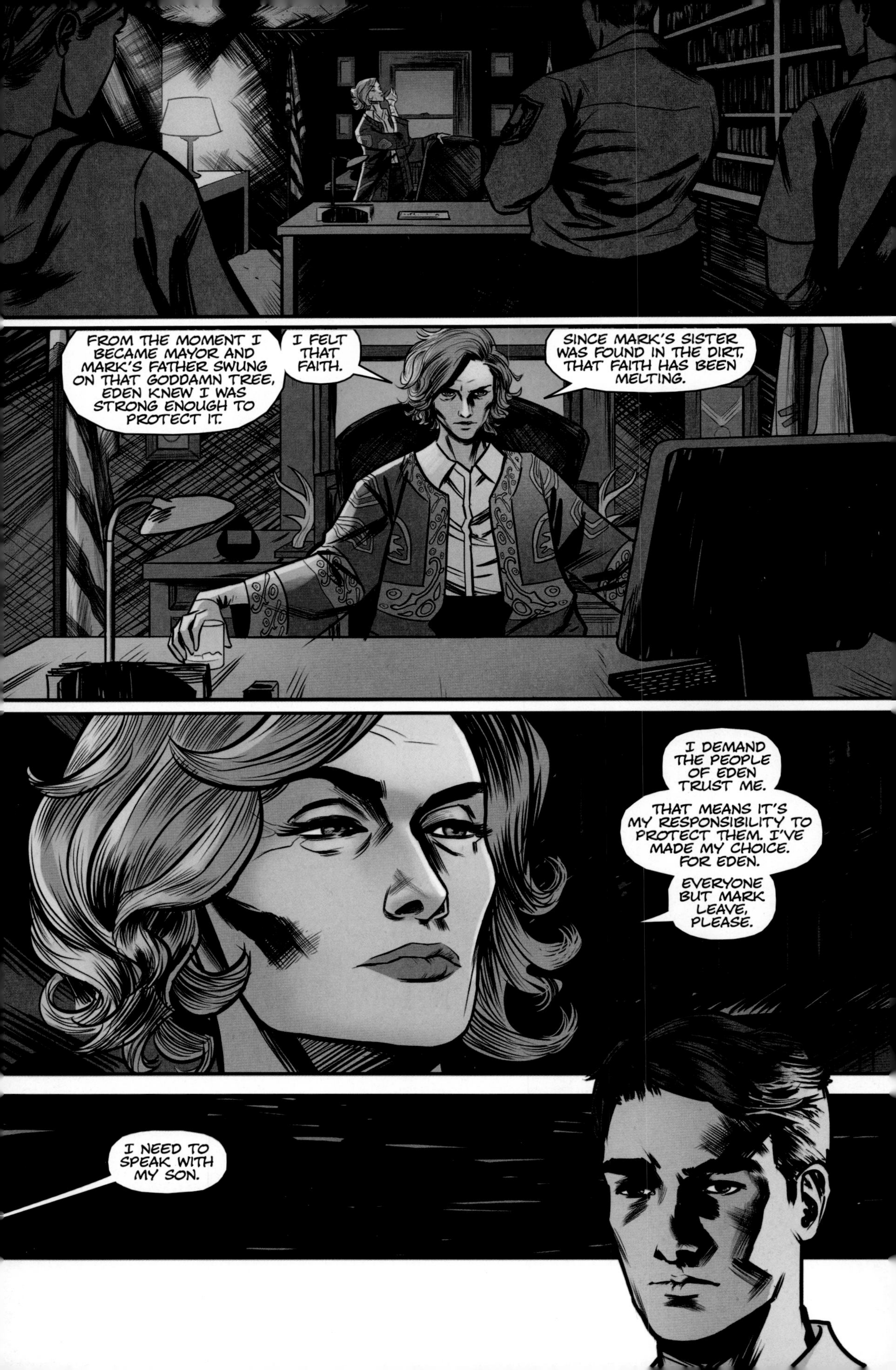
FROM THE MOMENT I BECAME MAYOR AND MARK'S FATHER SWUNG ON THAT GODDAMN TREE, EDEN KNEW I WAS STRONG ENOUGH TO PROTECT IT.
I FELT THAT FAITH.
SINCE MARK'S SISTER WAS FOUND IN THE DIRT, THAT FAITH HAS BEEN MELTING.
I DEMAND THE PEOPLE OF EDEN TRUST ME.
THAT MEANS IT'S MY RESPONSIBILITY TO PROTECT THEM. I'VE MADE MY CHOICE. FOR EDEN.
EVERYONE BUT MARK LEAVE, PLEASE.
I NEED TO SPEAK WITH MY SON.

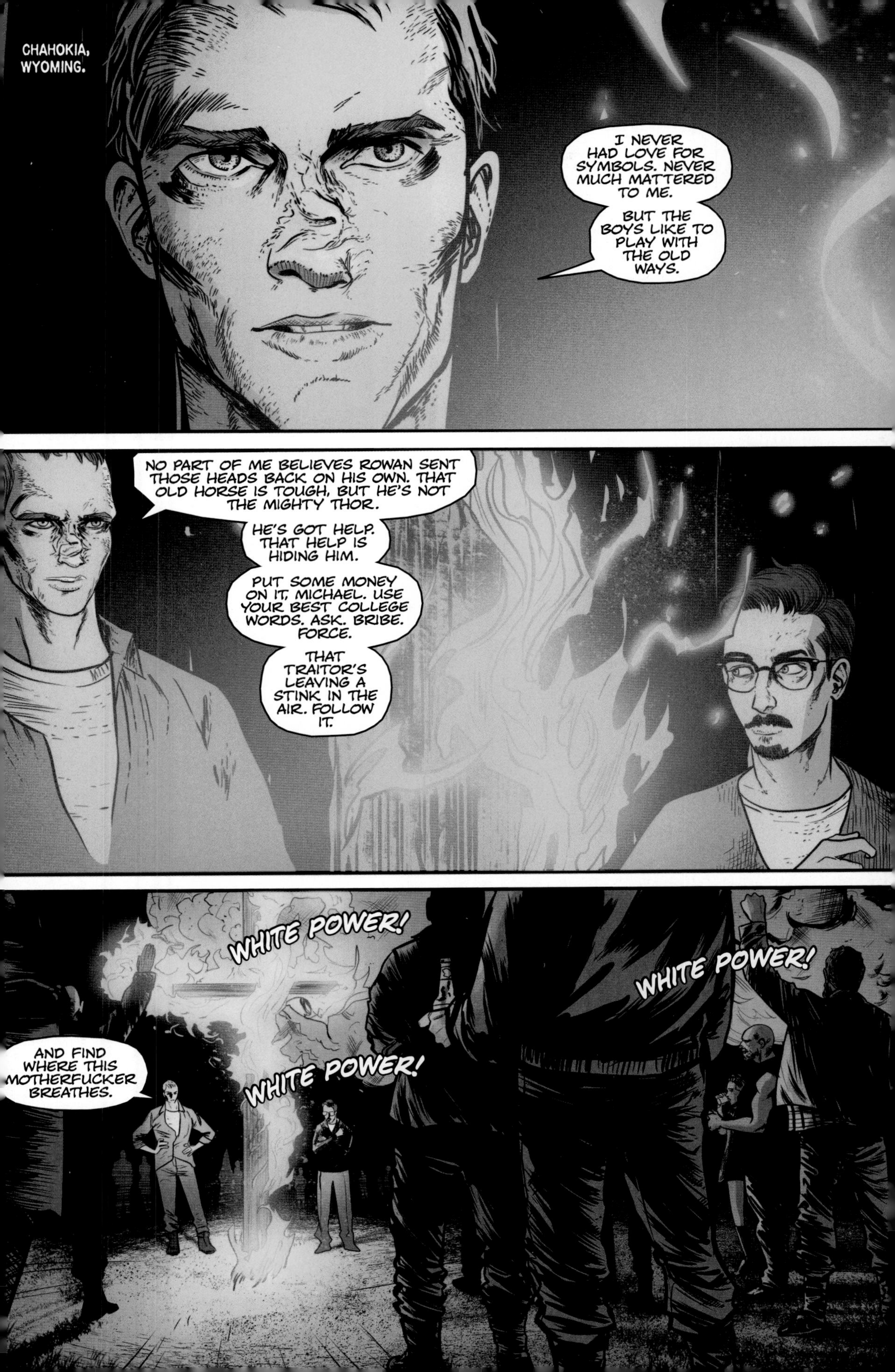
CHAHOKIA, WYOMING.
I NEVER HAD LOVE FOR SYMBOLS. NEVER MUCH MATTERED TO ME.
BUT THE BOYS LIKE TO PLAY WITH THE OLD WAYS.
NO PART OF ME BELIEVES ROWAN SENT THOSE HEADS BACK ON HIS OWN. THAT OLD HORSE IS TOUGH, BUT HE'S NOT THE MIGHTY THOR.
HE'S GOT HELP. THAT HELP IS HIDING HIM.
PUT SOME MONEY ON IT, MICHAEL. USE YOUR BEST COLLEGE WORDS. ASK. BRIBE. FORCE.
THAT TRAITOR'S LEAVING A STINK IN THE AIR. FOLLOW IT.
WHITE POWER!
WHITE POWER!
AND FIND WHERE THIS MOTHERFUCKER BREATHES.
WHITE POWER!

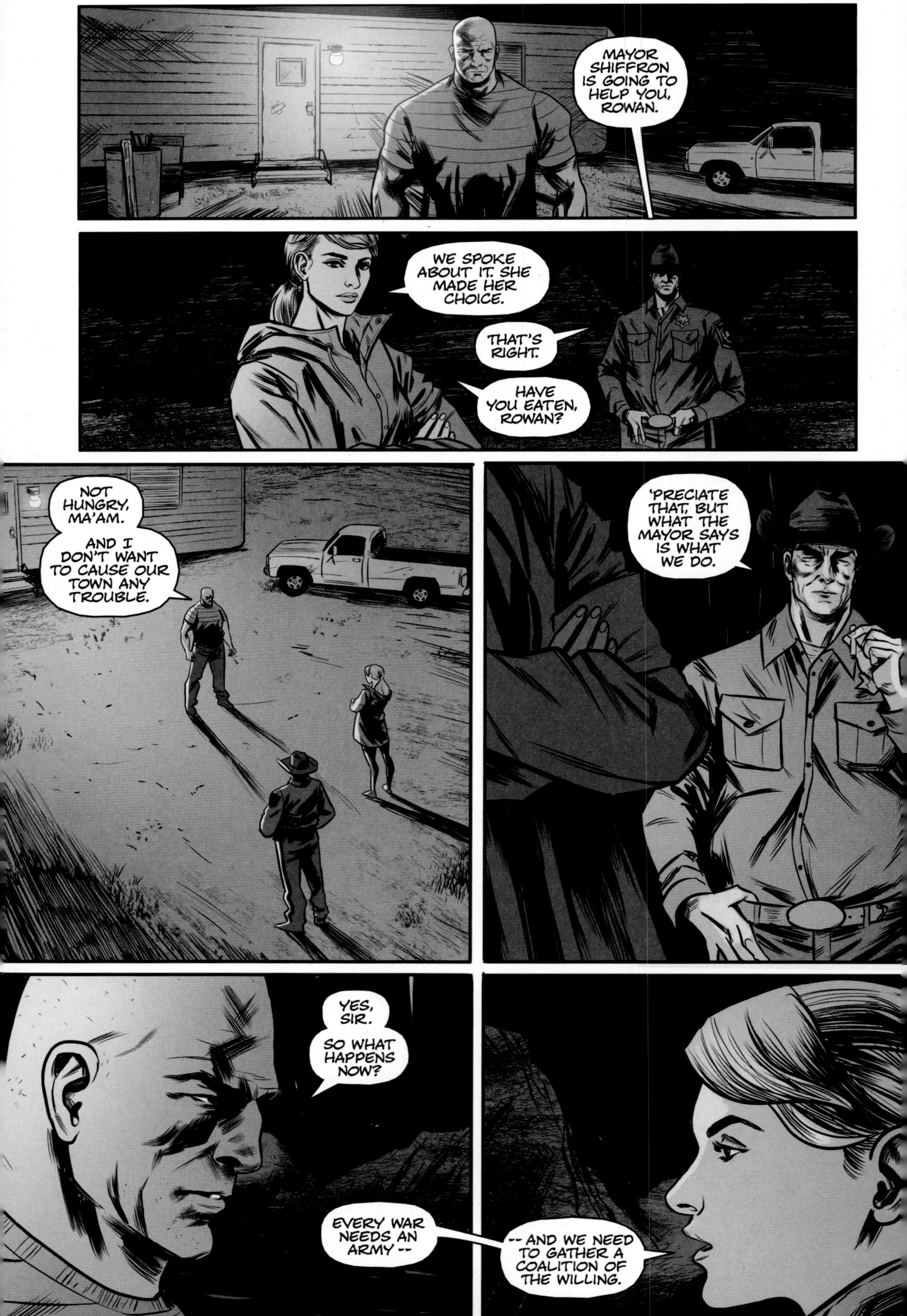
MAYOR SHIFFRON IS GOING TO HELP YOU, ROWAN.
WE SPOKE ABOUT IT. SHE MADE HER CHOICE.
THAT'S RIGHT.
HAVE YOU EATEN, ROWAN?
NOT HUNGRY, MA'AM.
AND I DON'T WANT TO CAUSE OUR TOWN ANY TROUBLE.
'PRECIATE THAT, BUT WHAT THE MAYOR SAYS IS WHAT WE DO.
YES, SIR.
SO WHAT HAPPENS NOW?
EVERY WAR NEEDS AN ARMY --
-- AND WE NEED TO GATHER A COALITION OF THE WILLING.

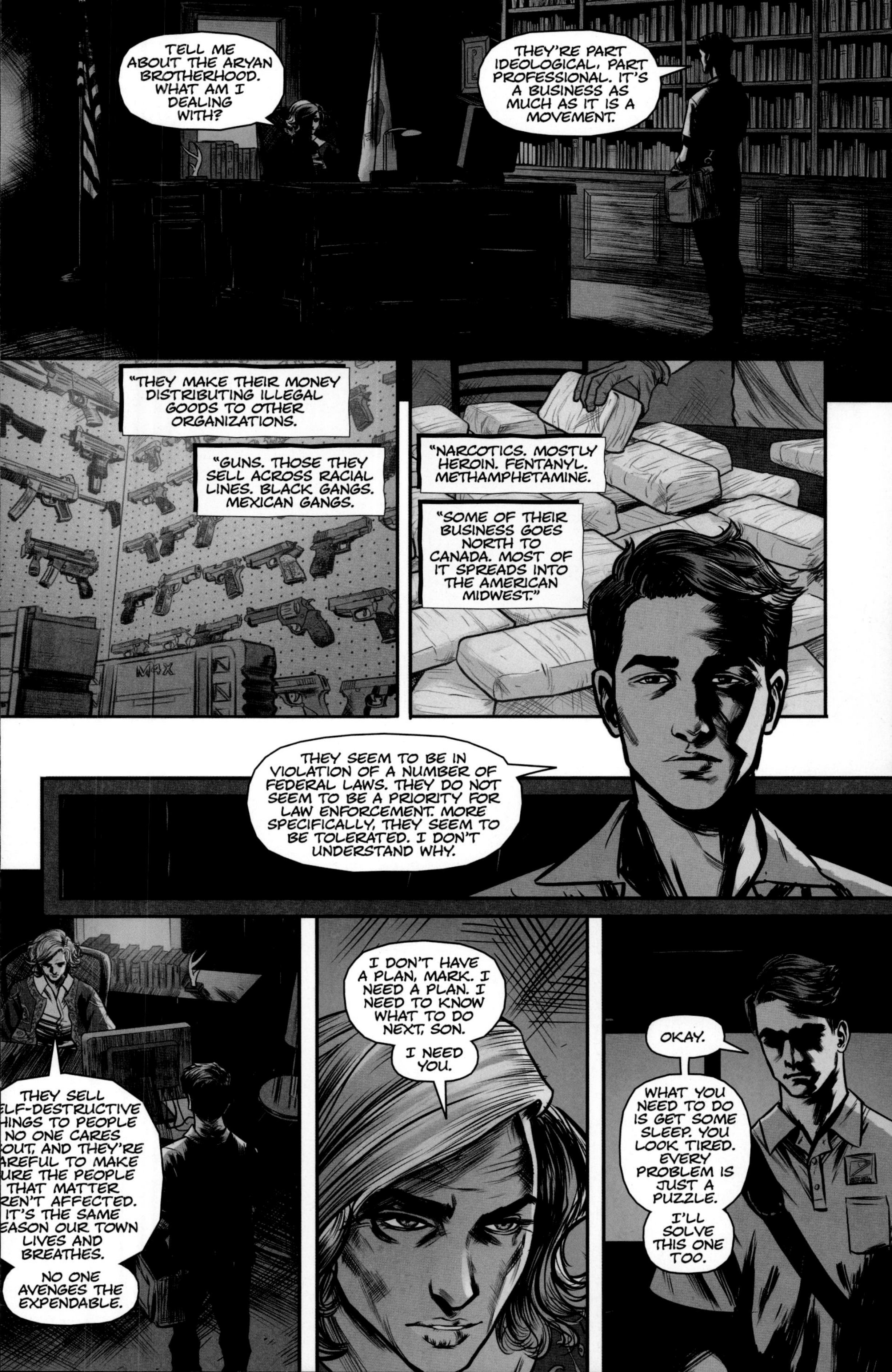

TELL ME ABOUT THE ARYAN BROTHERHOOD. WHAT AM I DEALING WITH?
THEY'RE PART IDEOLOGICAL, PART PROFESSIONAL. IT'S A BUSINESS AS MUCH AS IT IS A MOVEMENT.
"THEY MAKE THEIR MONEY DISTRIBUTING ILLEGAL GOODS TO OTHER ORGANIZATIONS.
"GUNS. THOSE THEY SELL ACROSS RACIAL LINES. BLACK GANGS. MEXICAN GANGS.
M4X
"NARCOTICS. MOSTLY HEROIN. FENTANYL. METHAMPHETAMINE.
"SOME OF THEIR BUSINESS GOES NORTH TO CANADA. MOST OF IT SPREADS INTO THE AMERICAN MIDWEST."
THEY SEEM TO BE IN VIOLATION OF A NUMBER OF FEDERAL LAWS. THEY DO NOT SEEM TO BE A PRIORITY FOR LAW ENFORCEMENT. MORE SPECIFICALLY, THEY SEEM TO BE TOLERATED. I DON'T UNDERSTAND WHY.
THEY SELL ELF-DESTRUCTIVE HINGS TO PEOPLE NO ONE CARES BOUT, AND THEY'RE AREFUL TO MAKE URE THE PEOPLE THAT MATTER REN'T AFFECTED. IT'S THE SAME EASON OUR TOWN LIVES AND BREATHES.
NO ONE AVENGES THE EXPENDABLE.
I DON'T HAVE A PLAN, MARK. I NEED A PLAN. I NEED TO KNOW WHAT TO DO NEXT, SON.
I NEED YOU.
OKAY.
WHAT YOU NEED TO DO IS GET SOME SLEEP. YOU LOOK TIRED. EVERY PROBLEM IS JUST A PUZZLE.
I'LL SOLVE THIS ONE TOO.

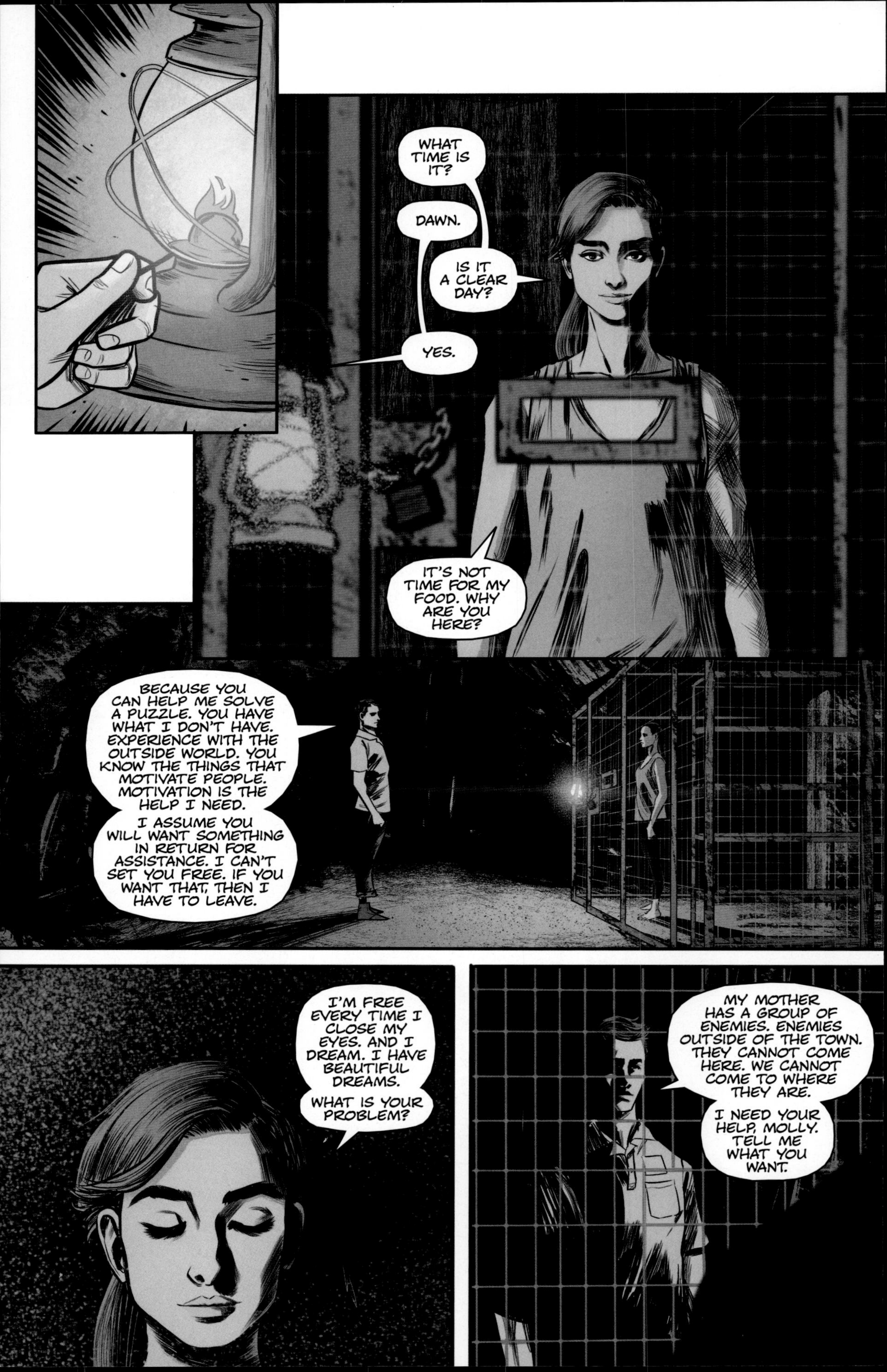
WHAT TIME IS IT?
DAWN.
IS IT A CLEAR DAY?
YES.
IT'S NOT TIME FOR MY FOOD. WHY ARE YOU HERE?
BECAUSE YOU CAN HELP ME SOLVE A PUZZLE. YOU HAVE WHAT I DON'T HAVE. EXPERIENCE WITH THE OUTSIDE WORLD. YOU KNOW THE THINGS THAT MOTIVATE PEOPLE. MOTIVATION IS THE HELP I NEED.
I ASSUME YOU WILL WANT SOMETHING IN RETURN FOR ASSISTANCE. I CAN'T SET YOU FREE. IF YOU WANT THAT, THEN I HAVE TO LEAVE.
I'M FREE EVERY TIME I CLOSE MY EYES. AND I DREAM. I HAVE BEAUTIFUL DREAMS.
WHAT IS YOUR PROBLEM?
MY MOTHER HAS A GROUP OF ENEMIES. ENEMIES OUTSIDE OF THE TOWN. THEY CANNOT COME HERE. WE CANNOT COME TO WHERE THEY ARE.
I NEED YOUR HELP, MOLLY. TELL ME WHAT YOU WANT.

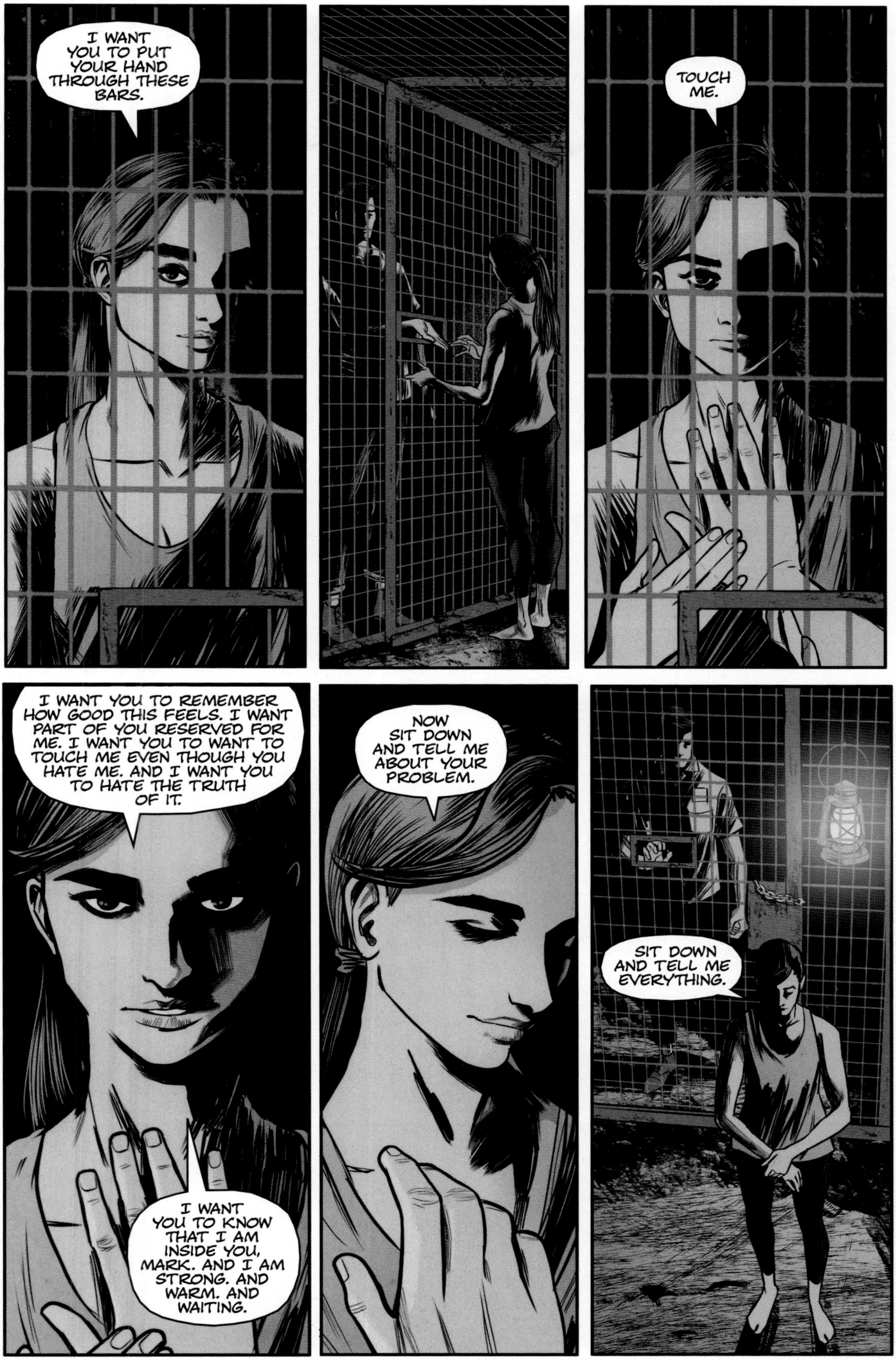
I WANT YOU TO PUT YOUR HAND THROUGH THESE BARS.
TOUCH ME.
I WANT YOU TO REMEMBER HOW GOOD THIS FEELS. I WANT PART OF YOU RESERVED FOR ME. I WANT YOU TO WANT TO TOUCH ME EVEN THOUGH YOU HATE ME. AND I WANT YOU TO HATE THE TRUTH OF IT.
I WANT YOU TO KNOW THAT I AM INSIDE YOU, MARK. AND I AM STRONG. AND WARM. AND WAITING.
NOW SIT DOWN AND TELL ME ABOUT YOUR PROBLEM.
SIT DOWN AND TELL ME EVERYTHING.

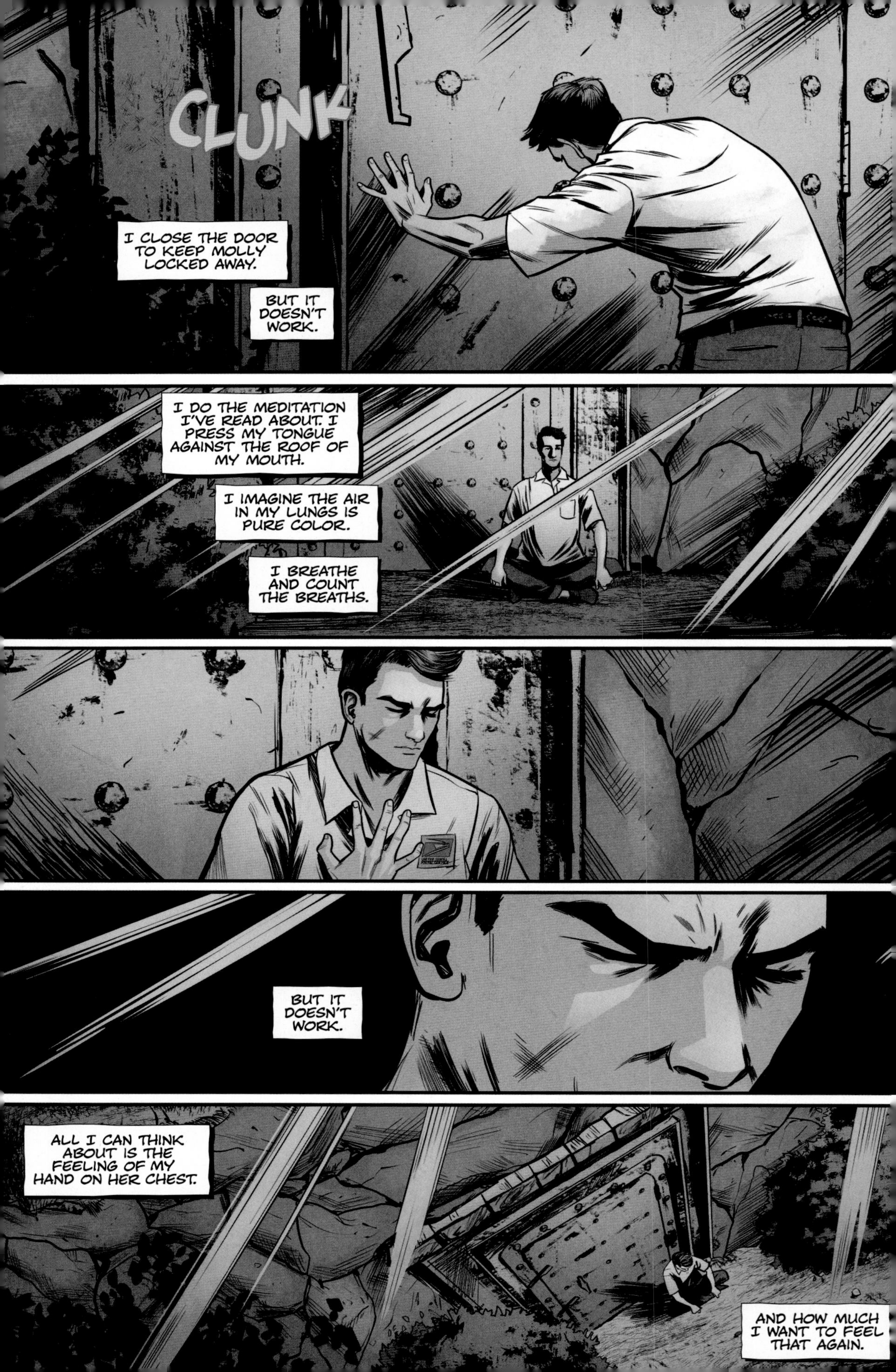
CLUNK
I CLOSE THE DOOR TO KEEP MOLLY LOCKED AWAY.
BUT IT DOESN'T WORK.
I DO THE MEDITATION I'VE READ ABOUT. I PRESS MY TONGUE AGAINST THE ROOF OF MY MOUTH.
I IMAGINE THE AIR IN MY LUNGS IS PURE COLOR.
I BREATHE AND COUNT THE BREATHS.
BUT IT DOESN'T WORK.
ALL I CAN THINK ABOUT IS THE FEELING OF MY HAND ON HER CHEST.
AND HOW MUCH I WANT TO FEEL THAT AGAIN.

Carpenter's **SCRAP SHOP**

ABNER.

YOU ONLY SEE ME WHEN THERE'S SOMETHING WRONG.

SO WHAT IS WRONG?

WE'RE AT WAR WITH SOMEONE. HE'S HIDING, BUT I'LL FIND HIM. WHEN I DO, I WANT YOU TO VISIT HIM.

YOU HAVE ROUTINELY REJECTED MY POINT OF VIEW, ABNER. YOU FIND ME ESOTERIC AND IRRELEVANT.

"FUCKING CRAZY" IS WHAT I REMEMBER YOU SAYING. I FOUND THAT HURTFUL.

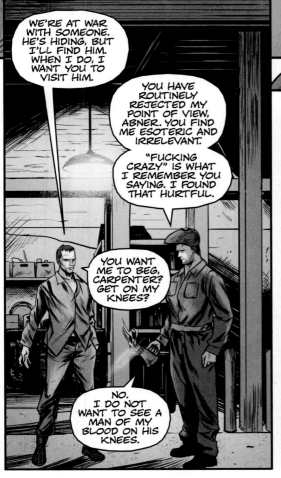

YOU WANT ME TO BEG, CARPENTER? GET ON MY KNEES?

NO. I DO NOT WANT TO SEE A MAN OF MY BLOOD ON HIS KNEES.

I'VE GOT A POT OF COFFEE I'M WILLING TO SHARE. TELL ME WHAT THREATENS YOU.

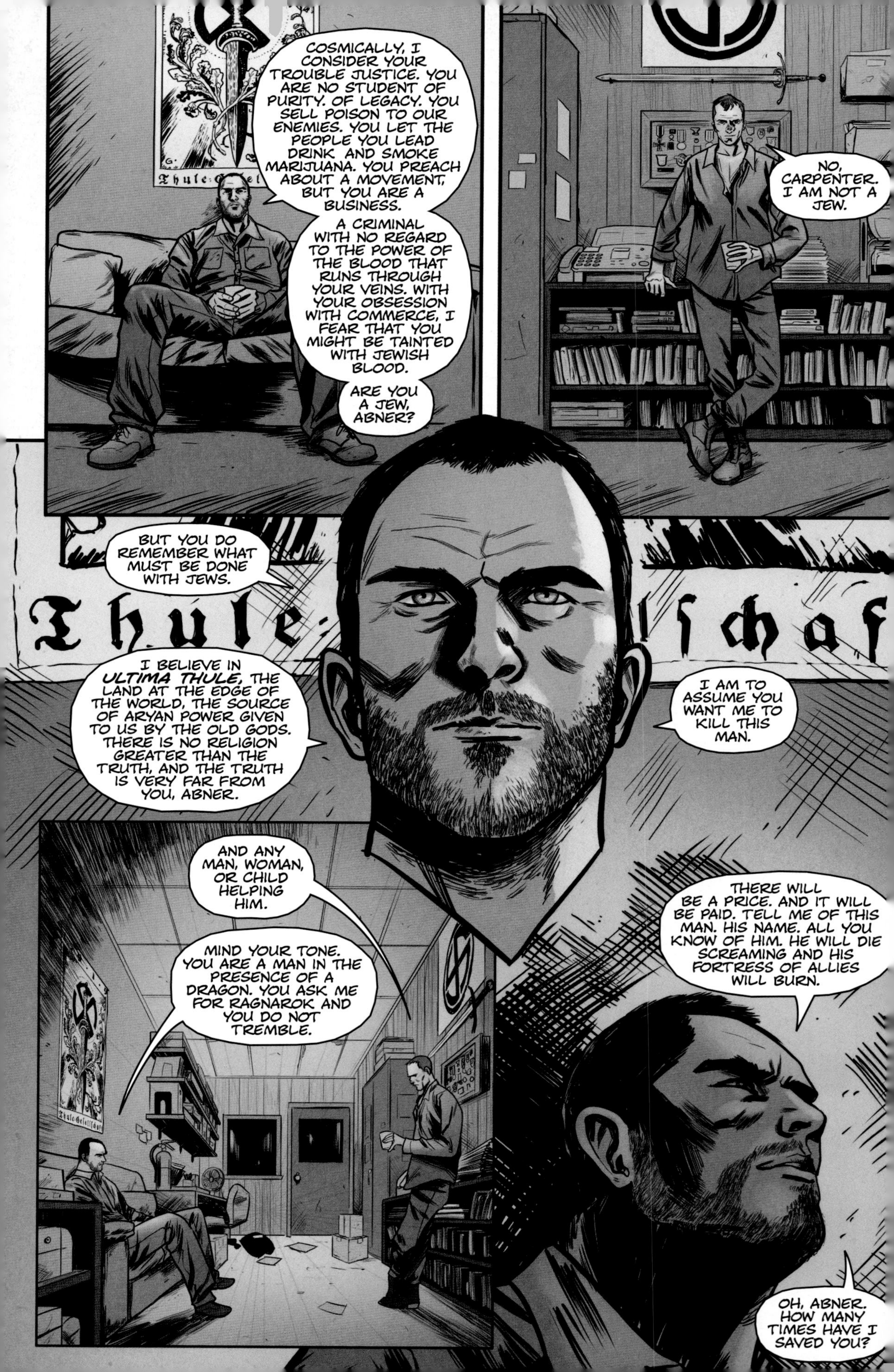
COSMICALLY, I CONSIDER YOUR TROUBLE JUSTICE. YOU ARE NO STUDENT OF PURITY. OF LEGACY. YOU SELL POISON TO OUR ENEMIES. YOU LET THE PEOPLE YOU LEAD DRINK AND SMOKE MARIJUANA. YOU PREACH ABOUT A MOVEMENT, BUT YOU ARE A BUSINESS.
A CRIMINAL WITH NO REGARD TO THE POWER OF THE BLOOD THAT RUNS THROUGH YOUR VEINS. WITH YOUR OBSESSION WITH COMMERCE, I FEAR THAT YOU MIGHT BE TAINTED WITH JEWISH BLOOD.
ARE YOU A JEW, ABNER?
NO, CARPENTER. I AM NOT A JEW.
BUT YOU DO REMEMBER WHAT MUST BE DONE WITH JEWS.
Thule
schaf
I BELIEVE IN ULTIMA THULE, THE LAND AT THE EDGE OF THE WORLD, THE SOURCE OF ARYAN POWER GIVEN TO US BY THE OLD GODS. THERE IS NO RELIGION GREATER THAN THE TRUTH, AND THE TRUTH IS VERY FAR FROM YOU, ABNER.
I AM TO ASSUME YOU WANT ME TO KILL THIS MAN.
AND ANY MAN, WOMAN, OR CHILD HELPING HIM.
MIND YOUR TONE. YOU ARE A MAN IN THE PRESENCE OF A DRAGON. YOU ASK ME FOR RAGNAROK AND YOU DO NOT TREMBLE.
THERE WILL BE A PRICE. AND IT WILL BE PAID. TELL ME OF THIS MAN. HIS NAME. ALL YOU KNOW OF HIM. HE WILL DIE SCREAMING AND HIS FORTRESS OF ALLIES WILL BURN.
OH, ABNER. HOW MANY TIMES HAVE I SAVED YOU?

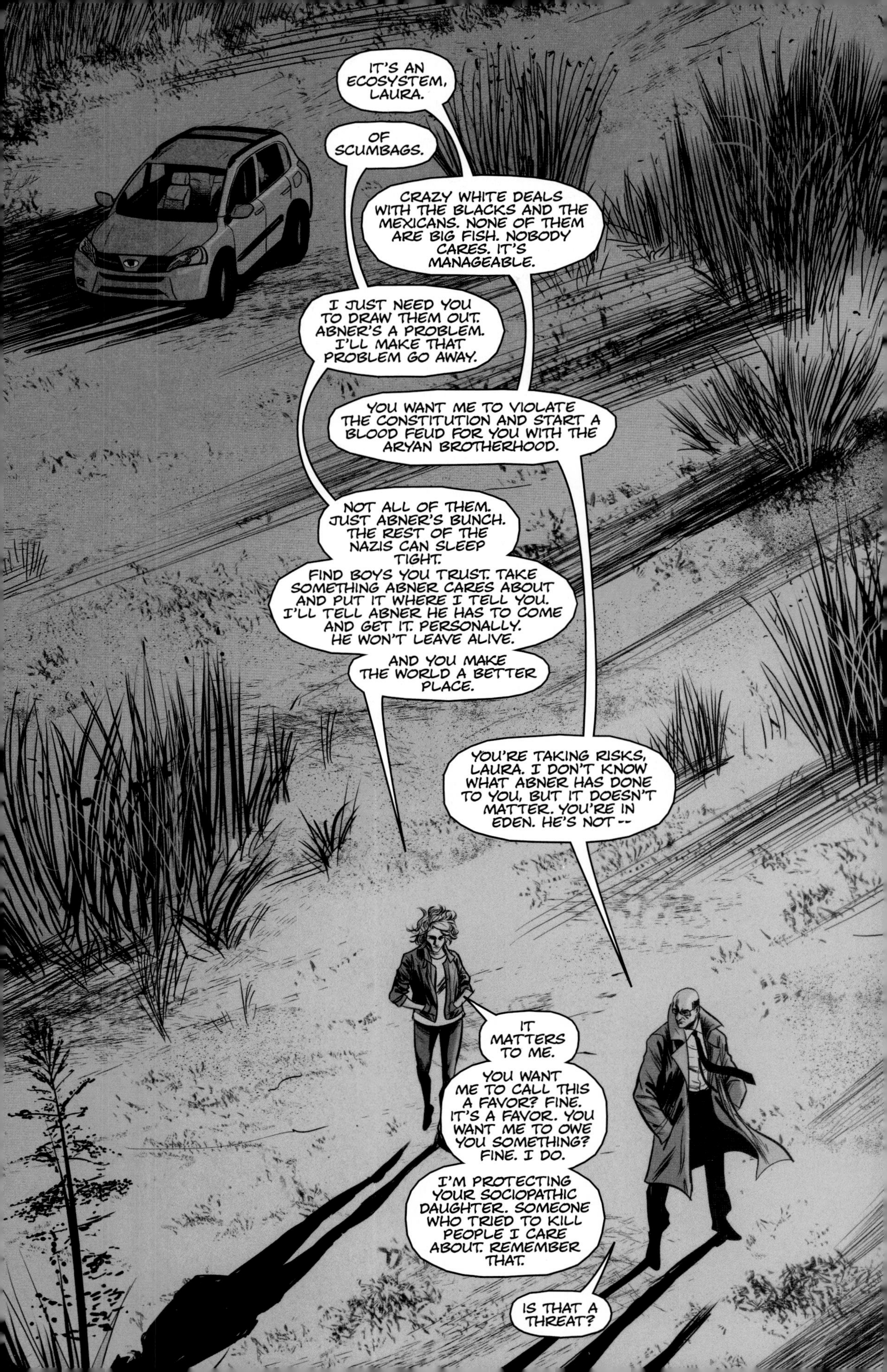
IT'S AN ECOSYSTEM, LAURA.
OF SCUMBAGS.
CRAZY WHITE DEALS WITH THE BLACKS AND THE MEXICANS. NONE OF THEM ARE BIG FISH. NOBODY CARES. IT'S MANAGEABLE.
I JUST NEED YOU TO DRAW THEM OUT. ABNER'S A PROBLEM. I'LL MAKE THAT PROBLEM GO AWAY.
YOU WANT ME TO VIOLATE THE CONSTITUTION AND START A BLOOD FEUD FOR YOU WITH THE ARYAN BROTHERHOOD.
NOT ALL OF THEM. JUST ABNER'S BUNCH. THE REST OF THE NAZIS CAN SLEEP TIGHT.
FIND BOYS YOU TRUST. TAKE SOMETHING ABNER CARES ABOUT AND PUT IT WHERE I TELL YOU. I'LL TELL ABNER HE HAS TO COME AND GET IT. PERSONALLY. HE WON'T LEAVE ALIVE.
AND YOU MAKE THE WORLD A BETTER PLACE.
YOU'RE TAKING RISKS, LAURA. I DON'T KNOW WHAT ABNER HAS DONE TO YOU, BUT IT DOESN'T MATTER. YOU'RE IN EDEN. HE'S NOT --
IT MATTERS TO ME.
YOU WANT ME TO CALL THIS A FAVOR? FINE. IT'S A FAVOR. YOU WANT ME TO OWE YOU SOMETHING? FINE. I DO.
I'M PROTECTING YOUR SOCIOPATHIC DAUGHTER. SOMEONE WHO TRIED TO KILL PEOPLE I CARE ABOUT. REMEMBER THAT.
IS THAT A THREAT?

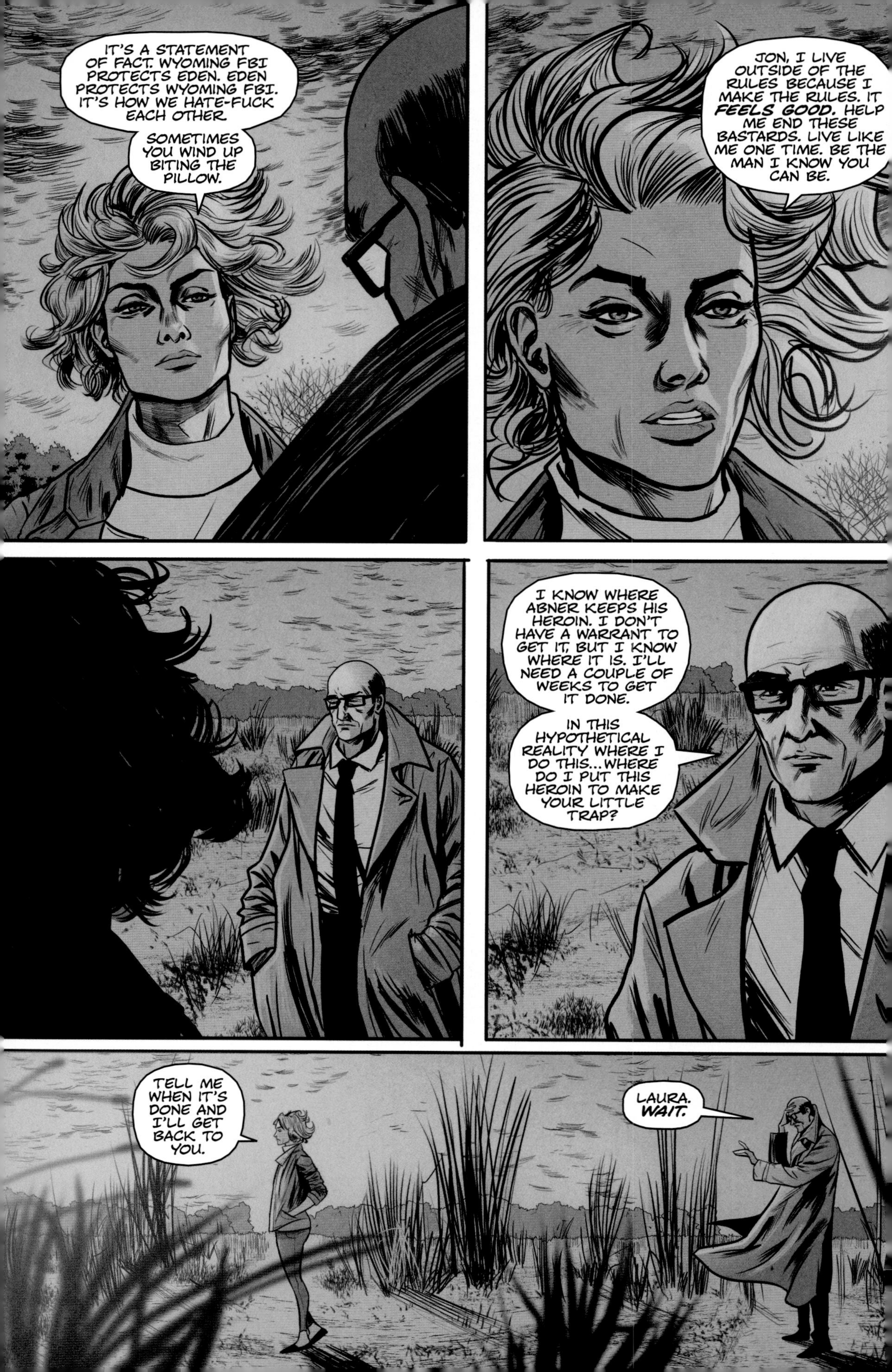
IT'S A STATEMENT OF FACT. WYOMING FBI PROTECTS EDEN. EDEN PROTECTS WYOMING FBI. IT'S HOW WE HATE-FUCK EACH OTHER.
SOMETIMES YOU WIND UP BITING THE PILLOW.
JON, I LIVE OUTSIDE OF THE RULES BECAUSE I MAKE THE RULES. IT FEELS GOOD. HELP ME END THESE BASTARDS. LIVE LIKE ME ONE TIME. BE THE MAN I KNOW YOU CAN BE.
I KNOW WHERE ABNER KEEPS HIS HEROIN. I DON'T HAVE A WARRANT TO GET IT, BUT I KNOW WHERE IT IS. I'LL NEED A COUPLE OF WEEKS TO GET IT DONE.
IN THIS HYPOTHETICAL REALITY WHERE I DO THIS...WHERE DO I PUT THIS HEROIN TO MAKE YOUR LITTLE TRAP?
TELL ME WHEN IT'S DONE AND I'LL GET BACK TO YOU.
LAURA. WAIT.

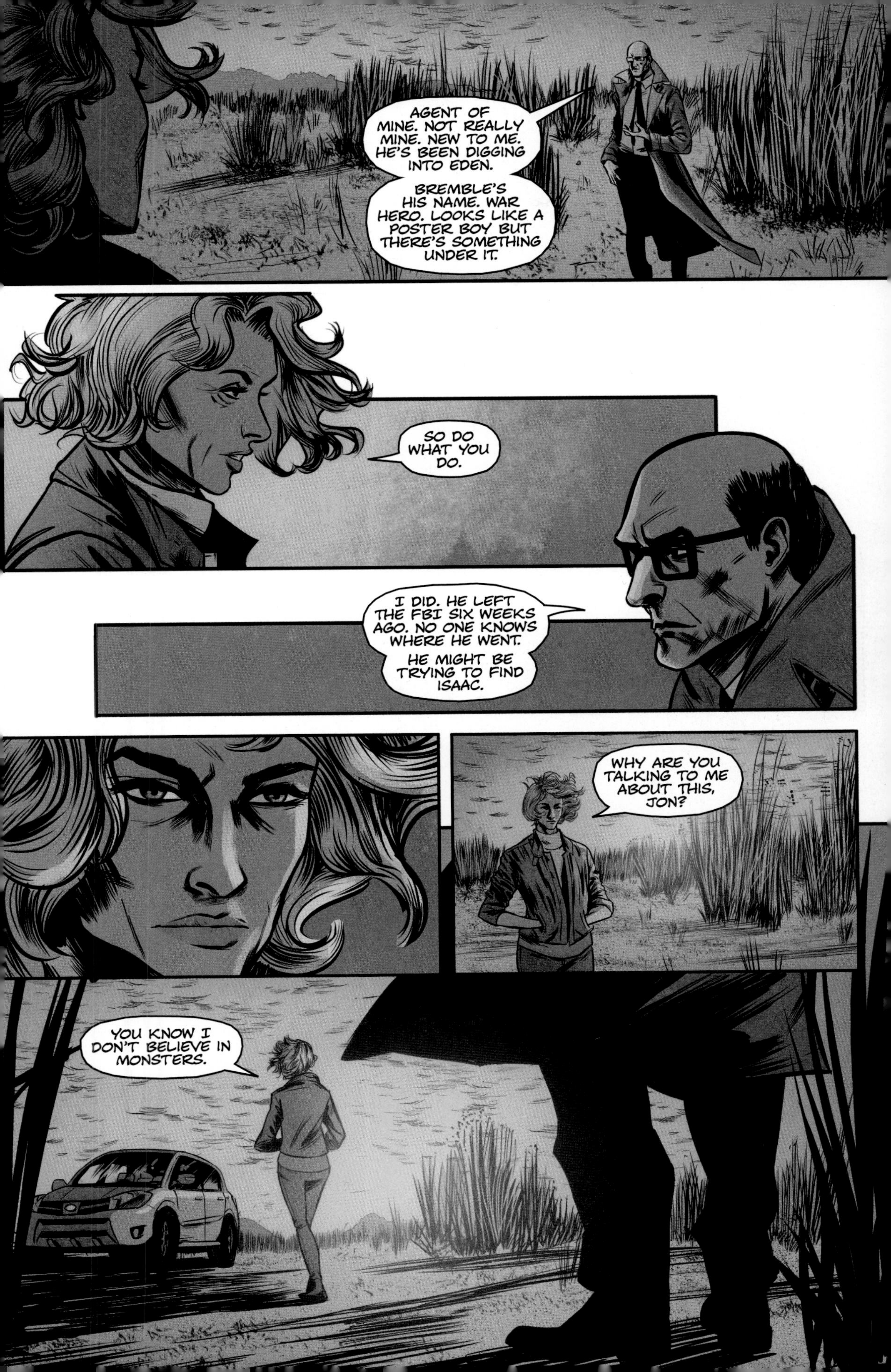

AGENT OF MINE. NOT REALLY MINE. NEW TO ME. HE'S BEEN DIGGING INTO EDEN.
BREMBLE'S HIS NAME. WAR HERO. LOOKS LIKE A POSTER BOY BUT THERE'S SOMETHING UNDER IT.
SO DO WHAT YOU DO.
I DID. HE LEFT THE FBI SIX WEEKS AGO. NO ONE KNOWS WHERE HE WENT.
HE MIGHT BE TRYING TO FIND ISAAC.
WHY ARE YOU TALKING TO ME ABOUT THIS, JON?
YOU KNOW I DON'T BELIEVE IN MONSTERS.

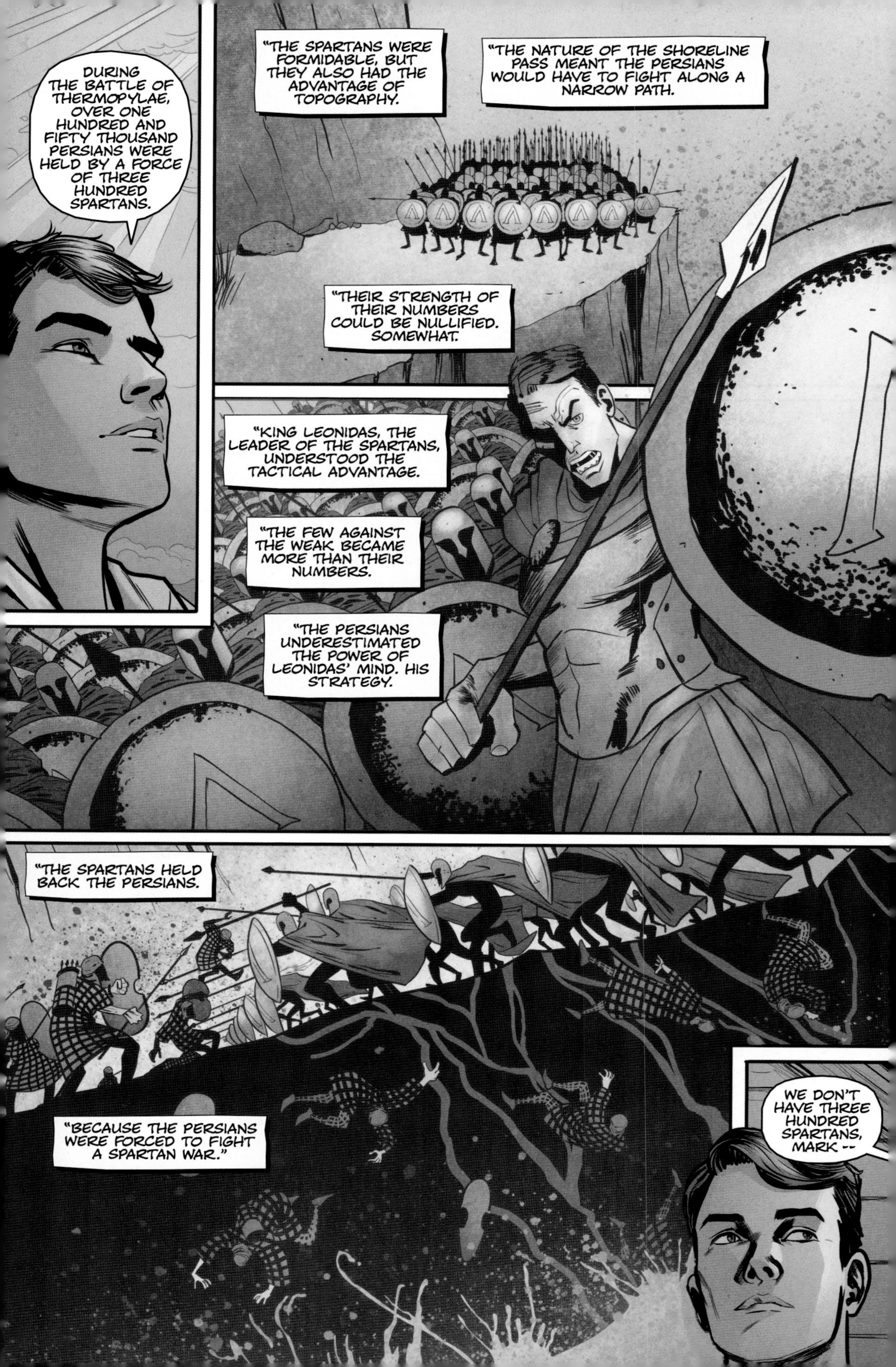

DURING THE BATTLE OF THERMOPYLAE, OVER ONE HUNDRED AND FIFTY THOUSAND PERSIANS WERE HELD BY A FORCE OF THREE HUNDRED SPARTANS.
"THE SPARTANS WERE FORMIDABLE, BUT THEY ALSO HAD THE ADVANTAGE OF TOPOGRAPHY.
"THE NATURE OF THE SHORELINE PASS MEANT THE PERSIANS WOULD HAVE TO FIGHT ALONG A NARROW PATH.
"THEIR STRENGTH OF THEIR NUMBERS COULD BE NULLIFIED. SOMEWHAT.
"KING LEONIDAS, THE LEADER OF THE SPARTANS, UNDERSTOOD THE TACTICAL ADVANTAGE.
"THE FEW AGAINST THE WEAK BECAME MORE THAN THEIR NUMBERS.
"THE PERSIANS UNDERESTIMATED THE POWER OF LEONIDAS' MIND. HIS STRATEGY.
"THE SPARTANS HELD BACK THE PERSIANS.
"BECAUSE THE PERSIANS WERE FORCED TO FIGHT A SPARTAN WAR."
WE DON'T HAVE THREE HUNDRED SPARTANS, MARK --

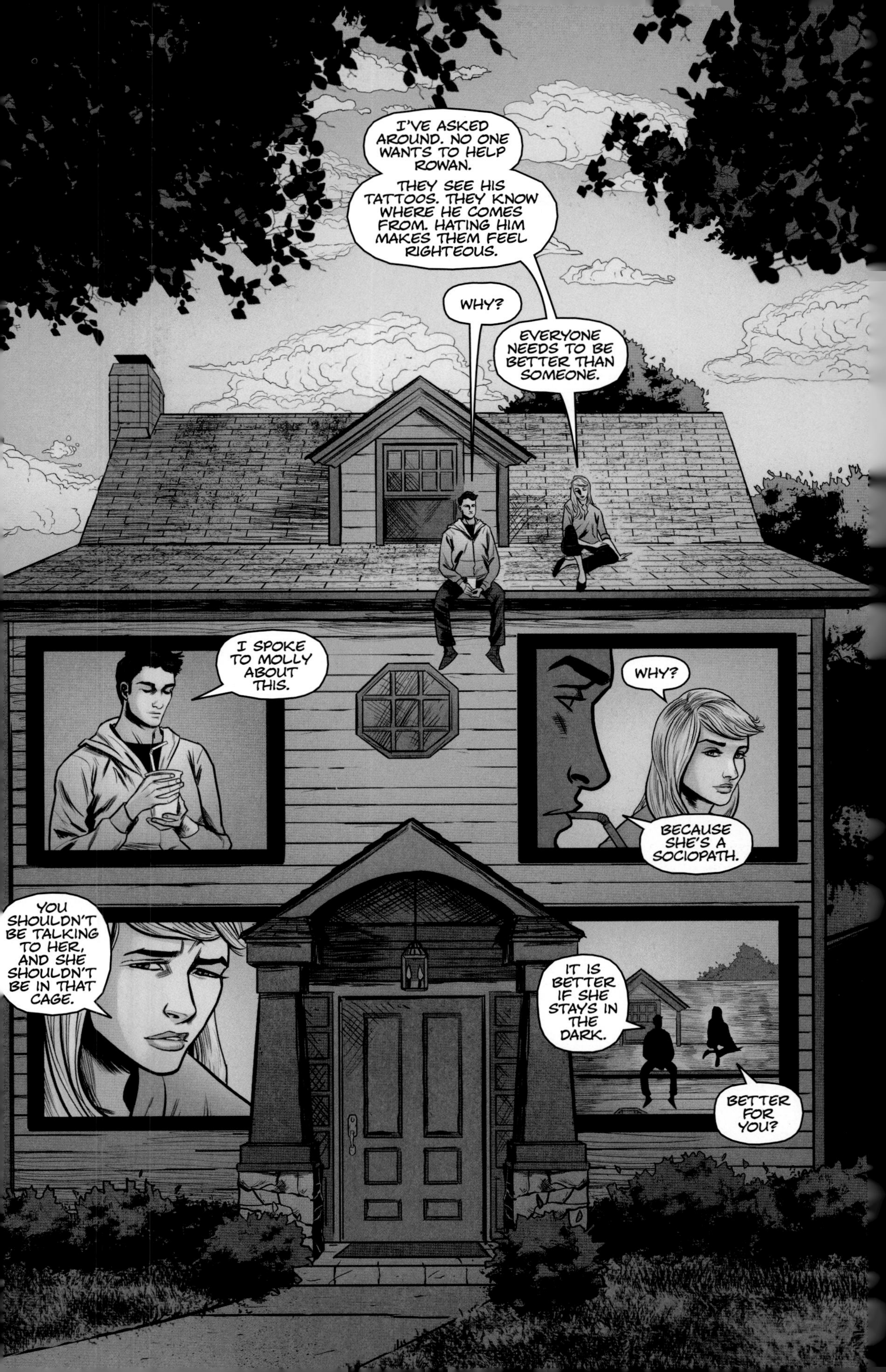
I'VE ASKED AROUND. NO ONE WANTS TO HELP ROWAN.
THEY SEE HIS TATTOOS. THEY KNOW WHERE HE COMES FROM. HATING HIM MAKES THEM FEEL RIGHTEOUS.
WHY?
EVERYONE NEEDS TO BE BETTER THAN SOMEONE.
I SPOKE TO MOLLY ABOUT THIS.
WHY?
BECAUSE SHE'S A SOCIOPATH.
YOU SHOULDN'T BE TALKING TO HER, AND SHE SHOULDN'T BE IN THAT CAGE.
IT IS BETTER IF SHE STAYS IN THE DARK.
BETTER FOR YOU?

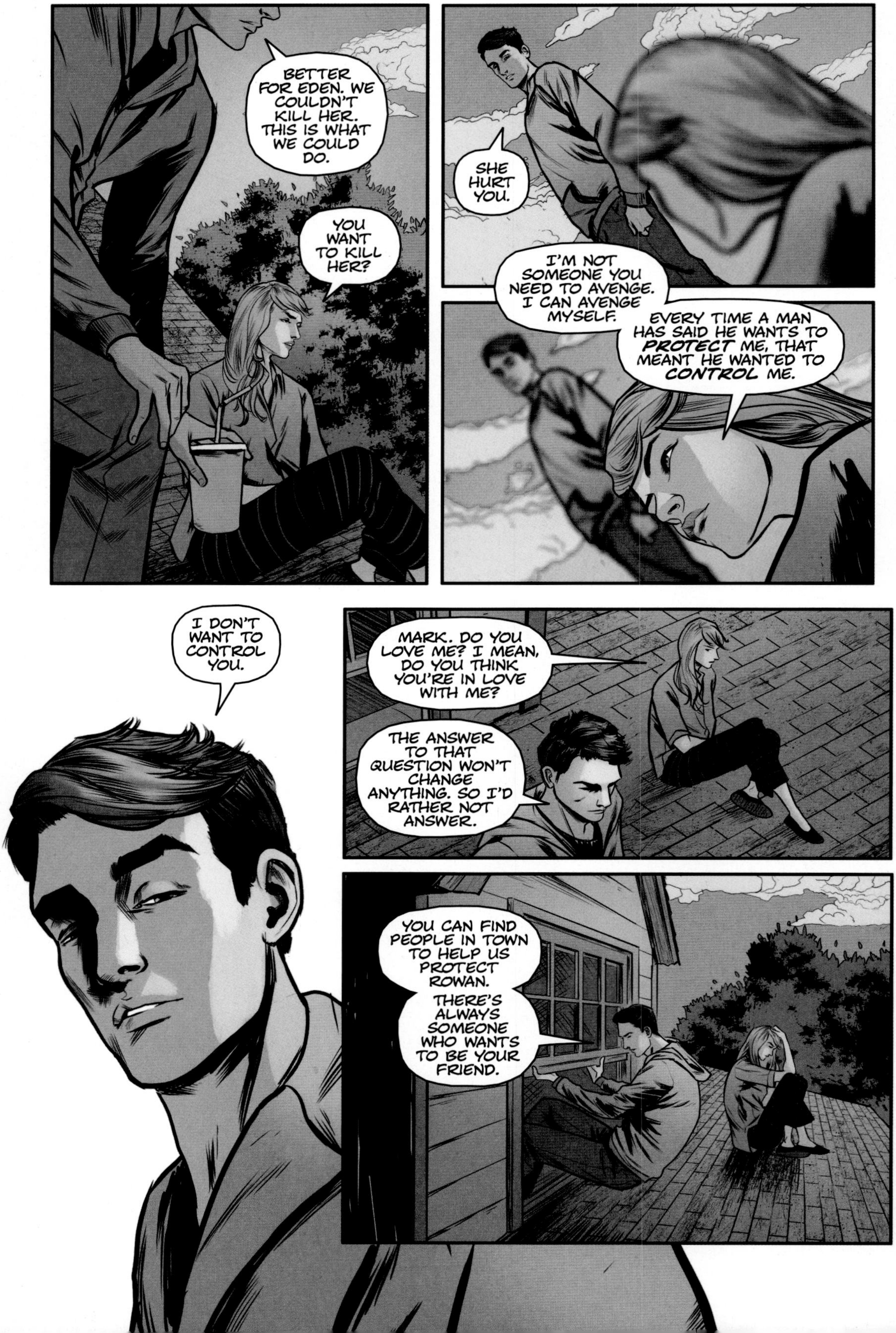
BETTER FOR EDEN. WE COULDN'T KILL HER. THIS IS WHAT WE COULD DO.
YOU WANT TO KILL HER?
SHE HURT YOU.
I'M NOT SOMEONE YOU NEED TO AVENGE. I CAN AVENGE MYSELF.
EVERY TIME A MAN HAS SAID HE WANTS TO PROTECT ME, THAT MEANT HE WANTED TO CONTROL ME.
I DON'T WANT TO CONTROL YOU.
MARK. DO YOU LOVE ME? I MEAN, DO YOU THINK YOU'RE IN LOVE WITH ME?
THE ANSWER TO THAT QUESTION WON'T CHANGE ANYTHING. SO I'D RATHER NOT ANSWER.
YOU CAN FIND PEOPLE IN TOWN TO HELP US PROTECT ROWAN.
THERE'S ALWAYS SOMEONE WHO WANTS TO BE YOUR FRIEND.

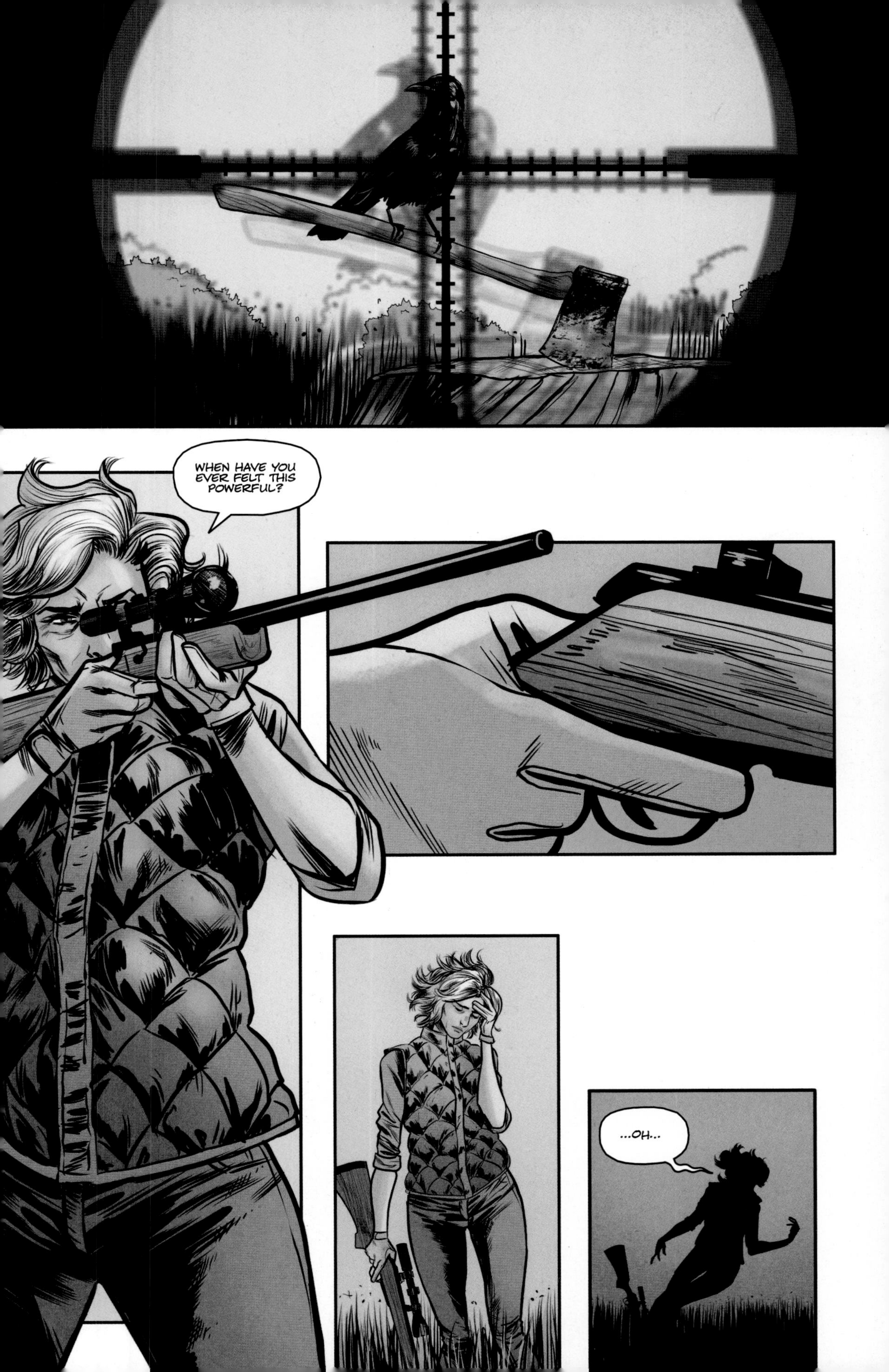
WHEN HAVE YOU EVER FELT THIS POWERFUL?
...OH...

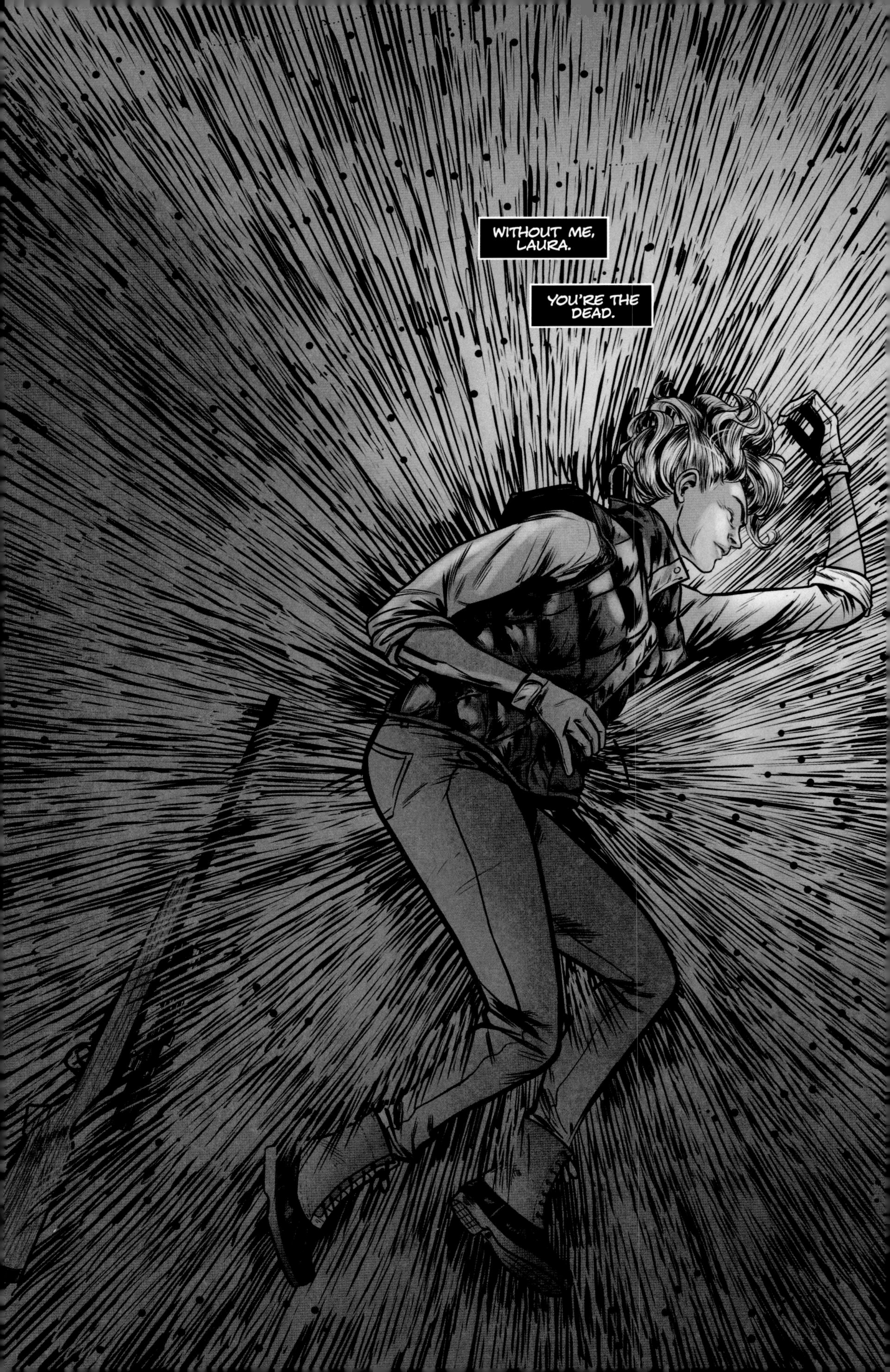
WITHOUT ME, LAURA.
YOU'RE THE DEAD.

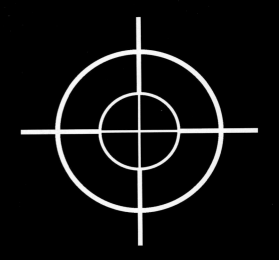

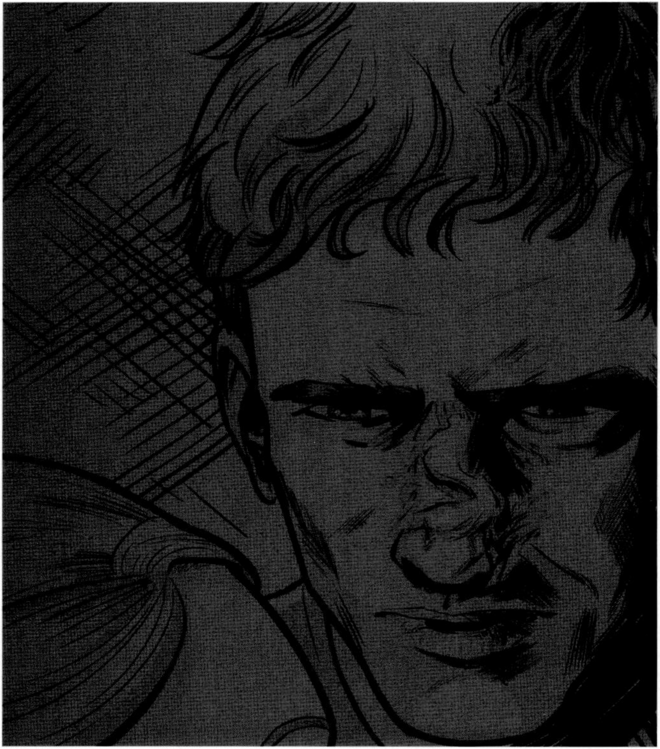

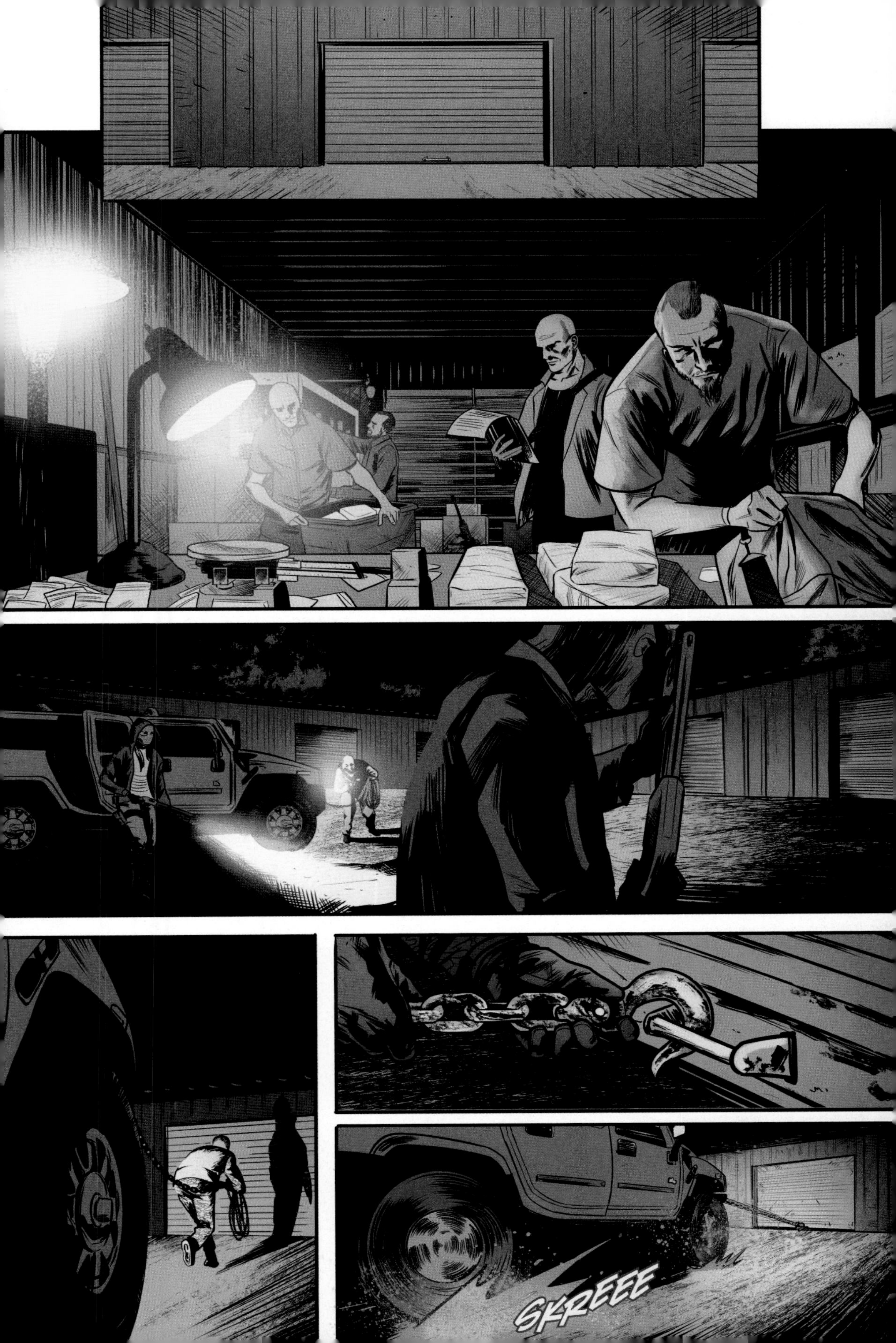
SKREEEE

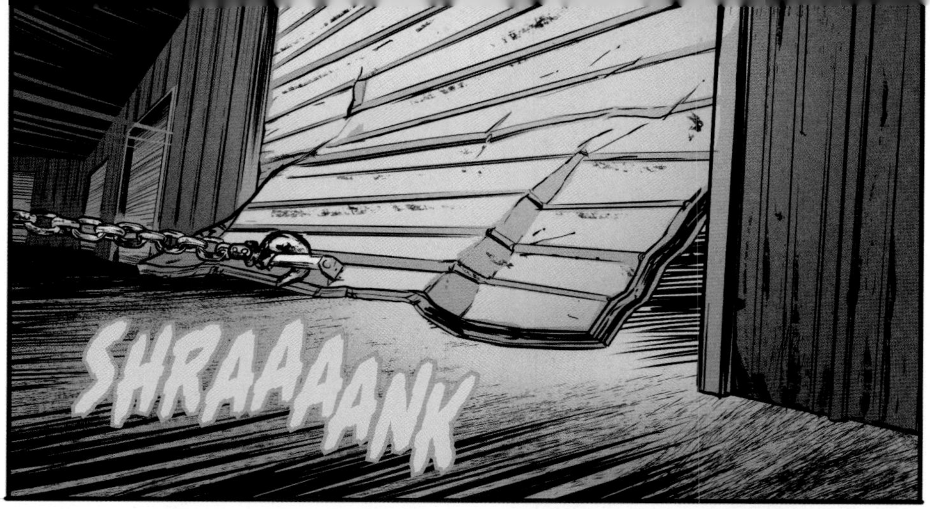
SHRAAAAANK

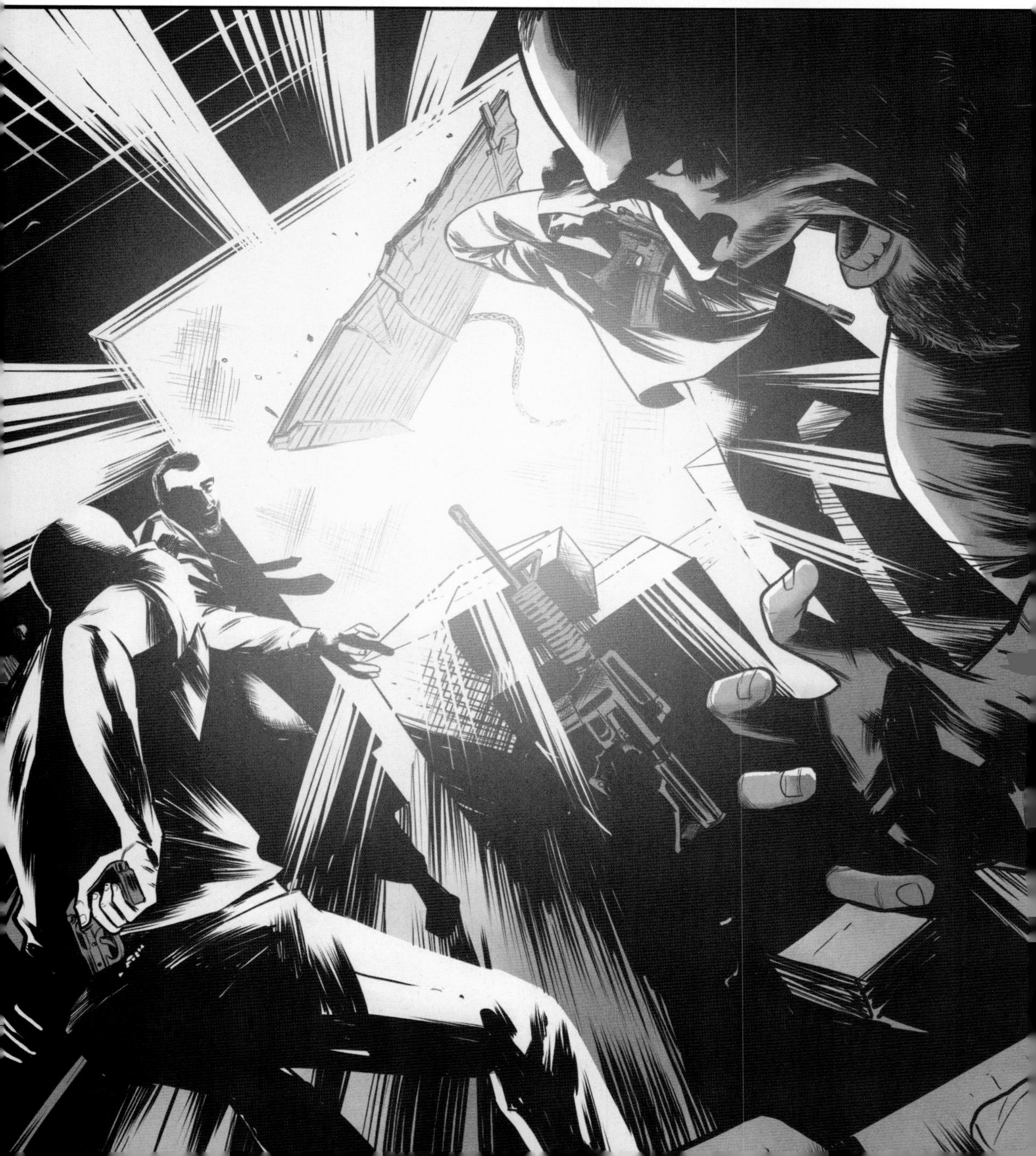

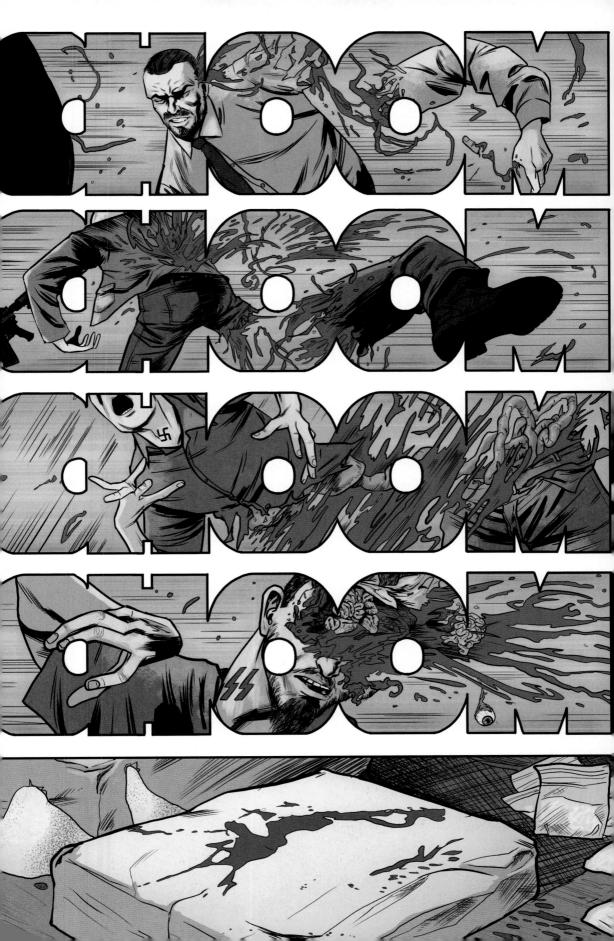

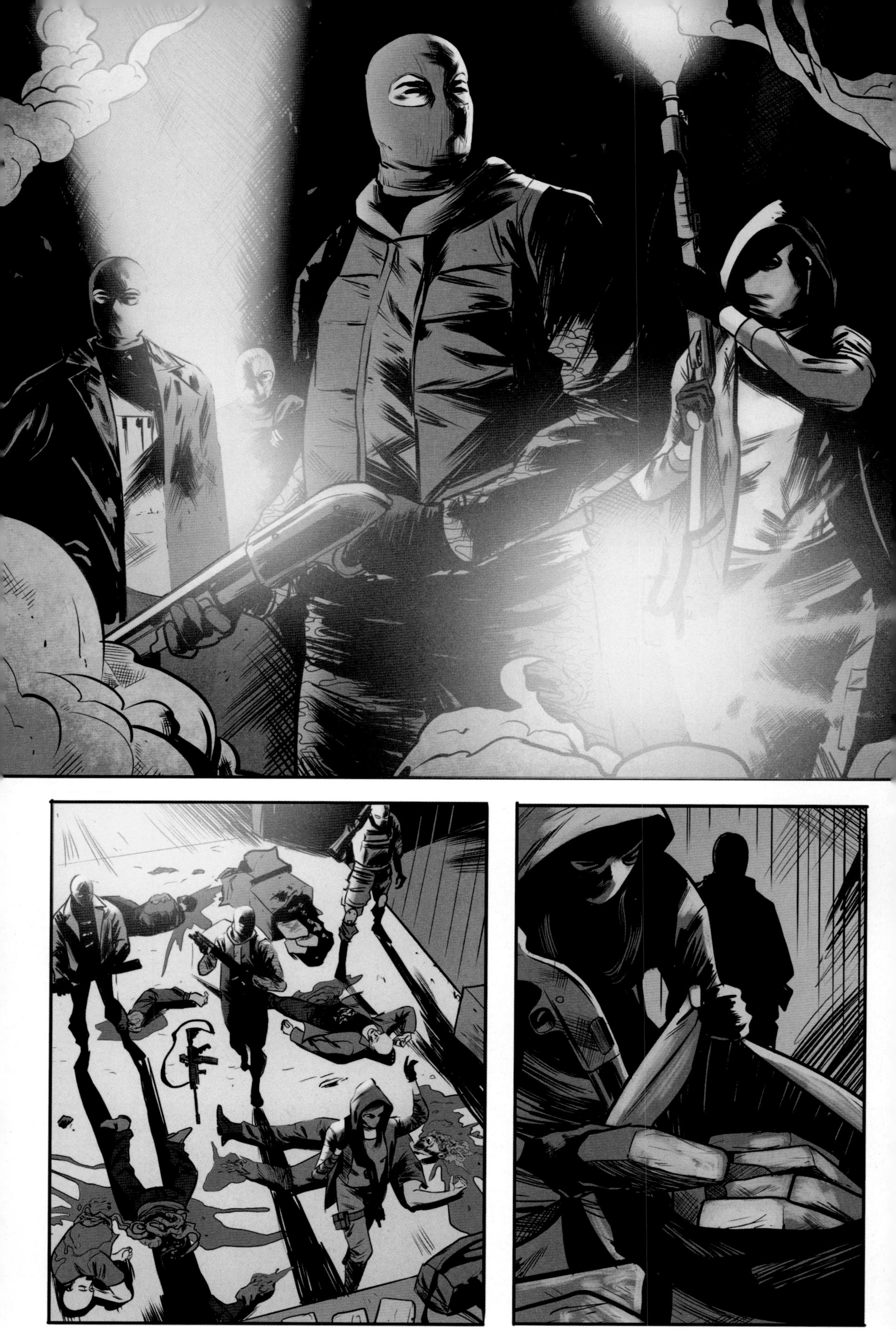

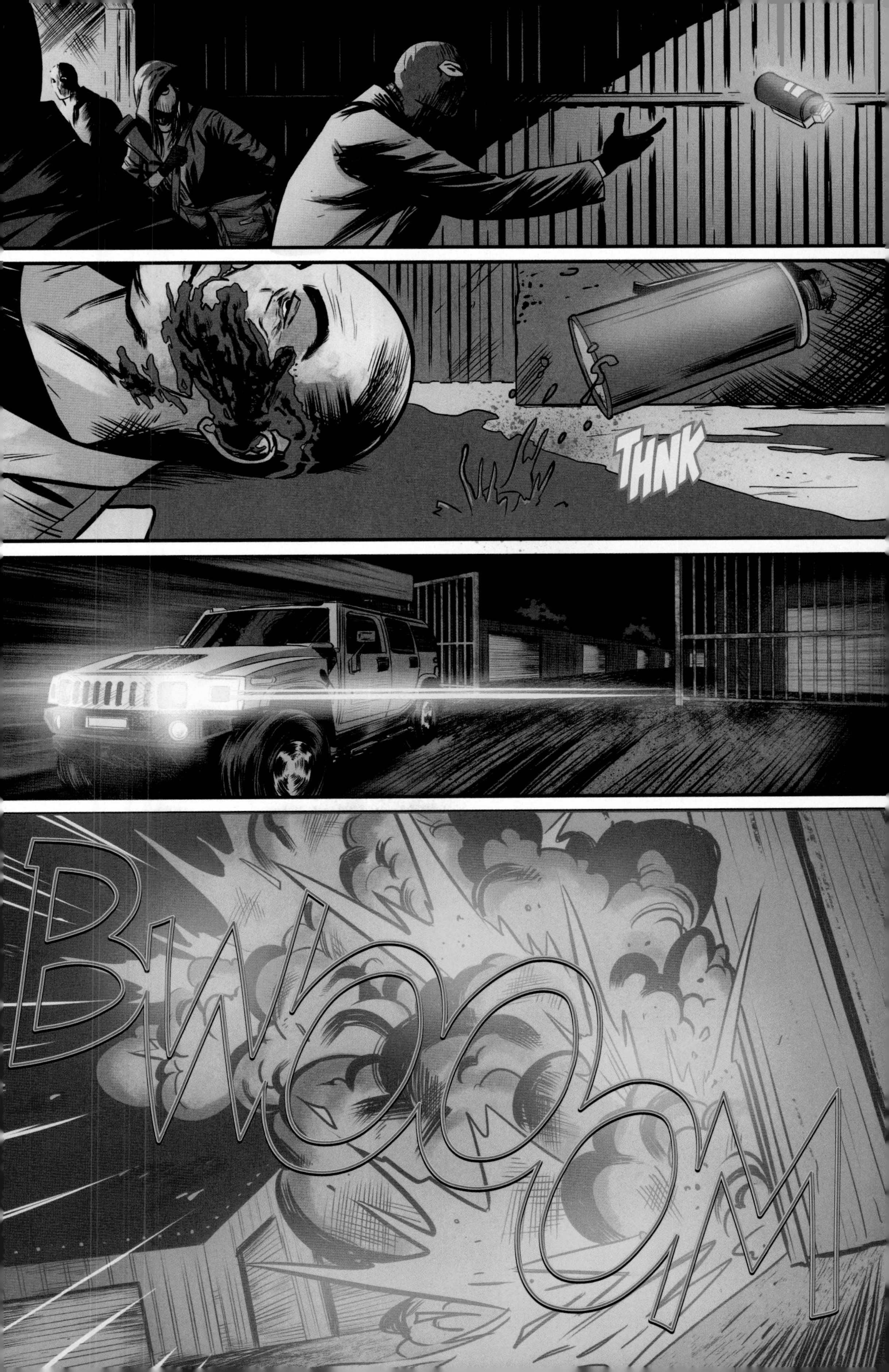
THNK
BWOOOM

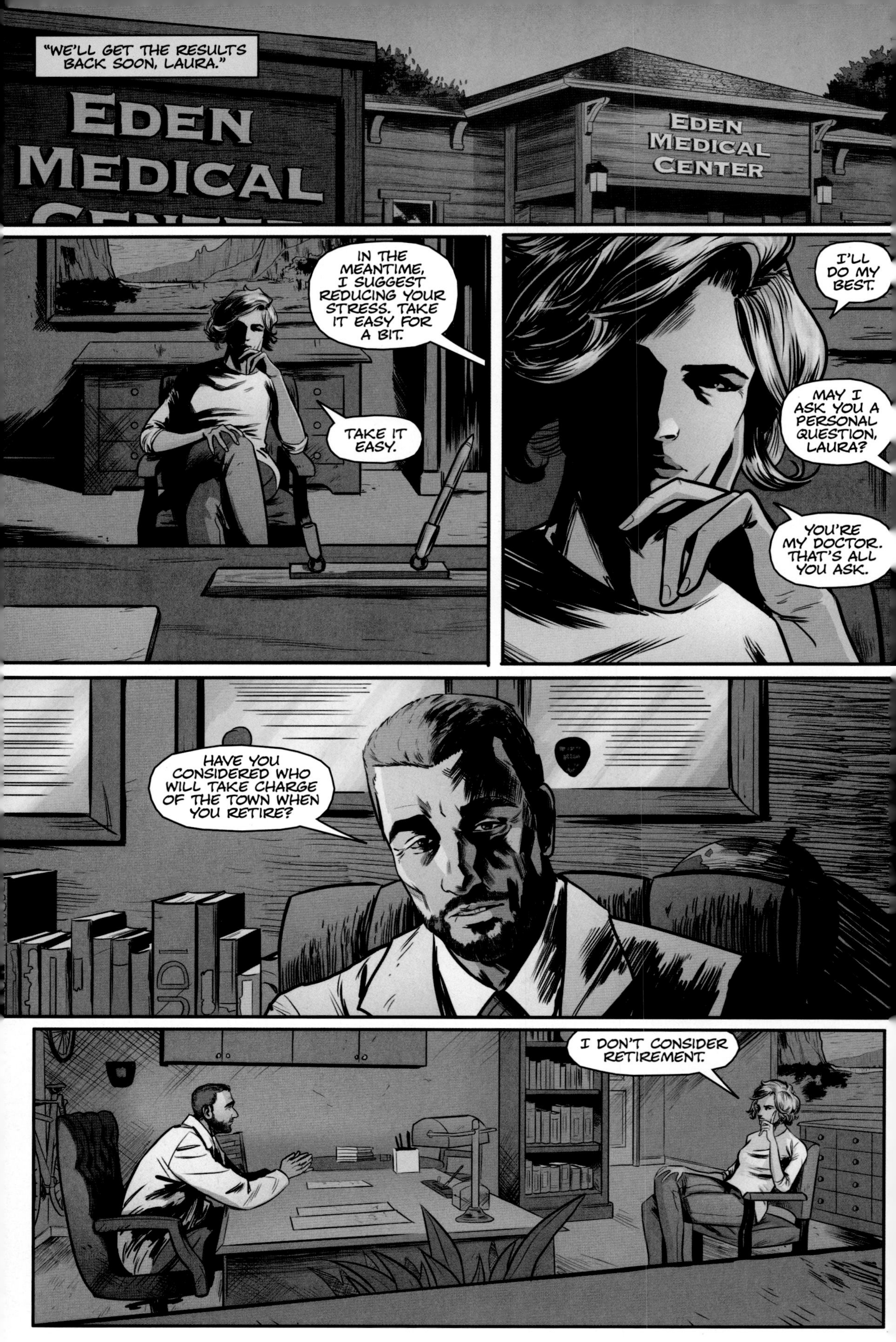
"WE'LL GET THE RESULTS BACK SOON, LAURA."
EDEN MEDICAL CENTER
EDEN MEDICAL CENTER
IN THE MEANTIME, I SUGGEST REDUCING YOUR STRESS. TAKE IT EASY FOR A BIT.
TAKE IT EASY.
I'LL DO MY BEST.
MAY I ASK YOU A PERSONAL QUESTION, LAURA?
YOU'RE MY DOCTOR. THAT'S ALL YOU ASK.
HAVE YOU CONSIDERED WHO WILL TAKE CHARGE OF THE TOWN WHEN YOU RETIRE?
I DON'T CONSIDER RETIREMENT.

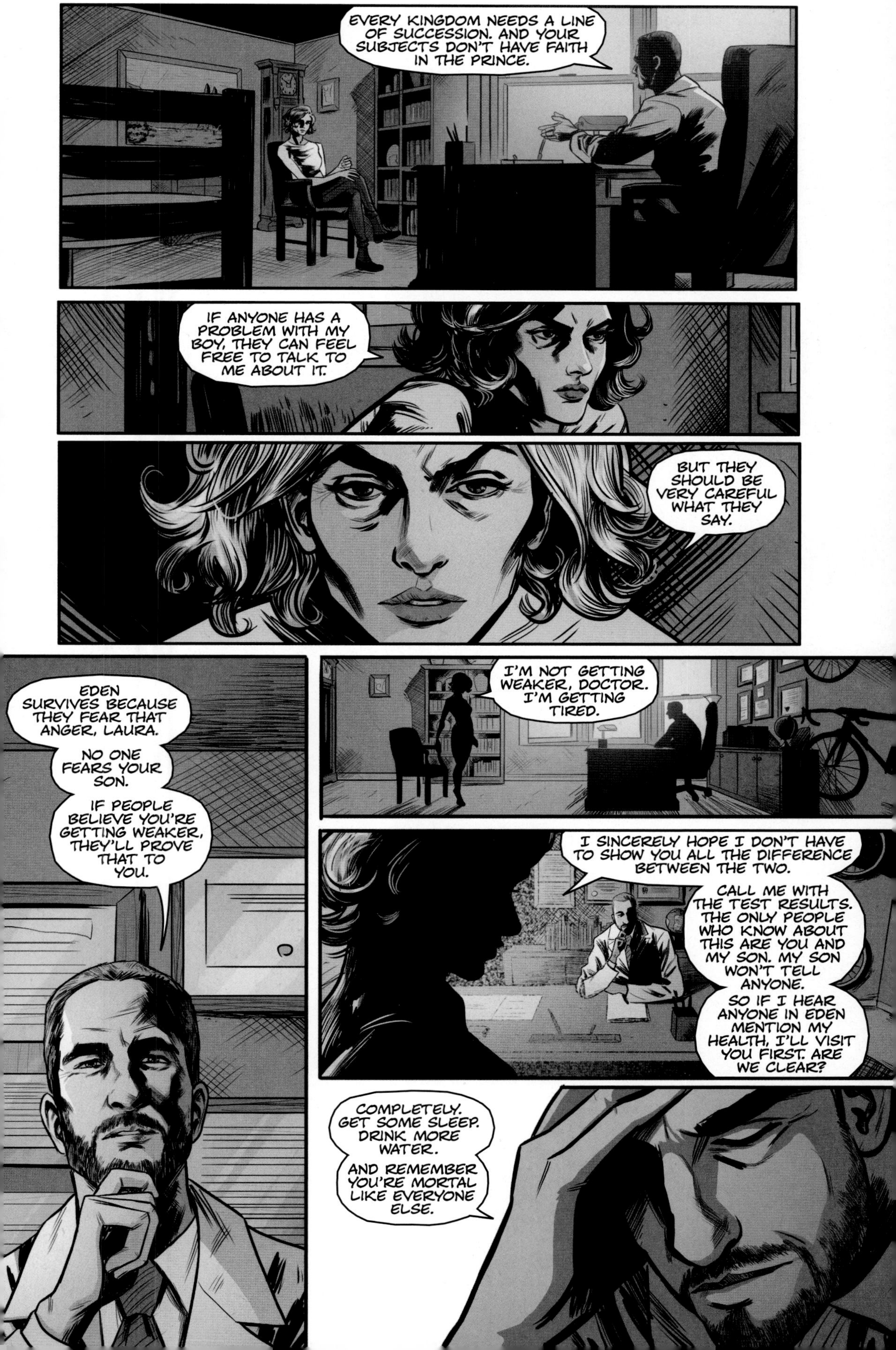
EVERY KINGDOM NEEDS A LINE OF SUCCESSION. AND YOUR SUBJECTS DON'T HAVE FAITH IN THE PRINCE.
IF ANYONE HAS A PROBLEM WITH MY BOY, THEY CAN FEEL FREE TO TALK TO ME ABOUT IT.
BUT THEY SHOULD BE VERY CAREFUL WHAT THEY SAY.
EDEN SURVIVES BECAUSE THEY FEAR THAT ANGER, LAURA.
NO ONE FEARS YOUR SON.
IF PEOPLE BELIEVE YOU'RE GETTING WEAKER, THEY'LL PROVE THAT TO YOU.
I'M NOT GETTING WEAKER, DOCTOR. I'M GETTING TIRED.
I SINCERELY HOPE I DON'T HAVE TO SHOW YOU ALL THE DIFFERENCE BETWEEN THE TWO.
CALL ME WITH THE TEST RESULTS. THE ONLY PEOPLE WHO KNOW ABOUT THIS ARE YOU AND MY SON. MY SON WON'T TELL ANYONE.
SO IF I HEAR ANYONE IN EDEN MENTION MY HEALTH, I'LL VISIT YOU FIRST. ARE WE CLEAR?
COMPLETELY. GET SOME SLEEP. DRINK MORE WATER.
AND REMEMBER YOU'RE MORTAL LIKE EVERYONE ELSE.

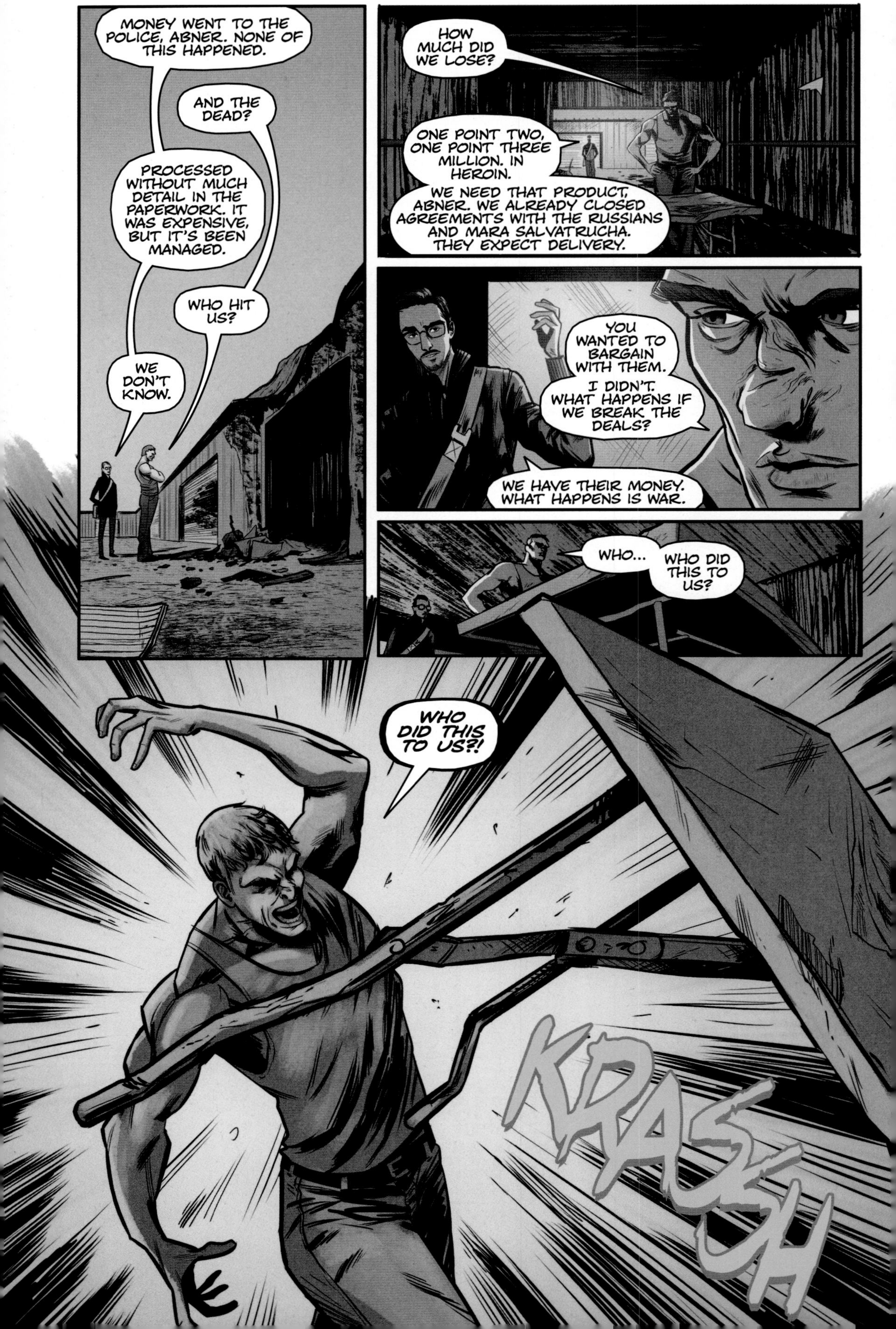
MONEY WENT TO THE POLICE, ABNER. NONE OF THIS HAPPENED.
AND THE DEAD?
PROCESSED WITHOUT MUCH DETAIL IN THE PAPERWORK. IT WAS EXPENSIVE, BUT IT'S BEEN MANAGED.
WHO HIT US?
WE DON'T KNOW.
HOW MUCH DID WE LOSE?
ONE POINT TWO, ONE POINT THREE MILLION. IN HEROIN.
WE NEED THAT PRODUCT, ABNER. WE ALREADY CLOSED AGREEMENTS WITH THE RUSSIANS AND MARA SALVATRUCHA. THEY EXPECT DELIVERY.
YOU WANTED TO BARGAIN WITH THEM.
I DIDN'T. WHAT HAPPENS IF WE BREAK THE DEALS?
WE HAVE THEIR MONEY. WHAT HAPPENS IS WAR.
WHO...
WHO DID THIS TO US?
WHO DID THIS TO US?!
KRASH

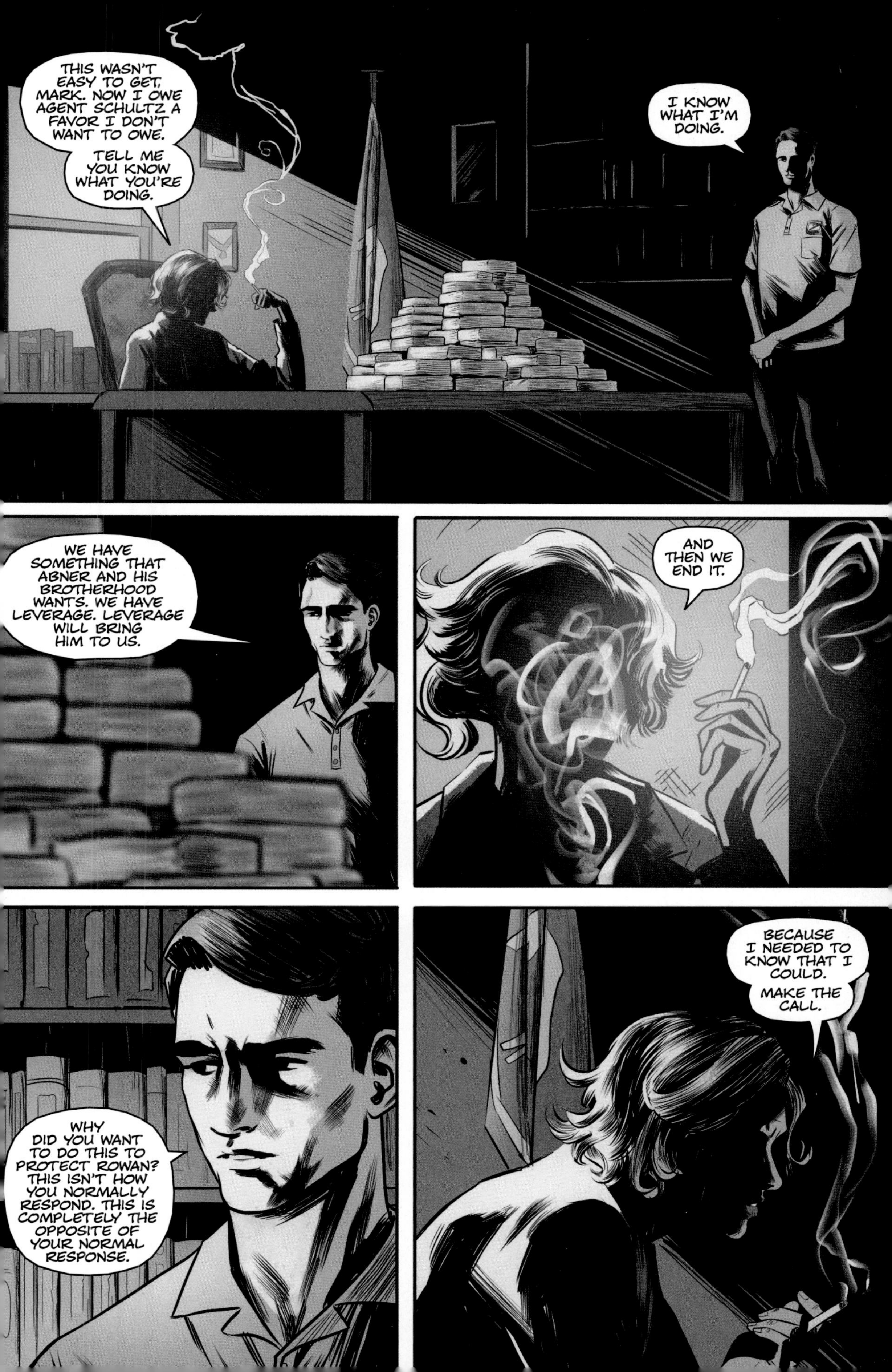
THIS WASN'T EASY TO GET, MARK. NOW I OWE AGENT SCHULTZ A FAVOR I DON'T WANT TO OWE.
TELL ME YOU KNOW WHAT YOU'RE DOING.
I KNOW WHAT I'M DOING.
WE HAVE SOMETHING THAT ABNER AND HIS BROTHERHOOD WANTS. WE HAVE LEVERAGE. LEVERAGE WILL BRING HIM TO US.
AND THEN WE END IT.
WHY DID YOU WANT TO DO THIS TO PROTECT ROWAN? THIS ISN'T HOW YOU NORMALLY RESPOND. THIS IS COMPLETELY THE OPPOSITE OF YOUR NORMAL RESPONSE.
BECAUSE I NEEDED TO KNOW THAT I COULD.
MAKE THE CALL.

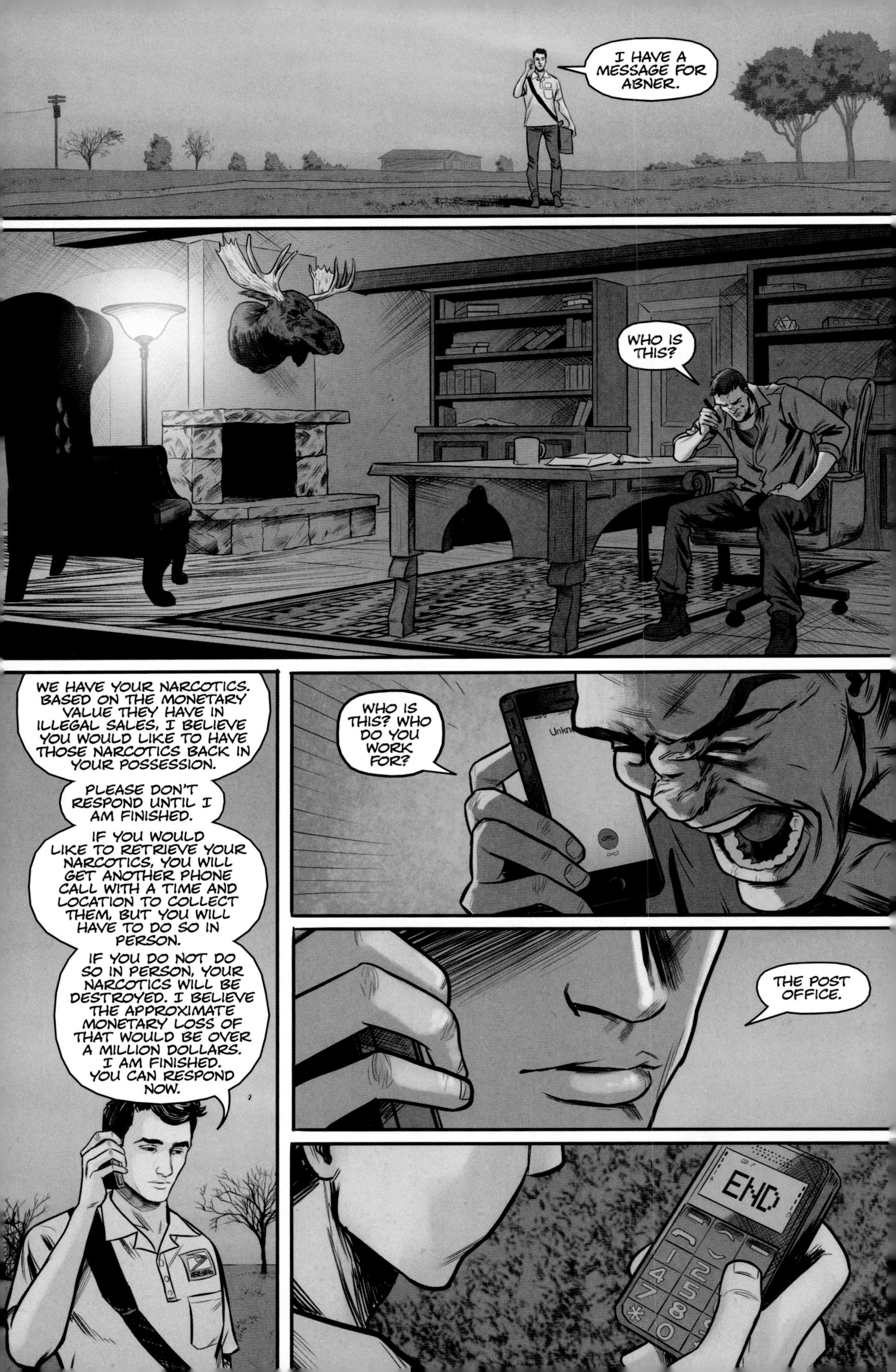
I HAVE A MESSAGE FOR ABNER.
WHO IS THIS?
WE HAVE YOUR NARCOTICS. BASED ON THE MONETARY VALUE THEY HAVE IN ILLEGAL SALES, I BELIEVE YOU WOULD LIKE TO HAVE THOSE NARCOTICS BACK IN YOUR POSSESSION.
PLEASE DON'T RESPOND UNTIL I AM FINISHED.
IF YOU WOULD LIKE TO RETRIEVE YOUR NARCOTICS, YOU WILL GET ANOTHER PHONE CALL WITH A TIME AND LOCATION TO COLLECT THEM, BUT YOU WILL HAVE TO DO SO IN PERSON.
IF YOU DO NOT DO SO IN PERSON, YOUR NARCOTICS WILL BE DESTROYED. I BELIEVE THE APPROXIMATE MONETARY LOSS OF THAT WOULD BE OVER A MILLION DOLLARS. I AM FINISHED. YOU CAN RESPOND NOW.
WHO IS THIS? WHO DO YOU WORK FOR?
THE POST OFFICE.
END

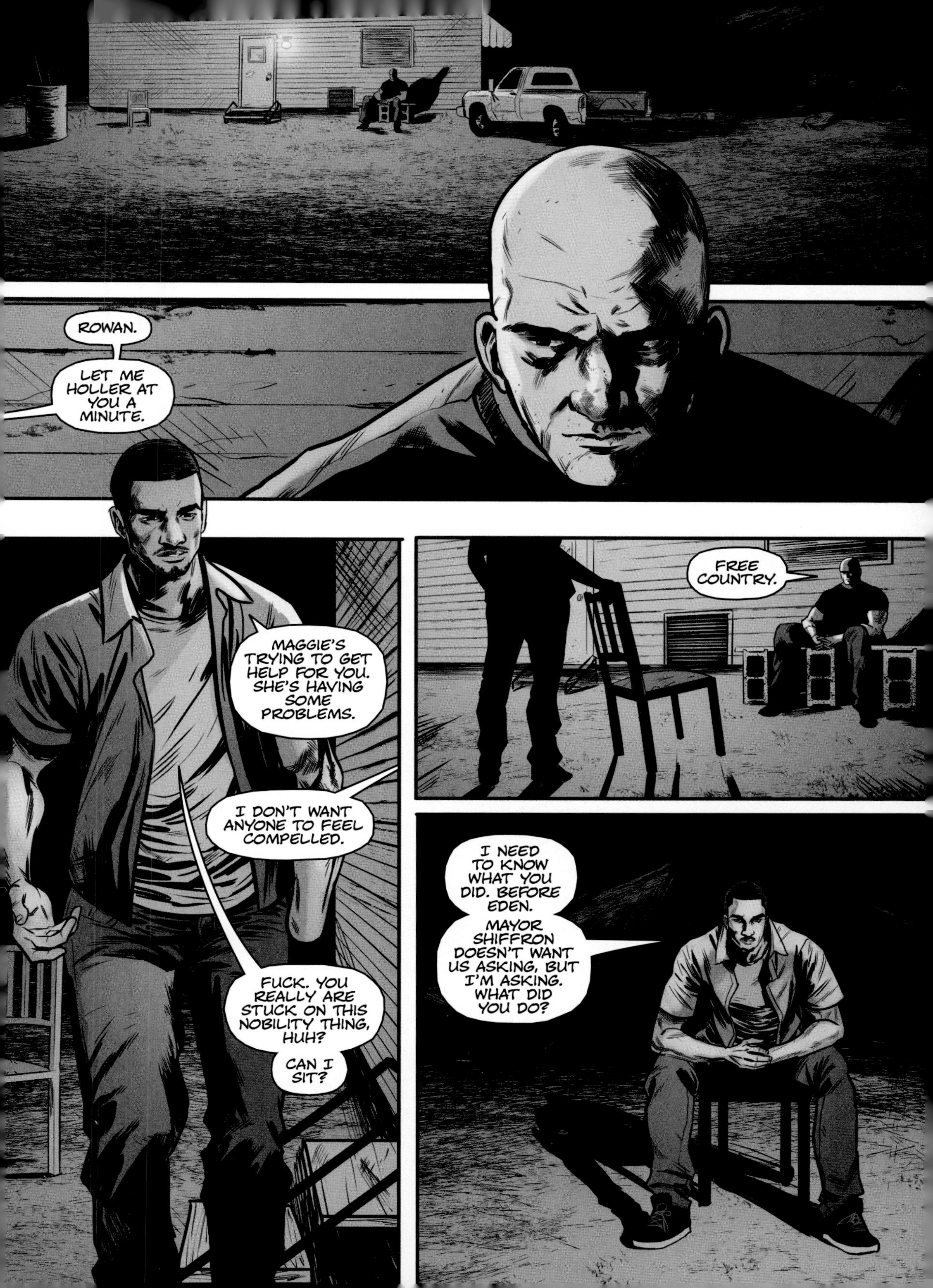
ROWAN.
LET ME HOLLER AT YOU A MINUTE.
MAGGIE'S TRYING TO GET HELP FOR YOU. SHE'S HAVING SOME PROBLEMS.
FREE COUNTRY.
I DON'T WANT ANYONE TO FEEL COMPELLED.
FUCK. YOU REALLY ARE STUCK ON THIS NOBILITY THING, HUH?
CAN I SIT?
I NEED TO KNOW WHAT YOU DID. BEFORE EDEN.
MAYOR SHIFFRON DOESN'T WANT US ASKING, BUT I'M ASKING. WHAT DID YOU DO?

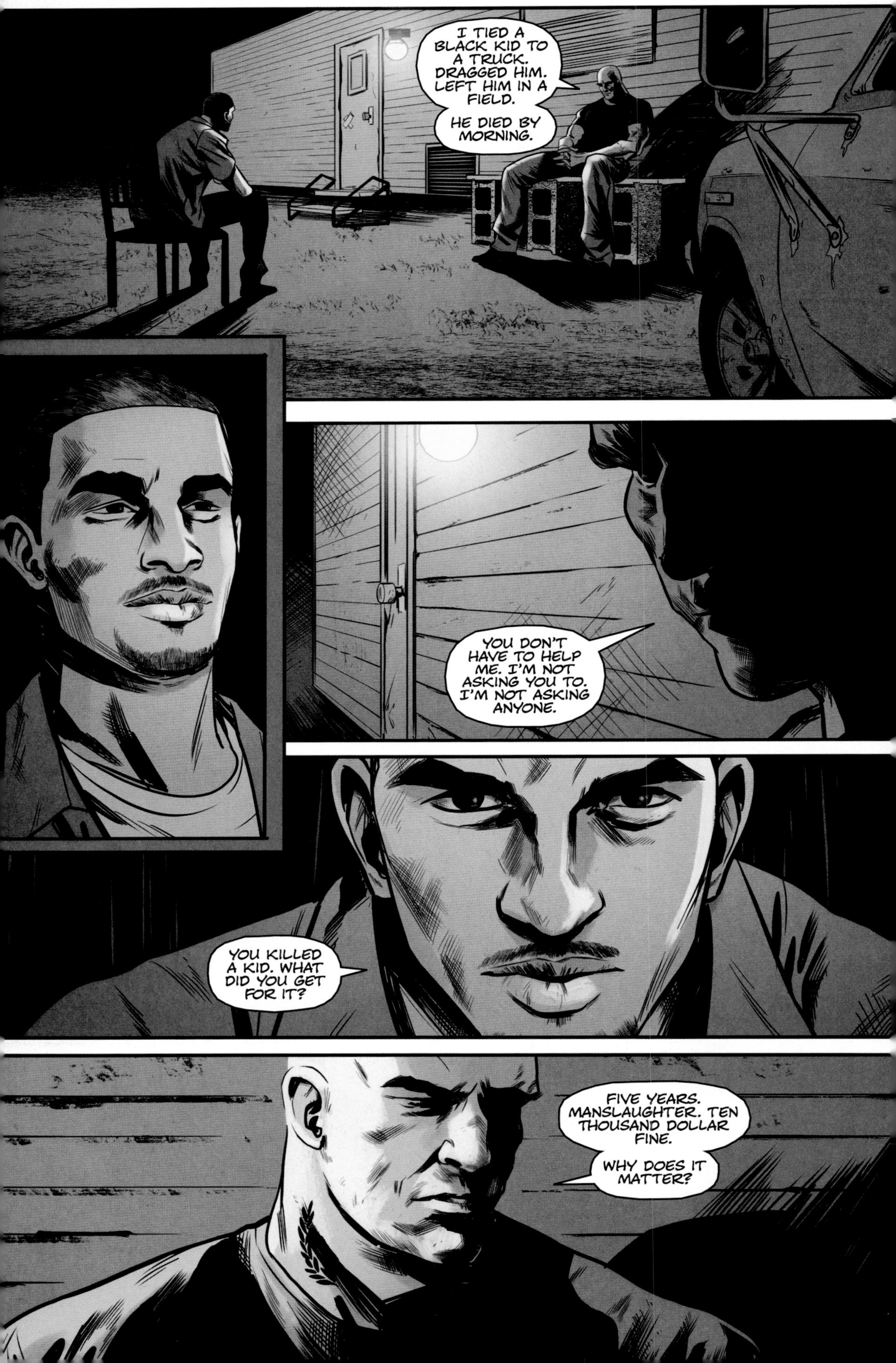
I TIED A BLACK KID TO A TRUCK. DRAGGED HIM. LEFT HIM IN A FIELD.
HE DIED BY MORNING.
YOU DON'T HAVE TO HELP ME. I'M NOT ASKING YOU TO. I'M NOT ASKING ANYONE.
YOU KILLED A KID. WHAT DID YOU GET FOR IT?
FIVE YEARS. MANSLAUGHTER. TEN THOUSAND DOLLAR FINE.
WHY DOES IT MATTER?

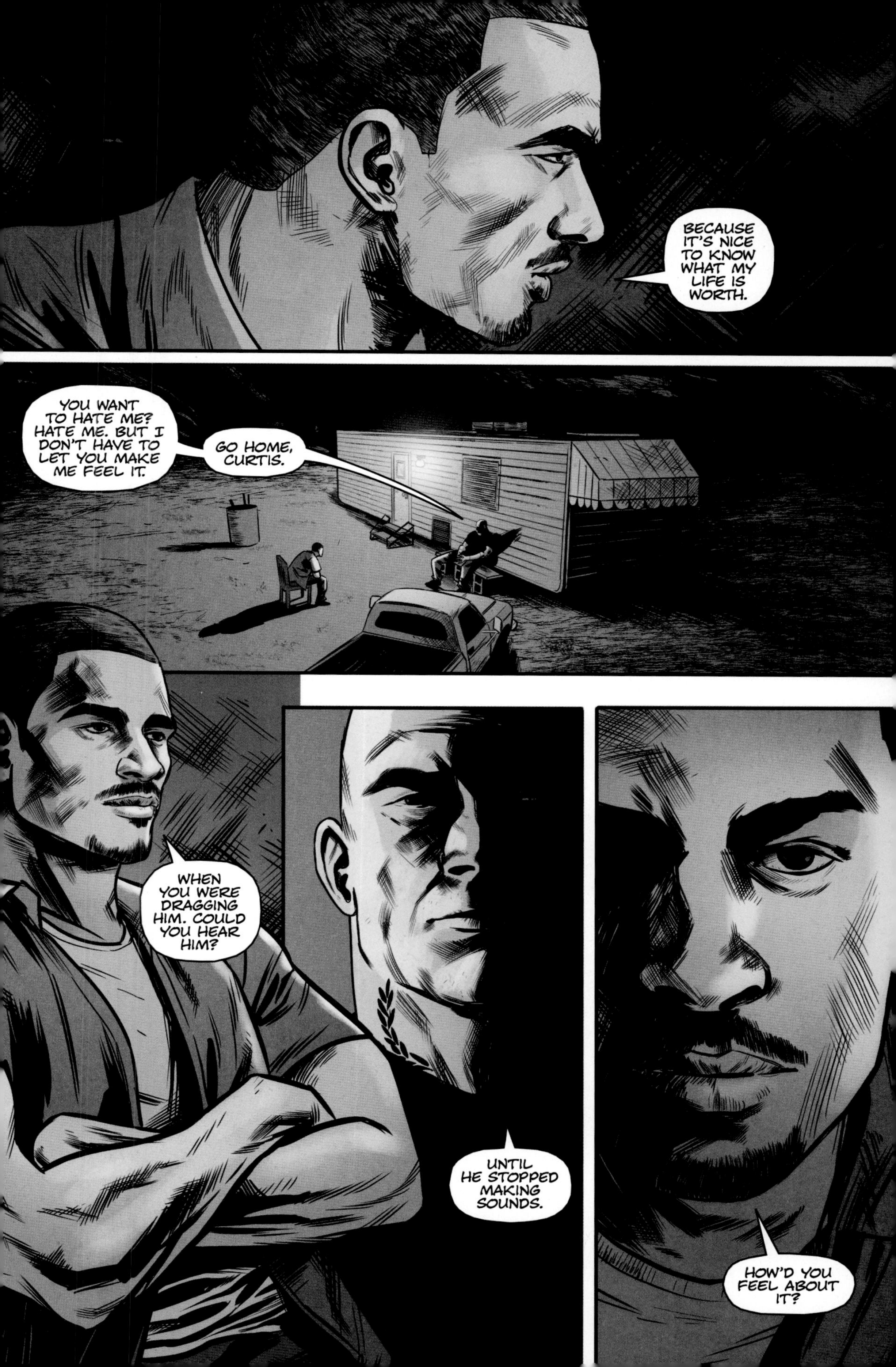
BECAUSE IT'S NICE TO KNOW WHAT MY LIFE IS WORTH.
YOU WANT TO HATE ME? HATE ME. BUT I DON'T HAVE TO LET YOU MAKE ME FEEL IT.
GO HOME, CURTIS.
WHEN YOU WERE DRAGGING HIM. COULD YOU HEAR HIM?
UNTIL HE STOPPED MAKING SOUNDS.
HOW'D YOU FEEL ABOUT IT?

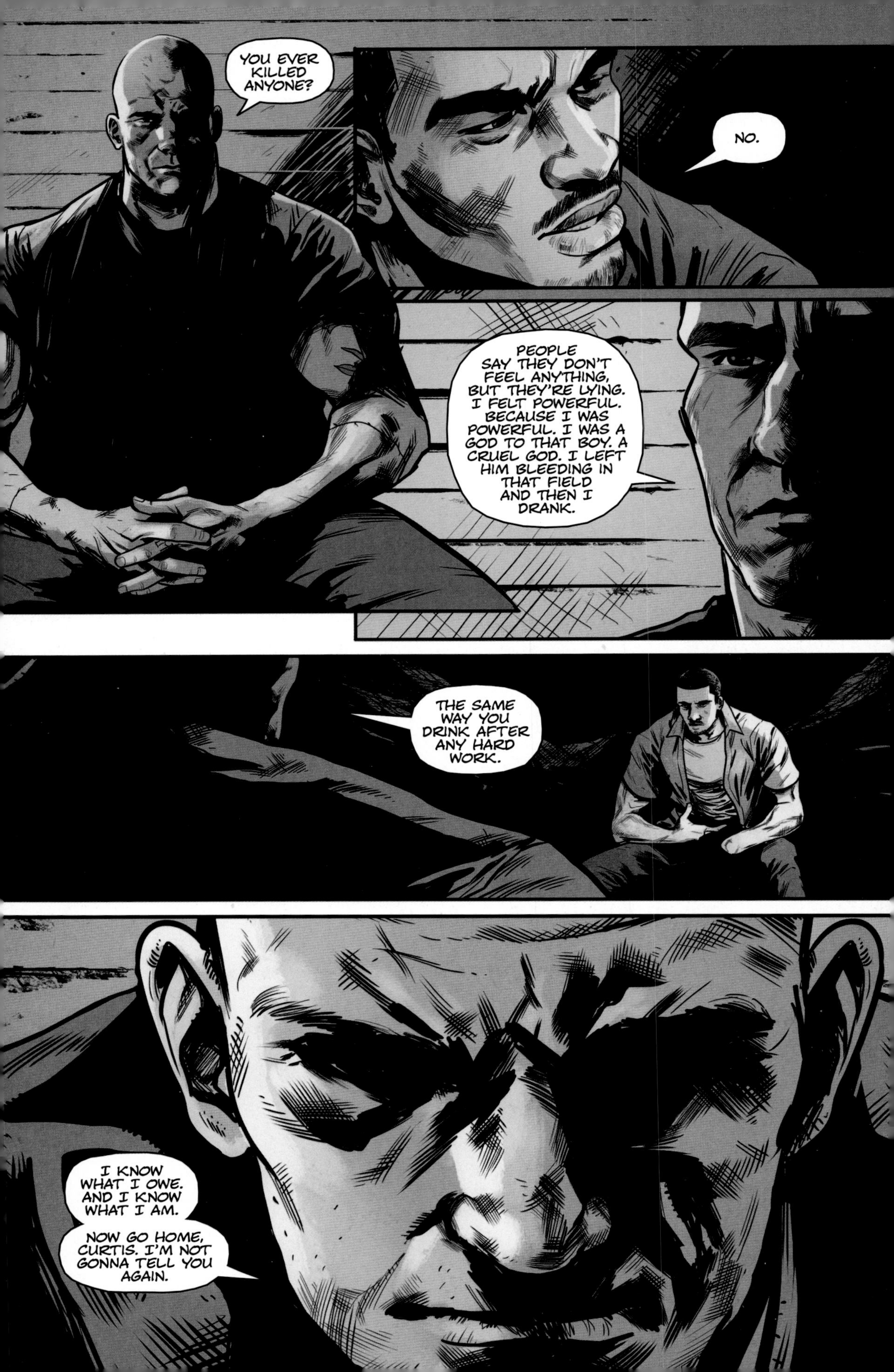
YOU EVER KILLED ANYONE?
NO.
PEOPLE SAY THEY DON'T FEEL ANYTHING, BUT THEY'RE LYING. I FELT POWERFUL. BECAUSE I WAS POWERFUL. I WAS A GOD TO THAT BOY. A CRUEL GOD. I LEFT HIM BLEEDING IN THAT FIELD AND THEN I DRANK.
THE SAME WAY YOU DRINK AFTER ANY HARD WORK.
I KNOW WHAT I OWE. AND I KNOW WHAT I AM.
NOW GO HOME, CURTIS. I'M NOT GONNA TELL YOU AGAIN.

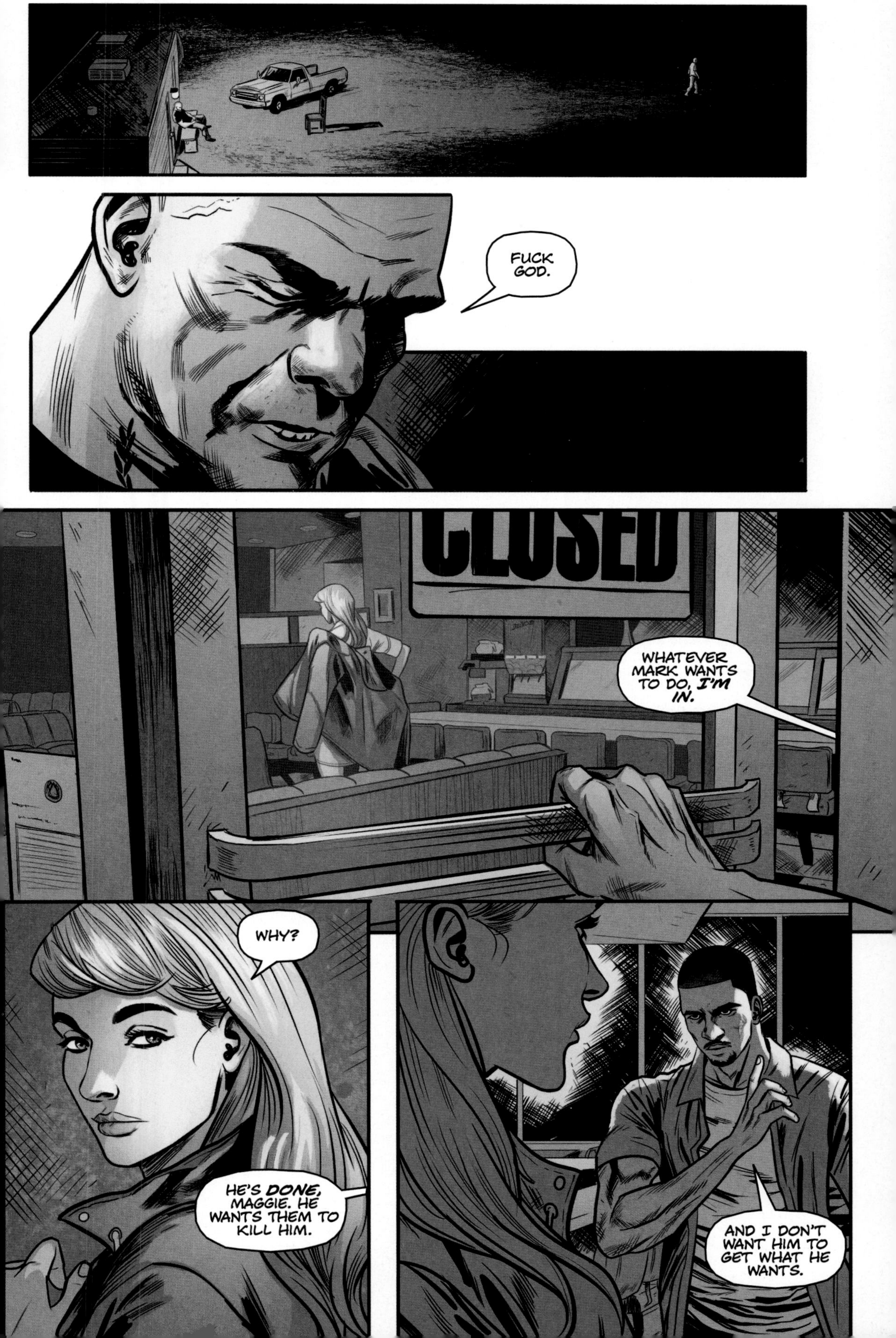
FUCK GOD.
CLOSED
WHATEVER MARK WANTS TO DO, I'M IN.
WHY?
HE'S DONE, MAGGIE. HE WANTS THEM TO KILL HIM.
AND I DON'T WANT HIM TO GET WHAT HE WANTS.

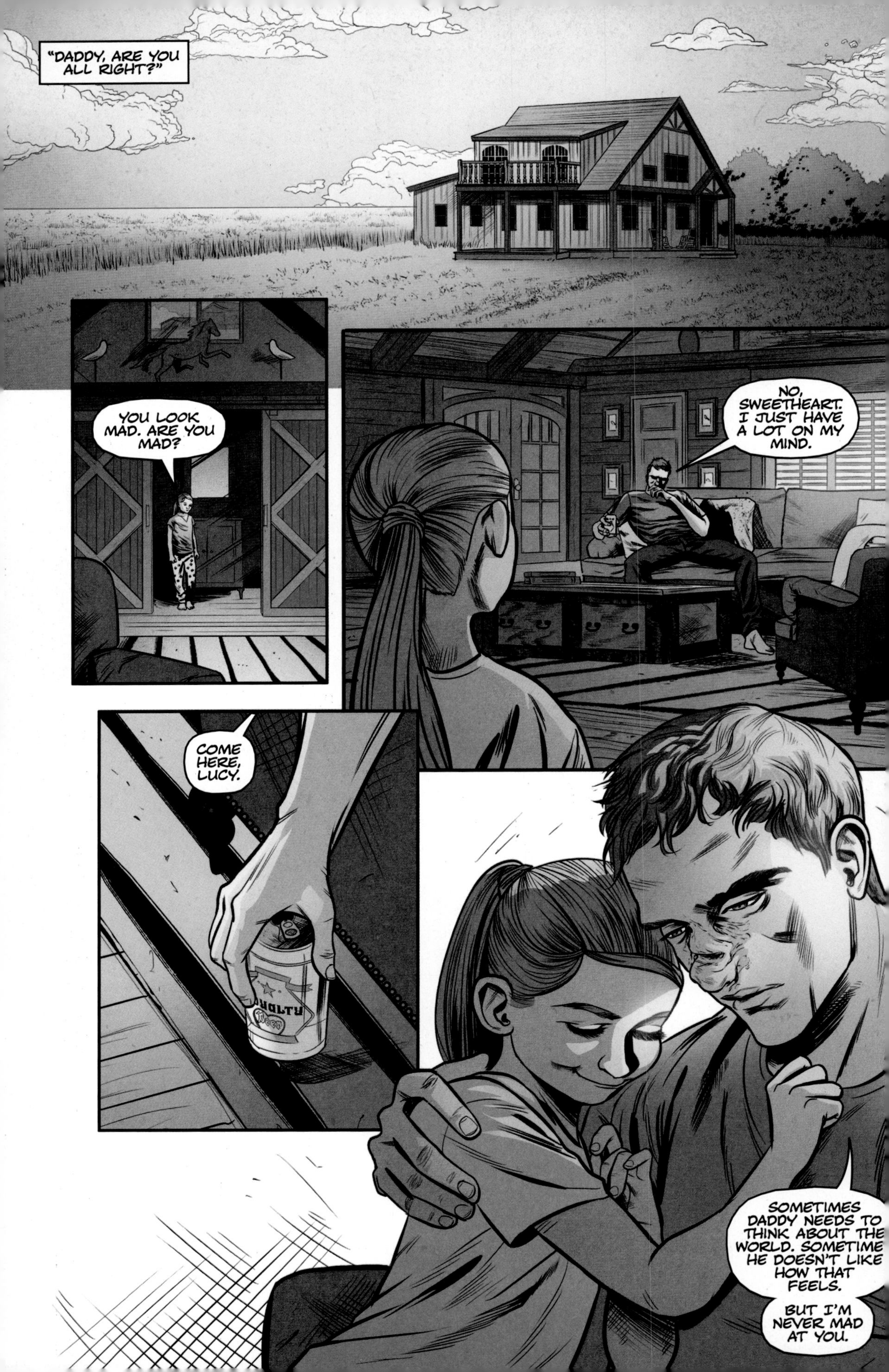
"DADDY, ARE YOU ALL RIGHT?"
YOU LOOK MAD. ARE YOU MAD?
NO, SWEETHEART. I JUST HAVE A LOT ON MY MIND.
COME HERE, LUCY.
SOMETIMES DADDY NEEDS TO THINK ABOUT THE WORLD. SOMETIME HE DOESN'T LIKE HOW THAT FEELS.
BUT I'M NEVER MAD AT YOU.

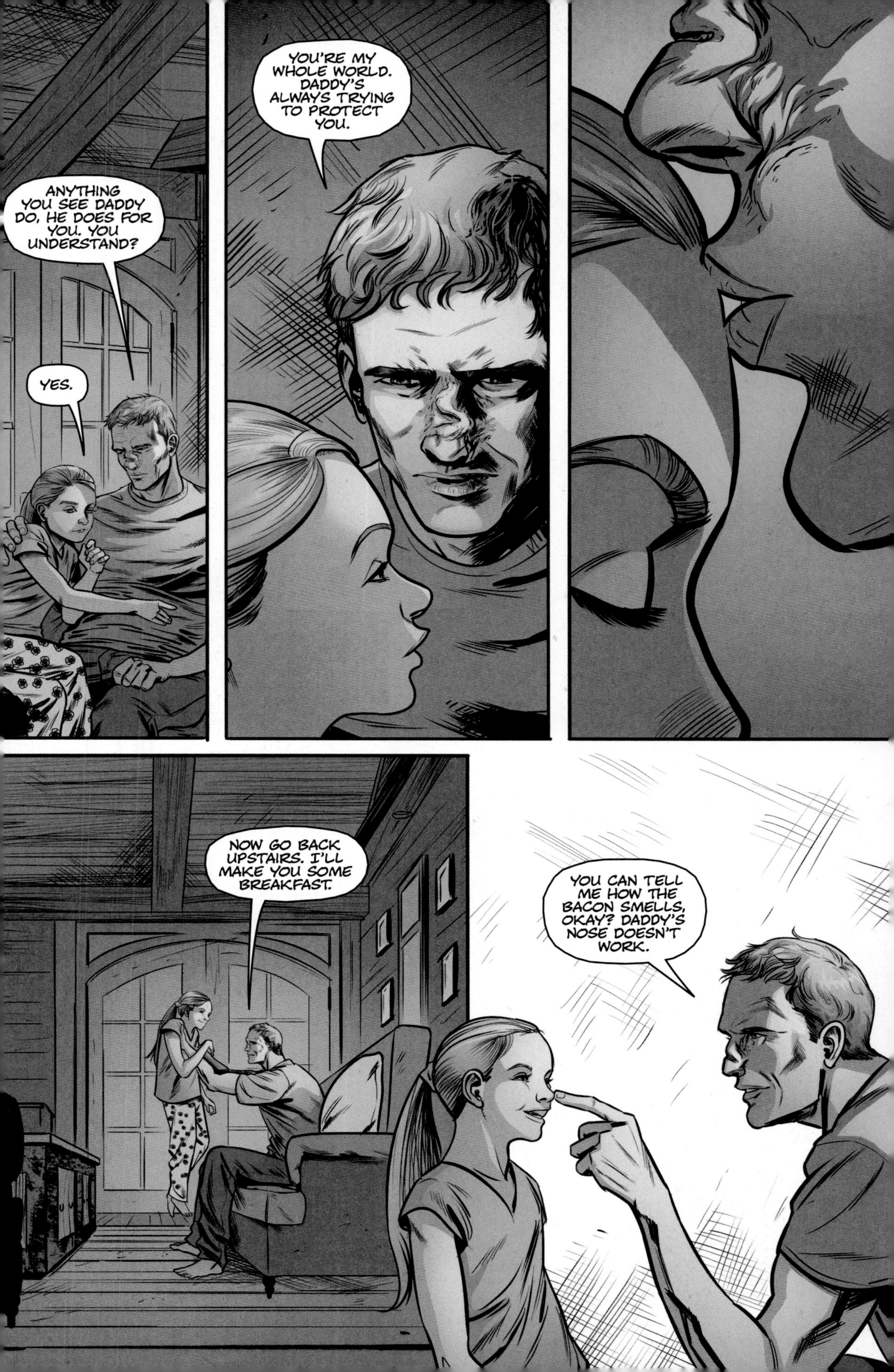
ANYTHING YOU SEE DADDY DO, HE DOES FOR YOU. YOU UNDERSTAND?
YES.
YOU'RE MY WHOLE WORLD. DADDY'S ALWAYS TRYING TO PROTECT YOU.
NOW GO BACK UPSTAIRS. I'LL MAKE YOU SOME BREAKFAST.
YOU CAN TELL ME HOW THE BACON SMELLS, OKAY? DADDY'S NOSE DOESN'T WORK.

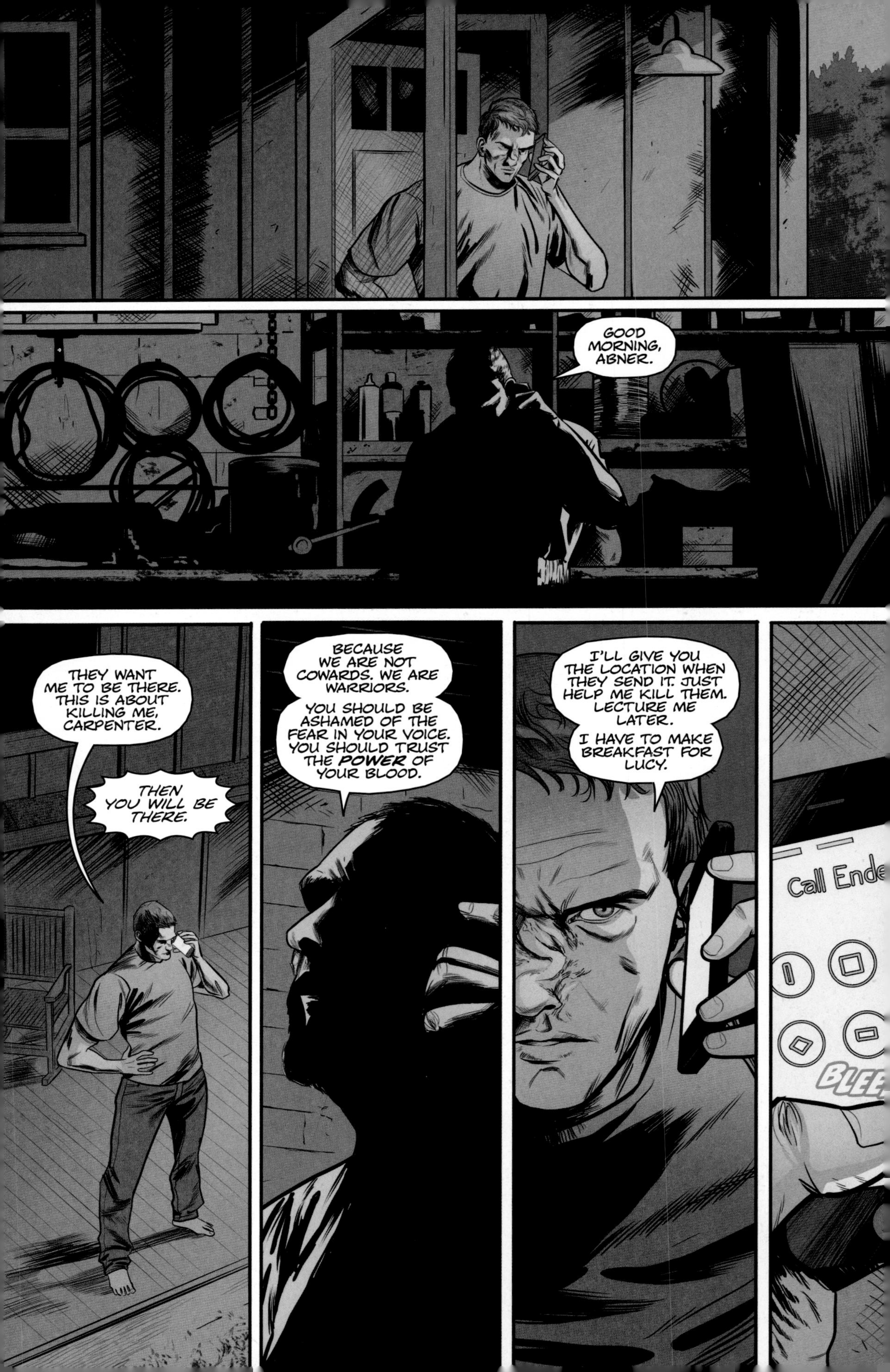
GOOD MORNING, ABNER.
THEY WANT ME TO BE THERE. THIS IS ABOUT KILLING ME, CARPENTER.
THEN YOU WILL BE THERE.
BECAUSE WE ARE NOT COWARDS. WE ARE WARRIORS.
YOU SHOULD BE ASHAMED OF THE FEAR IN YOUR VOICE. YOU SHOULD TRUST THE POWER OF YOUR BLOOD.
I'LL GIVE YOU THE LOCATION WHEN THEY SEND IT. JUST HELP ME KILL THEM. LECTURE ME LATER.
I HAVE TO MAKE BREAKFAST FOR LUCY.

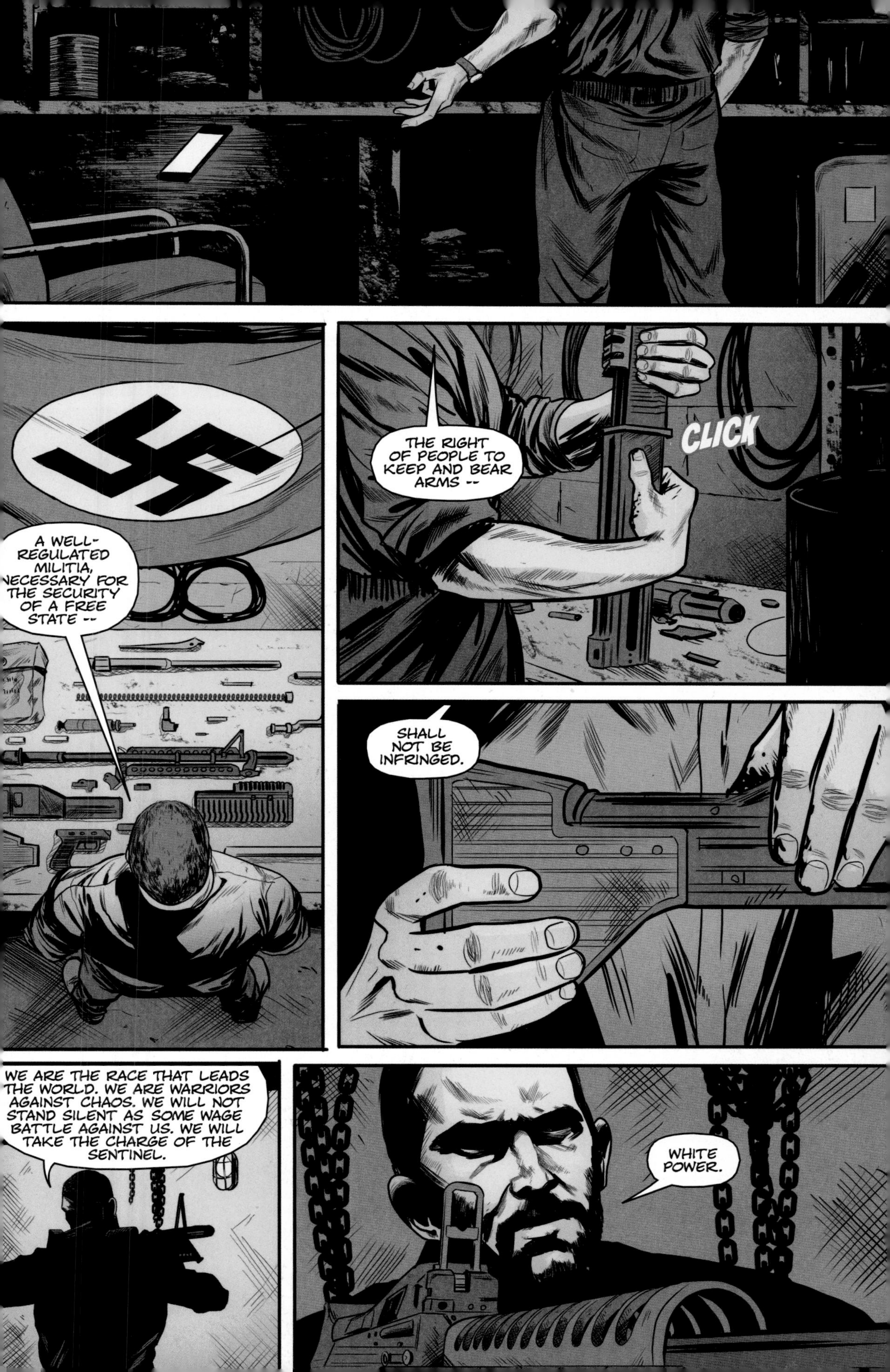
A WELL-REGULATED MILITIA, NECESSARY FOR THE SECURITY OF A FREE STATE --
THE RIGHT OF PEOPLE TO KEEP AND BEAR ARMS --
CLICK
SHALL NOT BE INFRINGED.
WE ARE THE RACE THAT LEADS THE WORLD. WE ARE WARRIORS AGAINST CHAOS. WE WILL NOT STAND SILENT AS SOME WAGE BATTLE AGAINST US. WE WILL TAKE THE CHARGE OF THE SENTINEL.
WHITE POWER.

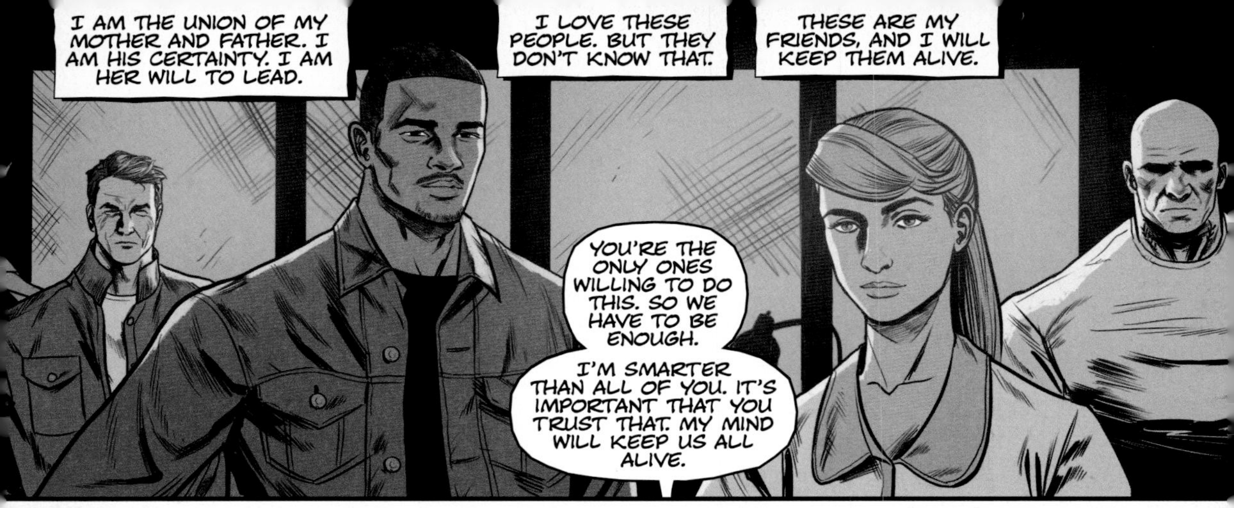
I AM THE UNION OF MY MOTHER AND FATHER. I AM HIS CERTAINTY. I AM HER WILL TO LEAD.
I LOVE THESE PEOPLE. BUT THEY DON'T KNOW THAT.
THESE ARE MY FRIENDS, AND I WILL KEEP THEM ALIVE.
YOU'RE THE ONLY ONES WILLING TO DO THIS. SO WE HAVE TO BE ENOUGH.
I'M SMARTER THAN ALL OF YOU. IT'S IMPORTANT THAT YOU TRUST THAT. MY MIND WILL KEEP US ALL ALIVE.

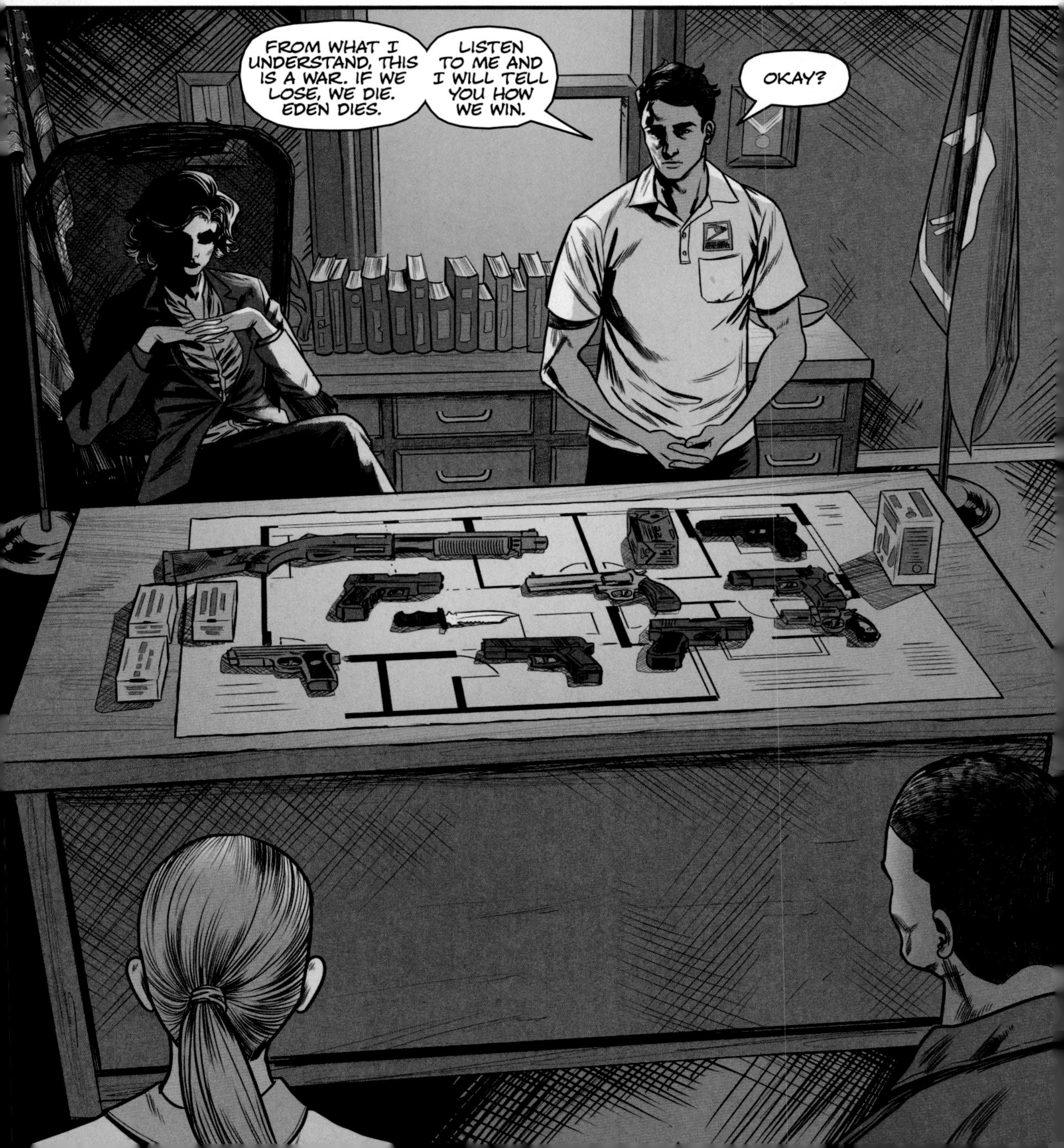
FROM WHAT I UNDERSTAND, THIS IS A WAR. IF WE LOSE, WE DIE. EDEN DIES.
LISTEN TO ME AND I WILL TELL YOU HOW WE WIN.
OKAY?

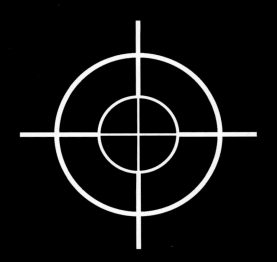

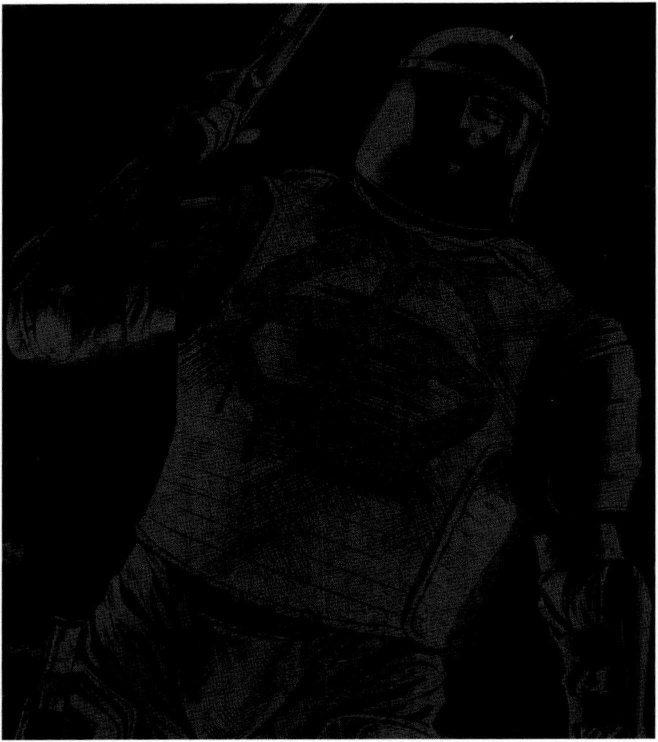

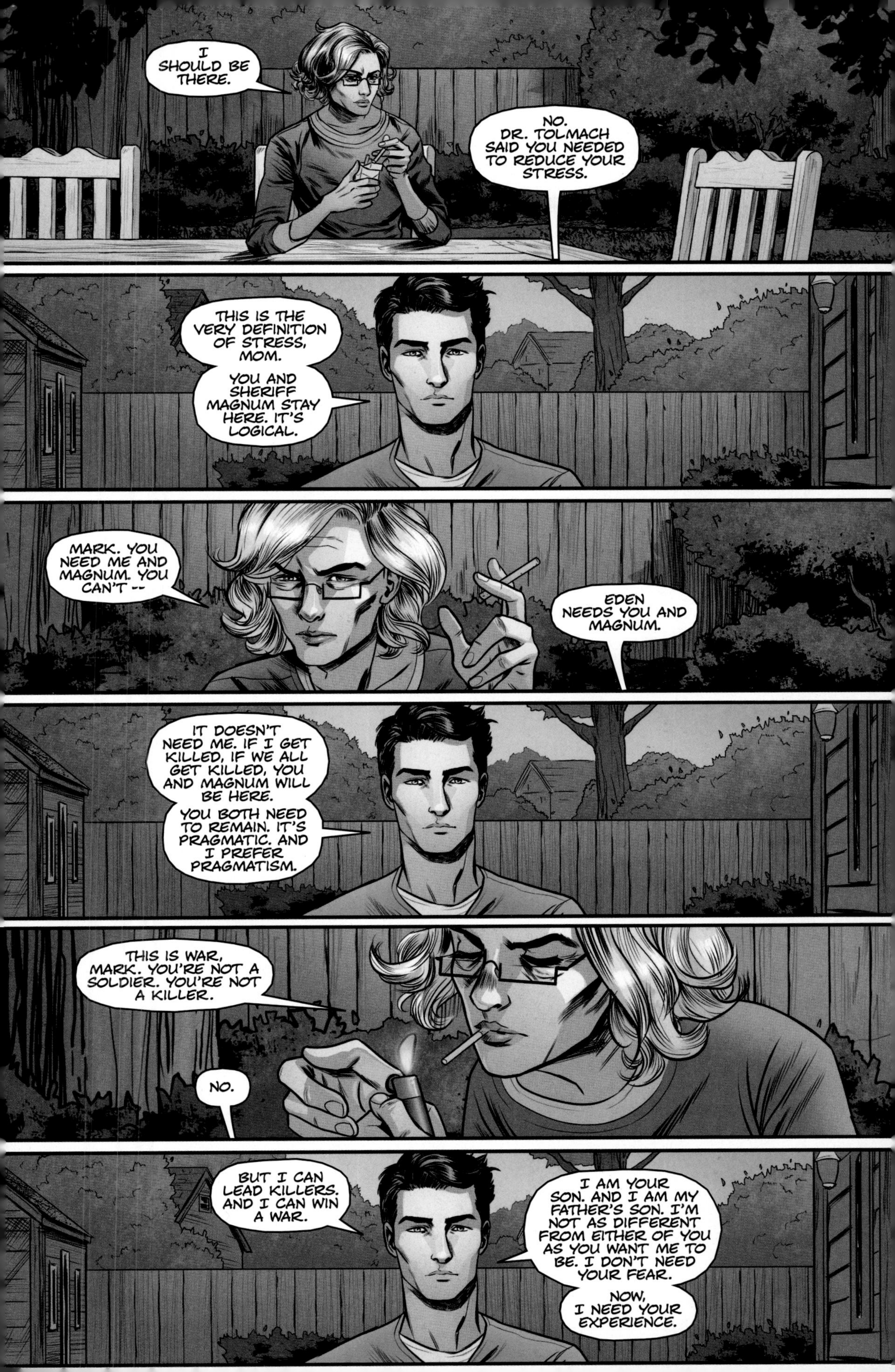
I SHOULD BE THERE.
NO. DR. TOLMACH SAID YOU NEEDED TO REDUCE YOUR STRESS.
THIS IS THE VERY DEFINITION OF STRESS, MOM.
YOU AND SHERIFF MAGNUM STAY HERE. IT'S LOGICAL.
MARK. YOU NEED ME AND MAGNUM. YOU CAN'T --
EDEN NEEDS YOU AND MAGNUM.
IT DOESN'T NEED ME. IF I GET KILLED, IF WE ALL GET KILLED, YOU AND MAGNUM WILL BE HERE.
YOU BOTH NEED TO REMAIN. IT'S PRAGMATIC. AND I PREFER PRAGMATISM.
THIS IS WAR, MARK. YOU'RE NOT A SOLDIER. YOU'RE NOT A KILLER.
NO.
BUT I CAN LEAD KILLERS. AND I CAN WIN A WAR.
I AM YOUR SON. AND I AM MY FATHER'S SON. I'M NOT AS DIFFERENT FROM EITHER OF YOU AS YOU WANT ME TO BE. I DON'T NEED YOUR FEAR.
NOW, I NEED YOUR EXPERIENCE.

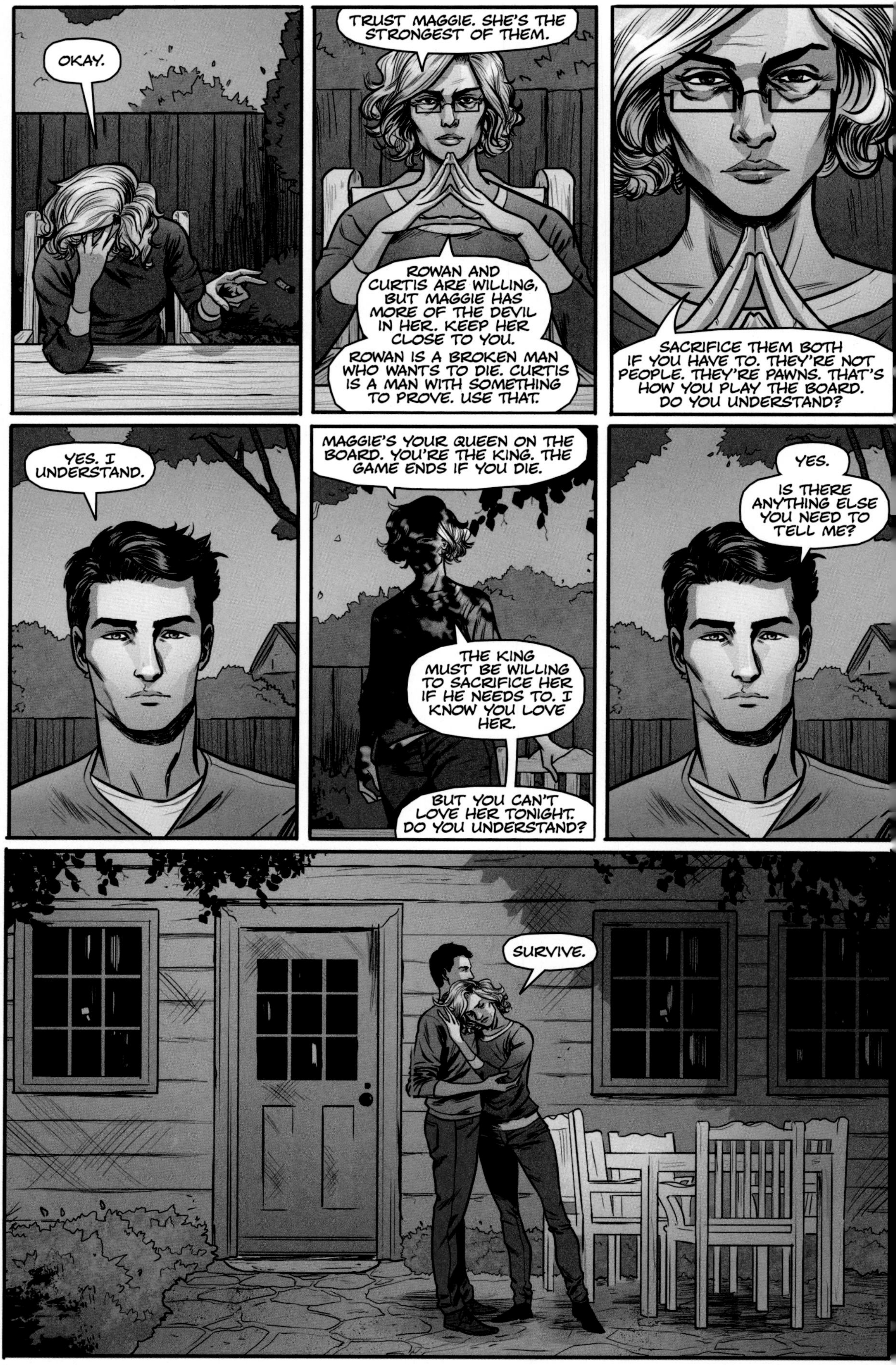
OKAY.
TRUST MAGGIE. SHE'S THE STRONGEST OF THEM.
ROWAN AND CURTIS ARE WILLING, BUT MAGGIE HAS MORE OF THE DEVIL IN HER. KEEP HER CLOSE TO YOU.
ROWAN IS A BROKEN MAN WHO WANTS TO DIE. CURTIS IS A MAN WITH SOMETHING TO PROVE. USE THAT.
SACRIFICE THEM BOTH IF YOU HAVE TO. THEY'RE NOT PEOPLE. THEY'RE PAWNS. THAT'S HOW YOU PLAY THE BOARD. DO YOU UNDERSTAND?
YES. I UNDERSTAND.
MAGGIE'S YOUR QUEEN ON THE BOARD. YOU'RE THE KING. THE GAME ENDS IF YOU DIE.
THE KING MUST BE WILLING TO SACRIFICE HER IF HE NEEDS TO. I KNOW YOU LOVE HER.
BUT YOU CAN'T LOVE HER TONIGHT. DO YOU UNDERSTAND?
YES.
IS THERE ANYTHING ELSE YOU NEED TO TELL ME?
SURVIVE.

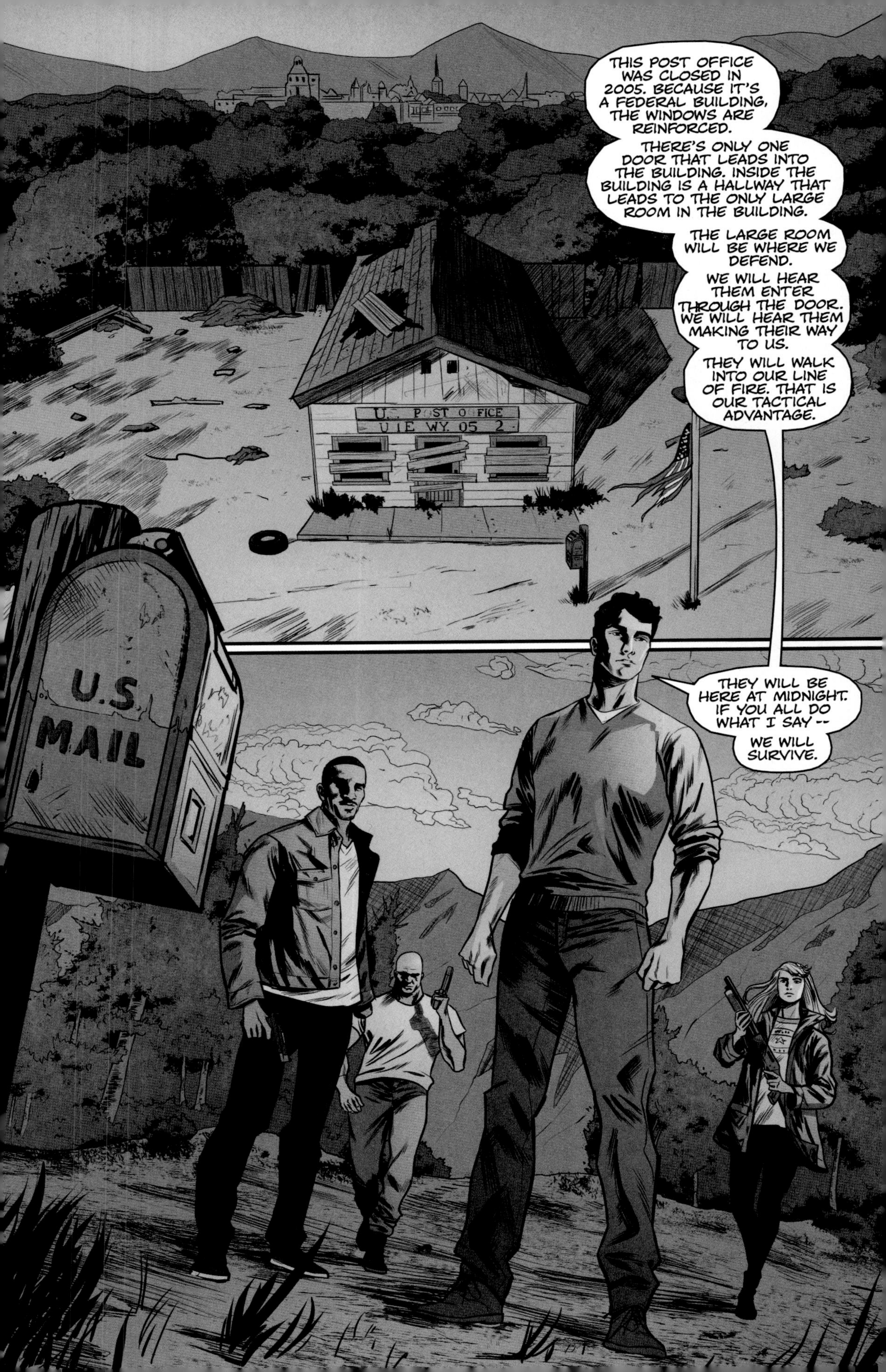
THIS POST OFFICE WAS CLOSED IN 2005. BECAUSE IT'S A FEDERAL BUILDING, THE WINDOWS ARE REINFORCED.
THERE'S ONLY ONE DOOR THAT LEADS INTO THE BUILDING. INSIDE THE BUILDING IS A HALLWAY THAT LEADS TO THE ONLY LARGE ROOM IN THE BUILDING.
THE LARGE ROOM WILL BE WHERE WE DEFEND.
WE WILL HEAR THEM ENTER THROUGH THE DOOR. WE WILL HEAR THEM MAKING THEIR WAY TO US.
THEY WILL WALK INTO OUR LINE OF FIRE. THAT IS OUR TACTICAL ADVANTAGE.
THEY WILL BE HERE AT MIDNIGHT. IF YOU ALL DO WHAT I SAY --
WE WILL SURVIVE.
U.S MAIL

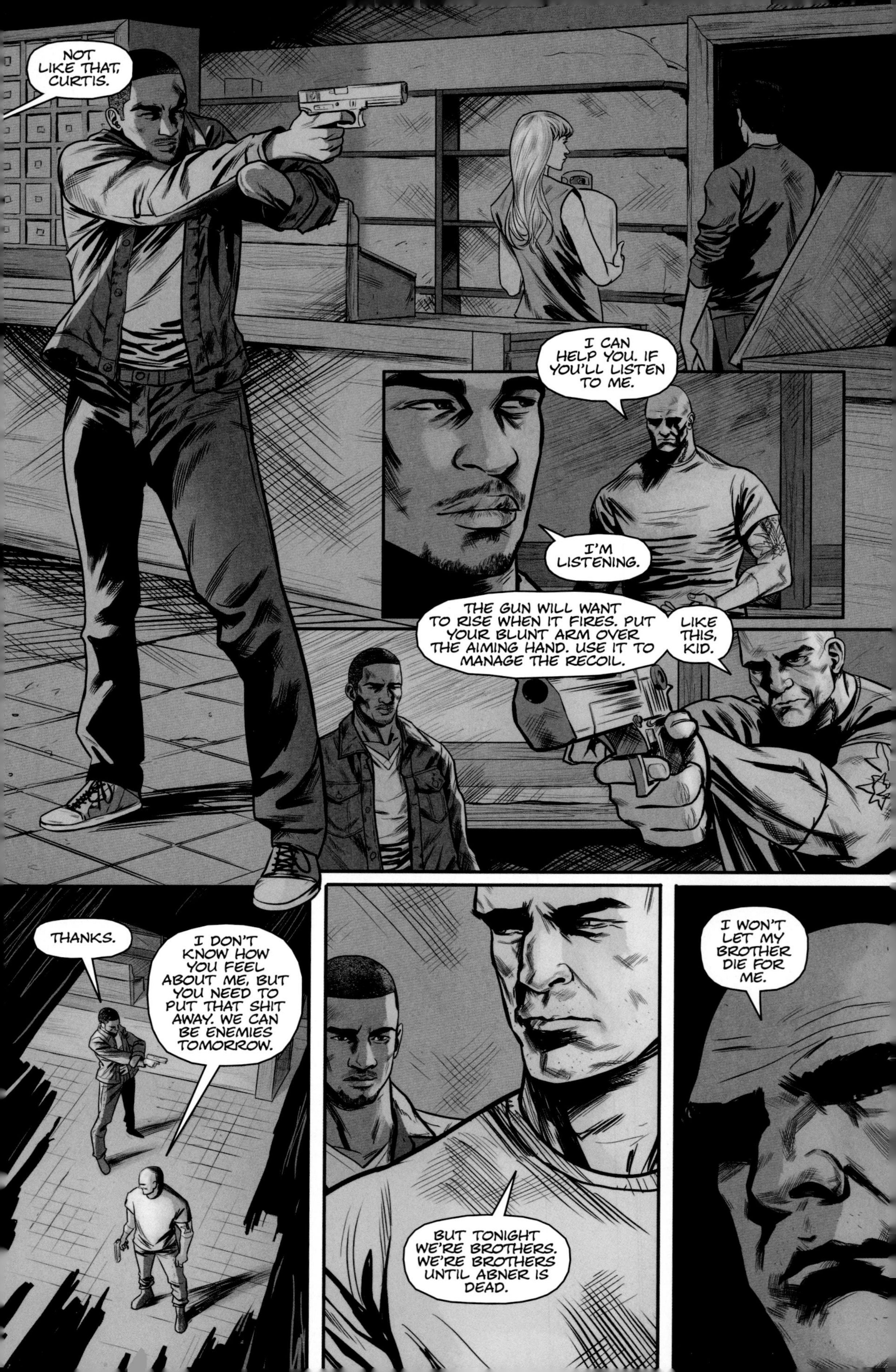
NOT LIKE THAT, CURTIS.
I CAN HELP YOU. IF YOU'LL LISTEN TO ME.
I'M LISTENING.
THE GUN WILL WANT TO RISE WHEN IT FIRES. PUT YOUR BLUNT ARM OVER THE AIMING HAND. USE IT TO MANAGE THE RECOIL.
LIKE THIS, KID.
THANKS.
I DON'T KNOW HOW YOU FEEL ABOUT ME, BUT YOU NEED TO PUT THAT SHIT AWAY. WE CAN BE ENEMIES TOMORROW.
BUT TONIGHT WE'RE BROTHERS. WE'RE BROTHERS UNTIL ABNER IS DEAD.
I WON'T LET MY BROTHER DIE FOR ME.

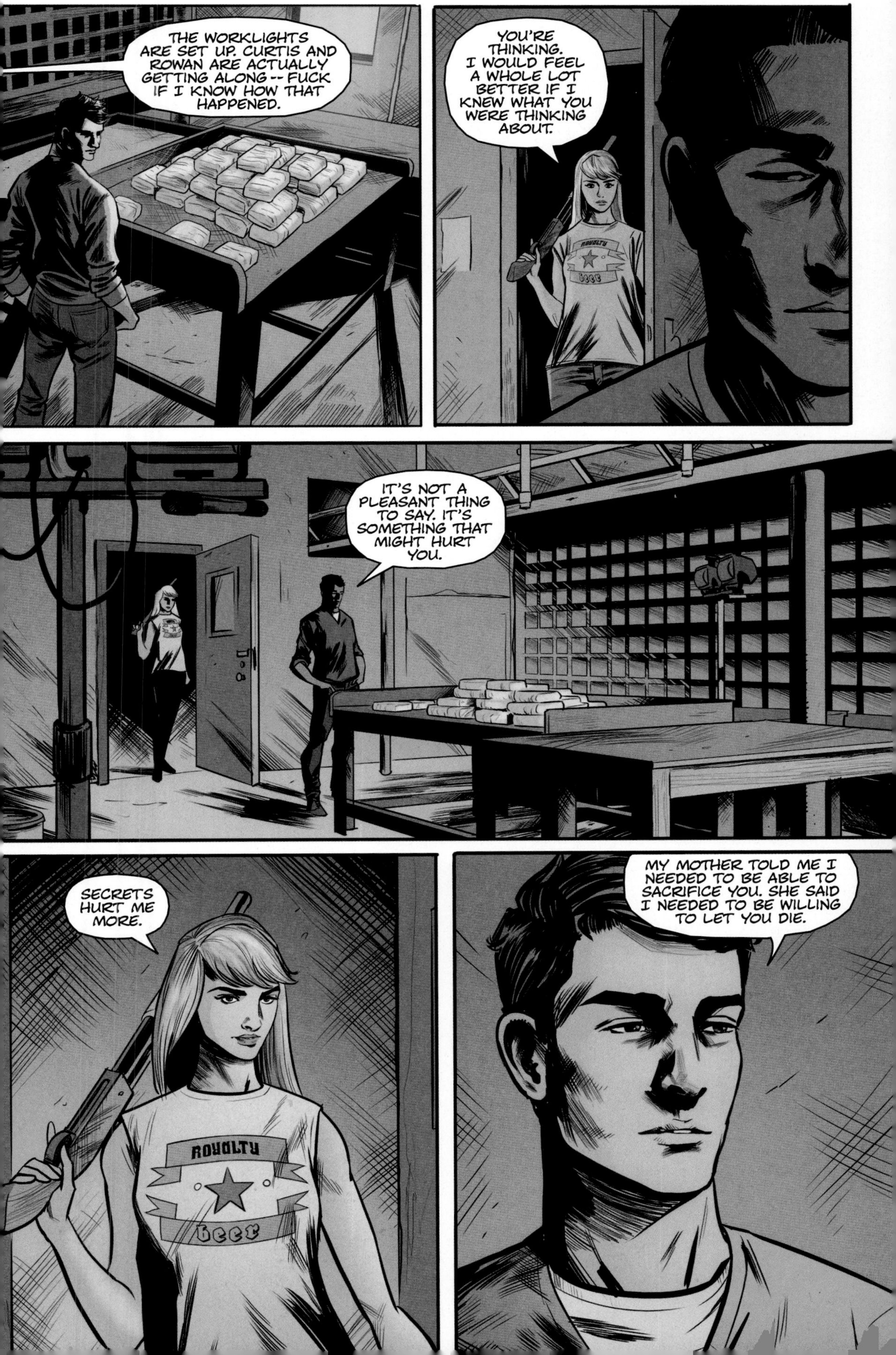
THE WORKLIGHTS ARE SET UP. CURTIS AND ROWAN ARE ACTUALLY GETTING ALONG -- FUCK IF I KNOW HOW THAT HAPPENED.
YOU'RE THINKING. I WOULD FEEL A WHOLE LOT BETTER IF I KNEW WHAT YOU WERE THINKING ABOUT.
IT'S NOT A PLEASANT THING TO SAY. IT'S SOMETHING THAT MIGHT HURT YOU.
SECRETS HURT ME MORE.
ROYALTY
beer
MY MOTHER TOLD ME I NEEDED TO BE ABLE TO SACRIFICE YOU. SHE SAID I NEEDED TO BE WILLING TO LET YOU DIE.

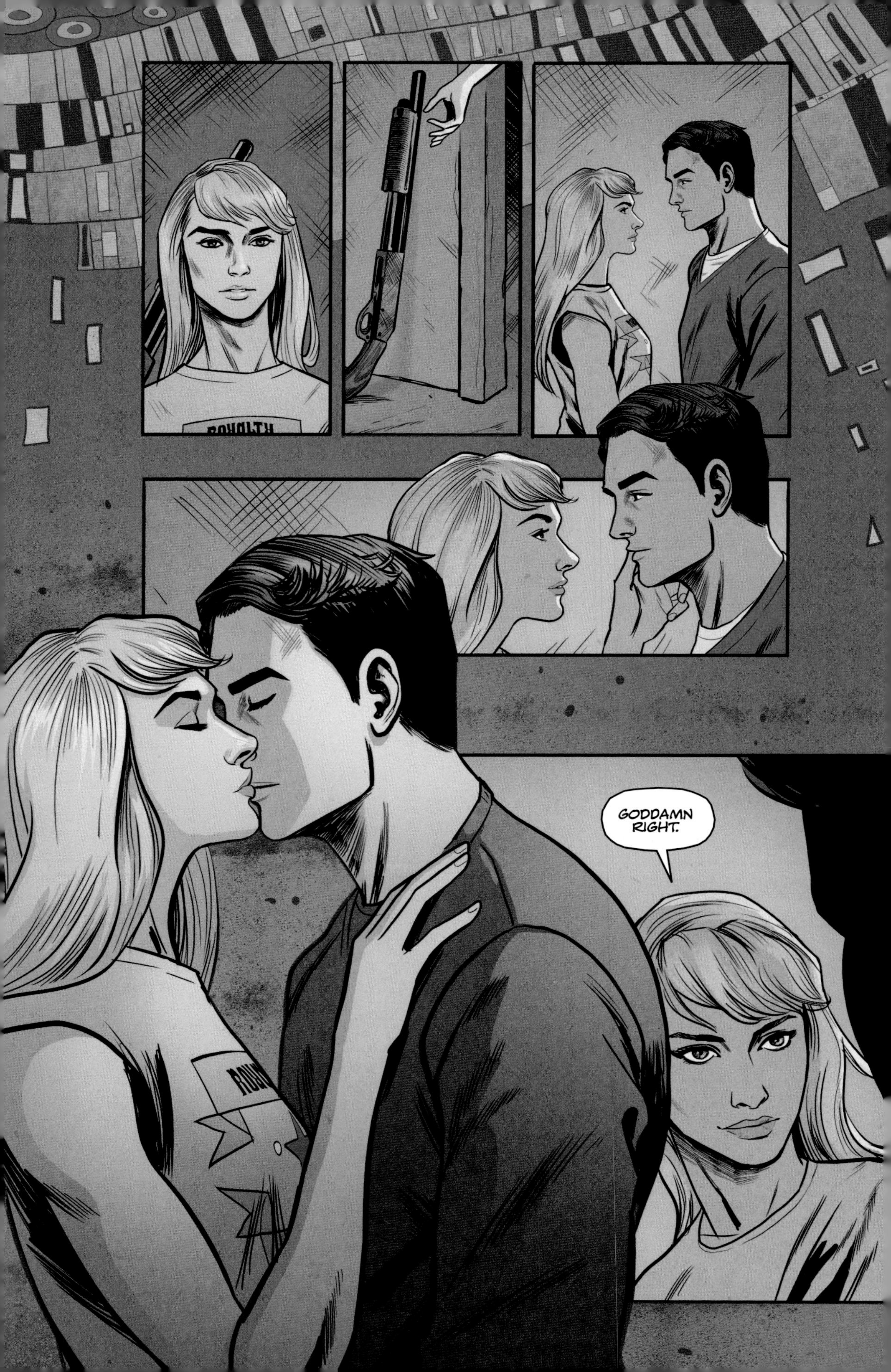
GODDAMN RIGHT.

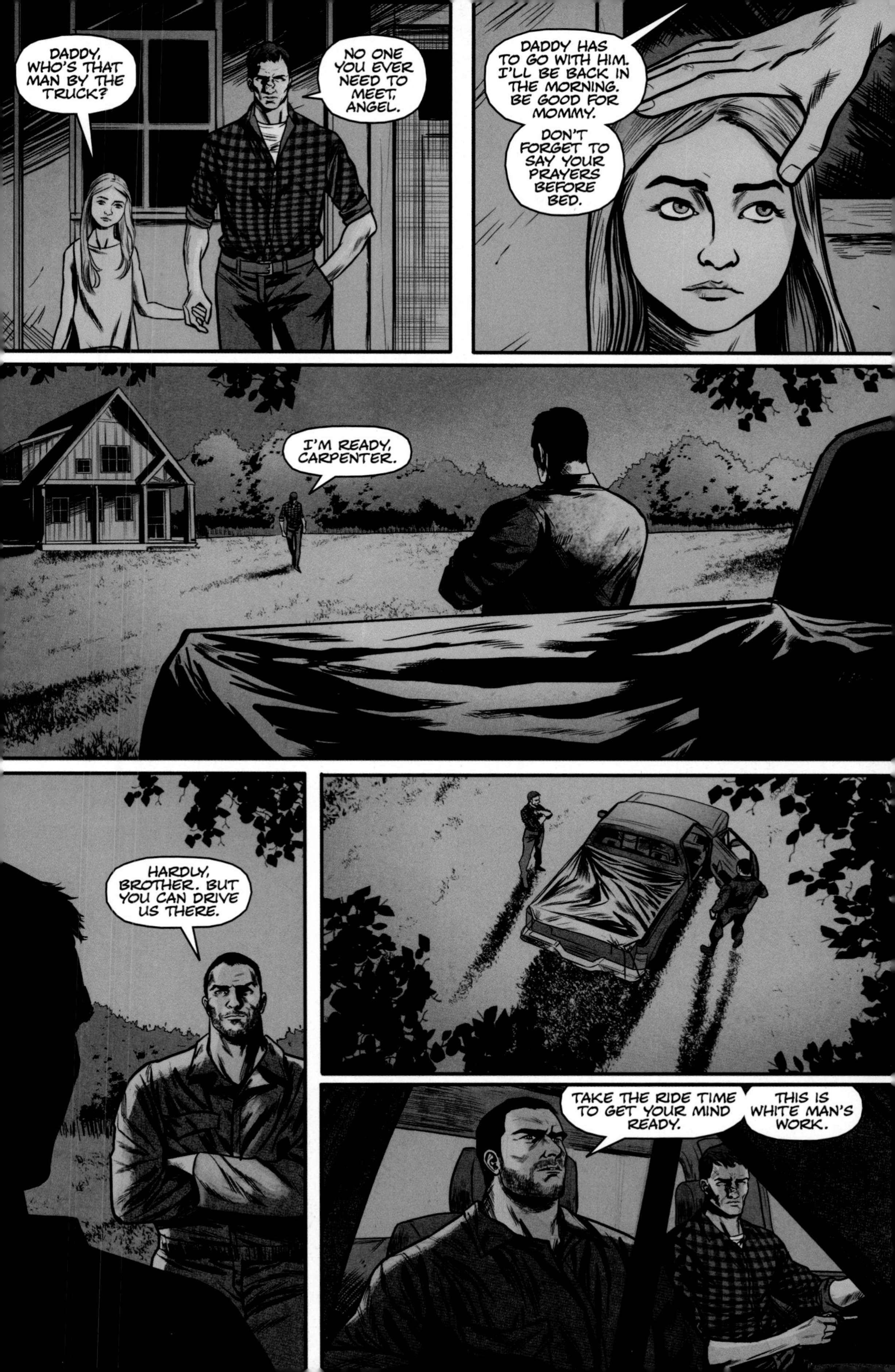
DADDY, WHO'S THAT MAN BY THE TRUCK?
NO ONE YOU EVER NEED TO MEET, ANGEL.
DADDY HAS TO GO WITH HIM. I'LL BE BACK IN THE MORNING. BE GOOD FOR MOMMY.
DON'T FORGET TO SAY YOUR PRAYERS BEFORE BED.
I'M READY, CARPENTER.
HARDLY, BROTHER. BUT YOU CAN DRIVE US THERE.
TAKE THE RIDE TIME TO GET YOUR MIND READY.
THIS IS WHITE MAN'S WORK.

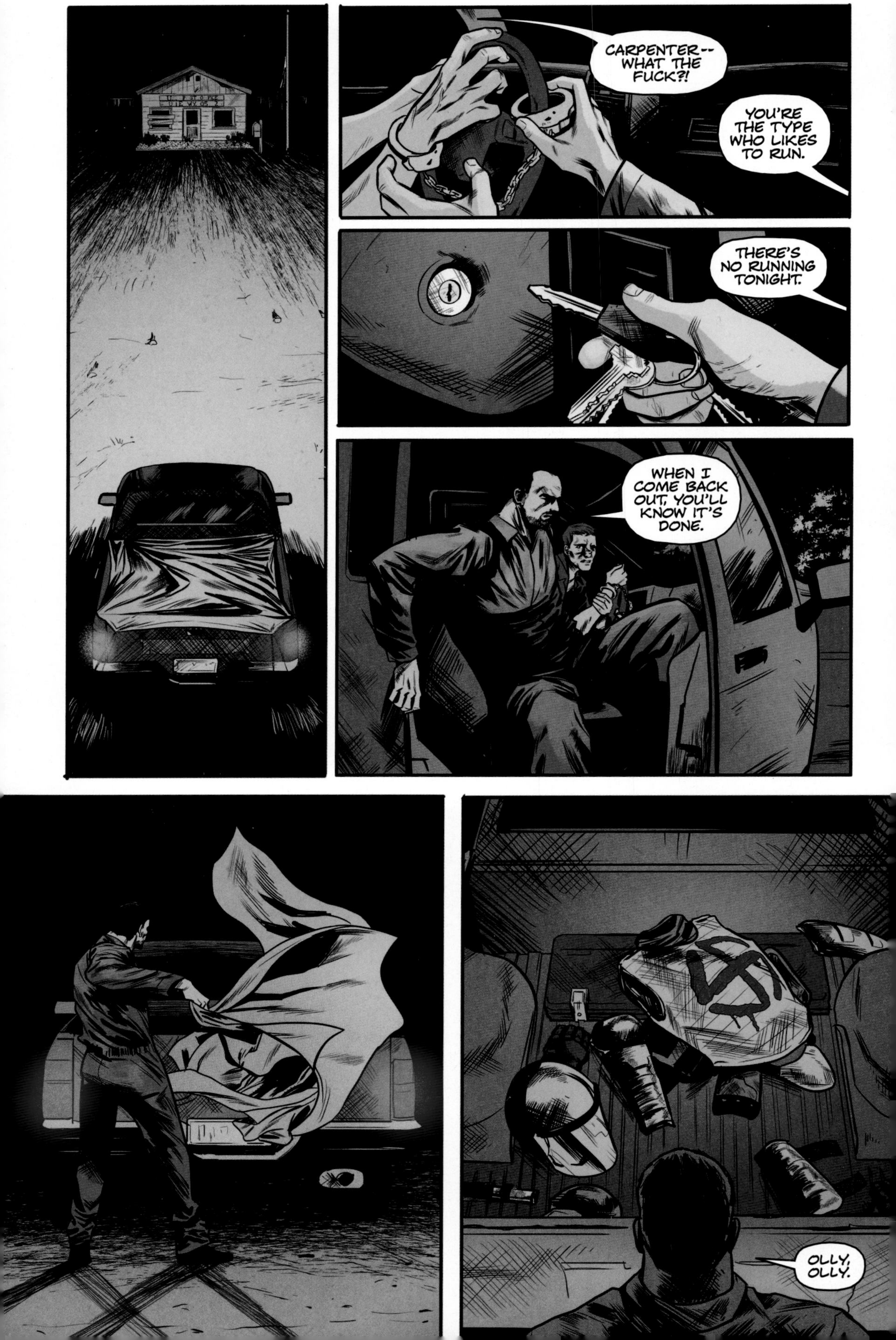
CARPENTER-- WHAT THE FUCK?!
YOU'RE THE TYPE WHO LIKES TO RUN.
THERE'S NO RUNNING TONIGHT.
WHEN I COME BACK OUT, YOU'LL KNOW IT'S DONE.
OLLY, OLLY.

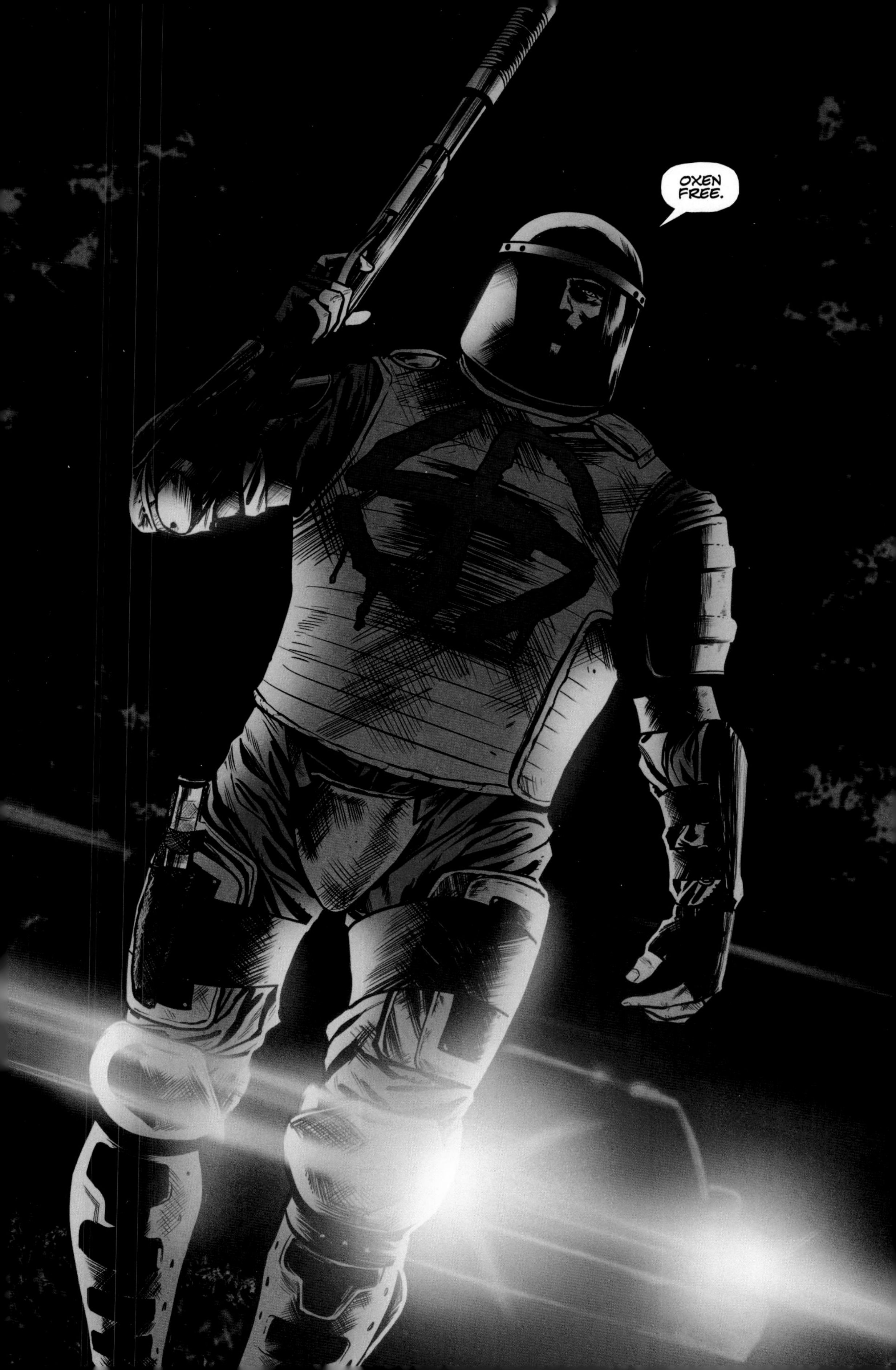
OXEN FREE.

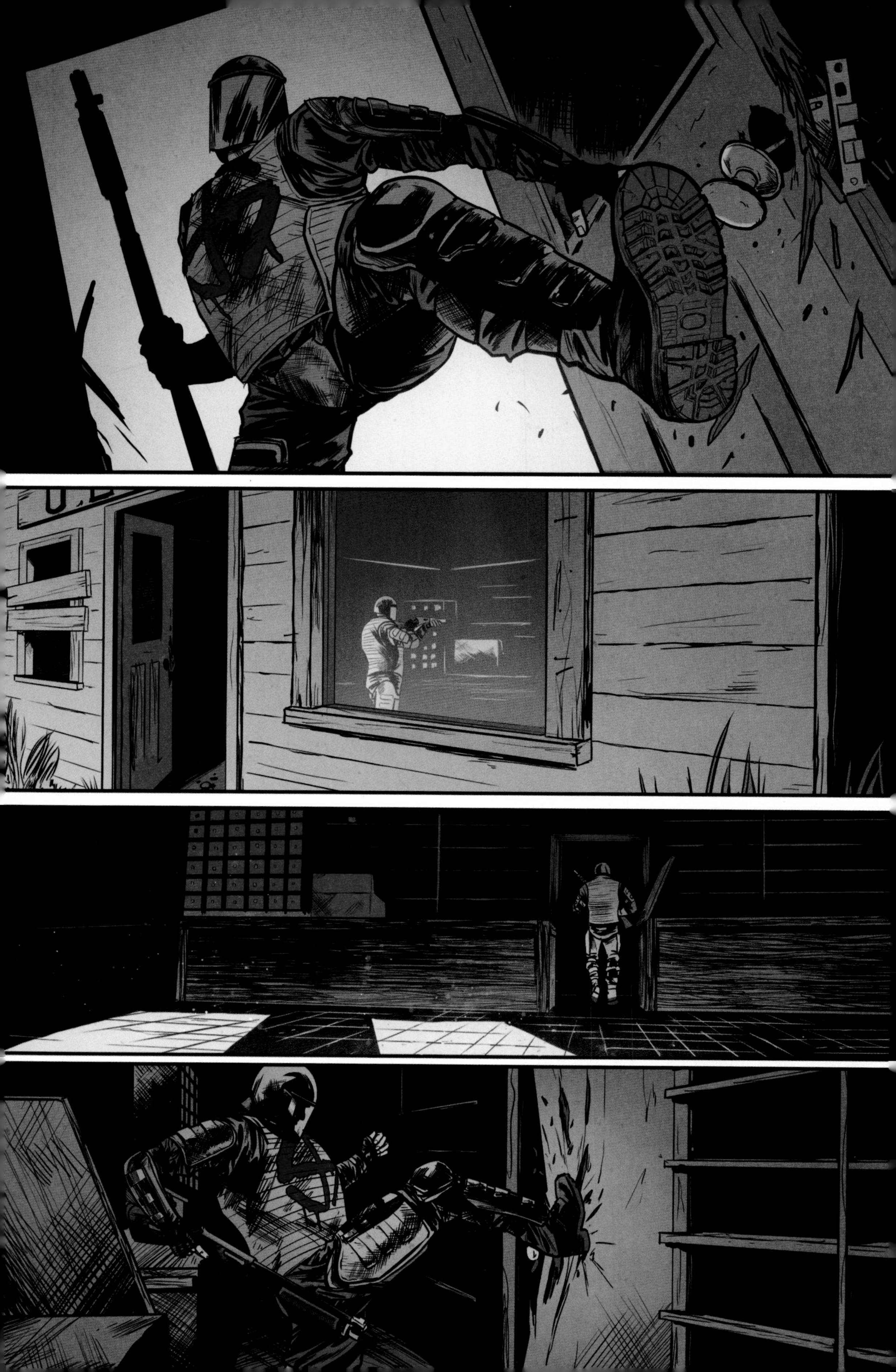

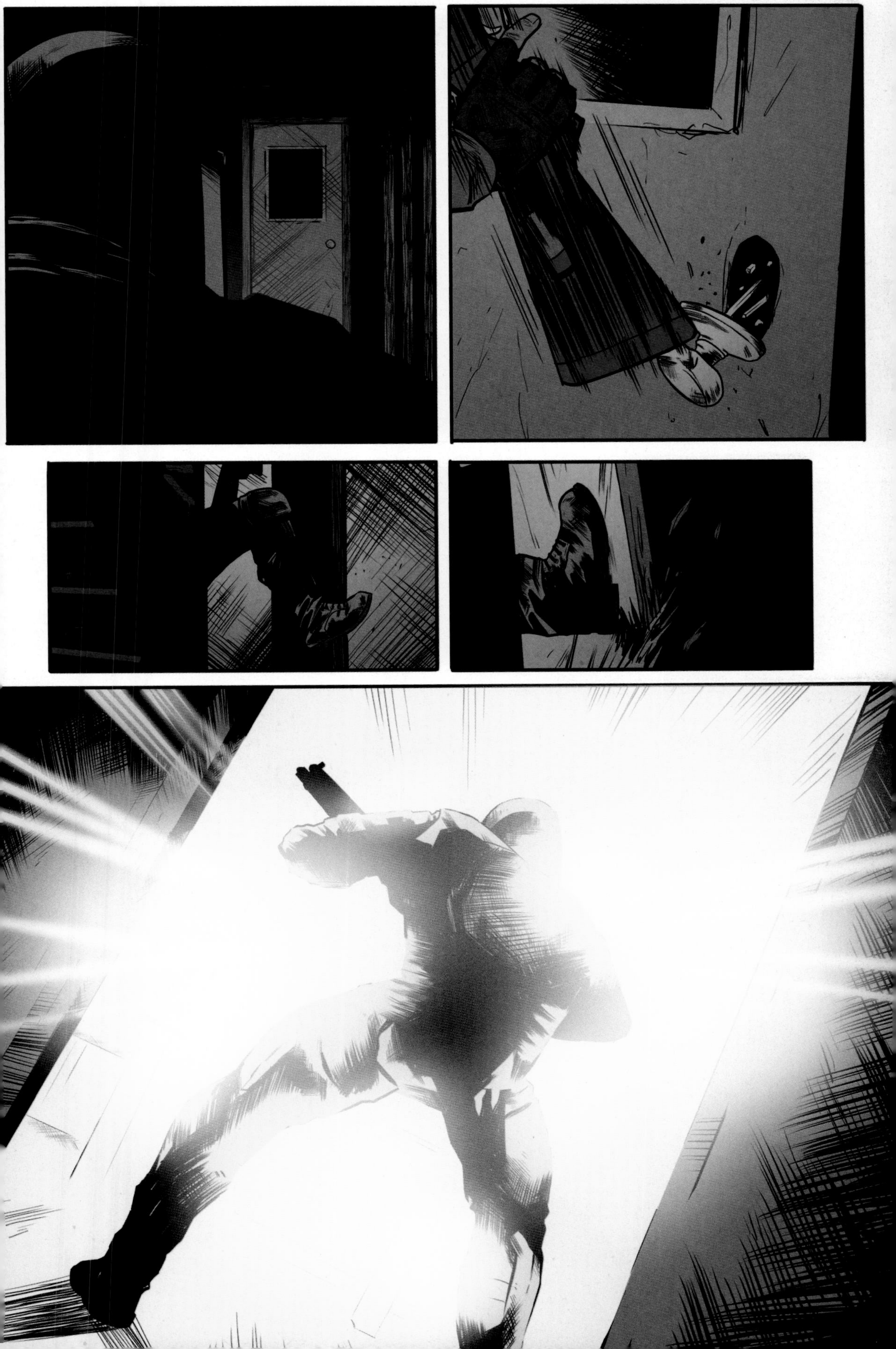

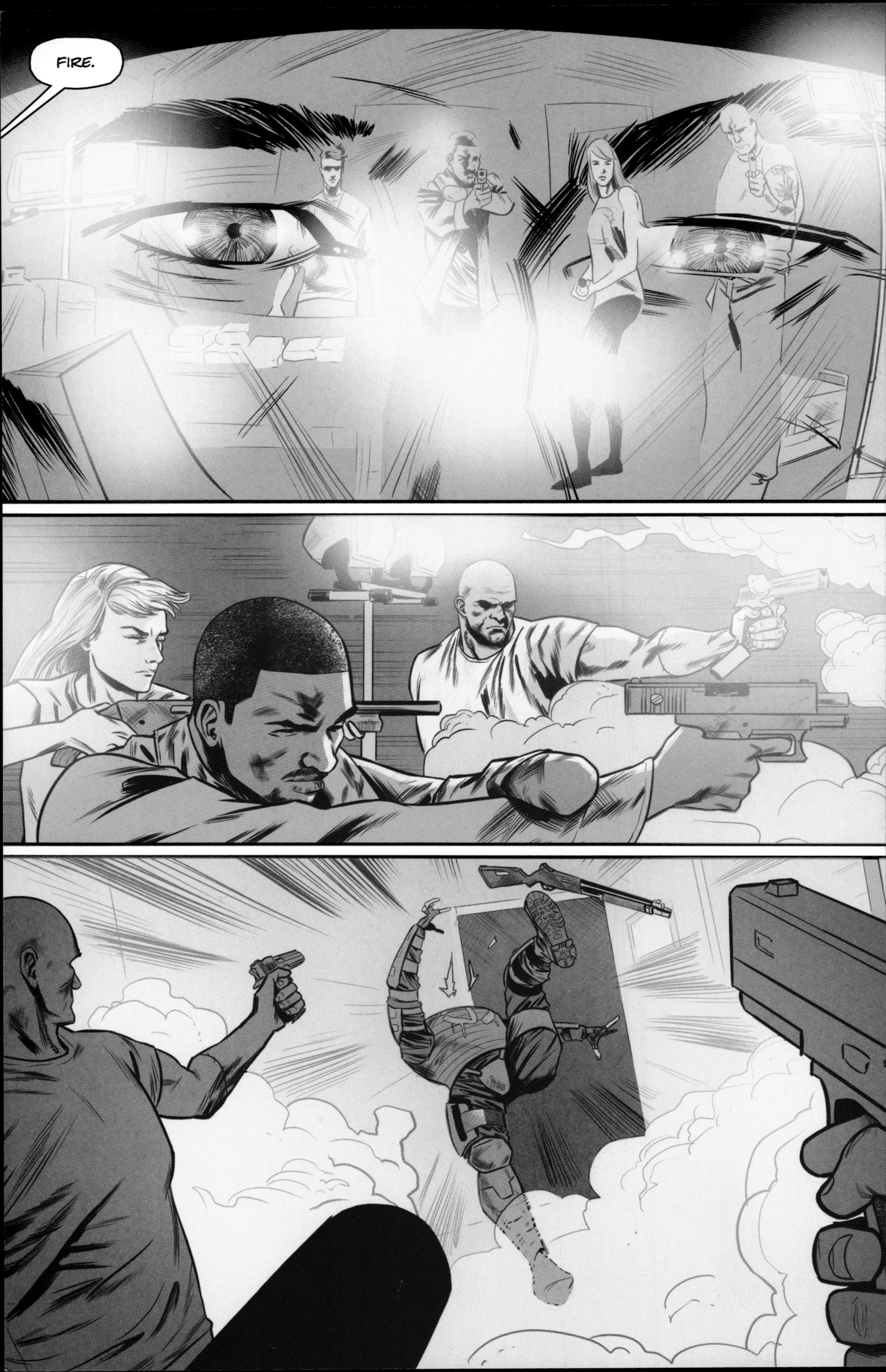
FIRE.

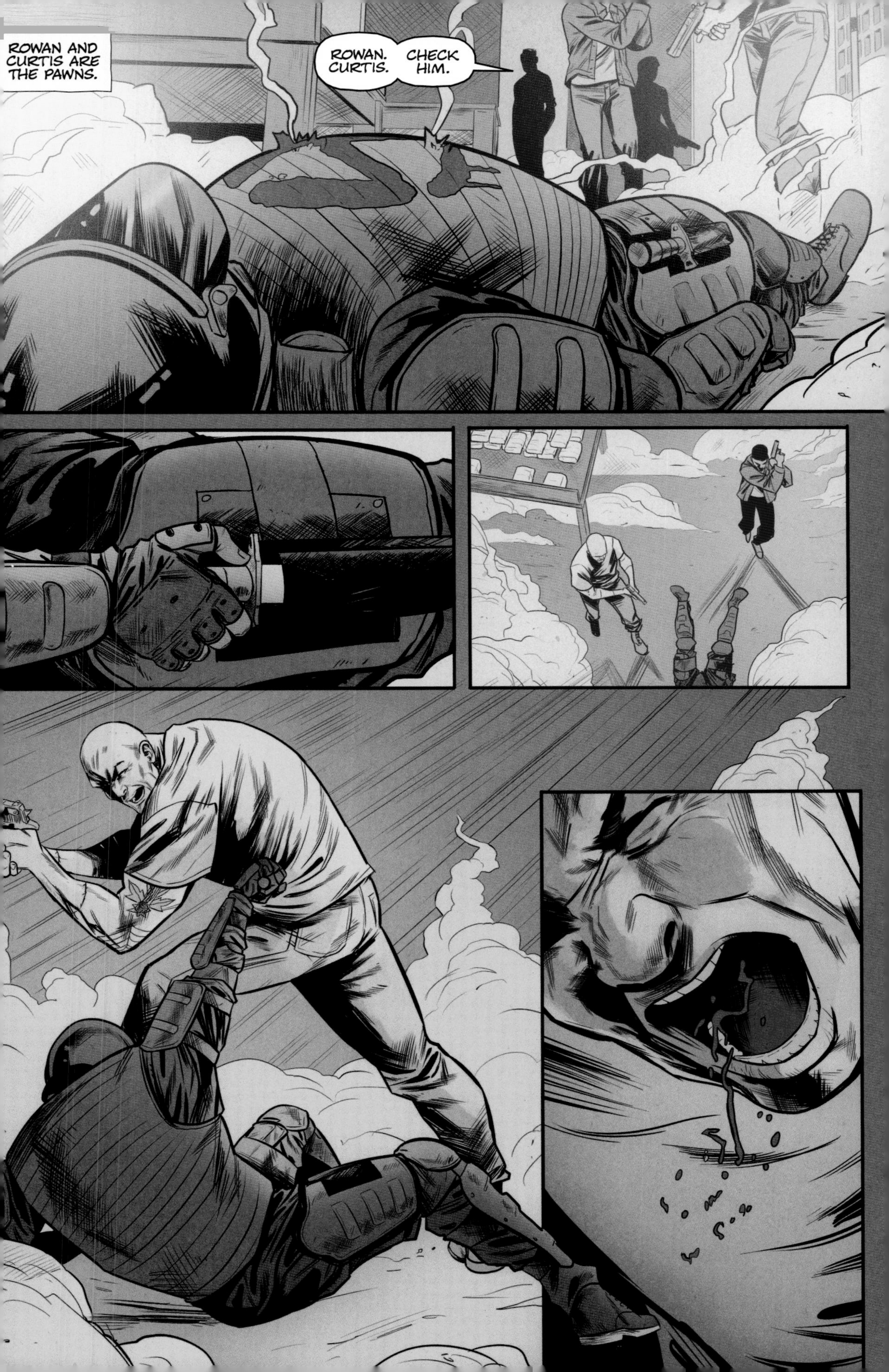
ROWAN AND CURTIS ARE THE PAWNS.
ROWAN. CURTIS.
CHECK HIM.

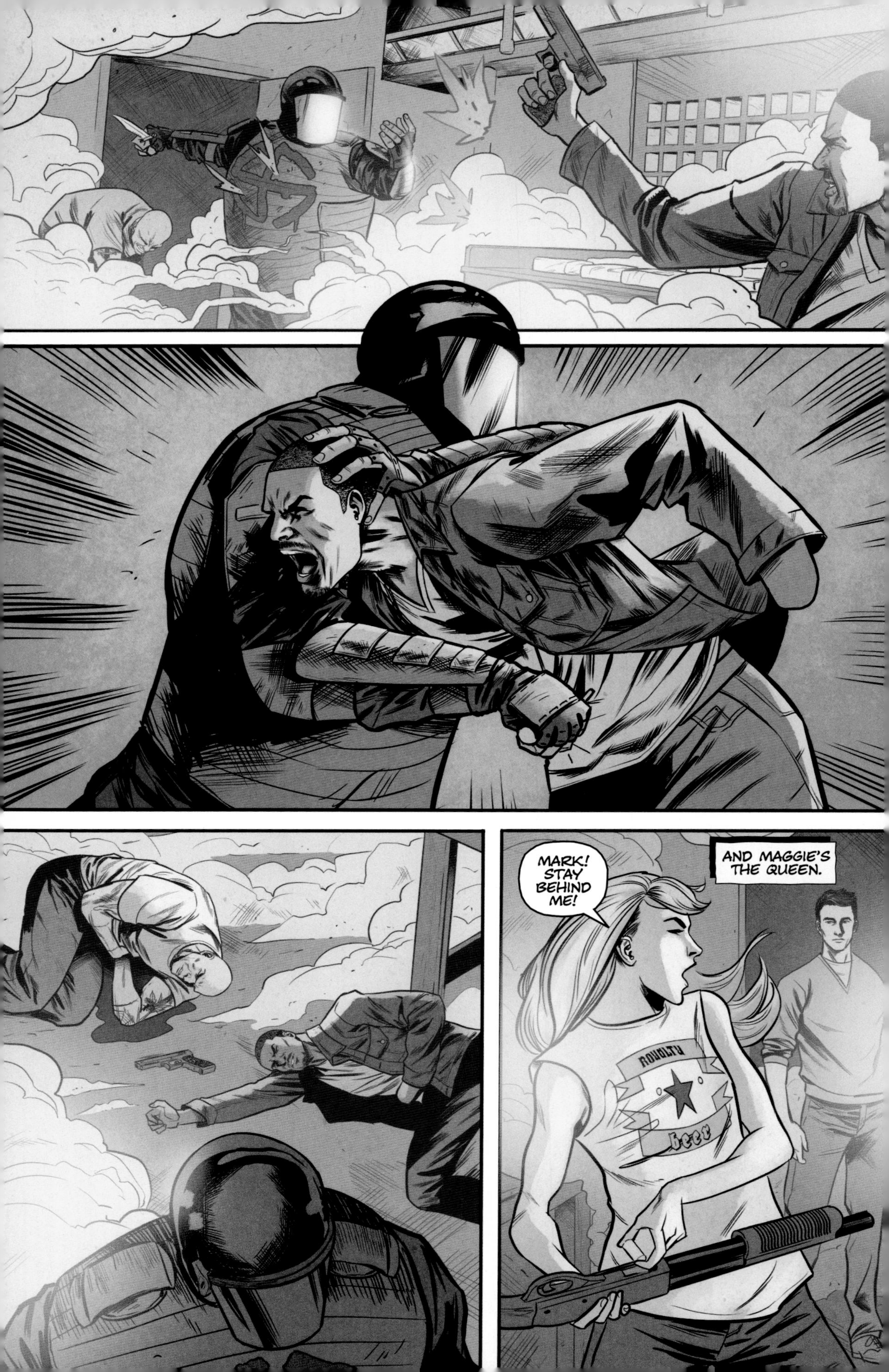
MARK! STAY BEHIND ME!
AND MAGGIE'S THE QUEEN.

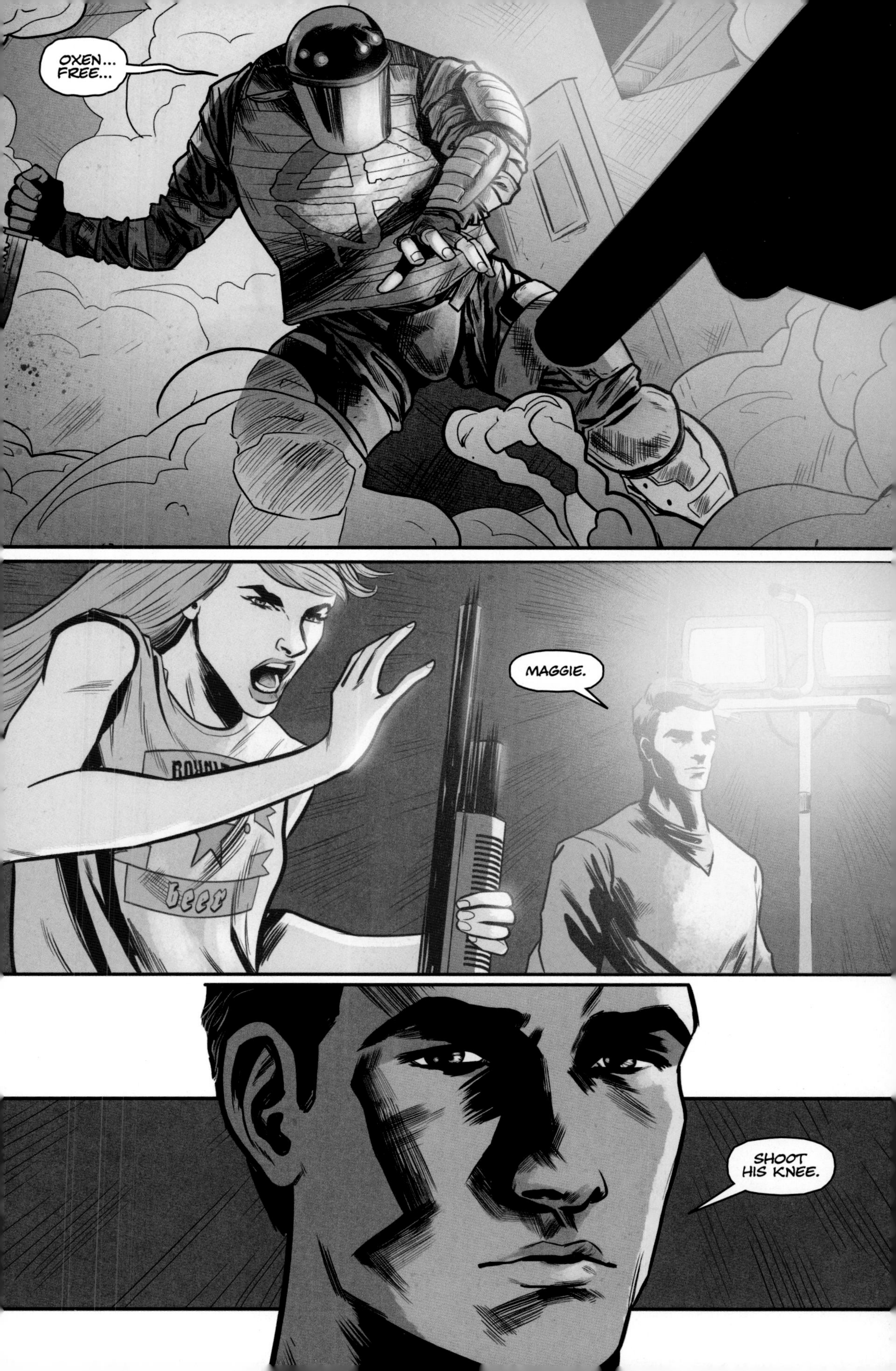
OXEN... FREE...
MAGGIE.
SHOOT HIS KNEE.

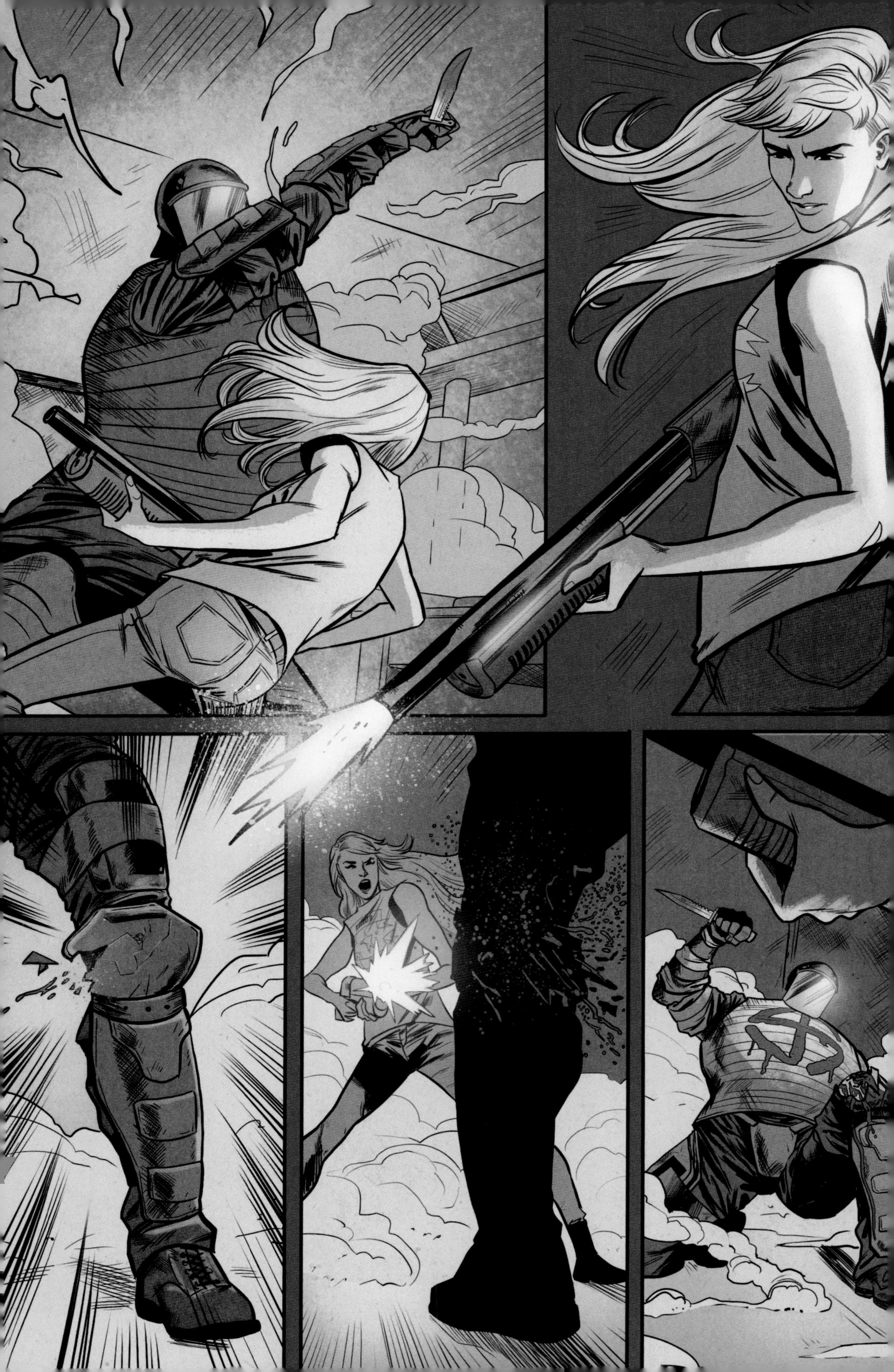

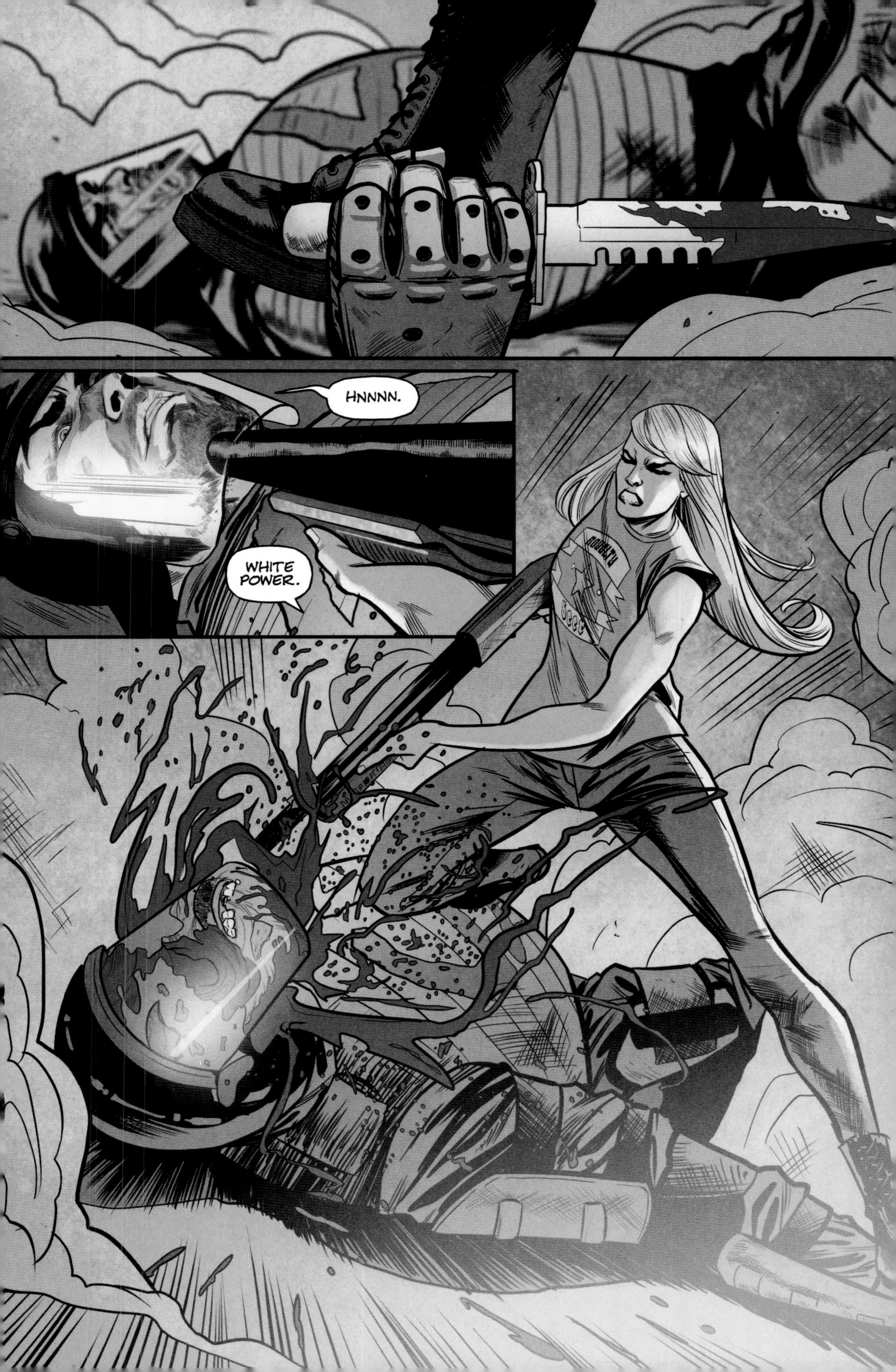
HNNNN.
WHITE POWER.

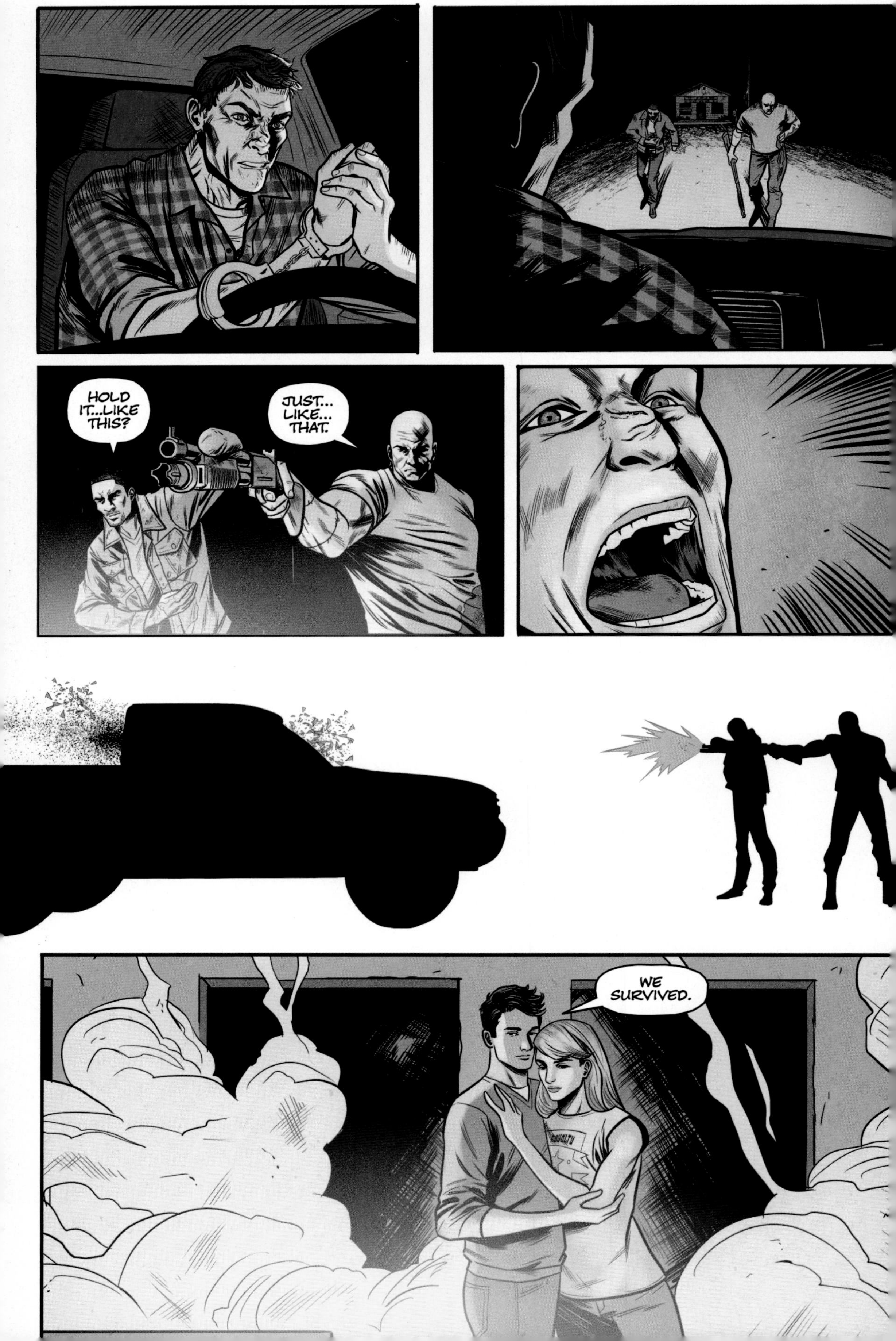
HOLD IT...LIKE THIS?
JUST... LIKE... THAT.
WE SURVIVED.

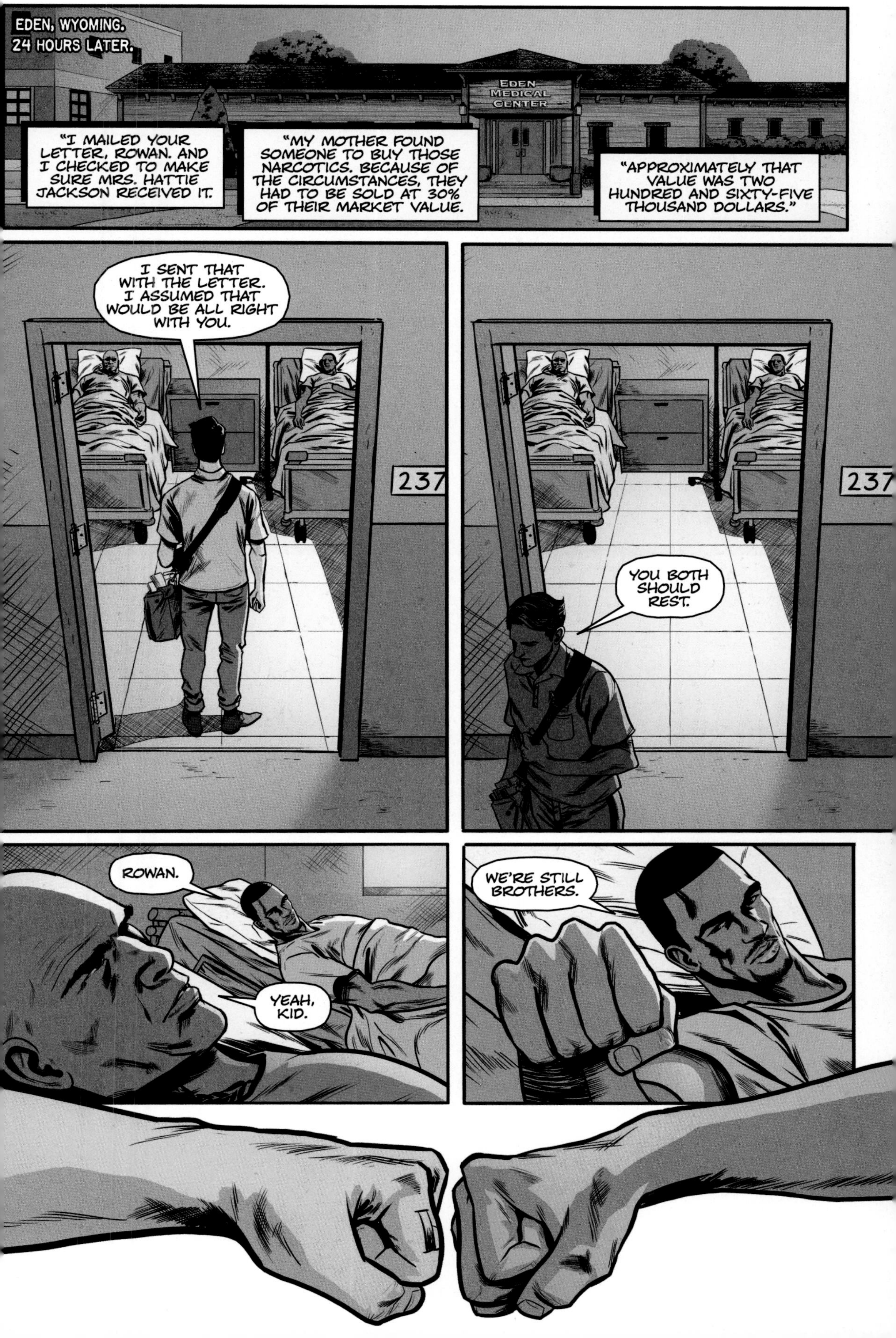

EDEN, WYOMING.
24 HOURS LATER.
EDEN MEDICAL CENTER
"I MAILED YOUR LETTER, ROWAN. AND I CHECKED TO MAKE SURE MRS. HATTIE JACKSON RECEIVED IT.
"MY MOTHER FOUND SOMEONE TO BUY THOSE NARCOTICS. BECAUSE OF THE CIRCUMSTANCES, THEY HAD TO BE SOLD AT 30% OF THEIR MARKET VALUE.
"APPROXIMATELY THAT VALUE WAS TWO HUNDRED AND SIXTY-FIVE THOUSAND DOLLARS."
I SENT THAT WITH THE LETTER. I ASSUMED THAT WOULD BE ALL RIGHT WITH YOU.
237
237
YOU BOTH SHOULD REST.
ROWAN.
YEAH, KID.
WE'RE STILL BROTHERS.

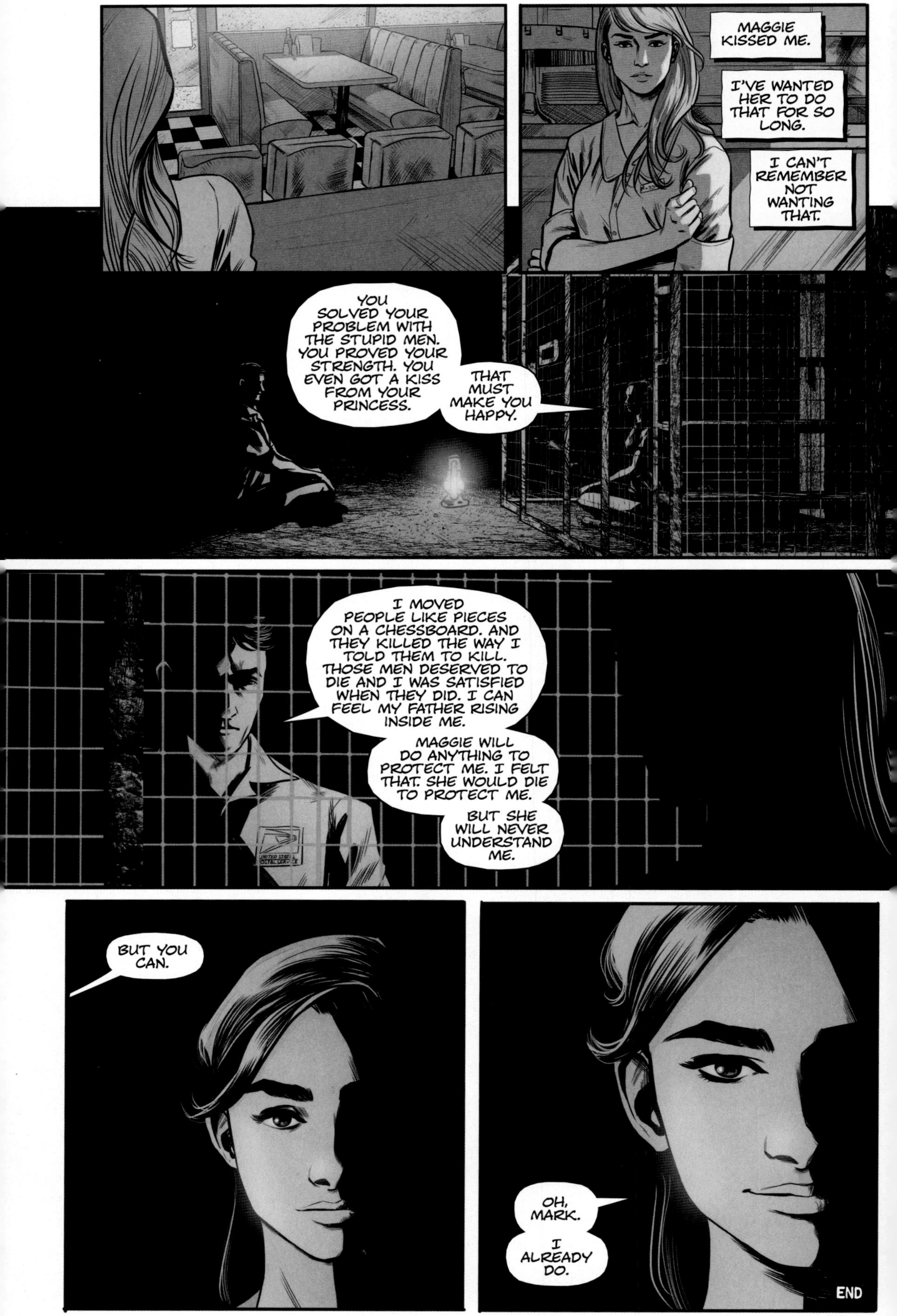
MAGGIE KISSED ME.
I'VE WANTED HER TO DO THAT FOR SO LONG.
I CAN'T REMEMBER NOT WANTING THAT.
YOU SOLVED YOUR PROBLEM WITH THE STUPID MEN. YOU PROVED YOUR STRENGTH. YOU EVEN GOT A KISS FROM YOUR PRINCESS.
THAT MUST MAKE YOU HAPPY.
I MOVED PEOPLE LIKE PIECES ON A CHESSBOARD. AND THEY KILLED THE WAY I TOLD THEM TO KILL. THOSE MEN DESERVED TO DIE AND I WAS SATISFIED WHEN THEY DID. I CAN FEEL MY FATHER RISING INSIDE ME.
MAGGIE WILL DO ANYTHING TO PROTECT ME. I FELT THAT. SHE WOULD DIE TO PROTECT ME.
BUT SHE WILL NEVER UNDERSTAND ME.
BUT YOU CAN.
OH, MARK.
I ALREADY DO.
END

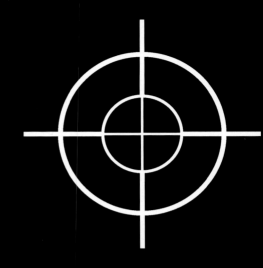

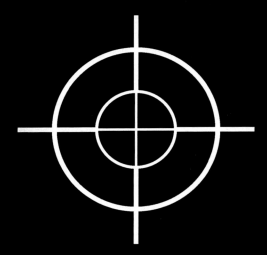

MAIL CALL

HEY THERE, POSTAL FANS!

Thanks so much for picking up this volume of *Postal*. It means so much to all of us here at Top Cow, and, as always, we ask that if you enjoyed this volume, please recommend it to your friends and put in on your pull list at your local comic shop! We love making this book, and we hope you love reading it, and we hope to keep putting it out for many issues to come!

First, let's give a big welcome to new series colorist **K. Michael Russell** — this dude is one of the greats, and if his first issue is any indication, he's bringing out the big guns for this exciting new story arc, a plot that **Bryan Hill** has been waiting to tell since the first issue of the series, as savvier readers will remember Rowan entering the town way back in issue #1.

In case you've forgotten, here's that fateful first meeting:

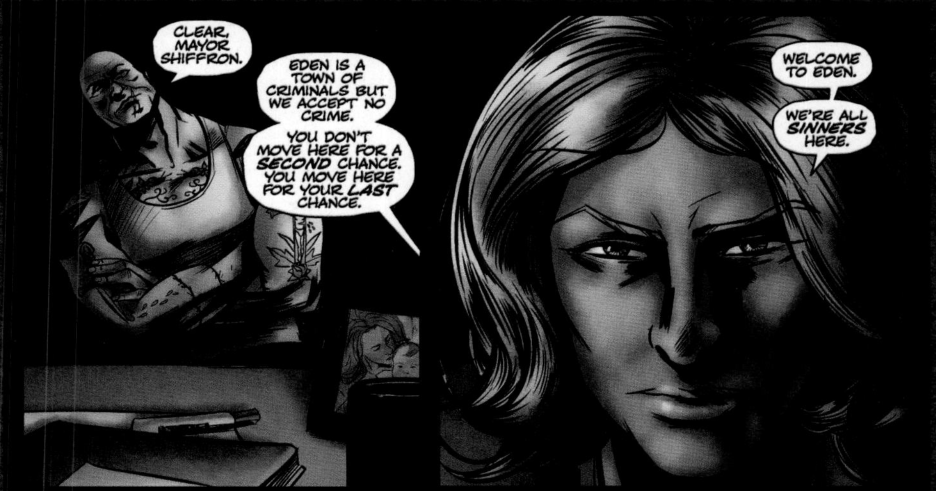
CLEAR, MAYOR SHIFFRON.
EDEN IS A TOWN OF CRIMINALS BUT WE ACCEPT NO CRIME.
YOU DON'T MOVE HERE FOR A SECOND CHANCE. YOU MOVE HERE FOR YOUR LAST CHANCE.
WELCOME TO EDEN.
WE'RE ALL SINNERS HERE.

But this storyline is also about some difficult topics, as Bryan discussed on Facebook:

"Social issues in comic books can be a mixed bag. Often they're presented in a myopic way, usually just preaching to the choir of people on one side of the issue. The work is well intentioned, but usually shallow. The naming of monsters. The scorning of monsters. The pride of being righteous.

That's easy. I've never been interested in what's easy.

[This arc] features a member of the fictional town of Eden, a former member of the Aryan Brotherhood, the cold patience of karma and the price of redemption.

It's NOT a diatribe or an oversimplification of cultural conflict in America. It's an examination of the roots of anger and fear that sprout into these movements. As we see the rise of populism and nativism in the world around us, my hope is it's a unflinching exploration of these issues, framed in a DAMN COOL CRIME STORY about a town full of fugitives trying on the skin of living new lives."

Have something to say about the new arc? We'd love to hear from you! Send your letters for the *Postal* team to **fanmail@topcow.com** (and if you want, mark them "**Okay to Print**," and we'll put them here for all to see)! Who knows, **Postmaster Mark** might even take a look at it himself.

MAIL CALL

If you've been following this book since *Volume 1*, you know that writer **Bryan Hill** can be a pretty insightful guy — it's safe to say that we're fans of his. If you want more of that insight, you can actually read Bryan in conversation with some other smart comic book people, and read interviews and op-eds conducted by him on at **comicsbeat.com** — there's one up there now with Jonathan Hickman and another with Greg Pak that'll knock your socks off.

But we know that comics is what you care about, which is why we want you to check out *Romulus* — **Bryan Hill** and **Nelson Blake II's** new creator-owned series, out now from Top Cow. Dig on this solicit text, and check out some art below:

"Our world isn't free. All of us, for generations, have lived under the secret control of The Ancient Order of Romulus. One young woman, raised by them, trained by them, betrayed by them, must push through her fear to take a stand against the silent evil that masters our world. Her name is Ashlar, and her war begins with the brutal first chapter of the new Image series ROMULUS, from writer BRYAN HILL (POSTAL) and artist NELSON BLAKE II (MAGDELENA)."

Pretty cool, right? But why should we leave you hanging with just one art preview?

Flip to the end of this book to read a quick preview of *Eden's Fall #1*, the first of a three-issue miniseries taking place in Eden, and featuring characters **from this book** — along with a few friends from *Think Tank* and *The Tithe*. It's in stores now, and co-written by **Bryan Hill** and **Matt Hawkins** — check it out!

"...Hooked me from
age one...don't miss
his tour-de-force..."

Greg Pak
otally Awesome Hulk,
ingsway West

BRYAN HILL

NELSON BLAKE II

ROMULUS

AVAILABLE NOW

we create...icons!
www.topcow.com

mulus 2016 Top Cow Productions. Image Comics and its logos
registered trademarks of Image Comics, Inc. All rights reserved.

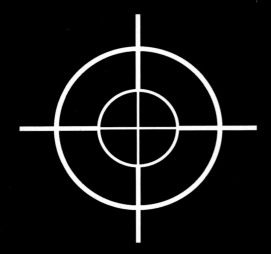

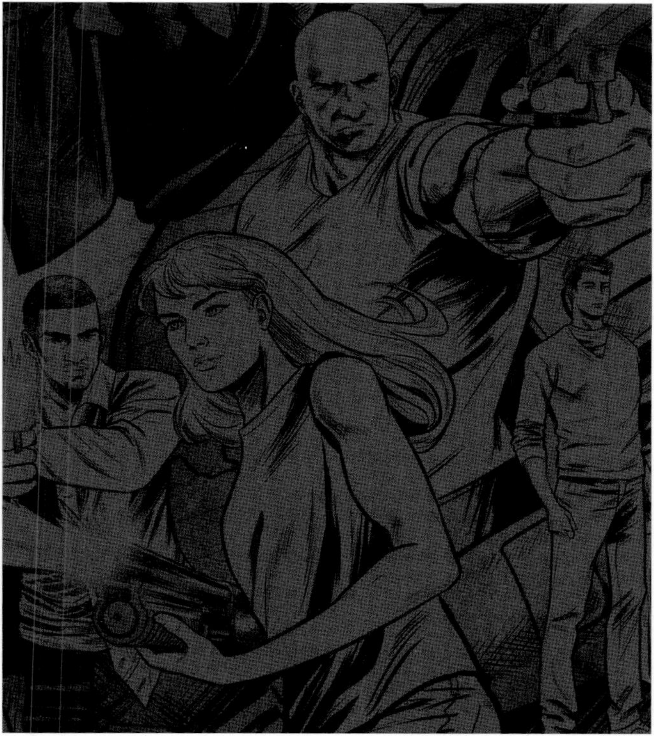

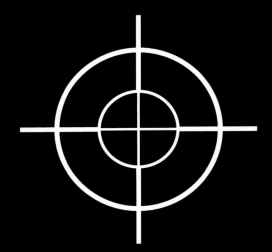

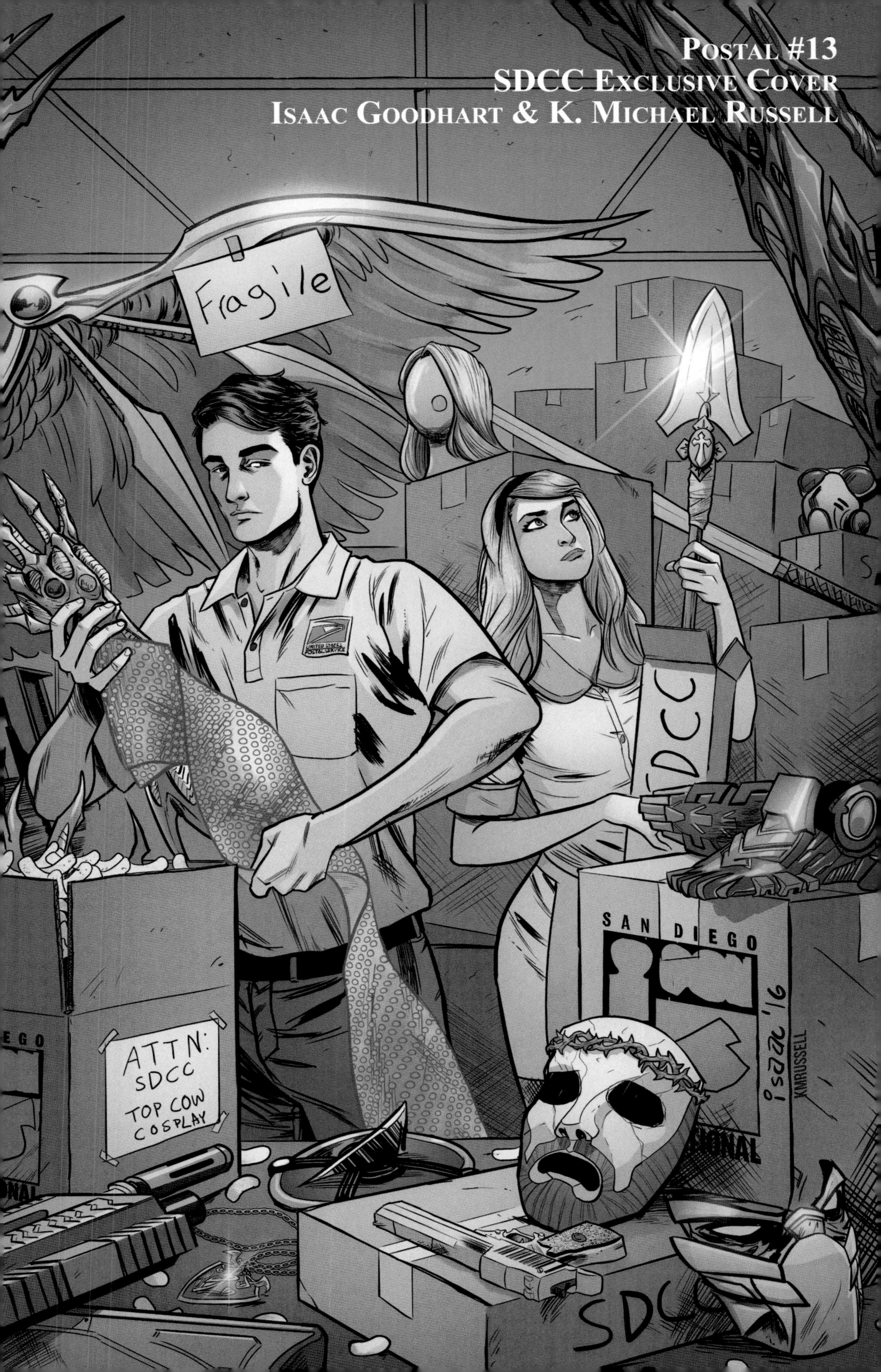
Fragile
SDCC
SDCC
SAN DIEGO
isaac '16
KMRUSSELL
ATTN:
SDCC
TOP COW
COSPLAY
SDCC

Postal #13
SDCC Exclusive Cover
Isaac Goodhart & K. Michael Russell

Postal #13
Cover A
Linda Sejic

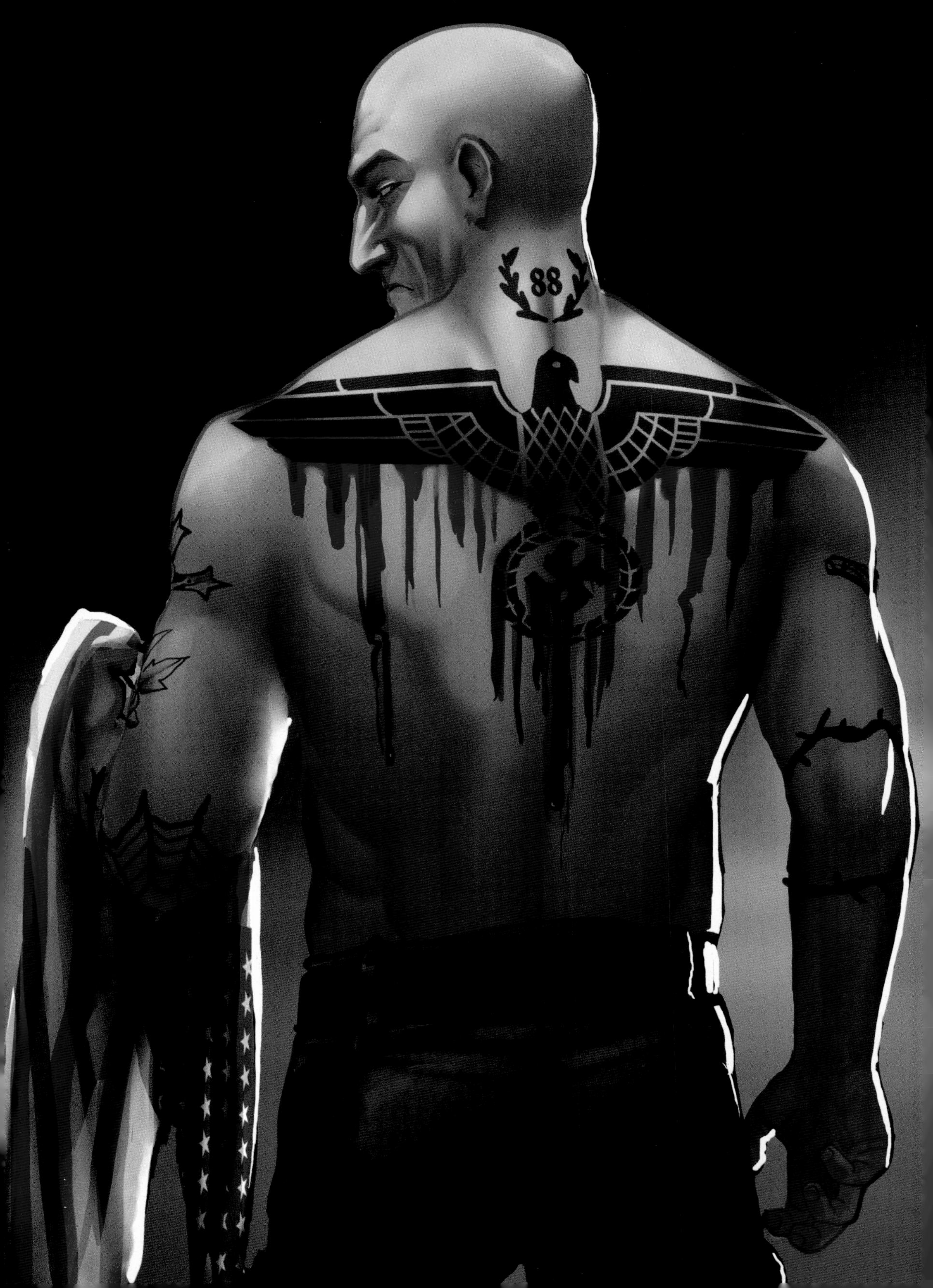
88

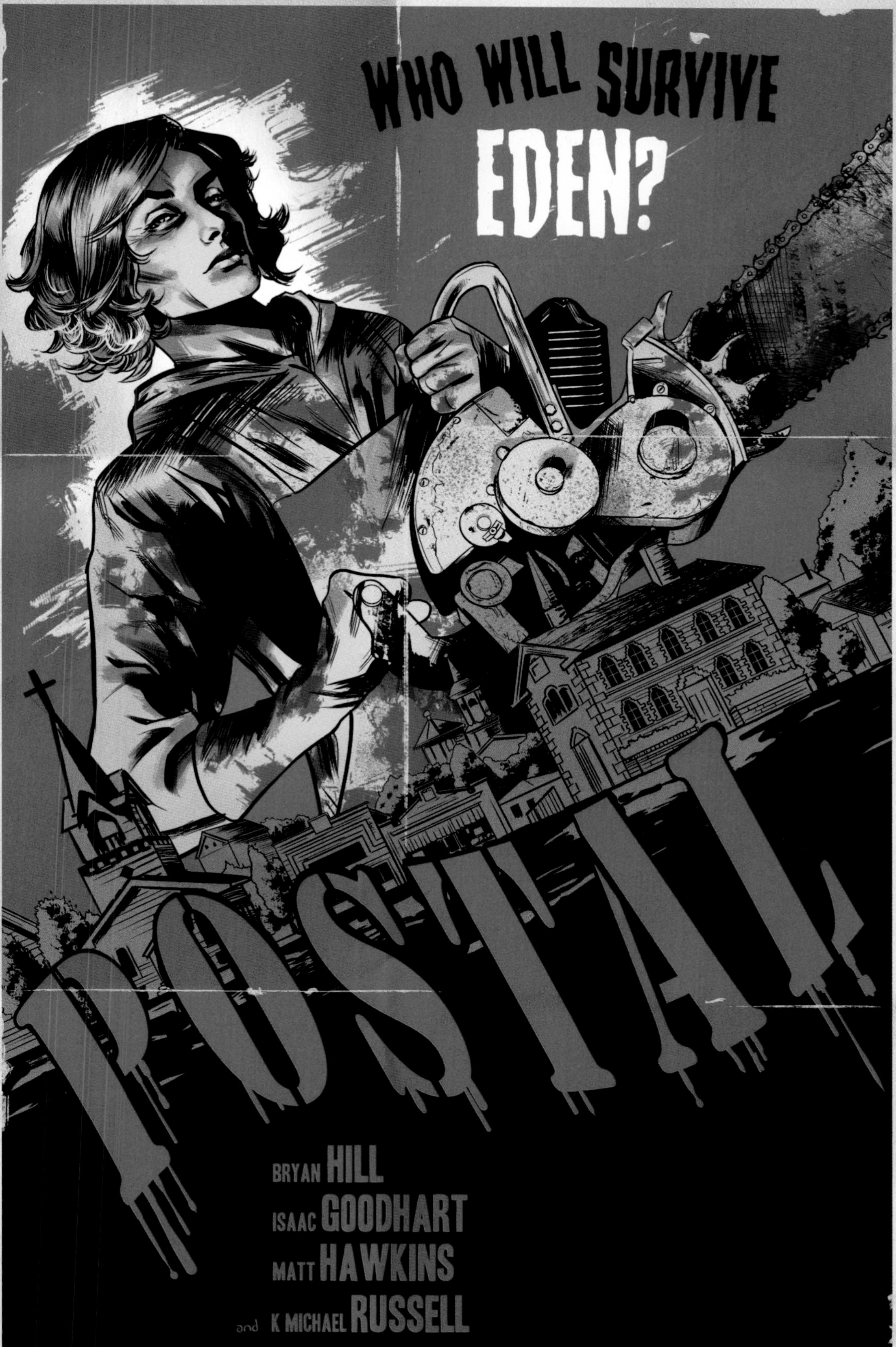
WHO WILL SURVIVE
EDEN?
POSTAL
BRYAN HILL
ISAAC GOODHART
MATT HAWKINS
and K MICHAEL RUSSELL

POSTAL #13 COVER B ISAAC GOODHART & K. MICHAEL RUSSELL

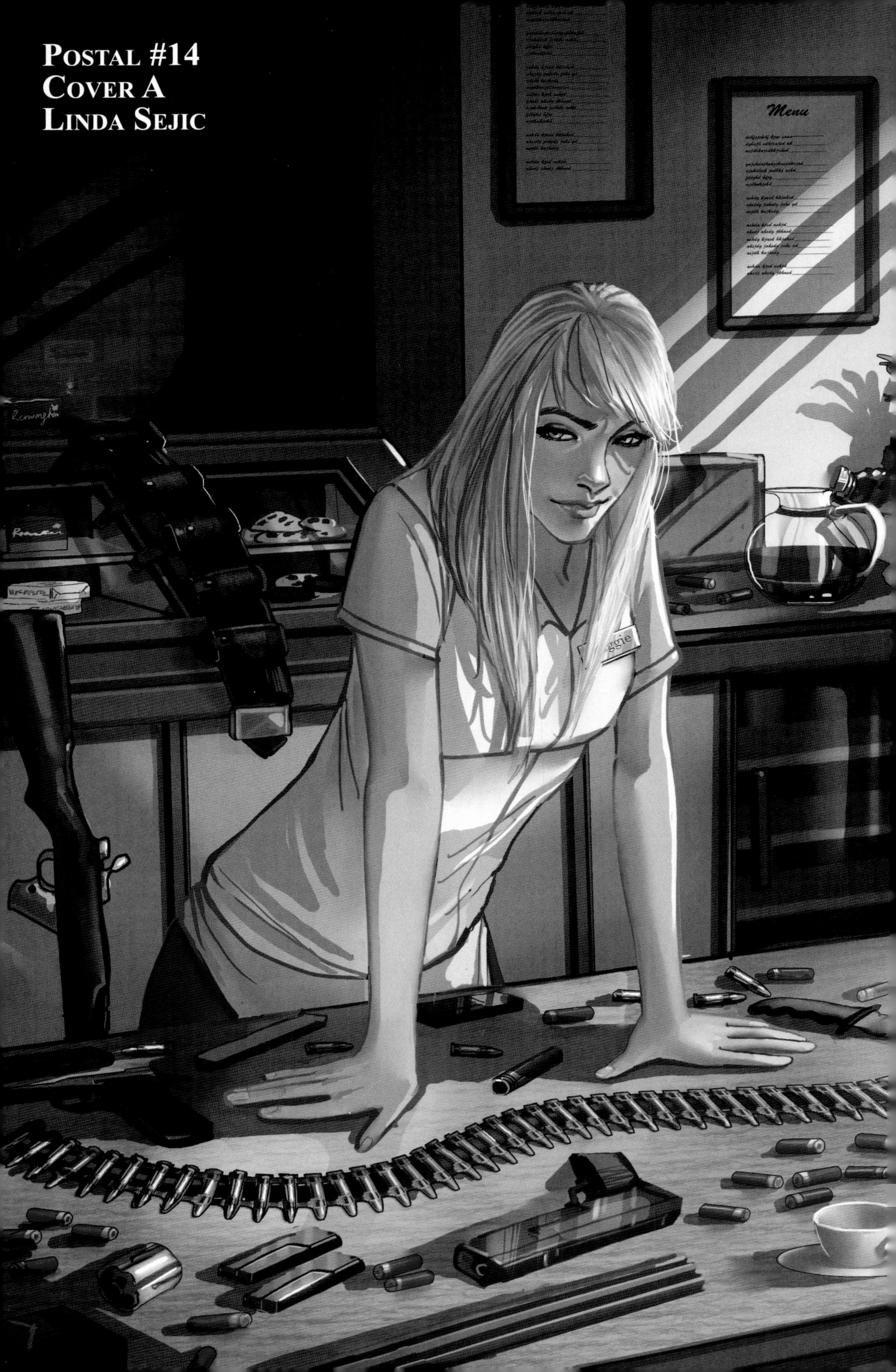
Menu

POSTAL #14
COVER A
LINDA SEJIC

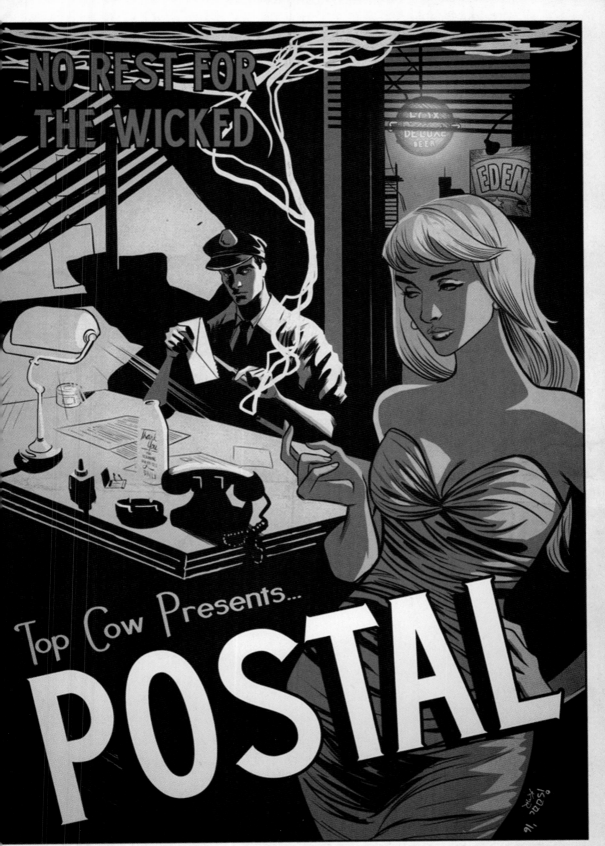

NO REST FOR THE WICKED

Top Cow Presents...

POSTAL

Bryan **HILL** · Isaac **GOODHART** · K Michael **RUSSELL** · Matt **HAWKINS**

POSTAL #14
COVER B
ISAAC GOODHART &
K. MICHAEL RUSSELL

POSTAL #15
COVER A
LINDA SEJIC

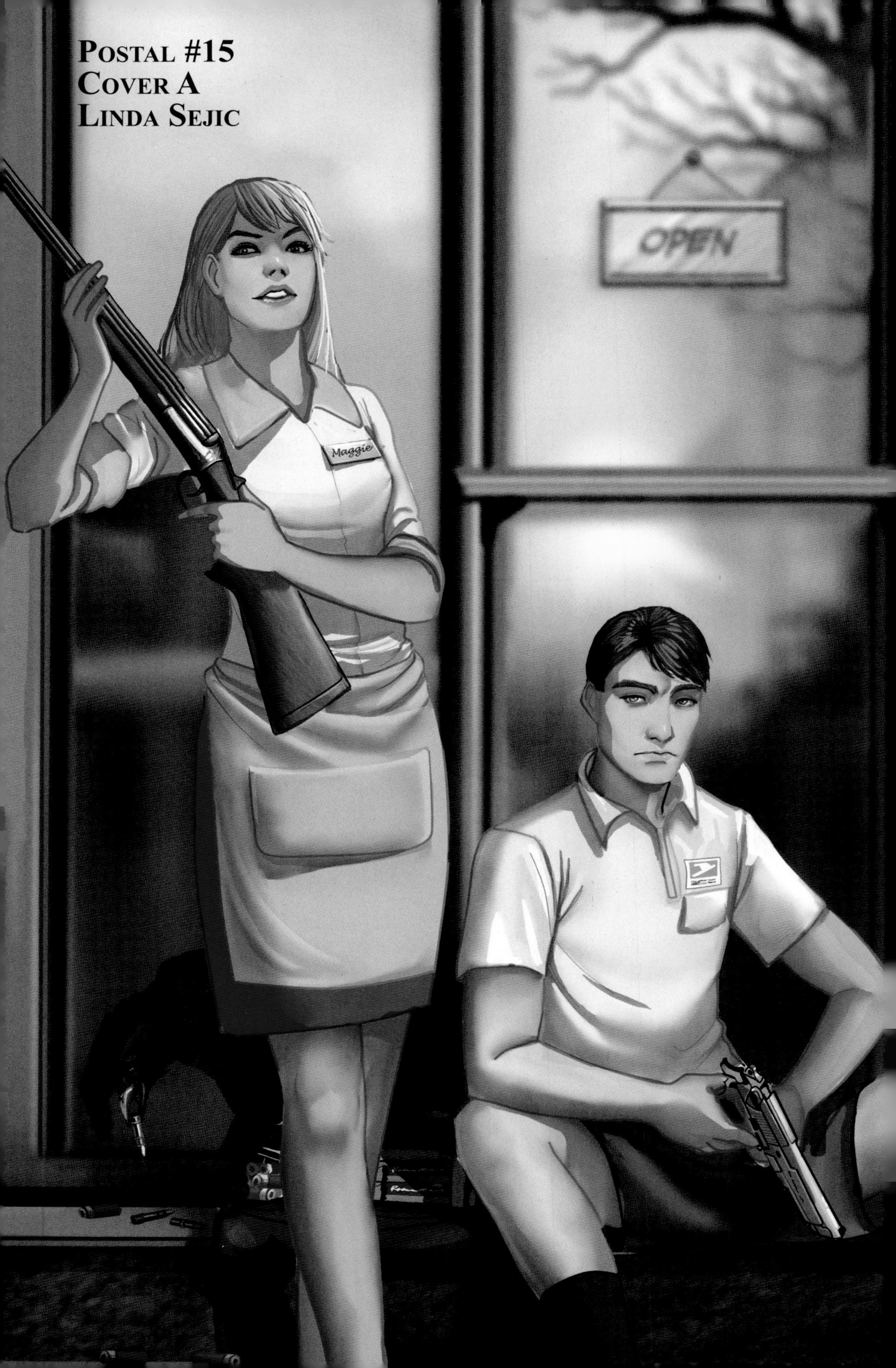
OPEN
Maggie

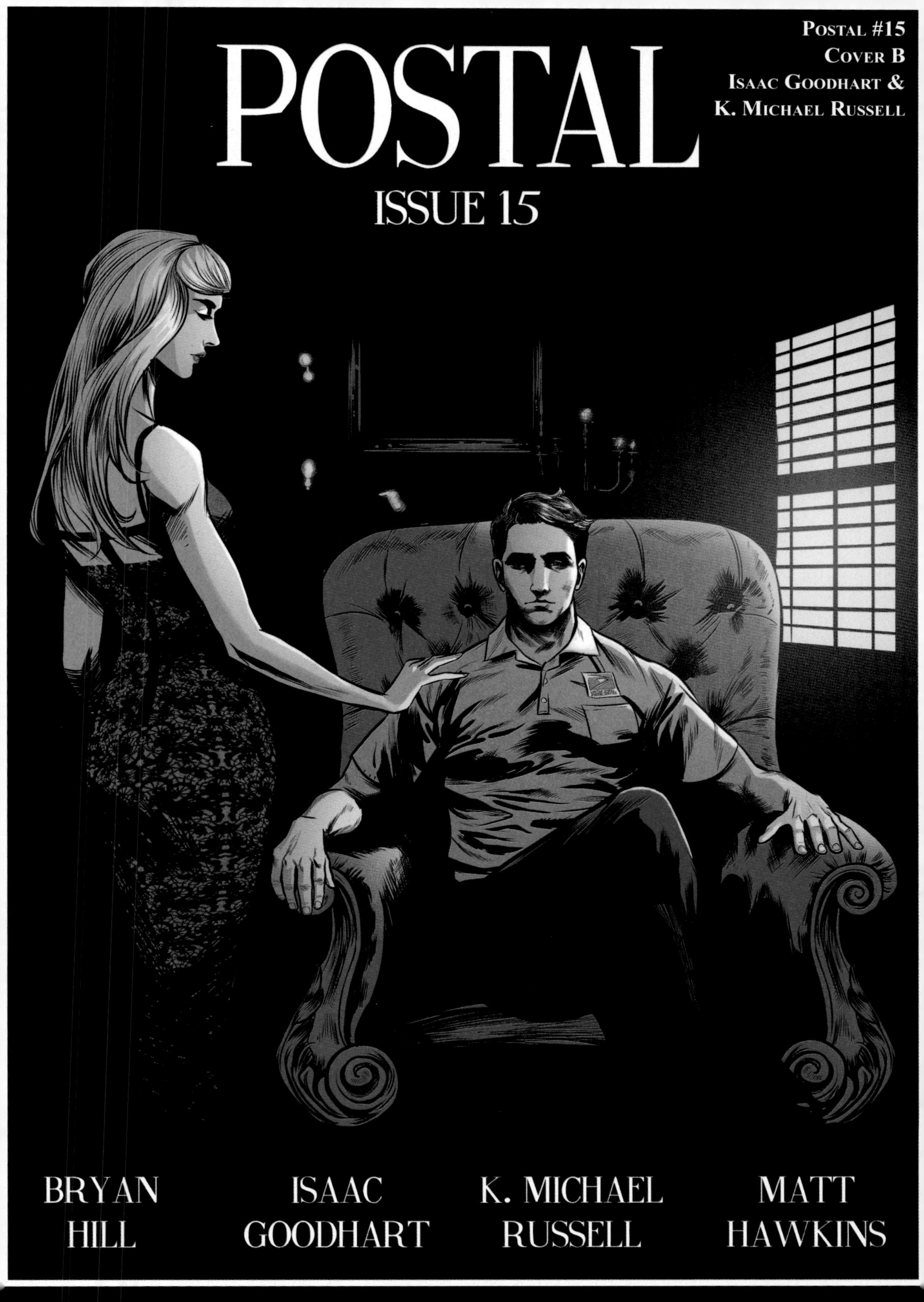
POSTAL
ISSUE 15
POSTAL #15
COVER B
ISAAC GOODHART &
K. MICHAEL RUSSELL
BRYAN HILL
ISAAC GOODHART
K. MICHAEL RUSSELL
MATT HAWKINS

TOP COW PRODUCTIONS INC PRESENTS AN EDEN-VERSE COMIC BOOK PRODUCTION CREATED BY MATT HAWKINS
WRITTEN BY BRYAN HILL DRAWN BY ISAAC GOODHART COLORED BY K. MICHAEL RUSSELL LETTERED BY TROY PETERI
EDITED BY RYAN CADY AND ASHLEY VICTORIA ROBINSON PRODUCED BY TRICIA RAMOS

Postal #16
Cover A
Linda Sejic

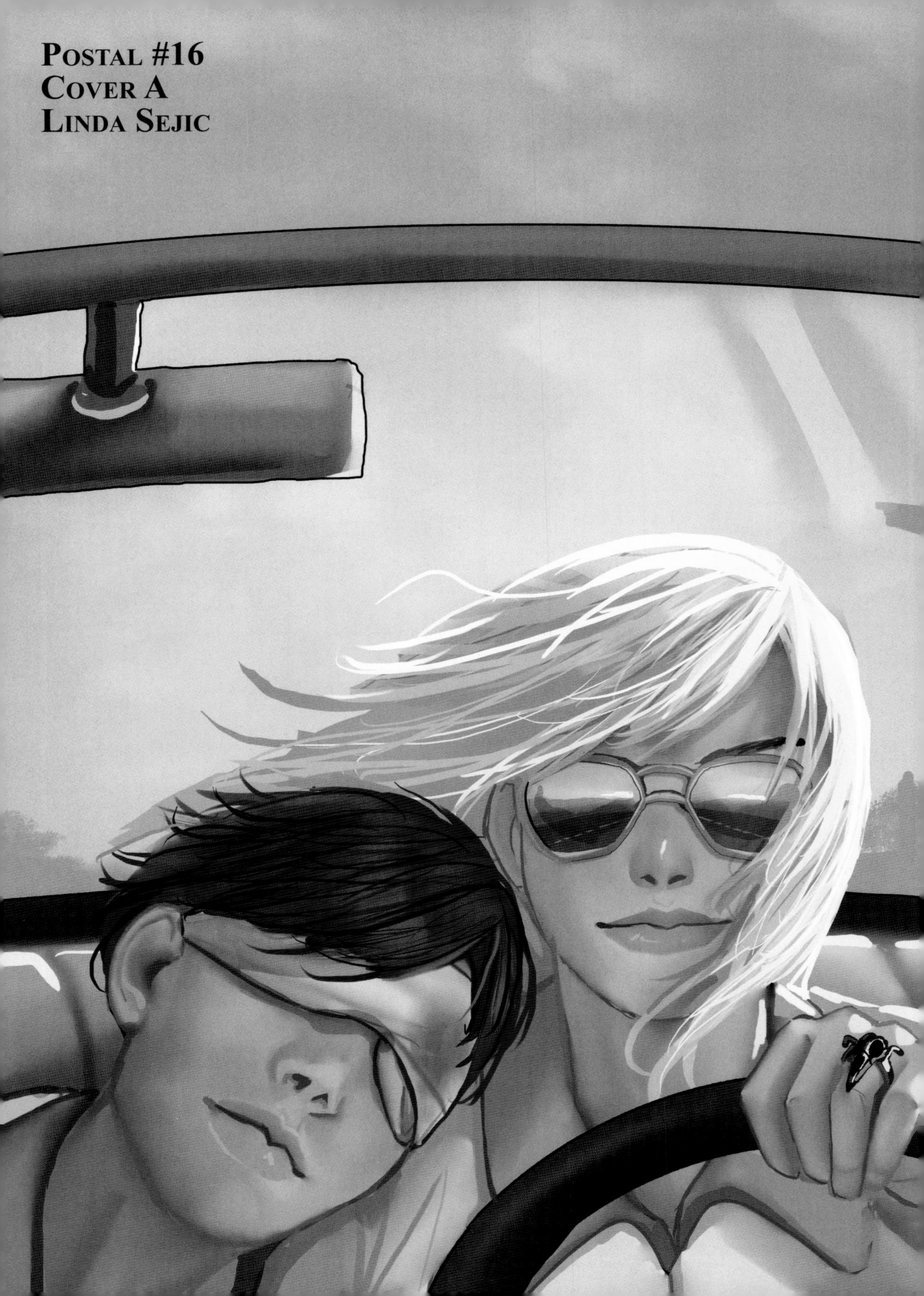

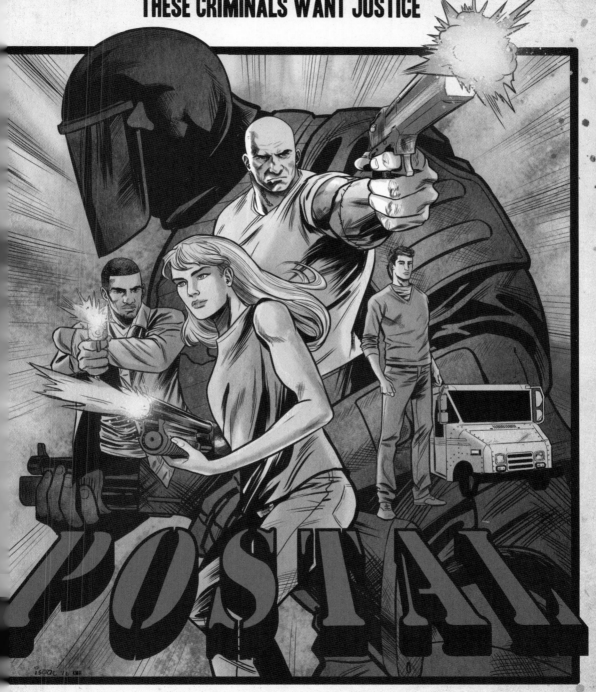

BRYAN HILL   ISAAC GOODHART   K. MICHAEL RUSSELL   MATT HAWKINS

THESE CRIMINALS WANT JUSTICE

POSTAL

TOP COW PRODUCTIONS INC. PRESENTS AN EDEN-VERSE COMIC BOOK PRODUCTION
WRITTEN BY BRYAN HILL DRAWN BY ISAAC GOODHART COLORED BY K. MICHAEL RUSSELL
LETTERED BY TROY PETERI EDITED BY ASHLEY VICTORIA ROBINSON PRODUCED BY TRICIA RAMOS

POSTAL #16   COVER B   ISAAC GOODHART & K. MICHAEL RUSSELL

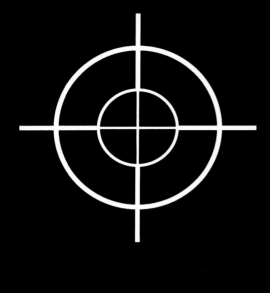

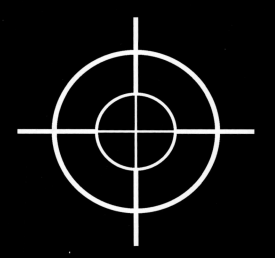

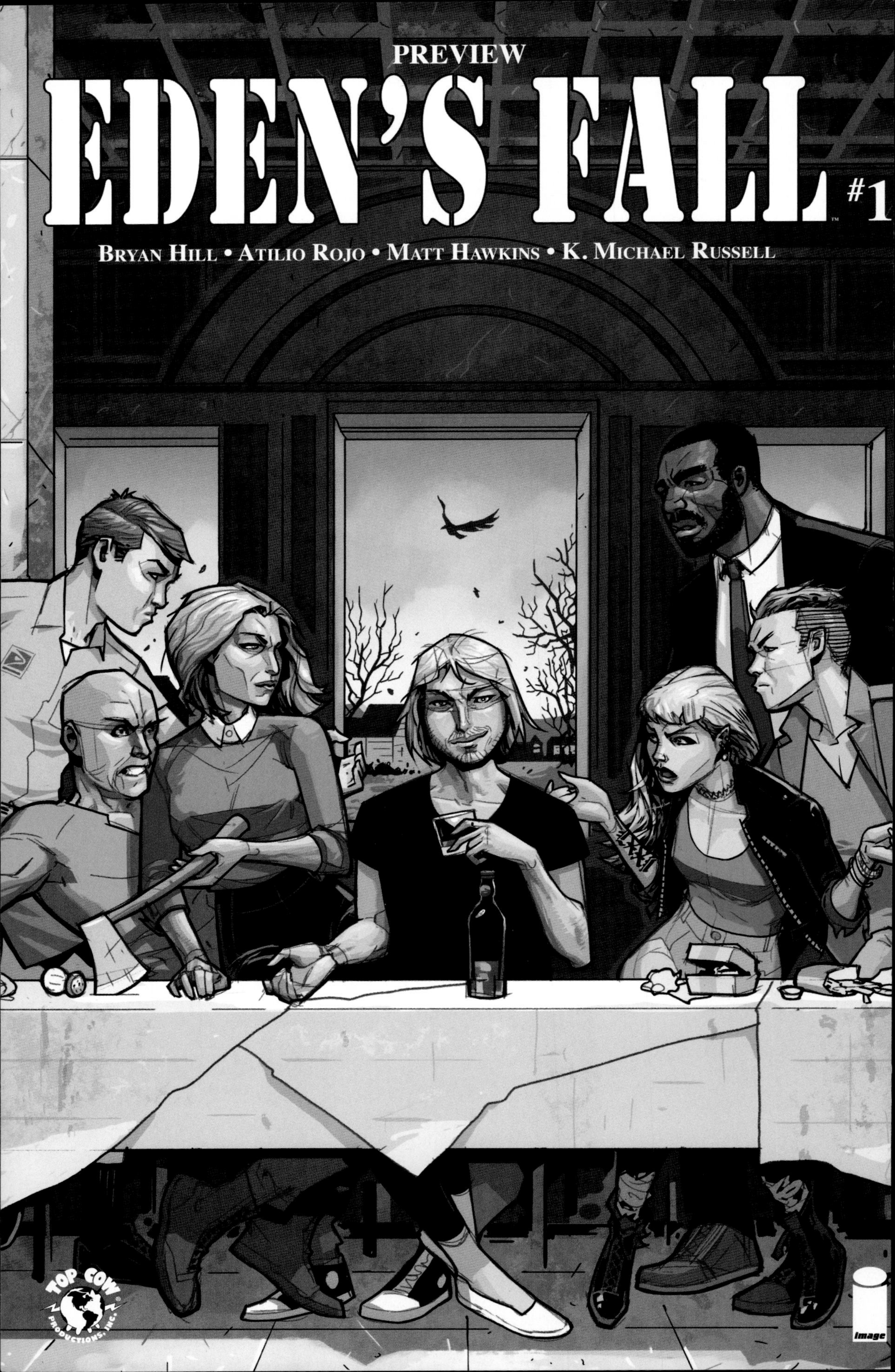
PREVIEW
EDEN'S FALL
#1
BRYAN HILL • ATILIO ROJO • MATT HAWKINS • K. MICHAEL RUSSELL
TOP COW PRODUCTIONS, INC.
image

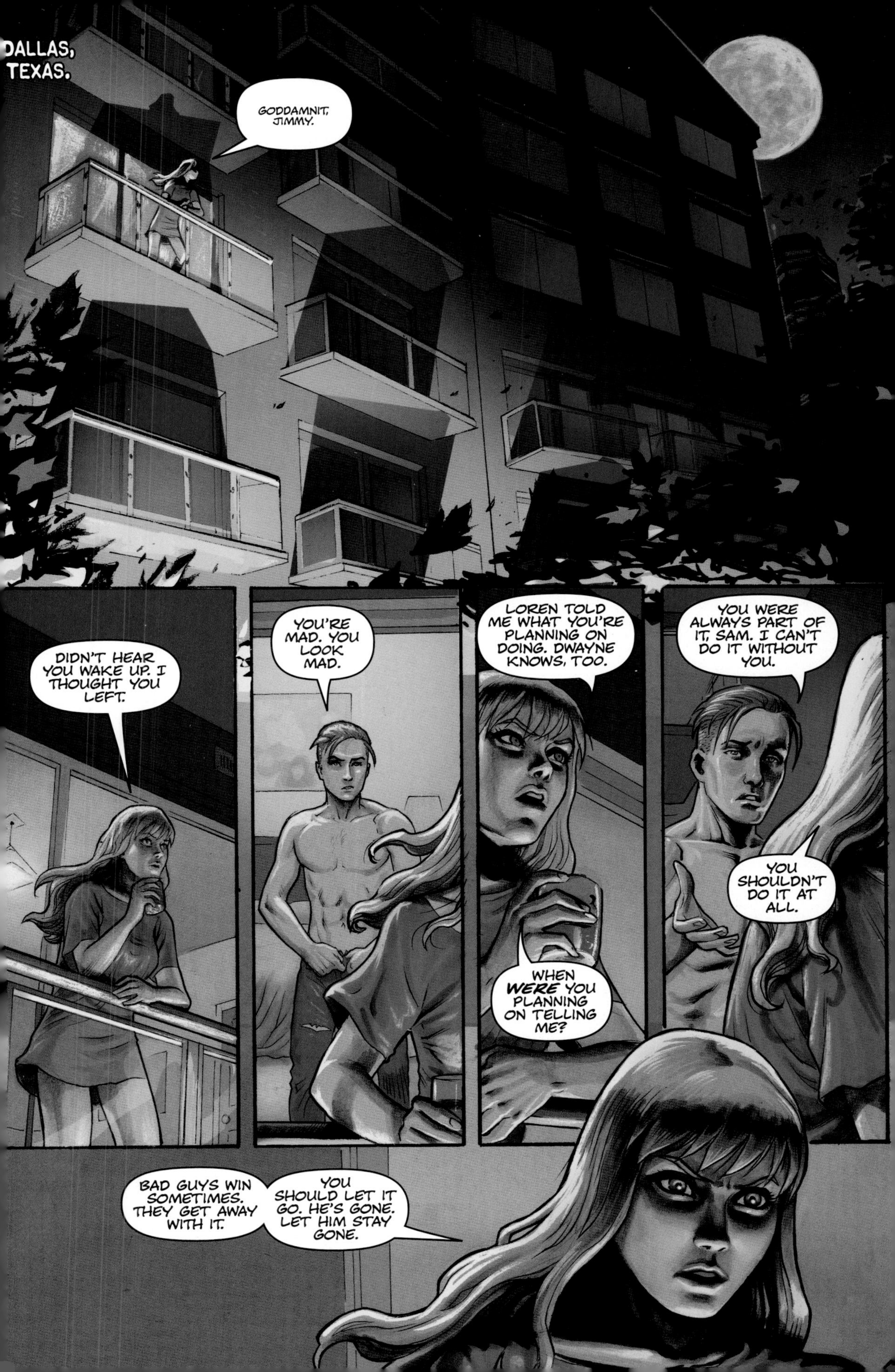
DALLAS, TEXAS.
GODDAMNIT, JIMMY.
DIDN'T HEAR YOU WAKE UP. I THOUGHT YOU LEFT.
YOU'RE MAD. YOU LOOK MAD.
LOREN TOLD ME WHAT YOU'RE PLANNING ON DOING. DWAYNE KNOWS, TOO.
WHEN WERE YOU PLANNING ON TELLING ME?
YOU WERE ALWAYS PART OF IT, SAM. I CAN'T DO IT WITHOUT YOU.
YOU SHOULDN'T DO IT AT ALL.
BAD GUYS WIN SOMETIMES. THEY GET AWAY WITH IT.
YOU SHOULD LET IT GO. HE'S GONE. LET HIM STAY GONE.

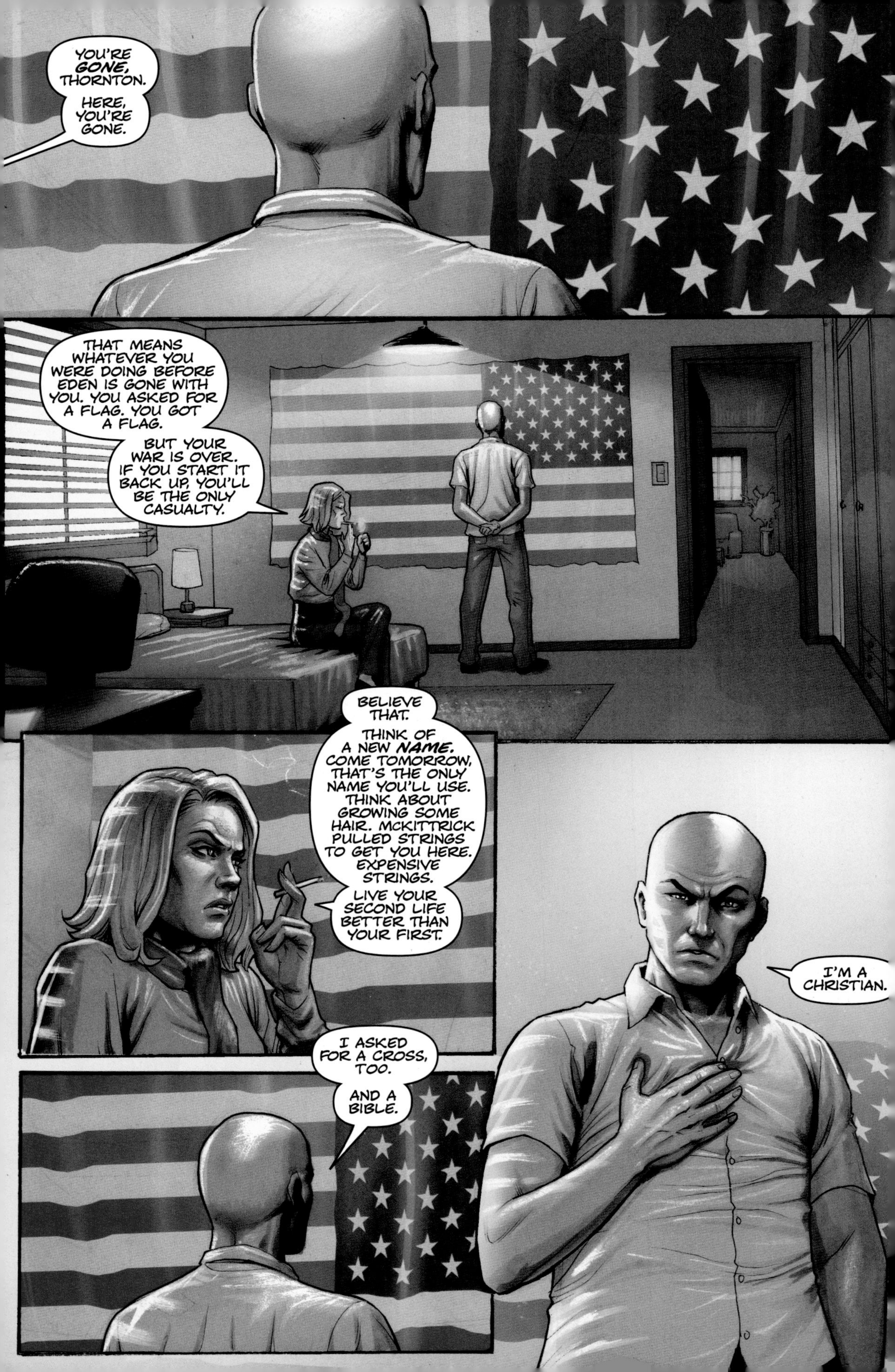
YOU'RE *GONE,* THORNTON.
HERE, YOU'RE GONE.
THAT MEANS WHATEVER YOU WERE DOING BEFORE EDEN IS GONE WITH YOU. YOU ASKED FOR A FLAG. YOU GOT A FLAG.
BUT YOUR WAR IS OVER. IF YOU START IT BACK UP, YOU'LL BE THE ONLY CASUALTY.
BELIEVE THAT.
THINK OF A NEW *NAME.* COME TOMORROW, THAT'S THE ONLY NAME YOU'LL USE. THINK ABOUT GROWING SOME HAIR. MCKITTRICK PULLED STRINGS TO GET YOU HERE. EXPENSIVE STRINGS.
LIVE YOUR SECOND LIFE BETTER THAN YOUR FIRST.
I'M A CHRISTIAN.
I ASKED FOR A CROSS, TOO.
AND A BIBLE.

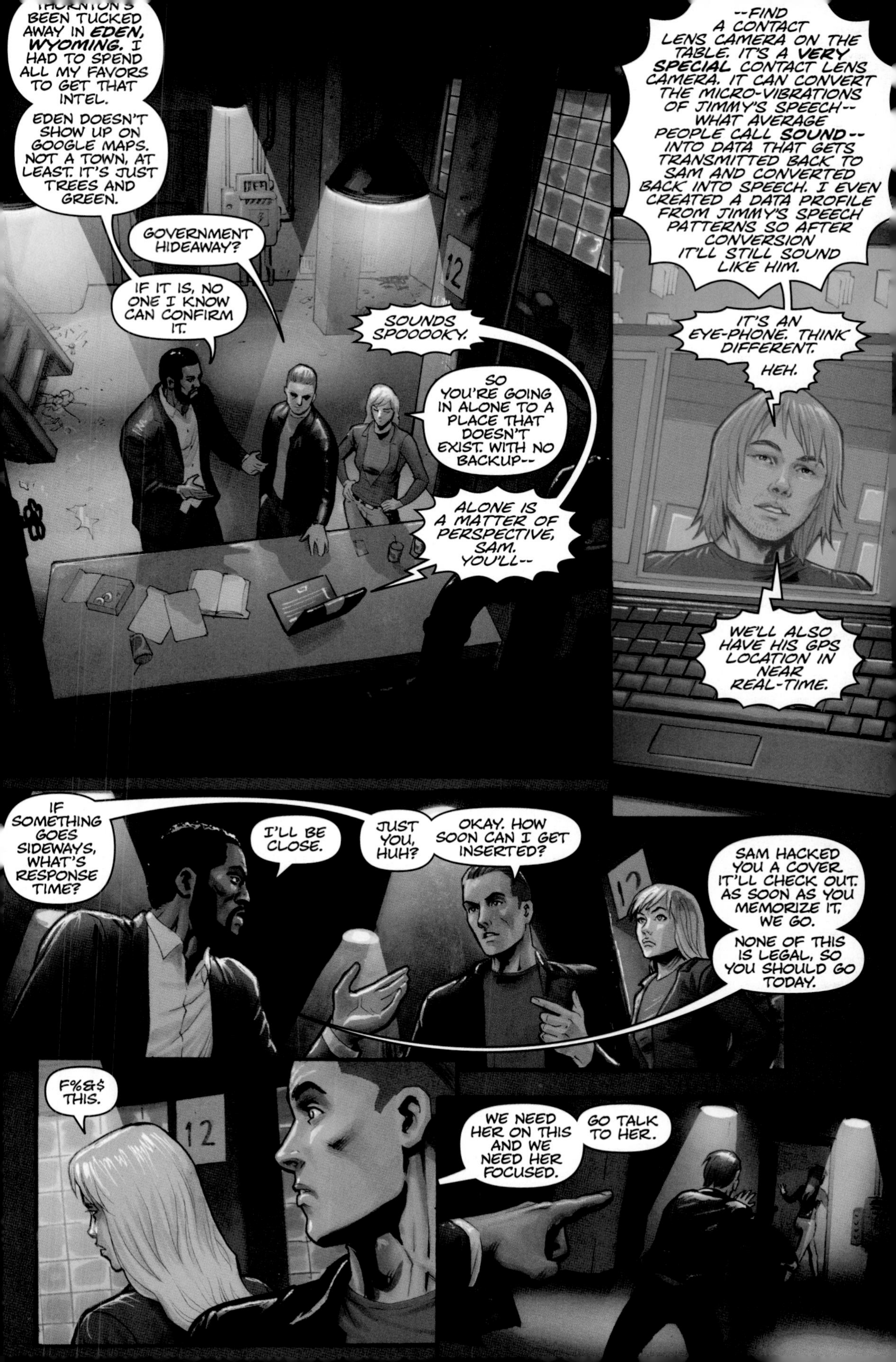
THORNTON'S BEEN TUCKED AWAY IN EDEN, WYOMING. I HAD TO SPEND ALL MY FAVORS TO GET THAT INTEL.
EDEN DOESN'T SHOW UP ON GOOGLE MAPS. NOT A TOWN, AT LEAST. IT'S JUST TREES AND GREEN.
GOVERNMENT HIDEAWAY?
IF IT IS, NO ONE I KNOW CAN CONFIRM IT.
SOUNDS SPOOOOKY.
SO YOU'RE GOING IN ALONE TO A PLACE THAT DOESN'T EXIST. WITH NO BACKUP--
ALONE IS A MATTER OF PERSPECTIVE, SAM. YOU'LL--
--FIND A CONTACT LENS CAMERA ON THE TABLE. IT'S A VERY SPECIAL CONTACT LENS CAMERA. IT CAN CONVERT THE MICRO-VIBRATIONS OF JIMMY'S SPEECH--WHAT AVERAGE PEOPLE CALL SOUND--INTO DATA THAT GETS TRANSMITTED BACK TO SAM AND CONVERTED BACK INTO SPEECH. I EVEN CREATED A DATA PROFILE FROM JIMMY'S SPEECH PATTERNS SO AFTER CONVERSION IT'LL STILL SOUND LIKE HIM.
IT'S AN EYE-PHONE. THINK DIFFERENT.
HEH.
WE'LL ALSO HAVE HIS GPS LOCATION IN NEAR REAL-TIME.
IF SOMETHING GOES SIDEWAYS, WHAT'S RESPONSE TIME?
I'LL BE CLOSE.
JUST YOU, HUH?
OKAY. HOW SOON CAN I GET INSERTED?
SAM HACKED YOU A COVER IT'LL CHECK OUT. AS SOON AS YOU MEMORIZE IT, WE GO.
NONE OF THIS IS LEGAL, SO YOU SHOULD GO TODAY.
F%&$ THIS.
WE NEED HER ON THIS AND WE NEED HER FOCUSED.
GO TALK TO HER.

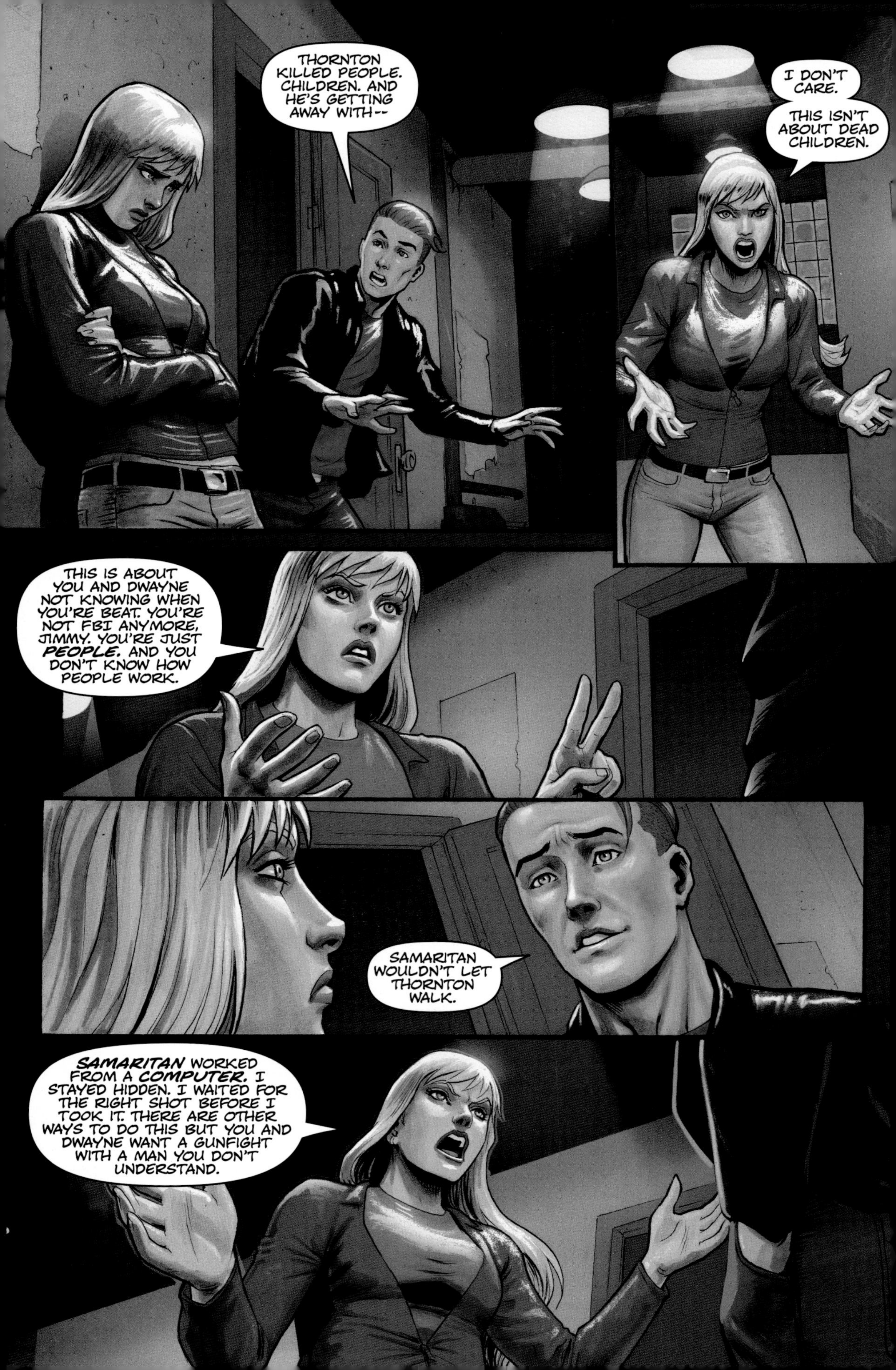

THORNTON KILLED PEOPLE. CHILDREN. AND HE'S GETTING AWAY WITH--
I DON'T CARE.
THIS ISN'T ABOUT DEAD CHILDREN.
THIS IS ABOUT YOU AND DWAYNE NOT KNOWING WHEN YOU'RE BEAT. YOU'RE NOT FBI ANYMORE, JIMMY. YOU'RE JUST PEOPLE. AND YOU DON'T KNOW HOW PEOPLE WORK.
SAMARITAN WOULDN'T LET THORNTON WALK.
SAMARITAN WORKED FROM A COMPUTER. I STAYED HIDDEN. I WAITED FOR THE RIGHT SHOT BEFORE I TOOK IT. THERE ARE OTHER WAYS TO DO THIS BUT YOU AND DWAYNE WANT A GUNFIGHT WITH A MAN YOU DON'T UNDERSTAND.

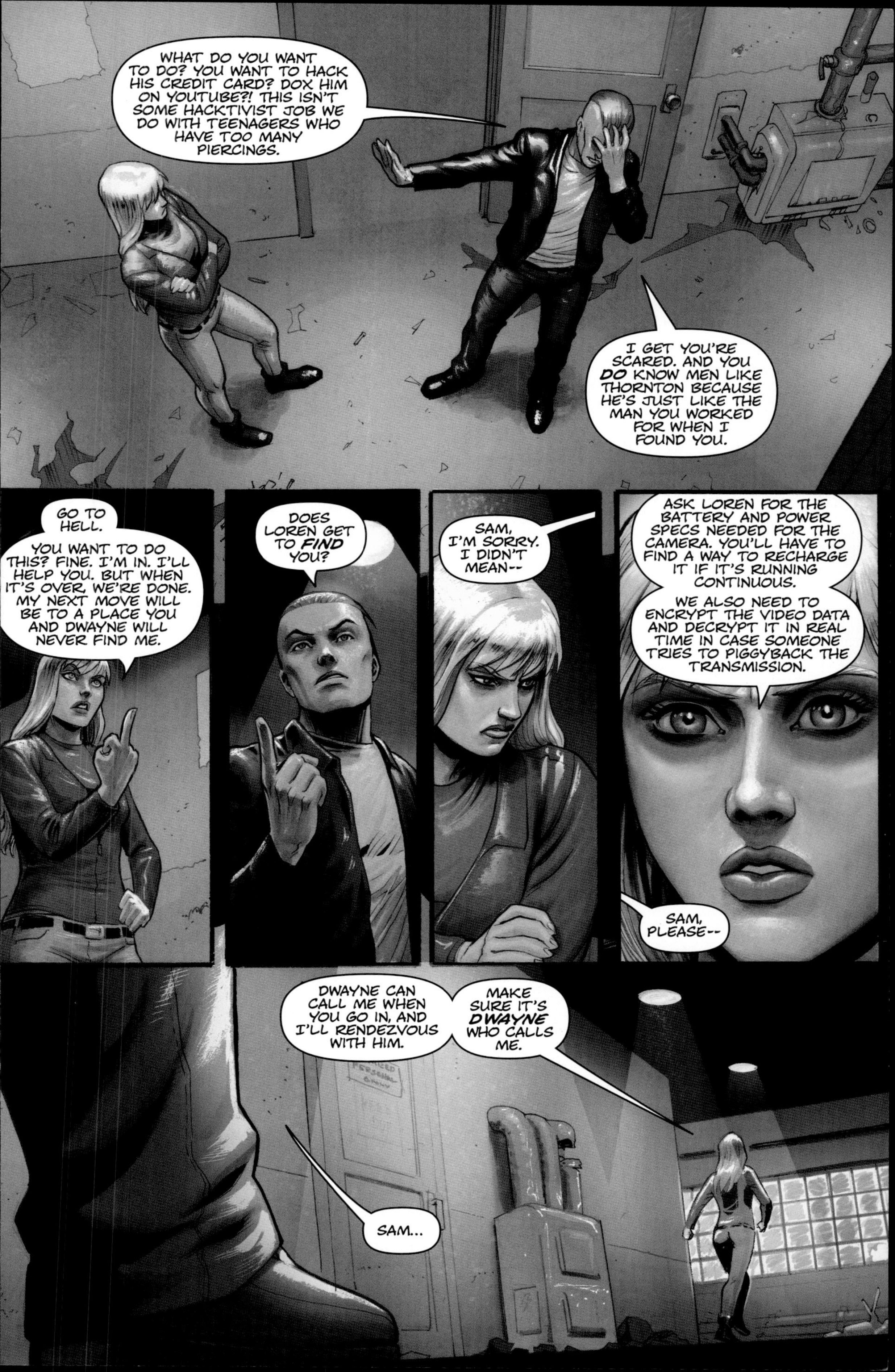
WHAT DO YOU WANT TO DO? YOU WANT TO HACK HIS CREDIT CARD? DOX HIM ON YOUTUBE?! THIS ISN'T SOME HACKTIVIST JOB WE DO WITH TEENAGERS WHO HAVE TOO MANY PIERCINGS.
I GET YOU'RE SCARED. AND YOU **DO** KNOW MEN LIKE THORNTON BECAUSE HE'S JUST LIKE THE MAN YOU WORKED FOR WHEN I FOUND YOU.
GO TO HELL.
YOU WANT TO DO THIS? FINE. I'M IN. I'LL HELP YOU. BUT WHEN IT'S OVER, WE'RE DONE. MY NEXT MOVE WILL BE TO A PLACE YOU AND DWAYNE WILL NEVER FIND ME.
DOES LOREN GET TO ***FIND*** YOU?
SAM, I'M SORRY. I DIDN'T MEAN--
ASK LOREN FOR THE BATTERY AND POWER SPECS NEEDED FOR THE CAMERA. YOU'LL HAVE TO FIND A WAY TO RECHARGE IT IF IT'S RUNNING CONTINUOUS.
WE ALSO NEED TO ENCRYPT THE VIDEO DATA AND DECRYPT IT IN REAL TIME IN CASE SOMEONE TRIES TO PIGGYBACK THE TRANSMISSION.
SAM, PLEASE--
DWAYNE CAN CALL ME WHEN YOU GO IN, AND I'LL RENDEZVOUS WITH HIM.
MAKE SURE IT'S ***DWAYNE*** WHO CALLS ME.
SAM...

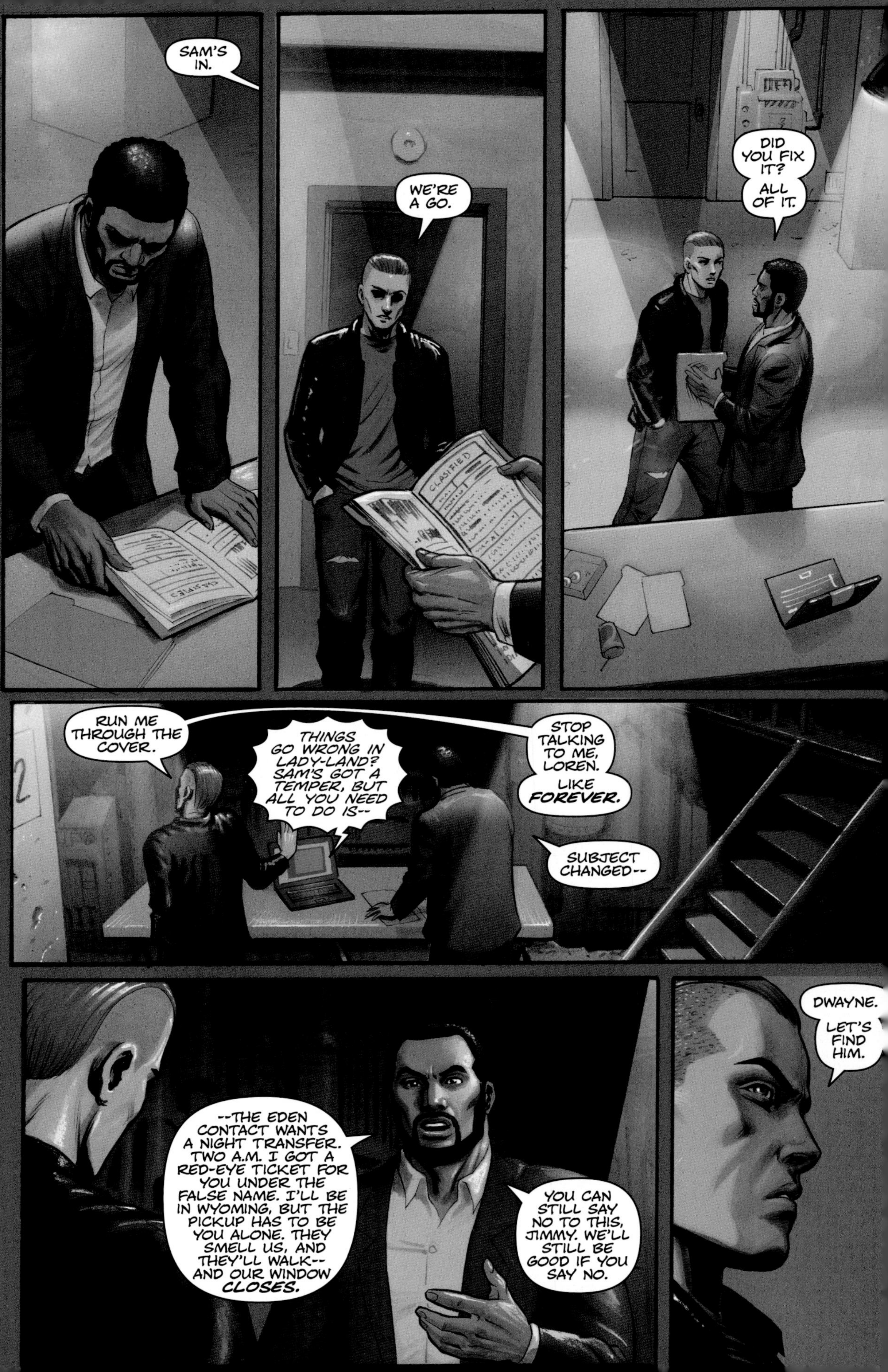
SAM'S IN.
WE'RE A GO.
CLASSIFIED
DID YOU FIX IT?
ALL OF IT.
RUN ME THROUGH THE COVER.
THINGS GO WRONG IN LADY-LAND? SAM'S GOT A TEMPER, BUT ALL YOU NEED TO DO IS--
STOP TALKING TO ME, LOREN.
LIKE *FOREVER.*
SUBJECT CHANGED--
--THE EDEN CONTACT WANTS A NIGHT TRANSFER. TWO A.M. I GOT A RED-EYE TICKET FOR YOU UNDER THE FALSE NAME. I'LL BE IN WYOMING, BUT THE PICKUP HAS TO BE YOU ALONE. THEY SMELL US, AND THEY'LL WALK-- AND OUR WINDOW *CLOSES.*
YOU CAN STILL SAY NO TO THIS, JIMMY. WE'LL STILL BE GOOD IF YOU SAY NO.
DWAYNE.
LET'S FIND HIM.

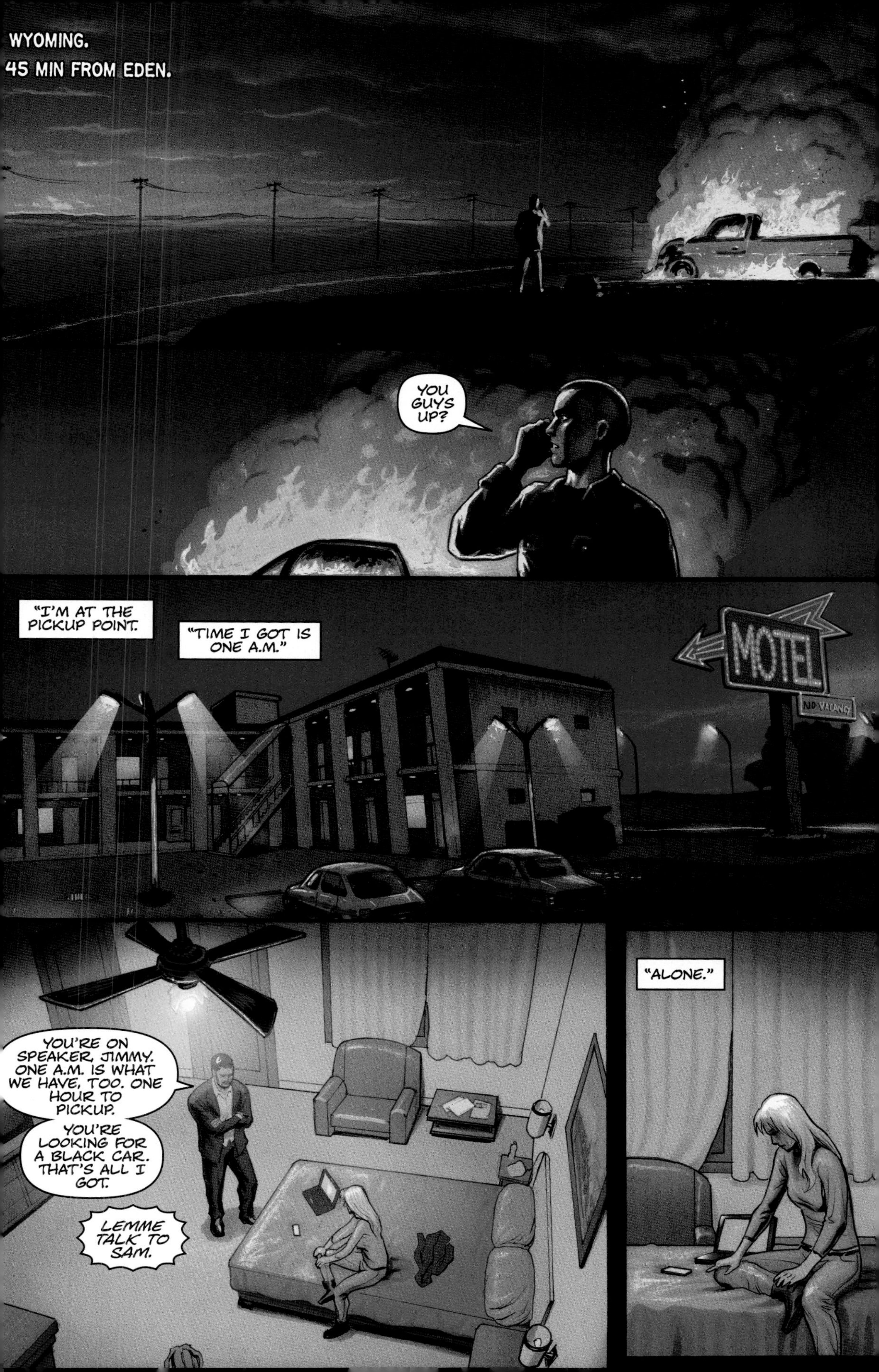
WYOMING.
45 MIN FROM EDEN.
YOU GUYS UP?
"I'M AT THE PICKUP POINT.
"TIME I GOT IS ONE A.M."
MOTEL
NO VACANCY
YOU'RE ON SPEAKER, JIMMY. ONE A.M. IS WHAT WE HAVE, TOO. ONE HOUR TO PICKUP.
YOU'RE LOOKING FOR A BLACK CAR. THAT'S ALL I GOT.
LEMME TALK TO SAM.
"ALONE."

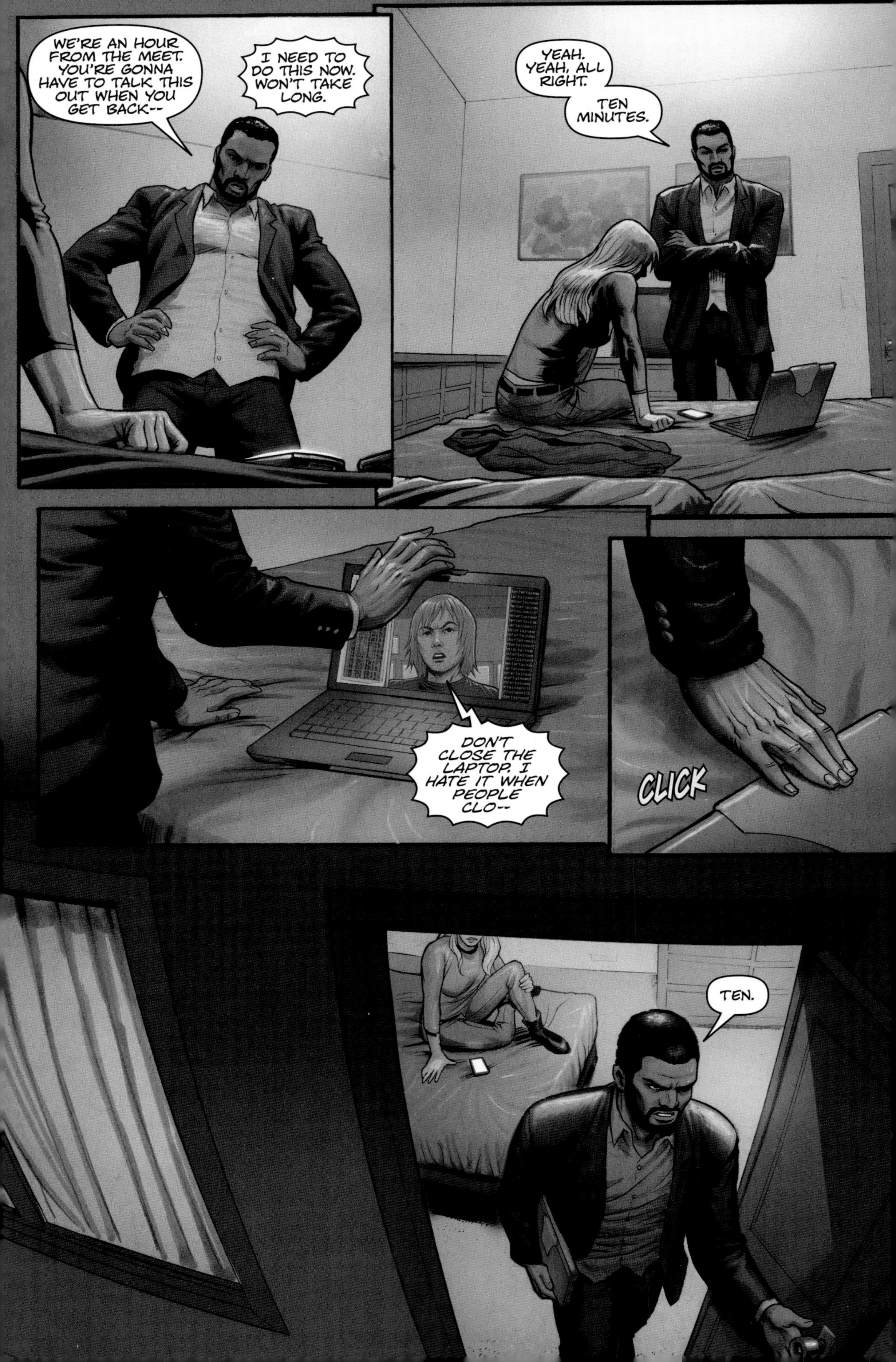
WE'RE AN HOUR FROM THE MEET. YOU'RE GONNA HAVE TO TALK THIS OUT WHEN YOU GET BACK--
I NEED TO DO THIS NOW. WON'T TAKE LONG.
YEAH. YEAH, ALL RIGHT.
TEN MINUTES.
DON'T CLOSE THE LAPTOP. I HATE IT WHEN PEOPLE CLO--
CLICK
TEN.

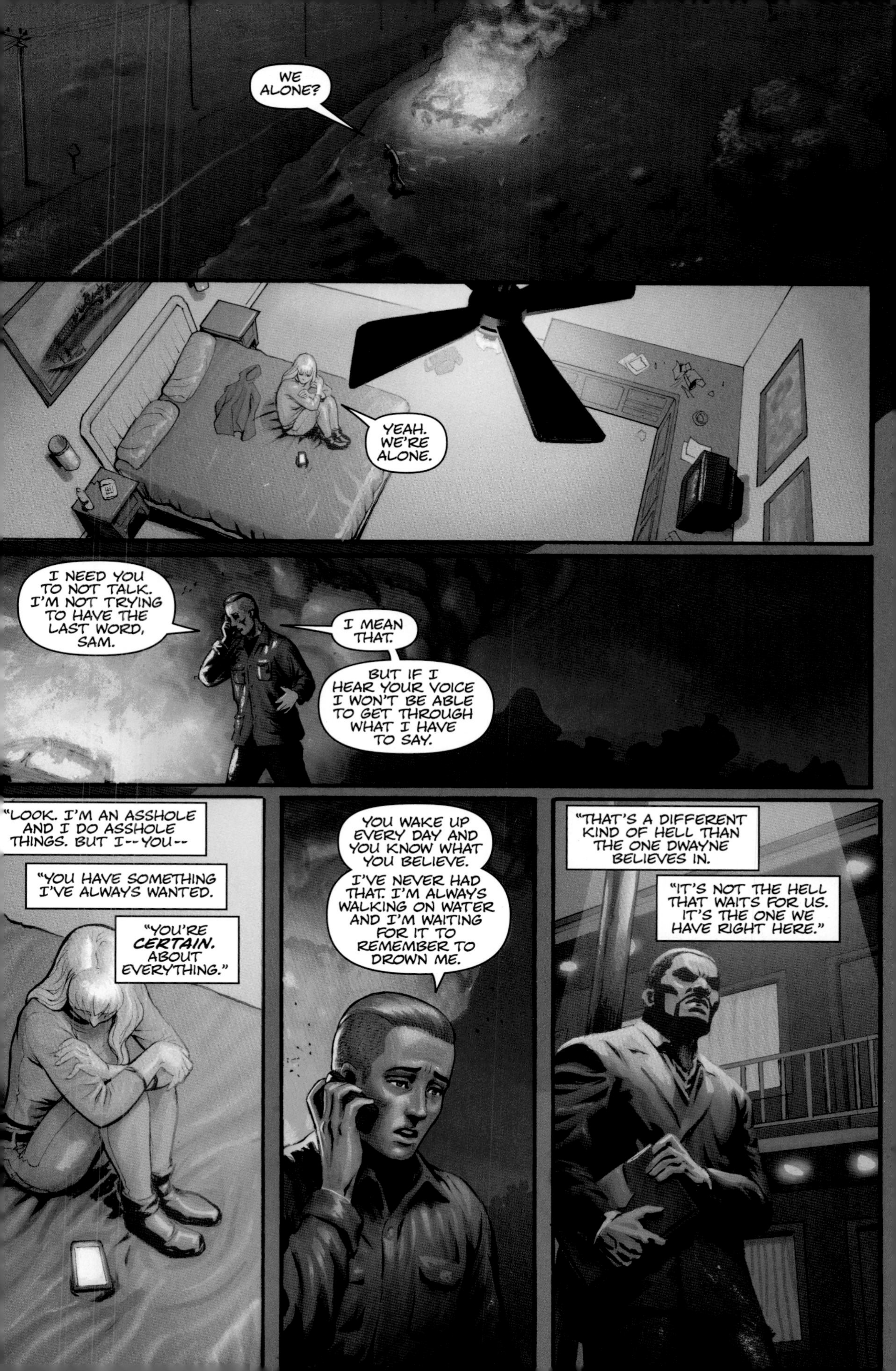
WE ALONE?
YEAH. WE'RE ALONE.
I NEED YOU TO NOT TALK. I'M NOT TRYING TO HAVE THE LAST WORD, SAM.
I MEAN THAT.
BUT IF I HEAR YOUR VOICE I WON'T BE ABLE TO GET THROUGH WHAT I HAVE TO SAY.
"LOOK. I'M AN ASSHOLE AND I DO ASSHOLE THINGS. BUT I--YOU--
"YOU HAVE SOMETHING I'VE ALWAYS WANTED.
"YOU'RE *CERTAIN.* ABOUT EVERYTHING."
YOU WAKE UP EVERY DAY AND YOU KNOW WHAT YOU BELIEVE.
I'VE NEVER HAD THAT. I'M ALWAYS WALKING ON WATER AND I'M WAITING FOR IT TO REMEMBER TO DROWN ME.
"THAT'S A DIFFERENT KIND OF HELL THAN THE ONE DWAYNE BELIEVES IN.
"IT'S NOT THE HELL THAT WAITS FOR US. IT'S THE ONE WE HAVE RIGHT HERE."

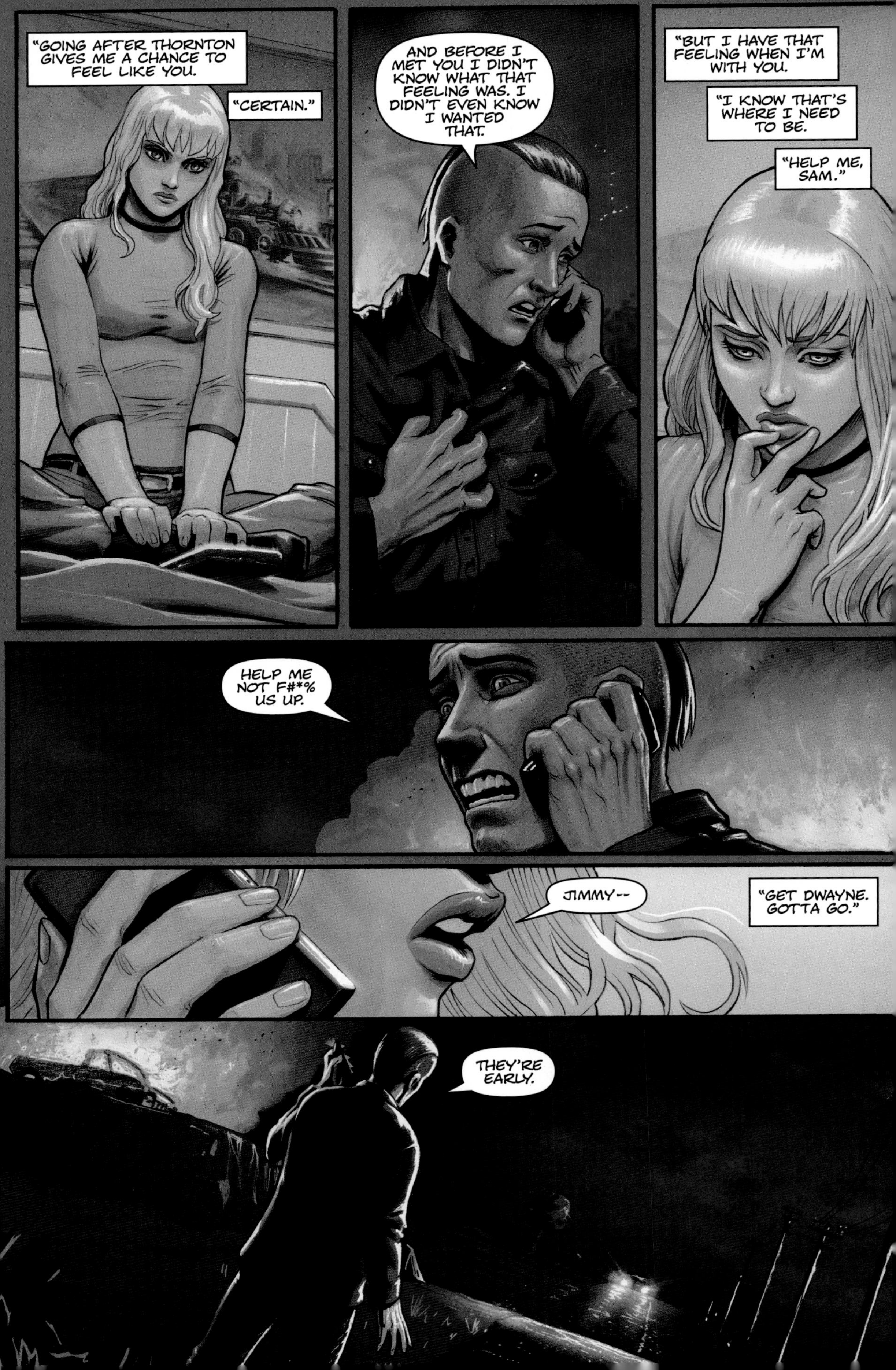
"GOING AFTER THORNTON GIVES ME A CHANCE TO FEEL LIKE YOU.
"CERTAIN."
AND BEFORE I MET YOU I DIDN'T KNOW WHAT THAT FEELING WAS. I DIDN'T EVEN KNOW I WANTED THAT.
"BUT I HAVE THAT FEELING WHEN I'M WITH YOU.
"I KNOW THAT'S WHERE I NEED TO BE.
"HELP ME, SAM."
HELP ME NOT F#*% US UP.
JIMMY--
"GET DWAYNE. GOTTA GO."
THEY'RE EARLY.

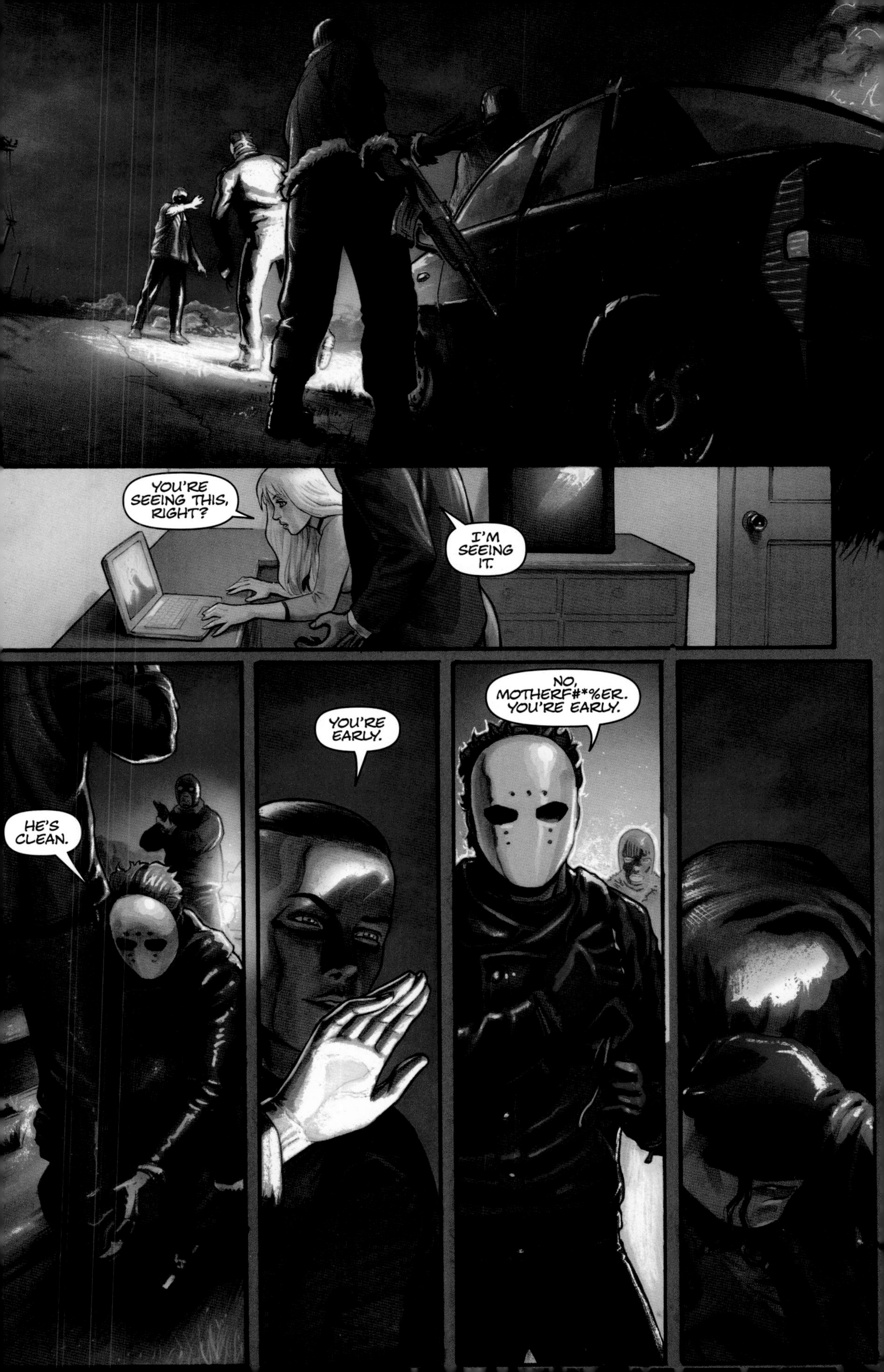
YOU'RE SEEING THIS, RIGHT?
I'M SEEING IT.
HE'S CLEAN.
YOU'RE EARLY.
NO, MOTHERF#*%ER. YOU'RE EARLY.

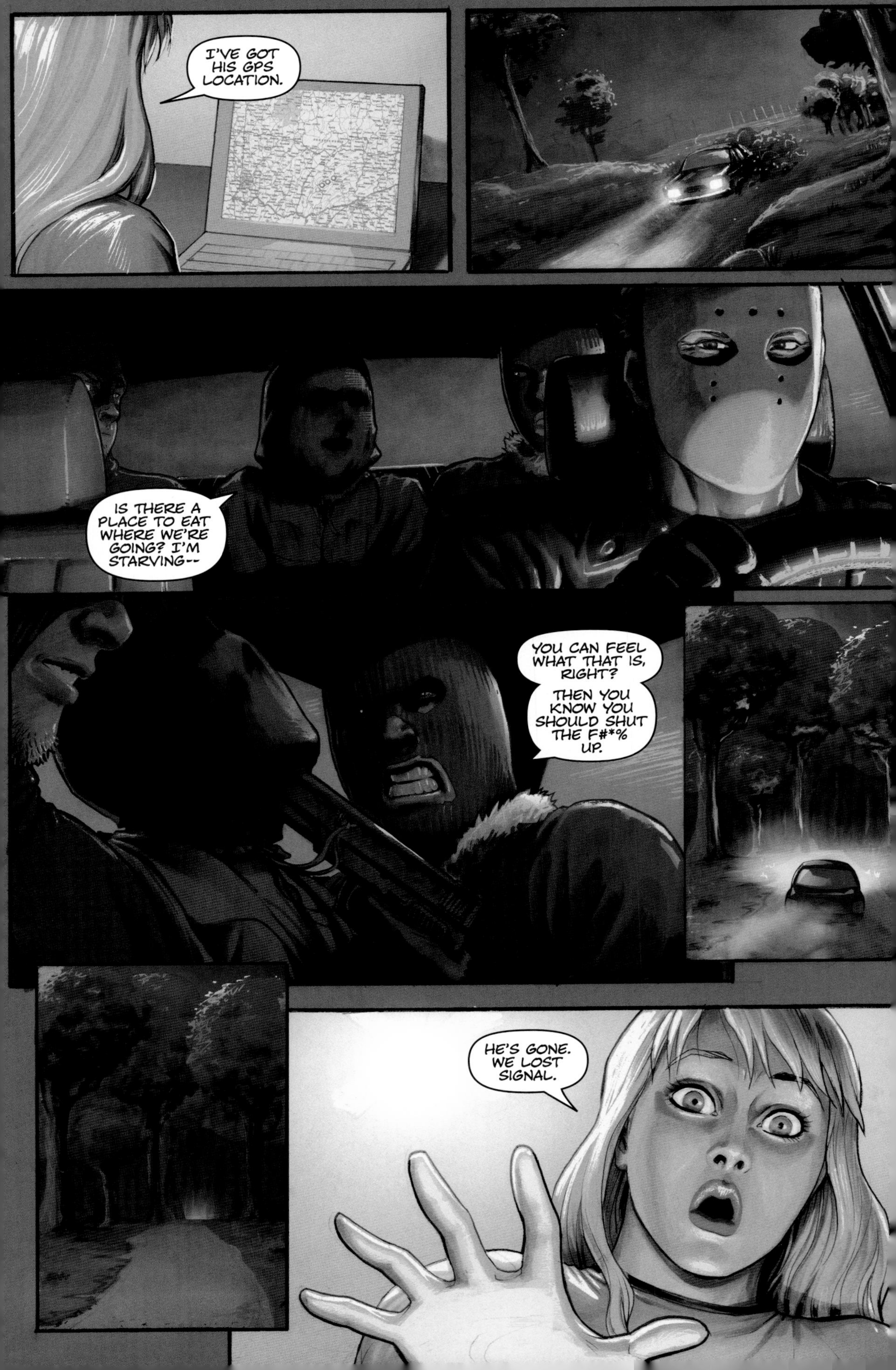
I'VE GOT HIS GPS LOCATION.
IS THERE A PLACE TO EAT WHERE WE'RE GOING? I'M STARVING--
YOU CAN FEEL WHAT THAT IS, RIGHT?
THEN YOU KNOW YOU SHOULD SHUT THE F#*% UP.
HE'S GONE. WE LOST SIGNAL.

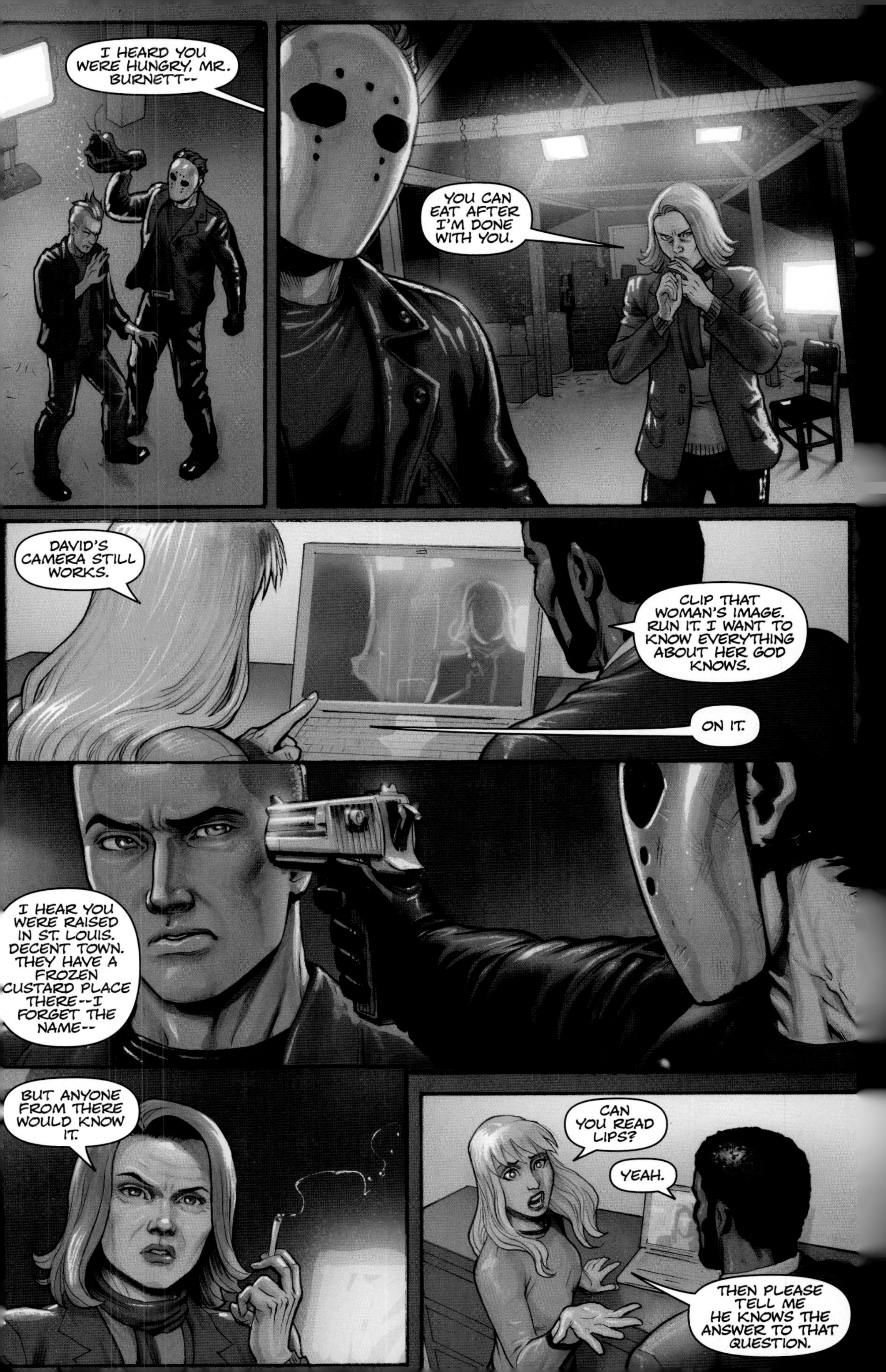
I HEARD YOU WERE HUNGRY, MR. BURNETT--
YOU CAN EAT AFTER I'M DONE WITH YOU.
DAVID'S CAMERA STILL WORKS.
CLIP THAT WOMAN'S IMAGE. RUN IT. I WANT TO KNOW EVERYTHING ABOUT HER GOD KNOWS.
ON IT.
I HEAR YOU WERE RAISED IN ST. LOUIS. DECENT TOWN. THEY HAVE A FROZEN CUSTARD PLACE THERE--I FORGET THE NAME--
BUT ANYONE FROM THERE WOULD KNOW IT.
CAN YOU READ LIPS?
YEAH.
THEN PLEASE TELL ME HE KNOWS THE ANSWER TO THAT QUESTION.

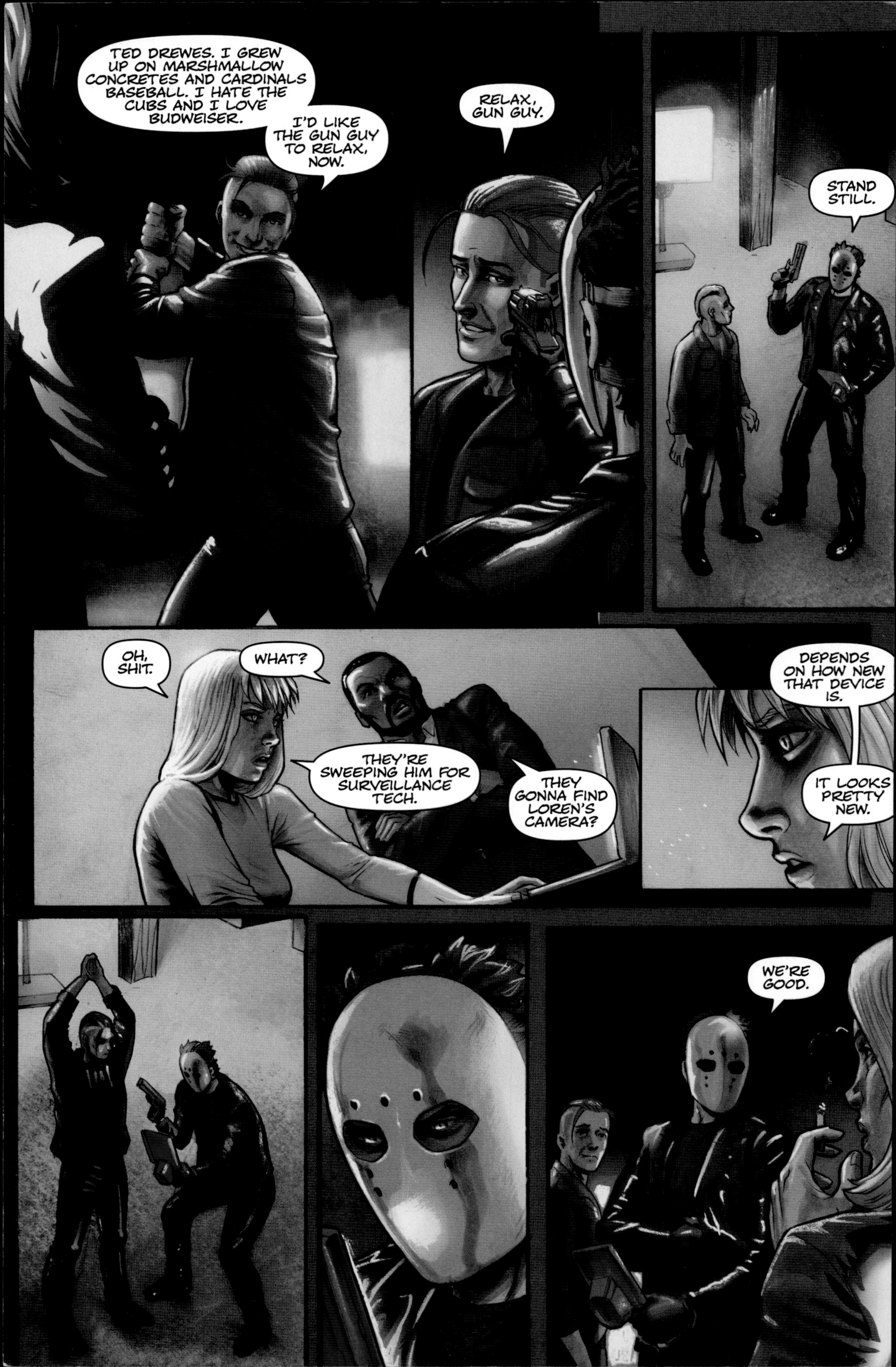

TED DREWES. I GREW UP ON MARSHMALLOW CONCRETES AND CARDINALS BASEBALL. I HATE THE CUBS AND I LOVE BUDWEISER.
I'D LIKE THE GUN GUY TO RELAX, NOW.
RELAX, GUN GUY.
STAND STILL.
OH, SHIT.
WHAT?
THEY'RE SWEEPING HIM FOR SURVEILLANCE TECH.
THEY GONNA FIND LOREN'S CAMERA?
DEPENDS ON HOW NEW THAT DEVICE IS.
IT LOOKS PRETTY NEW.
WE'RE GOOD.

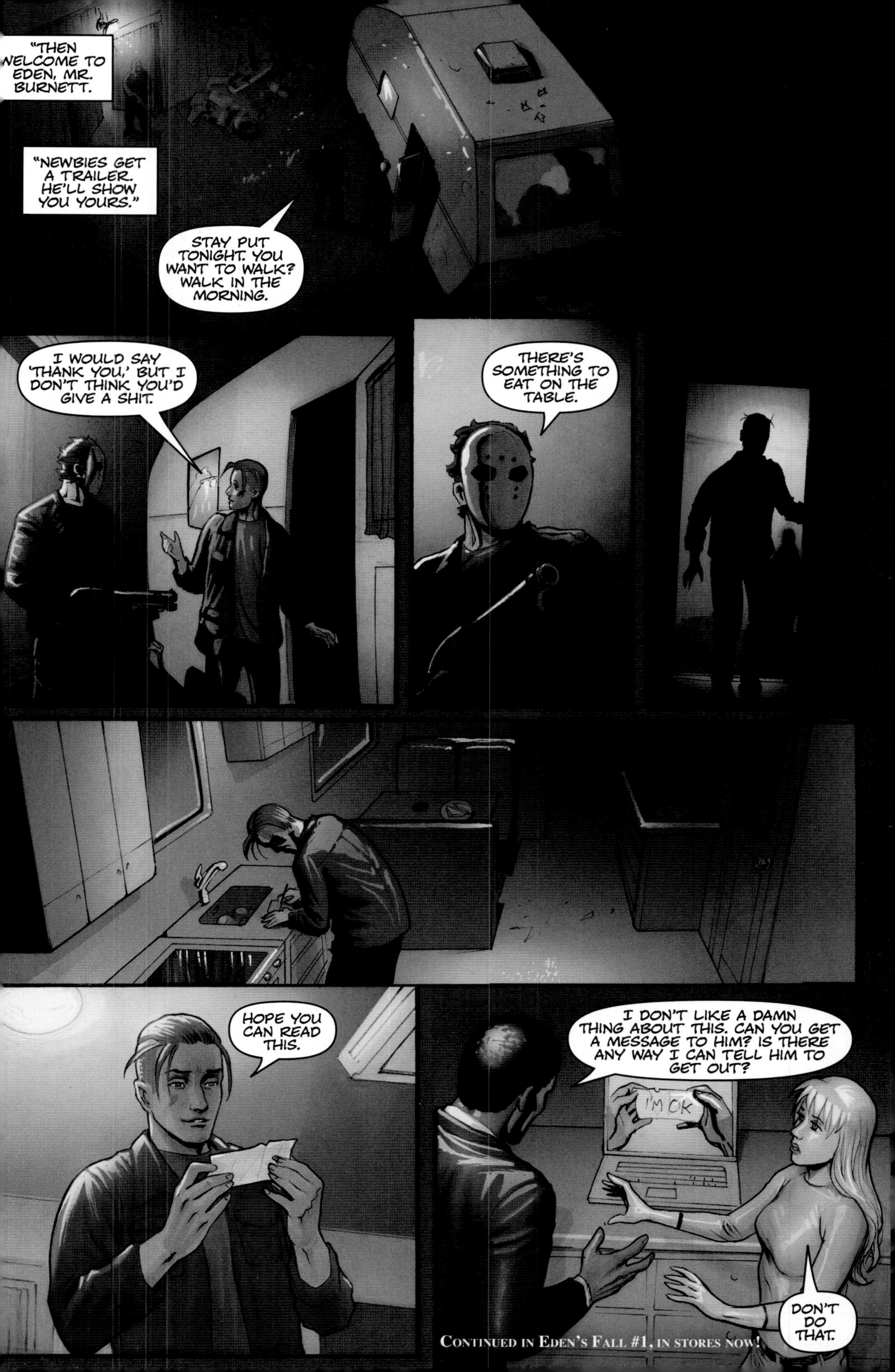

"THEN WELCOME TO EDEN, MR. BURNETT.
"NEWBIES GET A TRAILER. HE'LL SHOW YOU YOURS."
STAY PUT TONIGHT. YOU WANT TO WALK? WALK IN THE MORNING.
I WOULD SAY 'THANK YOU,' BUT I DON'T THINK YOU'D GIVE A SHIT.
THERE'S SOMETHING TO EAT ON THE TABLE.
HOPE YOU CAN READ THIS.
I DON'T LIKE A DAMN THING ABOUT THIS. CAN YOU GET A MESSAGE TO HIM? IS THERE ANY WAY I CAN TELL HIM TO GET OUT?
I'M OK
DON'T DO THAT.

CONTINUED IN EDEN'S FALL #1, IN STORES NOW!

Meet the Creators

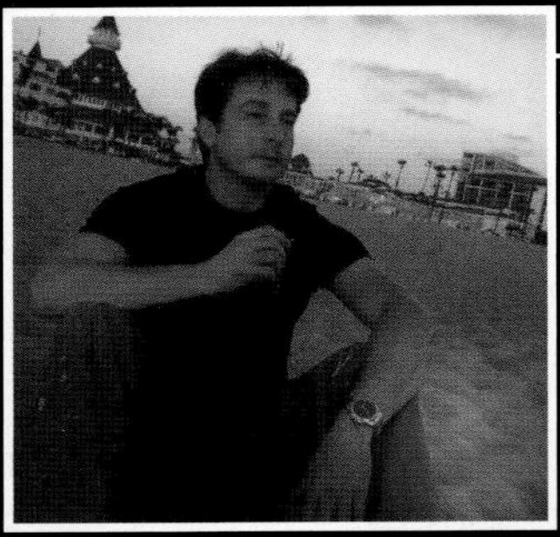

MATT HAWKINS

A veteran of the initial Image Comics launch, Matt started his career in comic book publishing in 1993 and has been working with Image as a creator, writer, and executive for over twenty years. President/ COO of Top Cow since 1998, Matt has created and written over thirty new franchises for Top Cow and Image including *Think Tank, Necromancer, VICE, Lady Pendragon,* and *Aphrodite IX* as well as handling the company's business affairs.

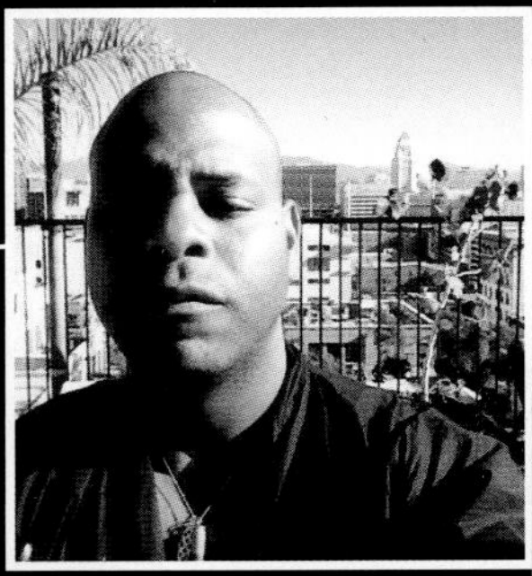

BRYAN HILL

Writes comics, writes movies, and makes films. He lives and works in Los Angeles. @bryanedwardhill | Instagram/bryanehill

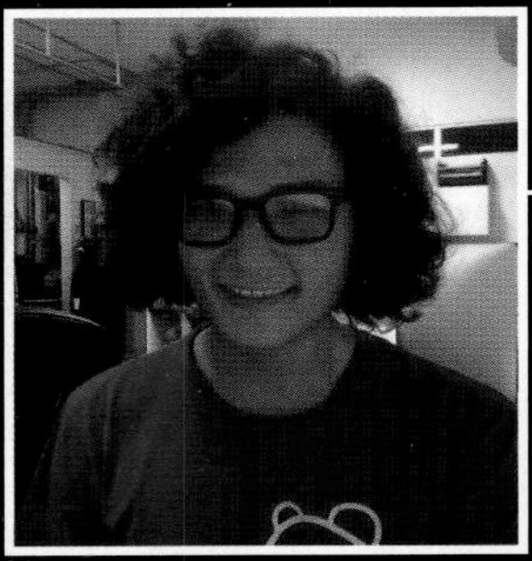

ISAAC GOODHART

A life-long comics fan, Isaac graduated from the School of Visual Arts in New York in 2010. In 2014, he was one of the winners for Top Cow's annual talent hunt. He currently lives in Los Angeles where he storyboards and draws comics.

K. MICHAEL RUSSELL

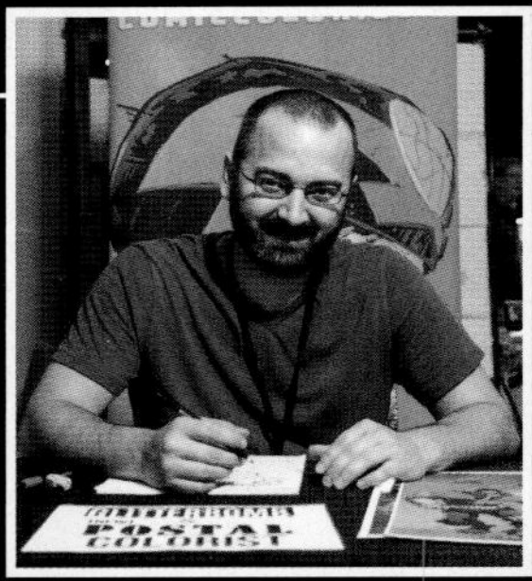

Michael has been working as a comic book color artist since 2011. His credits include the upcoming Image series *Glitterbomb* with *Wayward* & *Thunderbolts* writer Jim Zub, *Hack/Slash*, *Judge Dredd*, and the Eisner and Harvey-nominated *In the Dark: A Horror Anthology*. He launched an online comic book coloring course in 2014 at ColoringComics.com and maintains a YouTube channel dedicated to coloring tutorials. He lives on the coast in Long Beach, Mississippi, with his wife of sixteen years, Tina. They have two cats. One is a jerk. @kmichaelrussell

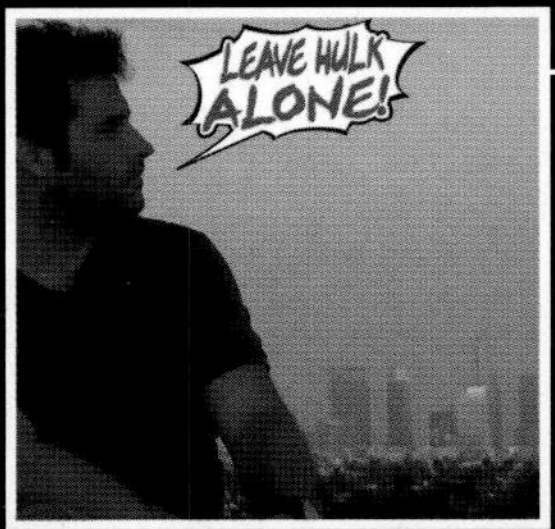
LEAVE HULK ALONE!

TROY PETERI

Starting his career at Comicraft, Troy Peteri lettered titles such as *Iron Man*, *Wolverine*, and *Amazing Spider-Man*, among many others. He's been lettering roughly 97% of all Top Cow titles since 2005. In addition to Top Cow, he currently letters comics from multiple publishers and websites, such as Image Comics, Dynamite, and Archaia. He (along with co-writer Tom Martin and artist Dave Lanphear) is currently writing (and lettering) *Tales of Equinox*, a webcomic of his own creation for www.Thrillbent.com. (Once again, www.Thrillbent.com.) He's still bitter about no longer lettering *The Darkness* and wants it back on stands immediately.